STAR WARS™

DARK DISCIPLE

STAR WARS™
DARK DISCIPLE

CHRISTIE GOLDEN

Based on *Star Wars: The Clone Wars*
Created and Executive Produced by George Lucas
Supervising Director: Dave Filoni
Produced by Cary Silver

"Lethal Alliance," "The Mission," "Conspirators,"
"Dark Disciple," "Saving Vos Parts I and II,"
"Traitor," and "The Path"

Written by Katie Lucas and Matt Michnovetz
and Dave Filoni

Lucasfilm Animation
A Lucasfilm Company

arrow books

1 3 5 7 9 10 8 6 4 2

Arrow Books
20 Vauxhall Bridge Road
London SW1V 2SA

Arrow Books is part of the Penguin Random House group of
companies whose addresses can be found at
global.penguinrandomhouse.com.

Penguin
Random House
UK

First published in Great Britain by Century in 2015

www.randomhouse.co.uk

A CIP catalogue record for this book is available from
the British Library.

ISBN 9780099580133

Printed and bound by Clays Ltd, St Ives Plc

MIX
Paper from
responsible sources
FSC® C016897

Penguin Random House is committed to a
sustainable future for our business, our readers
and our planet. This book is made from Forest
Stewardship Council® certified paper.

This book is dedicated to all of us who recognized early on that *Star Wars* was much, much more than just another science fiction movie—and loved it passionately for that.

STAR WARS

TIMELINE

I — THE PHANTOM MENACE

II — ATTACK OF THE CLONES
THE CLONE WARS (TV SERIES)
DARK DISCIPLE

III — REVENGE OF THE SITH
LORDS OF THE SITH
TARKIN
A NEW DAWN
REBELS (TV SERIES)

IV — A NEW HOPE
HEIR TO THE JEDI
BATTLEFRONT: TWILIGHT COMPANY

V — THE EMPIRE STRIKES BACK

VI — RETURN OF THE JEDI
AFTERMATH
AFTERMATH: LIFE DEBT
AFTERMATH: EMPIRE'S END
NEW REPUBLIC: BLOODLINE
THE PERFECT WEAPON (EBOOK ORIGINAL)

VII — THE FORCE AWAKENS

ACKNOWLEDGMENTS

So many people go into helping make a book what it is, from the first glimmer of an idea to the finished work. I'd like to thank, first and always, my wonderful readers, who make it possible for me to do work of the heart.

Special shout-out to my always fantastic editor, Shelly Shapiro, and to Erich Schoeneweiss, who offered both enthusiasm for the novel and insightful criticism to make it better. I'm grateful to Dave Filoni, for his fantastic work with *The Clone Wars* and for letting me hang out with two of the richest (and most fun) characters I've ever had the privilege to "meet." Extra gratitude to Katie Lucas, Matt Michnovetz, and Dave Filoni, whose scripts provided such a solid foundation for a great story. To Pablo Hidalgo and Leland Chee, thanks for helping me keep things true and accurate in this new incarnation of an old friend. And to Jennifer Heddle, who has aided my career in so many ways including this one.

Finally, so much appreciation to George Lucas, who, nearly forty years ago, gave this world one of its most beloved universes.

Thank you all!

FOREWORD

Star Wars has always loomed large in my life. I simply don't remember a time without it.

We began filming the prequels when I was eight years old and wrapped when I was fifteen. I spent a few adolescent summers as a PA on the sets of the prequels, watching and learning. I remember my baby brother training for days with Nick Gillard to execute an elaborate stunt as a fearless young Padawan. When he shot his scene, most of the actors came to the set to cheer him on—Hayden and Nick were so proud of him. The cast and the crew became an extended family of sorts. That was what *Star Wars* was built on—the collaboration and support of an entire community of passionate, talented people.

When I was seventeen, I was honored to have the opportunity to join that very community when I wrote my first ever episode of *Clone Wars,* "Jedi Crash." The positive response of the fans drove me to consider pursuing screenwriting in a more serious way. My run as a writer on *Clone Wars* ended up lasting almost ten years. During that time I had the pleasure of writing for some of the show's most exciting, not to mention most morally bankrupt, characters: Aurra Sing, Savage Opress, Darth Maul, and, of course, my favorite—Asajj Ventress.

I've always been drawn to resilient female characters having grown up obsessively watching *Buffy the Vampire Slayer,* and Ventress was the punk warrior witch of my dreams. Her strength and vulnerability resonated profoundly with me. I was thrilled to be assigned the *Dark Disciple* episodes and had a hell of a time writing them. I was in the throes of a bad breakup, and writing for Ventress and Vos was incredibly cathartic for me.

I was sad to see that *Clone Wars* was canceled before the episodes could air, but feel relieved that Ventress will finally be given her due with the publishing of this novel. At its core, *Dark Disciple* is a story of redemption; a story of how people can be unbelievably broken, and yet find a way to rebuild despite the odds. All of us are given chances time and time again to transform our lives, and it is our responsibility to seize those opportunities before they disappear.

Working with the incredible writers of *Clone Wars* and the incomparable Dave Filoni will always be one of the highlights of my career. *Clone Wars* gave me the tools to move forward on my own path and, most important, gifted me with the chance to serve the *Star Wars* universe for a brief time.

For as long as I live, I will never forget the times when my dad and I would sneak into the back of a darkened movie theater just as John Williams's unforgettable theme trumpeted from the speakers, holding hands while the crowd roared, raising their lightsabers into the air as the *Star Wars* logo flashed across the screen. I've never seen my dad happier.

May the Force always be with you.

Katie Lucas

A long time ago in a galaxy far, far away. . . .

STAR WARS
DARK DISCIPLE

For years, the galaxy-wide conflict known as the Clone Wars has raged. The struggle between the rightful government of the Galactic Republic and the Confederacy of Independent Systems has claimed the lives of untold billions.

The Force-wielding Jedi, for millennia the guardians of peace in the galaxy, have been thwarted at nearly every turn by the Separatists and their leader, the Sith Lord Count Dooku.

With the war showing no signs of ending, and the casualties mounting each day, the Jedi must consider every possible means of defeating their cunning foe. Whether some means are too unthinkable—and some allies too untrustworthy—has yet to be revealed . . .

CHAPTER ONE

Ashu-Nyamal, Firstborn of Ashu, child of the planet Mahranee, huddled with her family in the hold of a Republic frigate. Nya and the other refugees of Mahranee braced themselves against the repercussions from the battle raging outside. Sharp, tufted Mahran ears caught the sounds of orders, uttered and answered by clones, the same voice issuing from different throats; keen noses scented faint whiffs of fear from the speakers.

The frigate rocked from yet another blast. Some of the pups whimpered, but the adults projected calm. Rakshu cradled Nya's two younger siblings. Their little ears were flat against their skulls, and they shivered in terror against their mother's warm, lithe body, but their blue muzzles were tightly closed. No whimpers for them; a proud line, was Ashu. It had given the Mahran many fine warriors and wise statesmen. Nya's sister Teegu, Secondborn of Ashu, had a gift for soothing any squabble, and Kamu, the youngest, was on his way to becoming a great artist.

Or had been, until the Separatists had blasted Mahranee's capital city to rubble.

The Jedi had come, in answer to the distress call, as the Mahran knew they would. But they had come too late. Angry at the Mahranee government's refusal to cooperate, the Separatists had decided that genocide, or as close a facsimile as possible, would solve the problem of obtaining a world so rich in resources.

Nya clenched her fists. If only she had a blaster! She was an excellent shot. If any of the enemy attempted to board the ship, she could be of use to the brave clones now risking their lives to protect the refugees. Better yet, Nya wished she could stab one of the Separatist scum with her stinger, even though it would—

Another blast, this one worse. The lights flickered off, replaced almost instantly by the blood-red hue of the backup lighting. The dark-gray metal of the bulkheads seemed to close in ominously. Something snapped inside Nya. Before she really knew what she was doing, she had leapt to her feet and bounded across the hold to the rectangular door.

"Nya!" Rakshu's voice was strained. "We were told to stay here!"

Nya whirled, her eyes flashing. "I am walking the warrior path, Mother! I can't just sit here doing nothing. I have to try to help!"

"You will only be in the . . ." Rakshu's voice trailed off as Nya held her gaze. Tears slipped silently down Rakshu's muzzle, glittering in the crimson light. The Mahran were no telepaths, but even so, Nya knew her mother could read her thoughts.

I can do no harm. We are lost already.

Rakshu knew it, too. She nodded, then said, her voice swelling with pride in her eldest, "Stab well."

Nya swallowed hard at the blunt blessing. The stinger was the birthright of the Mahran—and, if used, their death warrant. The venom that would drop a foe in his tracks would also travel to his slayer's heart. The two enemies always died together. The words were said to one who was not expected to return alive.

"Good-bye, Mama," Nya whispered, too softly for her mother to hear. She slammed a palm against the button and the door opened. Without pausing she raced down the corridor, her path outlined by a strip of emergency lighting; she skidded to a halt when the hallway branched into two separate directions, picked one, and ran headlong into one of the clones.

"Whoa, there!" he said, not unkindly. "You're not supposed to be here, little one."

"I will *not* die huddled in fear!" Nya snapped.

"You're not going to," the clone said, attempting to be reassuring. "We've outrun puddle-jumpers like these before. Just get back to the holding area and stay out of our way. We've got this in hand."

Nya smelled the change in his sweat. He was lying. For a moment, she spared compassion for him. What had his life been like when he was a youngling? There had been no one to give him hugs or tell stories, no loving parental hands to soothe childhood's nightmares. Only brothers, identical in every way, who had been raised as clinically as he.

Brothers, and duty, and death.

Feeling strangely older than the clone, and grateful for her own unique life that was about to end, Nya smiled, shook her head, and darted past him.

He did not give chase.

The corridor ended in a door. Nya punched the button. The door slid open onto the cockpit. And she gasped.

She had never been in space before, so she was unprepared for the sight the five-section viewport presented. Bright flashes and streaks of laserfire dueled against an incongruously peaceful-looking starfield.

Nya wasn't sufficiently knowledgeable to be able to distinguish one ship from another—except for her own planet's vessels, looking old and small and desperate as they tried to flee with their precious cargo of families just like her own.

A clone and the Jedi general, the squat, reptilian Aleena who had led the mission to rescue Nya's people, occupied the cockpit's two chairs. With no warning, another blast rocked the ship. Nya went sprawling into the back of the clone's chair, causing him to lurch forward. He turned to her, his eyes dark with anger, and snapped, "Get off this—"

"General Chubor," came a smooth voice.

Nya's fur lifted. She whirled, snarling silently. Oh, she knew that voice. The Mahran had heard it uttering all sorts of pretty lies and promises that were never intended to be kept. She wondered if there was anyone left in the galaxy who didn't recognize the silky tones of Count Dooku.

He appeared on a small screen near the top of the main viewport. A satisfied, cruel smirk twisted Dooku's patrician features.

"I'm surprised you contacted me," his image continued. "As I recall, Jedi prefer to be regarded as the strong, silent type."

The clone lifted a finger to his lips, but the warning was unnecessary. Nya's sharp teeth were clenched, her fur bristled, and her entire being was focused on the count's loathed face, but she knew better than to speak.

General Chubor, sitting beside the clone in the pilot's chair, so short that his feet did not reach the floor, likewise was not baited. "You've got your victory, Dooku." His slightly nasal, high-pitched voice was heavy with sorrow. "The planet is yours . . . let us have the people. We have entire families aboard, many of whom are injured. They're innocents!"

Dooku chuckled, as if Chubor had said something dreadfully amusing over a nice hot cup of tea. "My dear General Chubor. You should know by now that in a war, there is no such thing as an innocent."

"Count, I repeat, our passengers are civilian families," General Chubor continued with a calmness at which Nya could only marvel. "Half of the refugees are younglings. Permit them, at least, to—"

"Younglings whose parents, unwisely, chose to ally with the Republic." Gone was Dooku's civilized purr. His gaze settled on Nya. She didn't flinch from his scrutiny, but she couldn't stifle a soft growl. He looked her up and down, then dismissed her as of no further interest. "I've been monitoring your transmissions, General, and I know that this little chat is being sent to the Jedi Council. So let me make one thing perfectly clear."

Dooku's voice was now hard and flat, as cold and pitiless as the ice of Mahranee's polar caps.

"As long as the Republic resists me, 'innocents' will continue to die. Every death in this war lies firmly at the feet of the Jedi. And now . . . it is time for you and your passengers to join the ranks of the fallen."

One of the largest Mahranee ships bloomed silently into a flower of yellow and red that disintegrated into pieces of rubble.

Nya didn't know she had screamed until she realized her throat was raw. Chubor whirled in his chair.

His large-eyed gaze locked with hers.

The last thing Ashu-Nyamal, Firstborn of Ashu, would ever see was the shattered expression of despair in the Jedi's eyes.

* * *

The bleakest part about being a Jedi, thought Master Obi-Wan Kenobi, *is when we fail.*

He had borne witness to scenes like the one unfolding before the Jedi Council far too many times to count, and yet the pain didn't lessen. He hoped it never would.

The terrified final moments of thousands of lives played out before them, then the grim holographic recording flickered and vanished. For a moment, there was a heavy silence.

The Jedi cultivated a practice of nonattachment, which had always served them well. Few understood, though, that while specific, individual bonds such as romantic love or family were forbidden, the Jedi were not ashamed of compassion. All lives were precious, and when so many were lost in such a way, the Jedi felt the pain of it in the Force as well as in their own hearts.

At last, Master Yoda, the diminutive but extraordinarily powerful head of the Jedi Council, sighed deeply. "Grieved are we all, to see so many suffer," he said. "Courage, the youngling had, at the end. Forgotten, she and her people will not be."

"I hope her bravery brought her comfort," Kenobi said. "The Mahran prize it. She and the others are one with the Force now. But I have no more earnest wish than that this tragedy be the last the war demands."

"As do all of us, Master Kenobi," said Master Mace Windu. "But I don't think that wish is coming true anytime soon."

"Did any ships make it out with their passengers?" Anakin Skywalker asked. Kenobi had asked the younger man, still only a Jedi Knight, to accompany him to this gathering, and Anakin stood behind Kenobi's chair.

"Reported in, no one has," Yoda said quietly. "But hope, always, there is."

"With respect, Master Yoda," Anakin said, "the Mahran needed more than our *hope*. They needed our help, and what we were able to give them wasn't enough."

"And unfortunately, they are not the only ones we've been forced to give short shrift," Windu said.

"For almost three standard years, this war has raged," said Plo Koon, the Kel Dor member of the Council. His voice was muffled due to the mask he wore over his mouth and nose, a requirement for his species in this atmosphere. "We can barely even count the numbers of the fallen. But this—" He shook his head.

"All directly because of one man's ambition and evil," said Windu.

"It's true that Dooku is the leader of the Separatists," Kenobi said. "And no one will argue that he is both ambitious *and* evil. But he hasn't done it alone. I agree that Dooku may be responsible for every death in this war, but he didn't actively commit each one."

"Of course not," Plo Koon said, "but it's interesting that you use nearly the same words as Dooku. He placed the blame for the casualties squarely upon us."

"A lie, that is," Yoda said. He waved a small hand dismissively. "Foolish it would be, for us to give it a moment's credence."

"Would it be, truly, Master Yoda?" Windu asked with a hard look on his face. As a senior member of the Council, he was one of the few who dared question Master Yoda. Kenobi raised an eyebrow.

"What do you mean, Master Windu?" asked Yoda.

"Have the Jedi really explored every option? Could we have ended this war sooner? Could we, in fact, end it right now?"

Something prickled at the back of Kenobi's neck. "Speak plainly," he said.

Windu glanced at his fellows. He seemed to be weighing his words. Finally, he spoke.

"Master Kenobi's right—Dooku couldn't have done this completely alone. Billions follow him. But I also stand by my observation—that this war is Dooku's creation. Those who follow him, follow *him*. Every player is controlled by the count; every conspiracy has been traced back to him."

Anakin's brow furrowed. "You're not saying anything we don't already know, Master."

Windu continued. "Without Dooku, the Separatist movement would collapse. There would no longer be a single, seemingly invincible figurehead to rally around. Those who were left would consume themselves in a frenzy to take his place. If every river is a branch of a single mighty one . . . then let us dam the flow. Cut off the head, and the body will fall."

"But that's what we've been—*oh*." Anakin's blue eyes widened with sudden comprehension.

No, Kenobi thought, *surely Mace isn't suggesting—*

Yoda's ears unfurled as he sat up straighter. "Assassination, mean you?"

"No." Kenobi spoke before he realized he was going to, and his voice was strong and certain. "Some things simply aren't within the realm of possibility. Not," he added sharply, looking at Mace, "for Jedi."

"Speaks the truth, Master Kenobi does," Yoda said. "To the dark side, such actions lead."

Mace held up his hands in a calming gesture. "No one here wishes to behave like a Sith Lord."

"Few do, at first. A small step, the one that determines destiny often is."

Windu looked from Yoda to Kenobi, then his brown-eyed gaze lingered on Kenobi. "Answer me this. How often has this Council sat, shaking our heads, saying, *Everything leads back to Dooku*? A few dozen times? A few *hundred*?"

Kenobi didn't reply. Beside him, Anakin shifted his weight. The younger Jedi didn't look at Kenobi or Windu, and his lips were pressed together in a thin, unhappy line.

"A definitive blow must be struck," Mace said. He rose from his chair and closed the distance between himself and Kenobi. Mace had the height advantage, but Kenobi got to his feet calmly and met Windu's gaze.

"Dooku is going to keep doing exactly what he has been," Windu continued quietly. "He's not going to change. And if *we* don't change, either, then the war will keep raging until this tortured galaxy is nothing but space debris and dead worlds. We—the Jedi and the clones we command—are the *only* ones who can stop it!"

"Master Windu is right," said Anakin. "I think it's about time to open the floor to ideas that before we would have never considered."

"Anakin," Kenobi warned.

"With respect, Master Kenobi," Anakin barreled on. "Mahranee's fall is terrible. But it's only the most recent crime Dooku has committed against a world and a people."

Mace added, "The Mahran who died today already have more than enough company. Do we want to increase those numbers? One man's life must be weighed against those of potentially millions of innocents. Isn't protecting the innocent the very definition of what it means to be a Jedi? We are failing the Republic and its citizens. We must stop this—*now*."

Kenobi turned to Yoda. The ancient Jedi Master peered at all those present, be it physically or holographically: Saesee Tiin, an Iktotchi Master; the Togruta Shaak Ti, her expression calm but sorrowful; the images of Kit Fisto, Oppo Rancisis, and Depa Billaba. Kenobi was surprised to see sorrow and resignation settle over Yoda's wrinkled green face. The diminutive Jedi closed his huge eyes for a moment, then opened them.

"Greatly heavy, my heart is, that come to this, matters have," he said. Using his cane, he rose and walked to the window. All eyes followed him. Below, Coruscant unfolded, and myriad small, personal vessels sped past, and the sun gazed down at it all as clouds drifted languidly by.

Yoda extended a three-fingered hand, indicating the view. "Each life, a flame in the Force is. Beautiful. Unique. Glowing and precious, it stands, to bravely cast its own small light against the darkness that would consume it." Yoda lifted his cane, pointing at a cloud that was grayer and larger than most of its fellows. "But grows, this darkness does, with each minute that Dooku continues his attacks." Yoda fell silent. No one interrupted as the cloud continued on its path, moving to hide the face of the sun. Its shadow leeched away the vibrancy of the city beneath it, turning its gleam to dullness, its bright colors to a muted, somber palette. It was nothing more than the sun and a shadow, but nonetheless, Kenobi felt his heart lurch within his chest.

"Stop him, we must," Yoda said solemnly. He closed his eyes and bowed his head. The moment hung heavy, and it seemed everyone was loath to break it.

Finally Mace spoke. "The question before us now is—who will strike the killing blow?"

Kenobi sighed and rubbed his eyes. "I, ah . . . may have a suggestion . . ."

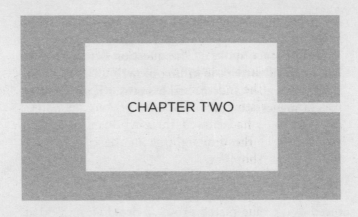

CHAPTER TWO

Things were going very well for Koorivar merchant
Sheb Valaad. Very well indeed. He had come to
Otor's Hub—*the* place to be if one dealt in certain
merchandise—a standard year before the war had
broken out. While others busied themselves with
choosing sides, Sheb had made himself a "powerful
friend" to both. Everybody liked trinkets: jewels,
paintings, statues, fancy hookah pipes made of exotic
materials and studded with gems from far distant
worlds. And if the makers of such exquisite items
happened to have met with unpleasant fates, well,
that simply caused what they had created to become
even more valuable. Most times, Sheb waited for the
unpleasant fates to occur and positioned himself to
benefit. Sometimes, he took a more . . . direct approach.

Oh, not he himself, no, no. His hands were made
for handling money and stroking valuable items.
There were plenty of others willing to take his credits
to do the ugly business of increasing the value of certain objects. He settled back in his chair and took a
pull on his hookah, absently reaching a hand to fin-

ger the ornate carvings on the horn that jutted from his skull.

A Koorivar's horn is a Koorivar's pride, his father had told him. It told the world everything it needed to know about the individual sporting it. Sheb's horn was large, twisting, and lavishly decorated. Great— *late*—artisans had carved their work upon it, and jewels caught the dim lighting in the smoky back room of his "shop."

He availed himself of one of the delicate pastries that were the specialty of his private chef, then gestured to the blue-plated protocol droid who stood at attention beside the door. Someone else stood at attention, too—the ever-reliable Thurg, a burly Gamorrean.

"Show our guest in, Blue," Sheb said.

"Of course, my most glorious master." Sheb had sprung for a customized version of the current protocol unit. Blue came equipped with two specialized programs: "Adul-8" and "B-Little." The former soothed Sheb, and the latter had proven vastly entertaining.

Blue stepped through the curtained door into the waiting room that lay beyond while Thurg, looking slightly bored, picked at his large, yellowed teeth. Sheb hoped Blue would catch him at it. The dressing-down the droid would give Thurg was sure to be a delight. Though Blue probably should be grateful it was only the Gamorrean's teeth that were being picked, not the bodyguard's porcine nostrils.

"Master Tal?" said the droid in his precise, clipped voice. "The most honorable, reputable, and *extremely* fair merchant of high-quality valuables and artifacts, Sheb Valaad, has graciously agreed to grant your request for an audience."

"Whoa, there," came Tal's cheerful voice. Sheb

took another pastry, smiling, and poured tea for his customer. Over these last couple of months, Tal had become a regular patron, and Sheb wondered what Tal's glib tongue had in store for poor Blue today. "I see you're set on verbal overload, Blue. And I've told you, don't call me master."

"Today's program setting will not permit me to override the designation, I fear, Master Tal." The droid strode through the curtain, politely holding it to the side so that Tal could enter easily.

Tal Khar was a tall, well-muscled Kiffar specimen who moved with an easy grace. As always, his eyes sparkled with good humor above the narrow yellow tattoo that ran the width of his face. Thurg blocked his way with a grunt and stood expectantly.

Tal rolled his eyes. "Sheb, call off your bantha. I've never brought a weapon in yet." The Gamorrean hesitated, looking back at his master, confused.

"Thurg, you know the rules."

Tal grinned at Thurg. "Go ahead. But you know I don't have any weapons."

"I know you no have weapons," Thurg said in guttural Basic, patting Tal down then stepping back. "He unarmed."

"You may now enter the radiant presence of my magnificent master," said Blue, sweeping his arm for good measure.

"Hey, Blue," Tal said, "how many synonyms for your name are there?"

"In Basic, there are—"

Tal waved a hand. "No, no, in *all* your languages. And can you tell me what they are?"

A slightly choked sound emanated from the droid, and he visibly slumped. Then: "Blue: My data banks register forty billion, eleven million, seven hundred forty-two thousand, nine hundred and eighty-three accepted synonyms for the color blue. Beginning with Basic, they are, in alphabetical order, ao, aqua, azure—"

"You don't have to obey that instruction, Blue," Sheb said.

"Oh, thank you, my most marvelous master, I am *exceedingly* grateful."

Sheb indicated the platter of pastries. "Tal, Tal," he said with a sigh. "Are you *trying* to short out my droid?"

". . . Maybe?" said Tal, his mouth full.

"Well, if you ever succeed, I shall expect to be compensated for repairs," the merchant said. "Now wipe your hands; I've something quite remarkable for you today."

Tal obliged with the enthusiasm of a child awaiting a gift, looking expectantly at Sheb. Sheb waved one of his assistants over. The Twi'lek female carried a tray, atop which sat something covered by a piece of cloth. With a flourish, Sheb unveiled the latest treasure.

Tal gasped quite satisfactorily, which did not surprise Sheb in the least. The item on the tray was millennia old but looked as if it had left the artist's studio but a few moments past. It was a small statuette of an aquatic creature, all memory of its species now forgotten, that had once frolicked—presumably it had frolicked, if the playful motion captured by the stone carving was to be trusted—in the oceans of a world that had been likewise lost to time. Small gems served it for eyes, and its tail curved beneath its four-flippered body to merge with a base that looked like a cresting wave.

Tal reached out to it, then paused, raising his eyebrows in question. Feeling like a benevolent deity,

Sheb nodded his permission to pick up the precious artifact. Tal did so, with great care.

"Boss? This scum say he need see you." Thurg forced his way through the curtains. His huge hands were clamped down on the furry arms of a Mahran, who didn't struggle at all. He looked around in appreciation.

"Nice, very nice," he said. His gaze fell on Tal.

Tal stared at him for a moment, then heaved a sigh. "Desh. What are you doing here?"

"Came to get you."

"Well, I'm busy."

Still held by the mammoth Gamorrean, the Mahran—who, apparently, knew Tal, and whose name was, apparently, Desh—actually managed a shrug. "Sorry."

"What . . ." Sheb struggled for words, trying to make sense of the absurd situation. "Tal, do you know this . . . this—"

"I do, from way back. He's not supposed to be here yet. Well, I guess what's done is done." Shaking his long black dreadlocked hair, Tal gently put the figurine on the table, sliding it a little bit away from him. He rose. "Too bad. I liked the pastries."

He extended a hand in Sheb's direction, then jerked it upward. The merchant let out a treble yelp of astonishment as he found himself squirming in midair. At the same instant the Mahran twisted and brought his arms up, breaking Thurg's grip as if it were nothing at all, then grabbed the Gamorrean's arm and flipped him over.

"Oh, I say," squeaked a panicked Blue, heading for the door with his arms raised, "help! Help—"

Four armed bodyguards charged in. The Rodian, huge black eyes fixed on Tal, slammed into the hapless droid. Blue went clattering into a corner, and the Rodian began firing at the interlopers.

"No, no blasters!" Sheb shouted, thinking of the irreplaceable items on display in the room, but they ignored him. Red blasterfire screamed through the room, and Sheb, still dangling in the air, screamed along with it, first in pain at seeing his beautiful merchandise obliterated, and then again when a bolt seared through his flapping robes dangerously close to his torso.

There were two other lights flashing about, as well, about a meter long, one green, one blue, that Tal and the interloper wielded like swords. Lightsabers! That meant—

Tal kept one hand extended, holding Sheb aloft, and with the other batted back the red bolts with an almost casual ease. Was the man . . . humming?

"Ahhh!" cried the Koorivar as a blast singed his thigh.

Tal winced. "Sorry," he said, smiling sheepishly up at Sheb, even as he executed a backward flip ending in a sharp, perfectly placed kick to the midsection of a bodyguard. The Gamorrean stumbled, then toppled as Tal slammed the butt of the lightsaber into his temple.

"I wasn't *done* yet," Tal said, directing his attention to Desh. The smaller, more slender Jedi—for such Sheb realized they both had to be—was on the table now. He splayed a four-fingered hand and lifted the Rodian into the air. For an insane second, he and his employer hovered eye-to-eye, the Rodian's tubular muzzle undulating with protests, and then the green-skinned bodyguard was slammed against the wall.

"Well, don't blame the messenger," the Mahran

said. He wasn't even breathing hard. "I was told you're to be reassigned."

"Two more weeks and I would have gotten the whole operation," Tal grumbled. He, too, was speaking as calmly as if the entire exchange were occurring in his own home over friendly drinks. "The Council couldn't wait that long?"

"It would seem not." Desh somersaulted from the table to the floor, grabbing two chairs in the process and hurling them at the four-eyed, arachnoid Aqualish firing steadily, though fruitlessly, at Tal. The furniture struck the bodyguard perfectly and he went sprawling to the floor, limbs entangled in the chair's back and legs at painful-looking angles. His blaster flew out of his hands.

The Mahran caught it effortlessly. He whistled as he examined it. "Nice."

"Oh, no, you don't, Blue," said Tal. The protocol droid had hastened over to one of the fallen bodyguards and clutched a comlink in his hand. Still keeping one hand turned toward Sheb, the Jedi leapt toward the droid and severed Blue's hand from his wrist. The droid gave a high-pitched shriek. "Oh, come on, that can be fixed," Tal said. "Don't be a baby."

"So, did I ruin the whole mission?" asked Desh. He thumbed his lightsaber, and with a *snap-hiss* the blade deactivated.

"Not the *whole* mission. Just the really satisfying wrap-up part of it." Miraculously, the statue of the oceanic creature had survived intact. Tal picked it up, smiling. "But this will do. I got a lot of useful information on a lot of very nasty sorts from this one."

"That touchy-feely stuff you do with things does come in handy."

"It's called psychometry, thank you very much."

Listening, Sheb realized why Tal—which, of course, wasn't this Jedi's name at all—had always been so eager to touch everything before purchasing it. Come to think of it, he hadn't purchased much, but he had certainly handled . . . Sheb whimpered.

"You know everything," he said, his voice taut.

"Well, not *everything*," said Tal-not-Tal. "I mean, I don't know every synonym for *blue*, for example. Blue, how about it?"

"Oh, dear," squeaked the droid.

"And as for you, Sheb, it's been a pleasure doing business with you. This might hurt a bit, but I'm sure the Jedi who will be here momentarily will take care of you."

Tal lifted his hand. And as the miserable protocol droid began to list the billions of synonyms for his name, Sheb almost thought he would welcome the unconsciousness that was about to claim him as Tal, looking apologetic, drew back his hand to send the black-market merchant hurtling into the wall.

CHAPTER THREE

It was not his birthplace, exactly, but the Jedi Temple was where Quinlan Vos had grown up. He'd raced through its corridors, hidden behind its massive pillars, found peace in its meditation hall, ended—and started—fights in rooms intended for striking blows and some that weren't, and sneaked naps in its library. All Jedi came here, at some point in their lives; for Quinlan, it always felt like coming home when he ran lightly up the stairs and entered the massive building as he did now.

He had enjoyed taking down Sheb's black-market operation back-to-back with his old friend, but that pleasure had been mitigated almost at once when they returned to Desh's ship. On their way back to Coruscant, Desh, whose formal name was Akar-Deshu, had soberly briefed him on Dooku's devastating attack on Mahranee. Vos didn't know what to say to offer comfort. The planet was now controlled by the Separatists, and they had made it clear that all Mahran were to be regarded as extremely hostile and killed on sight. A world and its people had fallen in the space of a few hours.

Obi-Wan Kenobi's normally modulated voice had had a slight edge of urgency to it when Vos and Desh had reported in, and it was that more than the cryptic words that made Vos decide to forgo anything resembling formal attire. Well, anything resembling *appropriate* attire, if he was being honest. After the refreshing scuffle, both his clothes and he could have used a good washing, but he figured there would be a chance to clean up once he'd pinned down Obi-Wan and found out what the hell was going on.

Everyone knew him here—even now, when he was often away for months, sometimes even a year, at a stretch. Vos grinned happily at seeing familiar faces and exchanged so many hugs, claps on the back, and handshakes that he was concerned he might be—

"Late, as usual," said Kenobi, in his usual put-upon tone.

Vos glanced up and smirked, used the Force to leap a dozen stairs, and landed gracefully before the Jedi Master.

"Nice to see you, too, Obi-Wan! I'm sure you've missed me."

"Not terribly," Kenobi said, but he smiled as he said it. "I do not recall our last adventure with particular fondness. Unfortunately, I don't think this next assignment will be nearly so pleasant, though I hope it is more successful." The two Jedi Masters had last been paired together to track down an escaped Hutt named Ziro. Unfortunately, someone had beaten them to the Hutt, with fatal results for the unpleasant Ziro.

Obi-Wan, as befitted a Jedi, was adept at concealing his feelings in the Force when he chose to. But now he did not, and even a non-Force-sensitive could have seen the concern in his gray-blue eyes.

"This isn't going to be good, is it?" Vos asked quietly.

"No, old friend," Kenobi said with a sigh. "It's quite far from good, actually."

"I'm listening."

Kenobi shook his head. "No, I . . . think I'll let the Council explain everything as they see fit."

Volumes were spoken in Kenobi's demeanor and word choice, and Vos didn't pry further. He had a bad feeling about this.

Kenobi found the hologram no easier to watch a second time. He instead concentrated on how Vos reacted. The other Jedi seldom opted to conceal his emotions, though he could when needed, and pain was in Vos's dark-brown eyes as the tragedy unfolded. And as before, there was silence when the hologram finished.

Vos exhaled and pressed his lips together. "Desh told me about the attack, but I had no idea this was why you asked me to come here. What does the Council wish of me?"

"A course of action that we reluctantly deemed necessary," said Mace. Vos's gaze flickered to Yoda, doubtless curious as to why Windu spoke instead of the head of the Council. "There's no way to phrase this other than bluntly. Master Vos—the Council wants you to assassinate Count Dooku."

For perhaps the first time since Kenobi had known Vos, the other Jedi was at an utter loss for words. He stared first at Windu, then at Yoda, then finally at Kenobi. He opened his mouth, possibly to protest or demand an explanation, then fell silent for a moment. When he spoke, he said quietly, "I think I understand. But . . . how do you propose I do this?"

"Get close to him, you will," said Yoda.

"Close enough to kill him? How am I supposed to manage that? I can't just walk into his palace."

"You have served the Republic well in previous undercover missions," Windu said.

"Well, sure—I've stopped some black-market shipments and blasted a few smugglers, but *this* . . . It's not a one-man job."

"Correct, Master Vos is."

Kenobi raised an auburn eyebrow. The plan had been for this to be a solo endeavor, but Yoda looked tranquil as he spoke, as if they'd intended this all along.

"Go alone, he will not. More than one it will take, to kill Dooku."

"Master Yoda, I volunteer to assist Master Vos," Anakin said at once. Before Kenobi could protest—he well knew that putting Anakin and Quinlan together on a mission was simply *asking* for trouble—Yoda shook his own head.

"One, there is, who has tried and failed," the old Jedi Master said. "Yet closer has she come than any other to killing Count Dooku."

Now it was Kenobi's turn to stare at the wizened Council leader. "You can't *possibly* mean Ventress!"

"Ventress?" Vos echoed. "Not Dooku's apprentice Ventress? The one who's been a thorn in our side for years?"

Yoda nodded serenely.

Asajj Ventress had indeed once been Count Dooku's Sith apprentice—and pet assassin. Kenobi and Anakin had crossed lightsabers with her on more than one occasion. Tall, lithe, exceptionally skilled in the Force, the former Nightsister was a formidable foe. But if anyone hated Dooku, it was her; Ventress's former Master had tried to kill her. Rumor had it she'd attempted more than once to return the favor.

"Wait, wait. I can't have heard this right," Vos said. "The Jedi Council wants me to work with a *Sith*?"

Kenobi shifted uneasily in his chair. Ludicrous as the idea sounded, when one set aside its very unexpectedness, it actually made a great deal of sense.

"*Failed* Sith," Kenobi corrected. "I wouldn't go so far as to call her trustworthy, but . . . it's true that our desires do align, on this one point. And no one knows him as well as she does. I must concur with Master Yoda. Asajj Ventress would be a tremendous resource, and one that could prove vital to the success of this mission."

"*Failed* is an interesting choice of words, considering Ventress has *failed* at more than being the perfect Sith," Windu snapped. He seemed surprised at Kenobi's words. "She's attempted to kill Dooku repeatedly and, obviously, not succeeded."

"She acted alone, before," Kenobi said. He turned to Vos. "This time, she won't be. She'll have you."

Vos's furrowed brow smoothed out and his dark eyes crinkled with their customary mischief above the yellow tattoo that crossed his face. "Didn't know you were such a romantic, Kenobi. Sure you won't be jealous?" Turning more serious, he asked, "How much help could she be? She hasn't been around Dooku for a while now. Why would she want to work with us, anyway? She won't be eager to help Jedi."

"The same man, our enemy is," Yoda said. "Aid us, she can—although she must not know she does so. His personality, his way of thinking, the places he knows and retreats to—knows all this, Ventress does." He leaned forward, his large eyes peering at Vos from beneath his deeply wrinkled brow.

"Ignorant of your pursuit, your quarry must be, of course. But ignorant also of her aid, must Asajj Ventress be."

"This is getting too complicated," Vos said. "Maybe this *is* a one-man job. No disrespect—but if I'm going to do this, I'm going to do it on my own, clean and simple. She'll just get in the way."

Yoda's face relaxed into a combination of gentleness and implacability. "Always know you to walk alone, the Council does," he said. "Underestimate Ventress, you do. Skilled, she is. Her help you must take, or fail you will."

Kenobi felt a not-unpleasant chill as Yoda uttered the words. He knew what that meant. Few were stronger in the Force than Yoda, and while the diminutive green-skinned Master was always humble and cautioned that one could never predict the ever-changing future with complete accuracy, there were some things that he simply knew to be the right path. This was one of them.

The rippling in the Force told Kenobi that his fellow Council members, all of whom were familiar with Yoda's unique insight, had sensed this, as well.

Picking up on the energetic shift in the room, Vos sighed. "All right—I accept the mission. I'll find Ventress and get her cooperation . . . somehow. And I will assassinate Count Dooku. But I can't promise that Ventress will survive this any more than Dooku will, once I'm through with him."

"See all ends, you cannot, young one," Yoda said.

"I can see the end of this session, Master Yoda," Vos said, "and it ends with me bowing, getting a shower and a meal, and likely getting more details from, I'm guessing, Master Kenobi."

Some frowned at Vos's impertinence, but Yoda's green-gold eyes were warm with amusement. "Correct you are, on all counts," he said. "Even the right order, have you determined." He sobered. "Cheers the spirit, humor does, even at the darkest times. Yet grave, this task is, and fraught with peril. May the Force be with you, Quinlan Vos."

The shower was welcome, the meal in the group dining hall even more so. All Jedi Padawans began their training at young ages, with little or no recollection of their families. Vos, brought to the Temple even younger than most, felt that he had hundreds of brothers and sisters, and it seemed that whenever he went into the dining hall he ran into at least half of them.

It was wonderful.

Popularity. Adulation. A Jedi, as Yoda might have said, craved not those things. Nor did Vos, really. But it made him happy to see his companions, to meet the overly solemn Padawans and squirmy-puppy younglings, and it was with reluctance that he left to go on his next assignment. He often thought that it was his ability to enjoy wherever he was and the company of whomever he was with that made him—perhaps ironically—so successful in jobs that took him to the worst places and saw him in the company of the worst people.

But Quinlan Vos had always ventured into stuffy, close rooms, darkened alleys, and isolated outposts alone. No one else to keep track of, to be beholden to, or to worry about. Once you realized that everyone with whom you associated was, potentially, happy to literally stab you in the back, all the wondering just . . . went away. Simple. Clean. Uncomplicated.

From everything he'd heard, Asajj Ventress was about as complicated as anyone could get. Obi-Wan,

Anakin, and Yoda had all gone toe-to-toe with her. There was clearly something about the woman that, on some level, they respected.

"Well, you're here long enough to shower and eat," Desh said as he plunked down a tray and sat across from Vos.

"Maybe even sleep!" Vos said, smiling as he sliced open a white-striped purple jogan fruit.

"Such luxury!" Desh winked and dived into a generous slice of steak. "Don't get used to it."

"I never do," said Vos.

"Don't suppose you can talk about it?"

"Can I ever?"

Desh thought about it, chewing, then shook his head. "Usually not. But there's something about it that concerns you."

"The perils of old friends," Vos said with a sigh. "I'm to have a partner."

"I know you prefer to work alone, but Jedi often work in pairs," Desh replied.

"That's just it. She's *not* a Jedi, and she's not even supposed to know that *I'm* one. Plus," Vos added, "this mission we're supposed to undertake together— it's extremely delicate and dangerous. I don't like wondering if my partner's more of a threat than the actual target."

"Well," Desh said, "the Temple can't prepare us for everything. That's part of the fun."

"And in what area is the Temple failing you at this moment, Master Vos?" It was Kenobi, smiling pleasantly as he joined them.

"You know, I'm glad you asked," Vos said.

"Oh, dear." Kenobi sighed.

"I know how to work with my fellow Jedi, and with civilians," Vos said. "I know how to deal with underworld scum and their hangers-on. But you know and I know that this 'partner' is unique, and I need to know what sort of interaction she's going to expect."

"Ah," said Kenobi. "Desh, can you excuse us? Vos will need to depart for his mission early tomorrow, and there are some . . ." He hesitated. ". . . things he should know about it."

"Of course, Master Kenobi," Desh said. "Later, Vos!" He picked up his tray and left them to it.

Kenobi turned to Vos. "Rather like you, Ventress appears to work alone. Frankly, we don't know how she'll react," Kenobi said. "But there are a few things about her personality I've learned. She's driven, focused, and hates Dooku. Once you've gained her trust, and she sees a real chance at killing her former Master, I think you'll be able to depend on her completely."

"Well, that's good. But how do I get to that part?"

"Asajj Ventress is highly intelligent and doesn't suffer fools gladly. Skill and competence impress her." Kenobi hesitated. "She's also a very striking woman, physically. It might tip her off if you, er, don't . . . *notice* her. And . . . she likes to trade barbs."

Vos snagged a fried kajaka root from Obi-Wan's plate and popped it into his mouth. "You were fighting her and chatting at the same time?"

Kenobi nodded. "It's . . ." He searched for the word. "Banter."

"You *flirted* with her?"

"Come now, Vos, you can't tell me you managed to go undercover in all sorts of shady places without flirting yourself. With Ventress, it's a power play, a way for her to exert control. It will serve you best if you engage in it with her."

Vos tapped his chest. "*Je-di,*" he said exaggeratedly. "No attachments, remember? How far is too far?"

"Be a little rough around the edges. Leer a bit. She'll make it plain enough she's not interested and take satisfaction in telling you so. She'll see it as a win."

Vos sighed. "I think," he said, taking another one of Kenobi's fried root strips, "that killing Dooku is going to be the easy part."

Kenobi did not contradict him.

CHAPTER FOUR

Level 1313 was so named because it was one thousand, three hundred, and thirteen levels from the core of the planet. Vos suspected it was easier to think of it that way rather than focusing on the weight of almost four thousand other levels between oneself and the surface. The difference between Coruscant's literal and figurative "underworld" and the one that saw the sun was sufficiently stark that they might as well be located in two different systems. Crimes that would be viewed as appalling above were everyday occurrences here. The Jedi wondered, not for the first time, how many would be born, live, and die here, never having glimpsed the sun, let alone the stars. He strode past shivering figures with hands outstretched to small fires burning in metal drums. Voices called out to him: *Please, sir, got anything to eat, or some credits to spare? Hey, handsome, I know what you want. Right this way, we've got what you're looking for, exotic items from across the galaxy . . .*

With a gentle brush of the Force, a flick of a finger, and a noncommittal smile, Vos caused each inquirer to forget they had seen him, focusing on his goal: a bar that looked—well, pretty much like every other bar Vos had patronized in the last few years.

He loved this part of a mission: when anything and everything could happen, when it was all new and exciting and hadn't yet devolved into something dirty, complicated, and usually far too banal.

The door hissed open to admit him. Though the air was hazy with the smoke of various substances being burned, Vos could nonetheless make out the forms of females of various species gyrating to the thump of loud, primal music. Quickly he scanned the place, looking for the individuals he had come to find.

One, a green-skinned, reptilian Trandoshan dressed in a yellow flight suit, sat at the bar. Vos spotted the others, nestled farther in the darker corners of the establishment, but they would come later.

Most of the patrons were huddled deep in conversation, but there was an empty space near the Trandoshan. Vos strode up, getting the server droid's attention and, gesturing to what appeared to be the drink of choice for the establishment, said cheerily to no one in particular, "Hey, how's it going?"

A couple of the patrons gave him sidelong glances, but no one replied. Undaunted, Vos took a seat, nodding to the droid who slid a cup filled with something thick and dark in his direction, and continued. "You gentlemen have any leads on any jobs?"

The Trandoshan (*Bossk,* Vos recalled: *known for hunting Wookiees with a viciousness and thoroughness that surpassed even that of most Trandoshans; member of the Bounty Hunters' Guild*) hissed in either amusement or annoyance—or perhaps both.

"This ain't no hospitality service, buddy. You're either in the know, or you ain't. And clearly . . . you ain't." With this pithy comment, he turned back to his drink, clearly feeling he had said all that needed to be said.

Vos gave it a beat, knocked back his drink as if he welcomed the horrible acidic taste, then said casually, "I guess the bald banshee is stealing everybody's gigs these days."

The constant murmur of voices and the clanking of ceramic ware and cutlery paused among those within earshot. Bossk turned to regard Vos again, stared at him stonily for a moment, then laughed.

"That woman is trouble!" He clapped Vos on the shoulder with a three-fingered, clawed hand, and gestured at the server droid. "Give my new friend another one of whatever he's drinking. On me."

Vos nodded his thanks. "So," pressed Bossk, "she stole a job from you, huh?"

Instead of answering directly, Vos inquired, "Where is she these days?"

The Trandoshan's eyes narrowed slightly. "No idea."

Gently, subtly, Vos extended a sense of camaraderie into the Force as he spoke. "I'd like to get a little *payback*. Know what I mean?"

Bossk regarded him for a moment longer, then seemed to make a decision. "I know someone who might know where she is. Come on."

He rose and started across the room, shoving his way through the crowd with no finesse and a great deal of confidence. Vos followed his new best friend to a booth back in one of the darkest corners of the bar. An anooba, its long tail curled almost twice around its pale-striped canine form, dozed under the table. It awoke at Vos's approach and started to snarl.

With a slight wave of his hand, Vos calmed it just enough. It wouldn't do for the beast to suddenly become overly friendly, but an attack wouldn't help his mission, either. It sniffed the air and its growl turned into a whine as it relaxed, though its ears and eyes showed that it remained alert.

Seated in the booth were a Theelin bounty hunter with strawberry-blond hair styled in deceptively innocent-looking pigtails (*Latts Razzi: preferred weapon the grappling boa*), a male Kyuzo with an enormous and doubtless heavy metallic hat (*Embo, utilizes the "hat" as both weapon and transportation; held in high regard among his fellow bounty hunters, owner of the anooba Marrok*), a droid (*Highsinger: extremely effective bounty hunter, believed to be unique*), and an earnest-looking, shaved-headed young man who had to be—

"Hey, Boba," said Bossk, "this guy is looking for No Name, the rookie."

Boba Fett was young, looking to be only in his late teens. "Rookie?" Fett snorted. "Don't you believe it. That woman knows *exactly* what she's doing."

"And what she's doing is . . ."

"Conning people. Why do you want to know, anyway?" Fett scowled into his drink, refusing to elaborate. Clearly, Ventress was a touchy subject. Vos was unsurprised.

"Like you, I got cheated out of a couple of big payouts," he offered.

"She didn't cheat us," Latts Razzi piped up. She swirled her cocktail, her eyes twinkling with humor as she peered up at Vos. "We got our pay. Just . . . not how the Boss here likes it."

"True enough," muttered Fett, "but I don't like her style." He drained his drink for emphasis.

"Agreed," Vos said mildly. He didn't attempt to directly influence any of the bounty hunters. They hadn't gotten their reputations by being weak-minded. He simply stood, exuding good cheer—which wasn't a pretense.

Fett looked Vos up and down. "You think you can give her a run? Make some trouble for her?"

"I'm certain of it."

Fett nodded, seemingly satisfied. "All right. I got a tip she took a job on Pantora, chasing down a Volpai named Moregi." He removed a holoprojector from his pocket, and the small image of a four-armed humanoid sprang to life on his outstretched palm. Fett's expression darkened as he regarded the figure. "I *was* going to take that job myself until I heard *she* got involved. You think you can handle her, be my guest." He tossed the holoprojector to Vos as if it were a discarded sabacc chip. Vos caught it deftly.

Bossk grinned at him. "Let's hope you're man enough."

Vos flipped the holoprojector in his palm, winked, and left. But not before he heard what Boba Fett doubtless thought was the final word on the subject: "He has no idea what he's getting himself into."

True enough, Vos thought with a mental shrug. *I never do.*

And that was half the fun.

Pantora was the primary moon in orbit around the planet Orto Plutonia. The moon was as temperate as the planet was icy and hostile, and had an elegant cityscape with the repeating pattern of domes shaped like teardrops—or, less poetically, onions. The Pantorans, for whatever reason, seemed inordinately fond of building on multiple levels. Parks, walkways, and other varieties of decorative architectural constructs adorned what on other worlds would be unremarkable rooftops.

Asajj Ventress was not a poetic woman, and the architecture of Pantora concerned her only inasmuch as it was making it difficult for her to track down her quarry. At the present moment, she stood atop a flattened version of such a tear-shaped dome, vision-enhancing goggles whirring and clicking as they readjusted.

She'd gotten a tip that her quarry preferred this part of the capital city, coming here to simply wander. A specific site would have been more helpful—a bar, a brothel, even a particular statue—but Ventress had learned to cultivate patience in the last several months.

Her augmented gaze traveled over the decorative buildings and multicolored trees that broke up the expanses of the red stone with which the Pantorans seemed to like to decorate their public spaces. The day was a pleasant one, and many Pantorans were out enjoying the sunshine. Speeders zipped overhead, though without the frantic urgency of those navigating the skylanes of Coruscant. There were clusters of family units, from adults to infants, setting out picnics in the shade of the trees while their younglings ambled about happily. Young lovers were here, too, strolling with their heads bent close to each other.

Ventress's gaze lingered a moment on a family—a male and female Mirialan with three younglings of various ages. The male was giving one of them a ride on his back, and the boy was clearly delighted. The adult female, presumably the mother, looked on, smiling fondly.

With a muttered oath of self-chastisement, Ventress returned to her search. But she couldn't shake the image. Once, she had belonged to a family—a sisterhood, strong and proud. Now they were dead, and she would never hold a sister's child, all because of Dooku.

Those Mirialans were fools. They did not understand how easily and completely a single moment could destroy everything. Let them laugh in their ignorance and play with their spawn while they could.

Slowly, Ventress moved her head, covered now with short, pale-blond hair, tracking along the open areas. A few lonely citizens sat on the steps of various buildings, eating their lunches. Some threw pieces of their meals to various small creatures, which survived by looking appealing to bored sentients who—

Ventress paused, adjusting the electrobinocular goggles slightly, and a smile curved her lips.

He was hunched over, four eyes blinking slowly, one hand holding a sandwich. A second arm held a cup, while the other two were plucking a crust to toss to the small, rodentlike creatures, whose tails flickered energetically as they consumed the food.

Moregi. "There's my Volpai," Ventress said softly, her voice a satisfied purr. She quickly calculated the best approach, fired a cable of plasma energy from her current rooftop to a lower one, then hooked the bow over it and slid down.

She landed gracefully and straightened, gazing down at her quarry. As if sensing her, the Volpai froze in his actions of feeding the animals and slowly turned his head.

Their eyes met. Ventress was unconcerned that she had been made. No bounty yet had escaped her. She dropped to the pavement and walked toward him casually, smiling as he leapt to his feet, bellowed at her, and took off.

Let the chase begin.

Moregi slammed deliberately into passersby, sending them tumbling behind him to block Ventress's pursuit. Four arms lent him extra dexterity as he leapt onto statuary, swung from overhangs, and frightened various mounts and their riders. While the chaos prevented Ventress from getting the clear shot she wanted, which would have ended the hunt in record time, she was not averse to giving chase. The Force buoyed her and guided her, and the prey was not so clever as to be entirely unpredictable to her keen senses. Moregi had to utilize his sheer physicality to shove his way through the crowd; Ventress, whose friend was the Force, conserved her energy for the final capture by simply soaring over the crowds of frightened, fallen pedestrians with a few well-timed leaps.

She thought she had him when the Volpai ran out of rooftop. Moregi hesitated, glancing over his shoulder at Ventress. Then he took a running jump and somehow made it to the next rooftop.

"Not bad," Ventress granted him, effortlessly making the leap herself. She let the Force tell her what Moregi would do next, and followed its guidance when she lost sight of him briefly. She cut a corner on one of the rooftops when he sought to throw her off by racing along the streets. She smiled to herself as she saw him emerge, and, arcing her body, she dived atop him.

They slammed hard to the ground. The impact forced her to tumble away from him, and she leapt lightly to her feet, facing him. The bounty was higher if she brought him in alive, so as Moregi stared at her, panting, Ventress was calculating the best way to bring him down.

Suddenly she caught a flurry of movement out of the corner of her eye and a figure sailed across her field of vision. Her Volpai went down beneath it.

Ventress was so taken aback she simply stared in

astonishment as the two grappled. Recovering, she demanded, "What is *this*?"

The dark-haired humanoid, struggling with his two arms to pin down the arms of a being who had four, turned his head and shot her a grin. "It's called a 'tackle.'"

CHAPTER FIVE

Fury surged within Ventress and her voice dropped to its lowest, most dangerous timbre. "Who. Are. You."

Moregi was still straining against the interloper. The man, though, again grinned up at Ventress. "Relax. I've got this one, honey." And he actually *winked*.

"Honey?"

Asajj Ventress stepped forward, yanked the laser-brain off her bounty, and punched him soundly in the jaw.

With a satisfying grunt, he went sprawling, staring up at her incredulously as his hand went to his mouth. Moregi, equally incredulous, stared wildly from Ventress to the intruder. Then, with a delighted cackle, he sprang to his feet and was off again in a heartbeat.

Ventress set off in pursuit, her outrage lending her speed. She didn't spare the interloper another glance. Whatever the idiot's goal had been, be it a serious attempt to steal her bounty or simply an excessive and ill-advised display of perceived masculine superiority, he had only delayed the inevitable.

Moregi had a couple of seconds' lead on her now.

An ordinary tracker would have lost him amid the unnecessary and vexing rooftop architecture, but Ventress was able to keep him in sight until he darted into a cluster of trees in yet another park area. She halted, catching her breath, trying to reach out in the Force to find him, but there were so many life-forms in close proximity that it wasn't possible. Silently, she moved around, senses alert. She was fairly certain he hadn't leapt to another forested rooftop; the gap would be too large for any non-Force-user to bridge without tools, and the Volpai had none.

Did any world really need this many trees on its rooftops? If it hadn't been for the stranger's interference, she'd have had Moregi three times over by this point. Granted, she'd been the one to lose her temper and surrender to the impulse to punch the cocky fool.

She sensed a presence behind her and closed her eyes, gathering strength.

"Do you normally go around stealing other people's bounties?" she snapped as the dark-haired idiot slipped in beside her, a blaster drawn. "Or was this just my lucky day?"

He stepped forward, moving with grace and skill as he peered around the trees. "Bounties are fair game. You must be new at this."

She arched a brow. He grinned. "Play nice, you may get lucky later!"

The flirtation attempt was so atrocious that Ventress couldn't even find it in her to be offended. "You're *lucky* I don't kill you right now," she muttered, slipping around a tree trunk. No Volpai.

"Luck is exactly what you'd need to kill *me*," he replied.

Crunch.

It was a faint sound, but both of them tensed. Moregi must have thought that they were so engaged in exchanging quips that he could sneak past them. Ventress's respect for the unnamed bounty-stealer went up a small notch. Few ears were sharp enough to have detected the soft noise. It was time to end this, and her patience—both with the Idiot and with the bounty—had worn out.

Ventress homed in on the source of the sound, extended a hand, and casually uprooted the tree behind which Moregi had been hiding. He stared at her, four eyes wide with shock, then fled toward the edge of the rooftop.

Ventress followed, and so did the Idiot. She shoved him aside in irritation. "Don't even think about it," she snapped. "He's mine."

She wondered what Moregi had in mind, if anything. He wouldn't be able to leap to the next rooftop, and the fall was—

He jumped.

Ventress and the Idiot slid to a halt at the edge and peered over to see the Volpai swinging nimbly from the hanging signs of various shops, putting his extra two arms to exceptional use. With the skill of a Wookiee, he went from OGGSOR'S FINE MILLINERY to FASHIONS BY F'JLK to A FIT FOR ALL FEET while Ventress and the Idiot paced him atop the roof. The chase had brought them from the public parks into what was clearly a high-fashion merchant area, and Ventress spared a moment to be amused at the looks of the wealthy, well-groomed Pantorans peering nervously up at the gymnastic Volpai.

Moregi hung from the swinging sign that proclaimed THE PAISLEY PIKOBI, having run out of convenient handholds, and as he hesitated about where to leap next, Ventress dived straight for him. Her hands closed on his shirt. Her momentum carried them forward, crashing through another sign with a depiction of various desserts.

Ventress shot out a hand and grabbed hold of a pipe that ran the width of the building. Moregi's shirt tore and he slipped from her grasp, but she reached out a second time and seized his hand. He clung to it, ready to take his chances with her rather than fall several stories to the unforgiving pavement.

Using the Force to lock her fingers in place on the pipe, Ventress tightened her grip on Moregi's hand. But his palm was sweaty from the chase, and he began to slide inexorably downward.

"You slippery, four-armed slimeball!" she shouted.

He fell, six limbs waving frantically like an insect, his mouth open in a scream.

Ventress was already moving her fingers to catch him with the Force when Moregi thumped down on the hood of a passing speeder. She gaped, stunned at the Volpai's impossibly good luck, as he clambered for a better grip aboard the vessel. He craned his neck and lifted one of his arms in a rude gesture.

"Me juuz ku, wermo!" See you, suckers.

You have got to be kidding me, Ventress thought. Unbelievable. Well, there was nothing for it but to start the chase. For the fourth time. Ventress dropped lithely to the street level and began to run. She was strong and fit, but she was beginning to think that this might be an exceptionally long chase and so emulated her prey by hopping onto the back of a bright-red vessel as it whisked past. She kept her gaze focused on the blue airspeeder to which her bounty clung like a burr on a bantha.

As it rounded a curve, the speeder disappeared from Ventress's view for the space of a heartbeat, and when her "own" speeder made the turn, the shiny blue surface of the vehicle was noticeably devoid of a Volpai hitchhiker.

Her gaze flickered to the sidewalks, where she caught some movement, and she nimbly leapt from the back of her hijacked speeder. But by the time she had rolled back to her feet, her quarry had disappeared into the crowd.

Ventress sighed. Slowing her pace to a less-attention-grabbing walk, she moved through the throng, constantly searching for Moregi. It seemed there was a street festival of some sort in the area today, if the profusion of vendors and the appetizing smell of food were reliable indicators.

She emerged into the city's main square, the center of which was dominated by an enormous statue. The bearded man with a kindly, paternal face had struck a dramatic pose atop a pillar. Four stone narglatches, fearsome predators with a mane of fleshy spines, roared silently at the base.

Ventress sensed the annoying interloper behind her again and, folding her arms, turned to regard him. He was easy on the eyes, with that mane of black dreadlocked hair, strong features with an unusual tattoo of a yellow stripe, and a lithe but muscular body. His pleasant looks didn't lessen her ire one whit, however.

"You just don't know when to quit, do you?"

"You know, this would be a lot easier if we worked together," he said, as if she hadn't even spoken. He extended a hand, ready to shake hers. She batted it aside and pushed forward.

"I work alone."

"Okay, partner!" he replied cheerily.

"I am *not* your partner!" she retorted, steaming ahead of him and jumping onto the topmost step of the monument. She scanned the crowd.

"You sure are dedicated," he said behind her.

Ventress pointed a stiff index finger directly into his face. "Don't. Test. Me." She held his gaze for a moment, then turned back to her search.

"Look, it's not *my* fault you lost him."

That did it.

She whirled and clamped her hand over his mouth. "Stay out of my way," she warned. She felt his lips move against her hand and tightened her grip, shaking him by the jaw like a dog she was muzzling. "I mean it."

Again the lips moved, but his eyes weren't on her and he lifted a hand to point. "Mmphrr," he said.

She turned to see that Moregi had caught yet another ride. Still gripping the Idiot's mouth closed, Ventress said, "Looks like you're useful after all." She shoved him backward, leapt onto the back of a stone narglatch, and then sprang onto an idling single-seat speeder. The Rodian driver protested, but Ventress kicked him in the chest and he fell to the pavement, recovering sufficiently to curse her as she took off after her quarry.

She closed the gap between them quickly. Before he could leap to another vehicle, Ventress rose in her seat and nocked her bow. Even moving, she couldn't miss at this range.

Moregi shocked her by not fleeing: He leapt directly at her. Ventress found herself flat on the back of a narrow vessel careening at full speed with a four-armed Volpai atop her, trying to crush her trachea with her own bow. They tumbled off her stolen speeder onto the hood of another one. Ventress grunted, air knocked out of her lungs yet again by the bulk of the surprisingly vigorous Moregi. She shoved upward, but he yanked the bow from her grip and tossed it away.

Ventress was done with finesse—that bow had been given to her by her fellow Nightsisters. Snarling like an animal, she used the Force to augment her own not-inconsiderable strength, flipped the Volpai over, and straddled him. She had two arms pinned, but the second pair and his powerful legs worked together to first seize her and then kick her over his head.

She nearly slid off the vessel—whose Pantoran driver was more than likely desperately regretting his decision to venture forth this morning—but levitated herself back onto it. A Volpai leg kicked at her, and as she rolled out of the way one of two flailing lower arms smacked her in the ribs; only her sharply honed instincts allowed her to pull back enough to take the worst out of the blow. Shooting to her feet, she followed with a good uppercut, but even using the Force to anticipate Moregi's moves, she was at a disadvantage fighting someone who had four fists. Ducking to avoid another punch, she reached for his shoulder to unbalance him—and was rocked by a left hook that connected solidly with her jaw. As she struggled to regain her balance, tightening her grip on him, she felt a piece of his shoulder plating come loose in her hand—and then she was falling.

Air whooshed by her. Her head still spinning from Moregi's blow, she reached out to the Force to slow her fall . . .

. . . and was caught by a strong hand that shot out of nowhere.

Dangling a few meters above the street, Ventress peered up to see the Idiot gazing down at her from another speeder. Deftly he lowered the vessel, releasing her to drop safely onto the pavement, and brought his stolen speeder to the ground.

Ventress touched her mouth and moved her jaw

cautiously. It wasn't broken, but it hurt like mad. "It's the fourth arm that always gets you," she muttered. She eyed the Idiot, waiting for the inevitable flippant comment.

Instead, he pressed his lips together and shook his head. "We would have caught him if you'd let me help you."

She scowled. It hurt her mouth. "I told you, I don't need your help!"

"Well," he said, reaching behind him. "It didn't look that way just now." He was holding her bow. Ventress eyed it, then him. She snatched the bow from his grasp.

"Am I supposed to be *grateful* that you stepped in? Meanwhile, you let the bounty get away!"

"Hey, *I'm* not the one who let him get away."

Ventress stepped forward with cool deliberation. "You should stop talking. *Now*," she said. The Idiot backed up as she approached. "Or I swear I will blast you back to whatever hole you crawled out of." She put a hand on his chest, let it linger there just long enough, then shoved him out of the way.

She felt him watching her as she strode off. She didn't care. Let him get an eyeful. The back of her was all he was ever going to see.

Her bounty had escaped, she was tired, her jaw was on fire, and she'd had to deal with someone who was the single most annoying man she had ever met.

A drink was definitely in order.

CHAPTER SIX

Vos was used to being told he didn't know when to quit. But those who said so were wrong. He *did* know when. Now, for instance, was an excellent time to quit. For a little while, anyway. Ventress's aquiline nose was far too out of joint for any progress to be made. He'd give her some time to cool off, then try again.

Vos was more than a little confused. He liked the persona he'd created for this mission. He was dashing, and witty, and strong, and flirty—okay, the "persona" was really pretty much his usual self. Except for the flirty part.

But what else was he supposed to do? Ventress—although more than a little scary, even Vos had to admit—was an attractive woman, slender but deceptively strong, with unusual ice-blue eyes and, well, a lot of other things that people might reasonably notice. Of course she'd get a lot of attention— unwanted, obviously, but she had doubtless come to expect it. And even Kenobi had pointed out that Vos couldn't afford to stand out too much. He was already pushing it by simply attempting to ally with her, he could see that now.

Vos followed Ventress easily, making sure she didn't spot him. It was a practice he had mastered long ago. That part of going undercover, at least, was familiar to him. She had no speeder, but went on foot, so he was spared the necessity of using the Force to convince someone to part with their vehicle—or of just stealing another.

His stomach rumbled. Chasing after the agile Moregi had worked up an appetite. He purchased a sandwich of roasted local vegetables and ate as he trailed his assignment. Once or twice, he thought she'd made him, and he'd ducked into a doorway or stepped behind a conveniently large pedestrian. By the time he finished his snack, wishing he had bought something to wash it down with, Ventress was approaching a bar.

"Perfect timing," he murmured, and smiled. Her half-hour walk ought to have allowed her space enough to cool her anger and maybe let her guard down a bit.

He slid into the seat beside her and tossed a credit onto the bar. Ventress turned to him, and her dismay would have been comical had it not been so obviously sincere.

"Can't I get a *moment* of peace?" she exclaimed, throwing her hands up in the air and then resting her face in them.

"Why do you want a moment of peace? I thought you were all on fire to go get that Volpai." He pointed to a pitcher of . . . something at the bartender's elbow.

"I *had* the Volpai, until you felt compelled to tackle him," she reminded him. "Your idiocy cost me twenty-five thousand credits."

Vos accepted the drink with a nod of thanks. "If

we had worked together, we would be splitting those credits right now," he said.

"I have this memory," she said, her husky voice dropping even deeper with dislike. "This memory of telling you that the bounty was mine, that I didn't need your help, and *to stay out of my way*."

"Funny, I have a memory where you told me I could be useful."

"And," she continued, as if he hadn't spoken, "I also told you that I wasn't your partner and that I work *alone*."

Vos imagined that just the venom in her words would have cowed an ordinary man. Fortunately, he wasn't one. "Doesn't have to be that way."

She opened her mouth. At that precise instant a small light on his right bracer began to blink. *Terrible timing, Kenobi*, he thought, then, *Actually, probably excellent timing*. He lifted a finger and said, "Hold that thought. I'm sure it'll be blistering. I'll be right back."

She looked disappointed—not, he knew, at the fact that he was leaving, but at the fact that she couldn't fire another volley of insults in his direction. Sighing, Ventress contented herself with saying, "I don't care."

If she truly didn't care, she wouldn't try to leave, and if she did attempt to sneak out, he'd follow her. Vos nodded and stepped out into the bustle of the street. A safe distance away, he activated the holo-projector.

A small, blue Obi-Wan Kenobi regarded him with a slight smile. "I must say, I'm relieved to see you're still alive," he said. "How are things progressing?"

How to answer that one? "She's everything you described . . . and more," Vos said.

Kenobi looked pleased. "Ah, so you've gained her trust? She's willing to work with you?"

Vos considered, recalling the incidents of the last hour. "I wouldn't say work with me so much as . . . allow me to be in the general vicinity of her."

"I can't say I'm surprised. No one expected this to be an easy mission. Something is better than nothing at all."

"Your lack of faith wounds me. I'll have her eating out of my hand in no time."

"With the Force, all things are possible," Kenobi said, adding, "except that."

"Okay, maybe I exaggerated a little."

Kenobi had that familiar, slightly pained expression, like he often did when Anakin piped up with something outrageous but exciting. "Only a trifle, I'm sure. Keep the Council and me apprised of the situation."

"Will do."

"May the Force be with you. No doubt you'll need it." Even though the hologram was only a few centimeters high, Vos could see the twinkle in Kenobi's eye. Despite the direness of the mission, the other Jedi was enjoying this.

"Ha, ha." Vos deactivated the holoemitter and stuck it back in his pocket. Obi-Wan hadn't said it, but Vos knew it was implied: He needed to seal the deal with Ventress, and quickly.

She was still there when he sauntered back into the bar, sparing him a brief glance before returning her attention to a green piece of metal plating.

"You know, funny thing," he mused, as if it had just occurred to him, "I don't even know the name of the woman who's been such a pain in my neck all day."

A ghost of a smile touched her full lips. "*Just* the neck?"

He shrugged, and for the first time that day the smile he gave her was genuine. "Well, for now."

She held his gaze, her ice-chip eyes regarding him not with anger and annoyance this time, but with evaluation. Vos had been raised in the Jedi Temple. He had been constantly tested, judged, and critiqued during his youth, and he knew that every time he stood before the Jedi Council they were considering his appropriateness for whatever mission they tasked him with. Being scrutinized was not a new experience for him. But this was different.

Kenobi had told him Ventress didn't suffer fools. And yet Vos knew he had been behaving like one around her since they had met. This was the moment, he realized, when his mission would either succeed— or fail spectacularly. Kenobi had also cautioned him against trying to use the Force to manipulate Ventress in any way. "She's extraordinarily strong-willed, and she's more experienced in the Force than many Jedi Knights," he had said.

Vos relaxed into the appraisal. He was coming to respect Asajj Ventress—she had demonstrated that she was good at what she did. And he'd already told her he thought she was a pain in the neck. These were real, true feelings, and he was comfortable with them both. He'd rolled the dice—now was the time to watch them land. He met her gaze evenly, and waited.

"Ventress," she said, finally.

"Vos." He extended a hand. She eyed it, and then they shook. It was the first time she'd touched him without anger or, at the very least, annoyance.

He gestured to the metal plating she had been examining. "What's that?"

She made a sour face and took a swig of her drink. "Oh, I pulled it off the Volpai."

Jackpot. "Can I see it?"

Ventress looked at him with mild curiosity, then shrugged. "Here. It's of no use, anyway."

Keeping an expression of mild curiosity on his face, Vos extended himself into the Force, closing his fingers around the object "of no use" and opening to what it had to tell him. He wasn't concerned about revealing himself to Ventress. His psychometry shell was so smoothly integrated in the Force that no one, not even fellow Jedi masters, had been able to detect it. The bar, with its music and conversations and clinking of glasses, retreated, growing faint and distant. Vos felt as if he were falling forward into a hole, but the sensation was a familiar and comfortable one. Images rushed up: A female Rodian, with gray-green skin, holding a blue youngling. It—he—bounced up and down in his mother's lap excitedly, clutching a small stuffed toy. He warbled as a hand reached out to caress his small cheek, and a face came into Vos's view.

Moregi's face. Only a glimpse, but it was enough; the Volpai's movements were gentle and slow, and his expression was kind. Occasionally Vos was able to sense emotions as well as see and hear, and his own heart was suddenly warm with Moregi's love for both mother and child.

Vos mentally disconnected from the Volpai's feelings and manipulated the image in his mind's eye, drawing back to take in the rest of the room. He focused on the details, memorizing them quickly: A narrow, bell-shaped window with a potted flowering plant and curtains of blue and yellow. The view out the window showed the angry zigs and zags of graffiti in green and purple paint, in a language he didn't know.

The image faded, and the sights and sounds of the bar returned. Only a few seconds had passed. He handed the of-great-use-after-all object back to Ventress with a noncommittal gesture.

"I don't think Moregi has left the planet. I might know where he is."

She eyed him skeptically. "Really," she said. "And how would you know that?"

"I got a tip."

"You might have said so earlier."

"Well," Vos said, "I only share that information with partners."

"I see."

He rose. "You coming?"

Again, the thorough scrutiny. Then Asajj Ventress tossed a couple of credits on the bar, rose, and followed.

"This tip must not have been very good," Ventress said about half an hour later as they stood, once again, on a rooftop. "You seem to just be wandering around."

Vos frowned. His gift was useful, but far from perfect. He didn't get to select what it revealed to him, though he could direct it somewhat. It would have been nice if he could have picked up a street address, but he had only a brief glimpse of run-down buildings to go on. Of course, he couldn't tell that to Ventress.

"I'm just . . . zeroing in on the right place," he said with as much confidence as he could muster. He recalled the details, and concentrated on looking for—

—graffiti in colors of purple and green.

"I think this is it." He pointed to a window several floors up in a tall, narrow building. The blue-and-yellow curtains were closed.

"Let's find out, shall we?" Ventress lifted her bow.

Both string and bolt glowed pink. As she fired, Vos realized that they were made of plasma energy—as was the cable that snaked across the distance between the two buildings.

"Oh, hey, that's handy," said Vos.

"Yes," Ventress agreed, "it is." She positioned the bow atop the plasma cable, grasped each end of the weapon, and slid down the cable to the ground without another word. Vos eyed her, sighed in minor annoyance. He had to go down the old-fashioned way, climbing like someone who couldn't use the Force so as not to tip her off. Ventress awaited him impatiently.

The door of the main entrance slid aside at a touch and they took a rickety lift up to the fourth floor. As they approached the apartment door, Vos, acting like the take-charge, assertive bounty hunter he was supposed to be, stepped in front of Ventress and banged on the door.

"Open up!" he demanded. Silence. He could sense life-forms on the other side of the door; no doubt Ventress was also picking up on them. "I said, open up!"

There was no response. The seconds ticked by. Slightly nonplussed, Vos gestured to Ventress. "Um . . . Open it."

The former Sith acolyte rolled her eyes, nocked an arrow, and fired it into the control panel. The panel sparked and sizzled as the door slid open.

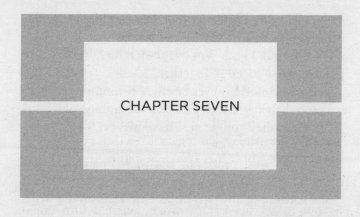

CHAPTER SEVEN

Vos knew whom he would see and was poised to charge when Ventress, grunting, sprang forward and kicked Moregi squarely in the midsection. Caught utterly off guard, the Volpai stumbled backward, but didn't run. Instead, he leapt in front of the pair of Rodians Vos had seen in his vision—a mother and child—and spread his four arms as wide as possible in an age-old gesture of defense.

"Don't hurt them!"

The baby shrieked, terrified, and the mother clutched him close. Her eyes, always large and expressive in Rodians, seemed huge to Vos as she stared at him and Ventress. He felt a twinge of remorse.

"I didn't do anything wrong!" Moregi cried.

From what Vos remembered, embezzlement was generally considered pretty "wrong" in most circles. But everyone always said they didn't do anything wrong. *That's what usually comes first: protestations of innocence.*

"I don't care," Ventress replied. She had drawn her bow and was pointing an arrow at Moregi's broad chest. Vos had his blaster trained on the Volpai. "The

Rang Clan put a price on your head so big, I'm lucky I found you first," Ventress continued.

"*We* found you," Vos reminded her. "*We*." He paused, then added, "Together."

Ventress closed her eyes briefly. Fortunately, Moregi was too distraught to try to take advantage of it.

"If it's money you want, I have plenty!"

Bribery: That comes second.

"I know," said Ventress. "But we're being paid well enough to get that money back to its rightful owner."

She hadn't put any particular emphasis on the word *we're,* but Vos brightened. "Thank you."

"I'm not the villain here," Moregi barreled on. "Can't you see? I was just trying to do what's best for my family. For my *child*!"

Vos winced inwardly at the words. The youngling was not Moregi's biological child; the infant appeared to be pure Rodian, yet that didn't matter. *My family. My child.* Like any good mate and parent, Moregi simply wanted what was best for those he loved. They weren't living in a palace; the family was obviously barely making enough to get by. Moregi had been desperate to change that, and Vos couldn't blame him. Not everyone had been raised with care and affection in a Temple, with plenty to eat and a roof over their heads.

Vos was passingly familiar with the Rang Clan, and he knew that Moregi had been right. Even though the Volpai had taken money that wasn't his, he wasn't the villain.

"How touching." Ventress's bored voice sounded even colder to Vos than usual. "But I'm afraid I can't help you."

Quickly, before things could escalate to violence in the close quarters, Vos lowered his blaster slightly and reached out toward Moregi with his other hand. "You're coming with us."

Moregi lashed out. Two arms came up. One knocked the blaster out of Vos's hand. A second landed a nasty punch to the Jedi's jaw. The other two arms shoved. Hard.

"Whoa!" Vos stumbled backward, almost knocking Ventress down. She dodged artfully.

Moregi glanced back at his wife, his four eyes filled with anguish. She wrapped her arms around their son.

"Run," she pleaded. "Just run." *I love you.* The words didn't need to be spoken to fill the room.

Moregi did run, leaping without a second's hesitation through the bell-shaped window, shattering the glass. Vos raced to the broken window just in time to see Moregi get to his feet, shake himself, and scamper off.

"You sure were right about that fourth arm," Vos muttered, rubbing his chin.

"You *idiot*!" Ventress's fists were clenched, and Vos braced himself for another one of her memorable punches. But she wasn't wasting time on him. She jumped down to the pavement and set off after their quarry.

Moregi had commandeered a bright-red, shiny speeder sled. The only problem was, it was facing the wrong direction. He glanced up to see Ventress racing after him on foot. Frantically jabbing at the controls and peering over his shoulder, he backed the speeder down the street. Ventress closed the gap between them.

Vos emulated his hopefully soon-to-be partner, jumping down from the apartment and using the Force to help him land softly. Glancing around, he spied a conveniently ownerless speeder bike with long handlebars and a low seat flanked by outrigger repulsor pods that he *borrowed*. He caught up to the running Ventress just as Moregi swung the speeder around and took off. Ventress slowed and stopped, wreathed in a gray cloud of fumes. She clenched her fist and snarled in frustration.

"Need a lift, partner?" Vos offered with a grin, pulling up beside her.

She glared at him, sighed heavily, and hopped on.

Ventress was *done* with Moregi. Vos could feel it through the Force coming off her in waves, a grim, frightening determination that made him glad he was not the primary target of it. He slid the speeder bike, highly maneuverable despite its overmuscled appearance, underneath the larger vehicle, then rose right in front of it. Moregi gasped. Ventress leapt as smoothly as an airdiver, her long, lean body arcing perfectly. She was a thing of beauty as her arms struck Moregi in the chest and she pulled, her momentum carrying both of them off the speeder to tumble onto the pavement below.

Moregi rose and turned to flee, but Vos was there, blocking his way. Whimpering, the Volpai turned to see Asajj Ventress triumphant, a glowing yellow lightsaber humming in her right hand.

"Hands up," she demanded, adding, "All four of them."

Like a cornered animal, even now Moregi tried to escape. He turned and ran—right into Vos's powerful punch. The force of the blow spun the Volpai around and he fell to the ground. He started to rise, only to find himself staring at a lightsaber and a blaster, both centimeters from his face.

"It's over, Moregi. We've got you."

Moregi looked at them, anguished. He tried a final

time. "Please—my family needs me. I'll give you triple what they're paying you."

"I already told you, it doesn't work that way," Ventress said. Her eyes narrowed. "And you've wasted my time making me run around this city. Triple won't even *cover* my fee."

"*Our* fee," Vos reminded her. "Let's go."

"Not to cast a shadow on this spectacular capture, but let's talk payment."

Vos lounged against the side of Ventress's *Banshee*, peering up at her as she descended. When she'd told him the name of the vessel, he'd been amused that she had obviously heard the term "banshee" applied to herself and had decided to embrace the reference. *Banshee* the ship was a flat, disc-shaped pursuit craft. Its two engine nacelles were powerful, but with a snub-nosed cockpit bristling with weapons, it was not particularly aesthetically pleasing. It sported a turret-mounted triple blaster atop it, and the cockpit had two anti-personnel blasters and two heavier laser cannons. The *Banshee* was made for two purposes—hitting hard, and getting away fast—and that was enough for her.

Moregi had offered no further resistance and now sat in the hold, trussed up and broken. Ventress simply could have retracted the ramp and taken off, but instead she found herself eyeing the interloper.

"I reckon it's an even split," Vos continued. He gave her one of his winning smiles. "After all, we do make quite a team."

She slitted her eyes and scrutinized him, thinking. He was quite attractive, but many men were. He was strong and fast—but he could be stronger and faster. He was genuinely amusing, which was rare, and she suspected that he was more intelligent than her private nickname for him—Idiot—reflected. And he wasn't easily discouraged. In the field of bounty hunting, that counted for a lot.

So instead of flat-out refusing again, Ventress planted her hands on her hips and asked, "Why are you so hot to be part of a team? Need someone to pick up your slack?"

His brown eyes widened and he placed a hand on his chest.

"Me? Are you kidding? *I* do the heavy lifting."

She waited.

"Well, it's a lot of work for one person," he said. "Even you have to admit that."

Ventress remained silent. His smirk, which had been perpetual until this point, slipped a little and he looked away. "It's just . . . I'm getting tired of being a loner. If that makes any sense."

Unexpectedly, memories flooded Ventress. Most of her life, she had been with someone, only to inevitably lose them in the cruelest of ways. First her Master, Ky Narec, then Mother Talzin and her sisters. Dead now, all of them; they had loved her, and they were slain.

Dooku had *not* loved her. She had thought he had—not as a woman, of course, or even as a daughter, but as an apprentice. Someone who showed promise, whom he enjoyed training and shaping. How eager she had been to learn, to serve him, to obey, and how quickly he had discarded her. She had meant something to him only when he could use her. There was, Ventress thought bitterly, something terribly askew with a universe in which, out of all her allies and mentors, Dooku was alive and the others breathed no more.

The painful reverie lasted but a moment. Ventress

knew her weaknesses, and knew how to bypass them. They were liabilities she had run across more than once in her solo career as a bounty hunter; once with Pluma Sodi, a young Kage girl who had been abducted from her family to be an unwilling bride, and again whenever a bounty's family had muddied the waters, as had happened earlier.

She should say no to the amusing idiot who stood before her; keep well away from partners, and entanglements, and trust.

Instead, Ventress found herself saying, "Fine. I'm game. We'll split it."

Vos's composure slipped. Adroit as she had seen him be earlier today, he actually slid a little where he leaned against the curving metal. He caught himself quickly. "Really?"

At his unabashed delight and surprise, a warning flare went up somewhere deep inside her: *Guard yourself*. It was too late now, though. Her voice was hard as she replied.

"But there's no way I'm carrying you." She shoved a stiffened finger pointedly into his broad chest. "If you want to partner with me, you've got work to do. This isn't playtime—this is a job. You're going to need to learn how to run faster and fight harder. No foolish errors. No lost quarries because you want to make a grand gesture. I won't tolerate laziness or stupidity. Got it?"

Surprise, quickly hooded, flashed in his eyes. The grin reemerged in its dazzling brilliance.

"Always feisty. But you might make a decent partner yet."

"*You* could use a little bit more training." She strode up the ramp and started to climb up the ladder.

He followed. "I think you'll find I'm . . . up to the

task," he said. Ventress glanced down at him to notice he was appreciatively eyeing her derriere.

"That won't be happening," she said drily. "I don't mix business with pleasure."

"You don't know what you're missing," he insisted.

"Then I'll have to remain happily ignorant. And *you'll* remain alive. For now, anyway. If you're going to get half the pay, you'll need to do half the work—and we'll need to line up twice as many jobs. Come on."

"Okay, *partner*!"

As she climbed quickly with Vos behind her, Ventress found herself hiding a smile.

CHAPTER EIGHT

Vos had thought Ventress had been teasing him with the whole *run faster, fight harder, you need training* bit. So when, within the first hour of their partnership, she handed him a list of running times to beat, weights to lift, and insisted on a regimen of daily hand-to-hand combat—with her—he'd laughed out loud.

"You're taking the joke too far," he said, tossing the pad back to her. She caught it and threw it back.

"I seldom joke."

Vos peered at her. "I thought my 'audition' with Moregi went pretty well."

"It did. That's why I agreed to take you on at all. But you've got a few things to learn before you're ready to play the part." He did not like her choice of words, as they hit too close to the truth. Vos had been careful not to use the Force around her, but he had been in physical training since he could walk. Was Ventress attempting to assert herself over him, as Kenobi had warned she might, or did she really just not see how good he was?

Or did she already suspect that he was a Jedi?

"I'm fine, thanks," he said.

Ventress folded her slender arms. "Tell you what. If you can knock me out, you can skip the extra training."

Oh, there is no way this is going to end well. "I don't like hitting a woman."

"Then every woman you fight is going to win. An enemy is an enemy, Vos, regardless of size, species—or sex."

There was no getting out of it. While the *Banshee* bore them through hyperspace, they went down into the cargo hold. Vos limbered up, cracked his neck, and while he was settling into position, she sprang. He darted to the right, his hand closing on her ankle. Deftly, she twisted in midair. Vos almost dodged her other foot as it descended onto his face, but reminded himself to be slower than usual and not use the Force. He did, however, turn his head so her kick struck his cheek and not his nose. His stumble was exaggerated, but the grunt of pain was not.

Ventress "let him catch his breath," and they circled. "Quick reaction, grabbing my foot," she said, grudgingly. Inwardly, he grimaced that it hadn't escaped her notice. Kenobi had said she was sharp.

He smirked, hoping he looked overconfident. "See? I'm better than you th—" He blocked the lightning-fast punch, but pulled his own. This was turning out to be more challenging than he'd expected. How hard was too hard to punch her? Should he really try to knock her out? While Vos was pondering, drawing his fist back for another blow, Ventress seized his other arm and pulled. Vos decided to let the whole mess conclude and permitted himself to be thrown. Honestly, he had to admit, it wasn't that hard; Ventress was unobtrusively using the Force. An ordinary opponent would never have noticed it.

He landed on the hard metal of the cargo floor and her knee was on his throat. Ventress rolled her eyes, then extended a hand to haul him to his feet.

"I guess I don't get to skip the extra training," Vos said, massaging his throat.

"You performed better than expected" was her reply. She picked up the pad with her instructions and tossed it to him. "But you can do better."

So now Quinlan Vos, Jedi Master, was once again in training. After the first few sessions, he found himself actually glad of it. Not only did Ventress fight dirty and ruthlessly, but she fought extraordinarily well. He'd seen a lot of it in their first hunt together, but that had only been the tip of the iceberg. Vos supposed it was only to be expected from someone trained by Count Dooku. He had wondered how it was that both Kenobi, a superb fighter, and Anakin, who was also excellent though a bit reckless, had been unable to take her down. Now he understood.

Vos made a point of utilizing the moves she had taught him on their next couple of hunts, so she'd see how much he'd "learned." The jobs were not particularly interesting in and of themselves; the usual routine of one rotten underworld sleemo putting a bounty out on another rotten underworld sleemo. Still, Vos discovered that hunting alongside Ventress— and showing her all the things he had "learned"— was a great deal of fun.

There had only been one time when he'd come close to blowing his cover. They'd been after a bounty, chasing him through the dark, dangerous, and very dirty streets of Coruscant's Level 1313, when they'd been ambushed. Well, Ventress maintained they'd been ambushed. Vos privately wondered if some of the denizens of the underworld were just bored that night.

It wasn't so much that their attackers were excellent fighters, but that there were simply so *many* swarming out of the shadowy corners. Vos and Ventress had their hands full, and at one point Vos had noticed that a leathery-faced Weequay whom Ventress thought she'd eliminated had woken up and was training a blaster on her.

Vos had no choice. He used the Force to knock the weapon out of the Weequay's hand, simultaneously leaping to close the distance between himself and the attacker. When Ventress turned around, Vos was in close enough proximity to later claim that he'd kicked the blaster away. Ventress had looked at him narrowly, but she made certain this time that the Weequay was dead, and had not asked Vos about it again. Since then, she had repaid the favor—more than once.

Vos was alternating between handstand push-ups and one-hand balancing—focusing on not using the Force—when he heard the ramp extend. He didn't stop his workout as he called, "Hey, got anything for us yet?"

Ventress came into view, upside down from his perspective, and peered at him critically. "I might," she said. "Let's try this with a little bit more weight." She grasped his feet and began to transfer her weight to her hands, bending her knees and leaning into the movement. He grunted, his legs quivering. "Oh, come on, I'm not putting that much weight on you. Keep going."

"Uhhhhhgggh," he said, but obeyed, still not using the Force.

Ventress grinned wickedly down at him, her short

tuft of blond hair falling slightly into her face. "We'll be working with pirates," she said.

"*With* them?" he grunted, managing another push-up. "Is that wise?"

"I've worked with this one before. She's got her own code of honor—and nothing in the galaxy can help you if you violate it." Ventress put more of her weight into her hands. If Vos had been able to use the Force, she could have done handstands of her own on his feet, but of course he had to use muscles alone. His arms were burning as he dipped again.

"She?"

"Don't tell me you've never heard of Lassa Rhayme?"

". . . nope?"

"The Blood Bone Order?"

"Oh . . . *them*, I've heard of. So that's Rhayme's crew?"

"It is. It's very egalitarian. She was voted into the position, and can be voted out at any time. No one has, so far, nor is likely to." Abruptly, Ventress put almost all her weight on his feet for a moment. Vos made a choking sound. "Keep going," she instructed, but eased off. For the moment. "She divides everything into equal shares. No cheating among the crew, no fighting on the ship. They'll follow her anywhere."

"No desertions allowed, I take it?"

"On the contrary. Anyone's free to leave, but most know a good thing when they see it. Our quarry, shall we say, left on a bad note." Again, she increased her weight.

"Oh? Uh—Ventress . . ."

"Her first mate—literally and figuratively—ran away three days ago with Rhayme's last intended target."

"The haul?"

"The haul, *and* the heiress they intended to take it from."

"I see. Ventress—"

"Captain Rhayme is taking this all very personally. So much so that there's quite a lucrative bounty on his head." Ventress appeared ignorant of Vos's imminent collapse.

"What will . . . *uhhng* . . . happen to him?"

"Even I don't particularly care to find out. Think pirate justice combined with jilted lover."

"I get the picture. Ventress, you really should—"

She let go, but not without yanking on his foot first. With a yelp, Vos collapsed into a heap. "Ouch," he said.

"Better do a few more."

"You just like watching me," he said, untangling himself.

"Never said I didn't," she replied.

"You *could* do more than watch," he said, and winked. For a terrible moment, she didn't reply, and he thought she was calling his bluff.

Then she rolled her eyes. "Since you brought it up . . . it's time I familiarize you with a new strategy. It's an easy one. This former lover of Rhayme's has an eye for women. So, we bait him."

It took Vos a second to figure out what she meant. "You mean . . . *you*?" As soon as he'd said it, he realized it could have sounded like an insult, which was not at all what he'd meant. Fortunately, Ventress appeared to let it slide.

"I have two approaches I like to employ," she continued. "The subtle one I call the nod and the wink. That's for the more sophisticated target—or one who wants to be discreet. The other's the full-on gambit, which is an obvious invitation. I've always been more than able to handle them alone, but with this approach, having a partner will make it even easier."

"Gotcha," he said, nodding.

Ventress eyed him thoughtfully. "You have no idea what I'm talking about, do you?"

Vos scoffed. "'Course I do. Hey, I bet I'd be great at this kind of thing," he said with feigned casualness.

A smile played on her full lips. "You think so?"

"Sure I do."

"All right, let's give it a shot, then." *Uh-oh,* Vos thought as a sense of panic rose in him. It was one thing to verbally flirt. What Ventress was proposing was entirely different.

"First, the nod and the wink." Ventress shifted her weight so one hip was slightly higher than the other. Casually, she ran a hand down her waist, along her thigh, then looked up at him from under her lock of blond hair. Her lips curving in a smile, she gave him a barely perceptible nod and closed one blue eye in a wink.

"Now you try," she said, dropping the seductress pose like a cloak. It was the Ventress he knew standing before him.

"I surrender," he said, putting his hands up. His cheeks were hot. He thought he would rather face a session with a torture droid than attempt what she had so easily demonstrated. "I can't top that."

"You haven't seen the full-on gambit yet."

"Don't have to."

She laughed and patted his cheek, offering him a genuine smile. "Your virtue is safe with me. Your discomfort is rather charming, actually, but I'm sure you'll get over it."

He had no response to her first comment and said

instead, "I'll let you handle this, if you really think it's necessary."

"For this one? Absolutely. A good bounty hunter uses whatever tools best suit the job. Sometimes it's a lightsaber, sometimes it's a sucker punch, and sometimes it's a nod and a wink. The idea is to catch our bounty effectively and in a timely manner, without unnecessary complications. Trust me, in this case, it's the perfect strategy."

They got the mark in fifteen minutes flat.

Ventress didn't even have to use the full-on gambit.

Ventress settled into the cockpit, with Vos in the seat behind her, and she found herself smiling. This mission had been an unqualified success. The bounty had been hefty, and having Lassa Rhayme's gratitude was no small thing. Vos had given up on his overdone persona, which was a blessing, and had relaxed into someone who was, actually, naturally appealing. She was glad he'd pushed his way into a partnership with her; not once had he given her cause to regret her decision.

Theirs was a relationship that was unique in her experience. Before, the roles of both parties had been clearly defined as master and servant. Sometimes, as with her Jedi Master, Ky Narec, and Count Dooku, she had been the servant, the apprentice. In her early years, she had quite literally been a slave. When Savage Opress, the Zabrak Nightbrother whom she had shaped, used Nightsister dark side magicks in order to destroy Dooku, she had been the undisputed master. The hallmarks of all those interactions had been discipline and gravity.

Vos was quite possibly the least serious person she'd ever met, except when he needed to be. He made her laugh, and she couldn't remember laughing since her time with Ky Narec. There was an ease in Vos's company she'd never found with anyone before, not even with the Nightsisters, and she realized she liked it.

It wouldn't last forever. None of her relationships did. But for now, Ventress decided, she would enjoy the ride.

"Hey," said Vos, in the seat behind her. "I just realized something."

"What's that?" Ventress plotted a course and entered the coordinates. A second later the stars turned into long, bright streaks, and then they were in the blue-and-white hyperspace lane.

"It's our anniversary!"

She peered around her chair at him. *"What?"*

"Well, not an anniversary, I suppose," he continued, "because it's not a certain amount of time we're celebrating. *But.* We have just successfully—wildly successfully, I might add—completed our fifth mission together. So . . . it's that kind of anniversary. What's that sort of thing called, anyway?"

"I don't know, and I don't care," Ventress replied. "We need to line up our next job." She settled back into her seat and suited task to word, calling up the current list of bounties on a small screen.

"Do you *ever* take your mind off the job? You know, relax a little?"

"I have a term for people who relax."

"Oh? What's that?"

She clicked a few more bounty subjects. "Dead."

"You are *so* much fun," Vos said.

"I know."

"Oh, come on," Vos said. He stepped around to her chair, leaning on the back of it. "Your friend Rhayme gave us a bottle of aged Tevraki whiskey. Let's crack it open. We won't be ready to do anything till tomorrow at the earliest, and we're in hyperspace."

Ventress sighed. "You go ahead if you want."

"No deal. We're partners. Split down the middle."

"I'd forgotten how persistent you were," she said, rising. "All right."

There wasn't much extra space aboard the *Banshee,* only two small cabins, a shared head, a tiny galley, and the cargo hold. They sat on the hard metal floor of the hold, opened the bottle, and Vos poured them each a shot.

"To the next hunt," Ventress said.

"To partnership," Vos replied, and they drank. The liquor burned like sweet fire, coating the tongue and sending warmth all through Ventress's limbs. It was far too easy to drink, and Ventress knew she'd have to be careful. She never drank to get drunk.

Vos's eyes widened. "Your friends have good taste," he said, his tone slightly tinged with awe. "Please let Captain Rhayme know that if she ever wants to hire us again, we'll be there."

Ventress chuckled a little and took another sip, while Vos poured himself another shot. Normally they dissected a hunt afterward, discussing what had worked, what hadn't, and what they might have done differently. This time, though, all had gone so smoothly there was nothing to criticize. So instead, Vos asked her about some of the weapons they were considering purchasing, and moves he'd seen her do. Ventress tensed slightly when he inquired about the lightsaber. By this point, her partner was a trifle worse—or better—for the alcohol, and she suspected it was making him less cautious. He'd never asked about her lightsaber before.

"I thought only Jedi used them," he said.

"You thought wrong. You can find them on the

black market easily enough. I would have thought you'd know that."

"Don't need to trade in the black market," he said. He waved a hand, indicating their stark vessel. "A simple existence, is ours." He slurred his words slightly, drained his glass, and reached for the bottle.

"You spill a single drop of that, it comes out of your pay," Ventress warned. He laughed.

"So," he continued, pouring with great focus, "you got it on the black market. Who trained you?"

"It's a sword. I know how to use swords." It wasn't exactly a lie. Vos stretched out on his back, using one arm for a pillow and propping the shot on his chest with the other. His gaze as he regarded her looked slightly unfocused.

Ventress turned the tables. "What about you, Vos? What's your story?"

She was expecting some kind of wisecrack. Instead, Vos looked as if he had no idea how to answer. He turned his head, gazing up at nothing. "You know," he said, his voice slightly slurred and touched with surprise, "I don't think I *have* a story."

"Everyone has a story," Ventress pressed, curious now.

He raised his head, drained the glass, and set it down. "Not me. I mean . . . I've done things, seen things. Things have happened to me. But . . . I don't think I have a story."

This had clearly never occurred to him. He seemed to be almost reeling from the revelation. Ventress wondered if it was the alcohol talking, or if Vos really did feel as lost as he sounded. "What about you?" he asked. "What's your story? Or do you not have one, either?"

"Oh, I have a story all right," Ventress said. "Quite a lot of stories, actually." The story of a girl given into slavery. Of a Jedi Padawan. Of a dark Master's apprentice. Of a Nightsister. "But none of them end well." She frowned into her glass. Maybe the delicious liquor was having an effect on her, too. She was seldom maudlin, and she didn't like it.

"I wonder," Vos mused, turning again to look at her. "What's worse . . . to have unhappy stories, or have no story at all?"

"Tonight's story ends with sleep." Ventress was done. She got to her feet. Vos didn't emulate her right away. "Vos? Can you get up?"

"Yep," he assured her.

"Are you lying?"

". . . maybe?"

Vos had permitted Ventress to help him to the door of his cabin, where she told him he'd better not have a hangover in the morning. He assured her he wouldn't, which was the truth, because he wasn't drunk.

It had been a necessity in undercover work to develop a strong tolerance for alcohol in order to blend in. The exquisite liquor so generously given to them by a pirate captain was strong, but nothing he couldn't handle. He had exaggerated his intoxication in the hope of getting Ventress to reveal some things about herself. It hadn't worked out quite as he'd intended.

Her casual query, "What's your story, Vos?" had blindsided him in a way he couldn't possibly have imagined. Of course he couldn't tell her the truth, but her word choice, *story,* made him realize that he truly didn't have one. He had a series of events from his life that he could relate, but somehow, they were never about him; never *his* stories, simply things he'd done. The distinction was subtle, so subtle he'd never even thought about it. Maybe it was the alcohol, maybe it was the time he'd spent in Ventress's company working as a team, but the realization shook him.

So Vos had said exactly what had sprung into his mind, and then attempted to refocus attention on Ventress. For the second time that evening, he got a shock: He was willing to bet a million credits that Ventress, too, had replied honestly—and her answer had surprised and shaken her, just as Vos's answer had rattled him.

He rubbed his tired eyes. He was likely reading too much into everything tonight. His belly was still pleasantly warm from the alcohol, but his thoughts were discordant. Vos stretched out on the cot, but sleep would not come right away. The words he'd spoken kept running through his brain: *What's worse . . . to have unhappy stories, or to have no story at all?*

Vos had no answer.

CHAPTER NINE

"You're late," said the man who sat in the seedy, ill-lit Level 1313 bar. He wore a fur-lined vest, a tan jacket, and gear that pegged him as a bounty hunter. Sharp eyes gazed out from under a hood. His voice was smooth and cultured, the exact opposite of his disheveled and dirty appearance.

"*You're* impatient," Vos replied. He waved at the bartender and pointed at the beverage his companion held in a grubby hand. A moment later a BD-3000 droid, her pale metal face smooth and her torso painted a garish scarlet, plunked a shot glass down in front of Vos. One articulated lid closed over a blank eye in a wink, then the droid sidled off.

Vos took a sip. Predictably, the beverage wasn't very strong. Obi-Wan Kenobi always eschewed the heavier stuff when he was on a mission.

"I am, rather," Kenobi said, "and I'm not alone. I've been getting pressure from the Council. How's it coming with Ventress? Have you made any progress?"

"Well, I'm her 'partner' now," Vos said, draining the weak drink and motioning for another. "We've been scoring marks together—and making quite the payday, I might add. Hey," he asked, keeping his face straight, "do I get to keep the money after this mission?"

Kenobi rubbed his eyes and gave a long-suffering sigh. "You can't play bounty hunter forever."

Vos mock-pouted, and winked at the BD-3000 as she set another glass of mostly water in front of him.

"Now that the two of you have established a rapport," Kenobi went on, "you must find a way to motivate her against Count Dooku."

Vos's joviality ebbed. Quietly, he said, "She has plenty of motivation."

Obi-Wan feigned obliviousness to Vos's sudden solemnity. "Well, then, help her tap into it. Soon."

"I'll find a way."

"I'm sure you will." Drink unfinished, Kenobi tossed a few credits on the table and rose. His hand descended on Vos's shoulder for a moment. Then he was gone. Vos was alone in the crowded bar, staring into his glass.

Vos ordered another shot and knocked it back, then rolled the glass between his fingers. Many Jedi would raise eyebrows at the thought of meditating in a bar, but Vos had done it before. It was simply a matter of being able to have part of his conscious mind alert while the rest of it sank deeper. And frankly, Vos sometimes wondered if other customers, crouched over their drinks and staring into them, weren't trying their own versions of the same thing.

He deliberately slowed his breathing and his heart rate, letting his gaze soften as he stared into the last few blue droplets in the glass.

The essence of his task could be summed up in two words: *Kill Dooku*. It expanded from there to *Get Asajj Ventress's help to do so*. Wider the ring spread, like ripples from a stone tossed into still water, to include, *Without her knowledge.*

His even breathing caught for an instant, then resumed. That was where the conflict came. He had gained her trust—and even grown to like her. That happened, sometimes, in this line of work. But Ventress was unique. Even the Council knew it, or else they wouldn't have asked him to pair up with her.

What were his key values? What did he owe, to himself and to others? To the Jedi Order as a whole, to the Council—to his "partner"? He was a Jedi, all but born in the Temple. Surely, he owed them his absolute obedience. The task was a worthy one. If anyone in the universe needed to be stopped, it was Dooku. Vos let himself imagine all the people slain by Dooku in one place, and the image was so horrific he felt his gut twist with real, physical pain.

But what about Ventress? She'd saved his life on more than one occasion during their bounty hunts. He owed her. And what about himself?

The thought instantly snapped Vos out of his meditation. Jedi did not think about themselves—their own wants, or needs, or desires. *Keep it together,* he told himself. *You're using her, yes, but you're not doing anything she doesn't want. And you know when it comes down to it, she's going to want to kill Dooku.*

Even his reasoning did not shake the feeling that he was doing something wrong, and he was unable to fall back into his meditation.

He ordered another shot and sat at the table for a long time.

Ventress paused in her welding as Vos approached. She had needed to take a couple of hours in relative safety to install some modifications to the *Banshee*. They had opted to land here, on a platform extending from the inner curve of one of the massive portals that burrowed its way into the Coruscant undercity. Vos had taken advantage of the chance to restock their supplies. Ventress permitted herself to silently marvel at the fact that she had let someone else take her hard-earned credits—and that she hadn't had a moment's concern about whether he and the supplies would return. She flipped up the protective visor and gave him a smile.

"You seem to be in a good mood," he said.

"I suppose I am," she replied. "No reason not to be. We're stocked up, the new modifications to the ship are almost complete—*and* I've managed to secure another job for us." She extinguished the torch and removed the visor.

Striding up the *Banshee*'s ramp, Vos caught up to her and they fell into an easy step together. "Oh? Where we headed?"

"We're going to Oba Diah. To see the Pykes."

Vos made a sour face. Ventress supposed she couldn't blame him. Vos was almost annoyingly cheerful—no, she amended, strike the "almost"—and the Pykes were not anybody's idea of fun. The Pyke Syndicate liked to call itself a family, but it was driven by anything other than familial love. It was a crime syndicate whose focus was on the distribution of highly illegal spice of all types, from the mild to the mind destroying.

"A barrel of laughs, being your partner."

"No one says you need to stick around," Ventress offered.

"Ah, but you'd miss me. You know you would."

She didn't reply, only arched a brow. But she had to admit, if only to herself . . . he was right.

* * *

"Looks like we've got a welcoming committee," Vos observed. Oba Diah was a world as unwelcoming as its inhabitants. Wreathed in mist, the major city was carved out of the jutting obsidian crags of the inhospitable terrain. Centuries ago, the Pykes had built structures from material that resembled deep green smoked glass. From these looming yet eerily beautiful structures, the wealthy and powerful gazed from luminous blue-green windows down at those less fortunate. Ventress settled the *Banshee* down onto one of the many landing plaftforms erected on spokes that jutted out from the main Pyke citadel and peered out the viewport.

"Fife," she said. "He's Marg Krim's majordomo. I've worked with him before. Usually he thinks he's more than enough to handle a situation. This should be interesting. Come on."

No fewer than eight heavily armed guards flanked the strutting Fife. Ventress strode forward, Vos just a step behind her, and came to a stop in front of the Pyke. No matter how often one interacted with them, the species always took getting used to. Taller and slighter than an average human, Pykes had long, spindly legs and arms that bore three fingers. Their heads were large, sleek, and elongated, with a tapered skull, yet their faces were undersized, small as a child's. The overall effect was unsettling.

"Fife," she said coolly.

He didn't acknowledge her. His glowing magenta eyes were turned toward Vos, who stayed silent— thankfully, Ventress thought—though his arms were folded across his chest and he met Fife stare for stare.

Ventress regarded Fife for a moment, then, hoping that a brief acknowledgment would be enough for the openly curious Pyke, said flatly, "My partner, Vos."

Fife's head drew back in the characteristic Pyke gesture for surprise. He stared at Ventress. "A partner? You? That's new." He looked Vos up and down and said to him, "You must be pretty good for this one to trust you."

"I am," Vos replied matter-of-factly.

Fife motioned for them to follow. The eight guards tramped in silent menace behind them as Fife led them through the halls of the Pyke Palace.

They strode through a marble entrance, the warm, sand-colored stone floor flanked by massive dark pillars that emitted green illumination. While the design and artistry of the entranceway was beautiful, Ventress caught glimpses of languid movement in alcoves on each side and the brief gleam of glazed eyes. It was hard not to cough from the sickly sweet smell of spice. Attractive the place was, but what went on here was unpleasant indeed.

She returned her attention to Fife. "We've known each other awhile," she said, quickening her steps to keep pace with him. "Anything you can fill me in on before we hear it from your boss?"

He looked at her for a moment, then spoke quietly. "What I can say is that Black Sun is trying to move in on the Pyke Syndicate. Marg Krim has been put in a terrible position. Much is on the line for him. Black Sun wants all his business. He risks both losing face with our syndicate and . . . well, the rest I will leave for him to share."

They reached the foot of the throne. Marg Krim blinked at them, his body twitching with anxiety. In the Force, worry, anger, and fear rolled off him. He wore the headdress that marked his station, a metallic mask affixed to his huge skull that looked like rays of the sun or the plumes of a bird.

Fife bowed low, his gangly arms sweeping. "O Illustrious Imperator, Marg Krim," he said, "I have brought the bounty seekers you requested."

Krim continued to stare at Vos and Ventress for so long that Ventress thought the Illustrious Imperator might be too heavily drugged to have a coherent conversation. Then he spoke, and he wasted not one word.

"My mate and two younglings have been captured by Black Sun and taken to Mustafar."

"Oh, boy," Vos muttered under his breath.

"You will find them, and bring them back alive." His voice quivered with emotion, and he took another puff on his hookah in an attempt to steady himself.

Ventress chose her words carefully. "Before we begin," she said, exuding calmness in the Force, "there are a few things we need to know. For instance—"

"Why aren't you sending your own men to bring them back?" Vos interrupted.

Ventress jabbed him with an elbow and whispered harshly in his ear: "Because then *we* wouldn't get paid!"

Fortunately Marg Krim was too lost in his own turmoil to notice the exchange. "I should be able to, shouldn't I? But I cannot. My supposedly devoted men are willing to let my family *die* if it means they do not have to join Black Sun. That hateful group sees this attack on my family as a victory either way, because they know it will hurt me. My family must be returned safely . . . and secretly. This will show both Black Sun and my own men that Marg Krim is still a powerful member of the Pyke Family." He closed his eyes and murmured, "Family . . ."

"Don't worry," Vos said warmly. "We'll get your family back alive."

"Provided that's the way we find them," Ventress added. She did not want to be held responsible for failure if Black Sun kidnappers got trigger-happy.

"Bring them home," Krim said, his voice hollow. Then he added, in a whisper, "Please."

CHAPTER TEN

"You're awfully quiet," Vos said as they prepped the ship for takeoff.

"I don't have anything to say."

Apparently, Vos did. "I know. It rattled me, too. We're so used to bringing in sleemos and criminals, it's hard to adjust to rescuing someone's mate and kids."

"As long as the credits are good, I'll bring in who-ever anyone wants." The pat words were easily spoken, but Ventress knew it was a lie, and not the first she had told Vos. Not that long ago, Ventress had not worked alone; she had been part of a team of bounty hunters led by Boba Fett. The team had been tasked with the delivery of a crate of mysterious but precious cargo. Ventress had discovered that the "cargo" packed in the crate was a young woman named Pluma Sodi. The girl, who looked to be only in her teens, had been abducted from her family and was being delivered to a greedy and lecherous Belugan named Otua Blank, who planned to make her his bride against her will. Ventress had *not* delivered Pluma Sodi like a wrapped present to the disgusting

Belugan. She'd released Pluma and placed Boba Fett in the container in the girl's stead. Sometimes, Ventress wondered if the boy would ever forget that incident, but she had no regrets. Even so, she did not like the memory. In that moment, Ventress had been soft, and life had taught her that the universe was not kind to the soft.

Vos eyed her. "Really?"

"Really."

He shrugged. "If you say so."

"Shut up and enter the coordinates for Mustafar."

"Ah yes, scenic Mustafar, because everyone looks good in red lighting. Become a bounty hunter, see the galaxy!"

She would never admit it, but, while there were times when she wanted to throttle Quinlan Vos, who never seemed to have a bad minute, let alone an entire bad day, there were also times when his ebullience was welcome. Ventress was none too keen on visiting Mustafar. No one in her right mind would be. The only thing it was good for was lava, and the only people who lived there were those who had the dangerous job of harvesting the molten export, Black Sun (who found the lava handy as well, specifically for convenient disposal of evidence), and various and sundry beings who either didn't want to be found or had control of others they didn't want found.

Standing in the throne room, hearing that the destination was Mustafar and the obstacle toward recovering the bounty was Black Sun, Ventress had been tempted to walk. But Marg Krim was very powerful in his current position, and while everything had to be kept on the down-low, earning his gratitude could be lucrative over and above the already exorbitant fee they'd been promised.

Well. Who wanted to live forever, anyway?

They came out of hyperspace with the red planet looming before them. Vos opened his mouth to speak and Ventress turned to him with a finger raised in warning.

"Not one word about the color," she said.

He laughed brightly. "How did you know?" He sounded delighted.

"If there's a bad joke to be made, you'll make it. More than once."

Vos heaved an exaggerated sigh. "Guilty as charged." He shrugged, as if he hadn't been about to make another joke about the color. Ventress maneuvered the *Banshee* through thick clouds of black smoke to settle on a landing platform at the edge of a rough-looking mining town.

The platform, and the town itself, were precariously perched on a ledge overlooking a river of orange liquid. Had this been Naboo or any other more hospitable world, and the liquid the cool blue of water, it would be prime real estate. But here, it was just a collection of shanties to house the unfortunates whose job it was to harvest the lava. Ventress debated putting on a breath mask, but decided against it. The masks were vital if one was constantly exposed to the fumes, but a few hours here wouldn't harm them.

The heat was oppressive, but endurable. The natives of this world, the Mustafarians, did wear breath masks while working near the lava. It made them all look mysterious and uniform. As passersby peered up at them curiously, Ventress realized, belatedly, that the masks could have helped camouflage them.

"I hate small towns," she muttered as she and Vos hurried toward a cluster of the rideable lava fleas that the Mustafarians had long ago domesticated. "Everybody knows everybody's business."

"Yeah, but in this case that's going to help us."

"Except within an hour, everyone will know we're here."

They approached a stooped Mustafarian who clearly owned the fleas. A price was agreed on, and credits changed hands.

"It's a bit warm here, isn't it?" Vos commented as they mounted their rented fleas. The Mustafarian glared at him and did not reply. Vos persisted: "Makes you thirsty. Where can we get a drink?"

"The Last Resort," the Mustafarian said, his voice sounding muffled through the breath mask.

"That the best bar in town?" Ventress asked.

The Mustafarian laughed. "*Only* bar in town."

"Guess that's the place to be," Vos said. "Thanks."

He tugged gently on the reins, and the creature gave an obedient leap in the direction of town. Ventress copied Vos's motions, but her flea just shuffled awkwardly and gave a couple of hesitant hops. She placed a hand on its shiny carapace and thought: *You're not too big to squash.* She was no telepath, but she pushed her intention at it through the Force, and it began to lurch sullenly after Vos and his mount.

Ventress's eyes watered from the smoke. She refrained from coughing by sheer determination, and concentrated on guiding her flea through the town. The narrow streets were growing increasingly packed with workers of an astounding variety of species, and most of them, she observed, seemed to be headed in the same direction.

"It must be quitting time at the mine," she commented. "Let's just follow the crowd."

The mass of miners flowed like the lava, and the two rented fleas didn't take much encouraging to join the current. Sure enough, The Last Resort appeared shortly. It was a large building, just as run-down as the rest of the town.

"Looks like we found our bar," Vos mused as he reined in and urged his mount to join the other lava fleas tied to the hitching post. He and Ventress dismounted.

Inside, the bar smelled little better than the fumes exuded by the lava, and Ventress reflected that no matter what their décor or patron variety, places like this all had the same feel about them: a sense of despair, sullen resentment, and hunger, spiked here and there with a sharp upswing of short-lived euphoria.

Here, though, a dull exhaustion was the dominant sensation, eclipsing the other emotions. The miners were being ground down, a little each day, to a sort of bitter lethargy that was—

Ventress turned her head, following a thread of bright arrogance that wove throughout the blunter emotions. Her gaze fell on a group of burly Falleen. They wore nothing that definitively marked them as members of Black Sun, but they didn't need to. Their posture and physiques, powerful not just from physical exertion but also from good nourishment, set them apart from the majority of the bar's patrons, most of whom slumped over their glasses as if already half dead.

One of the Falleen sat in a corner by himself, legs outstretched, draining a mug as he regarded his fellow drinkers with a thinly veiled expression of contempt on his mottled, green face.

As if reading her thoughts, Vos murmured, "I think we've found a winner."

It was almost too easy. "Sit back and relax," Ventress said. "I've got this one."

"So what do you think? The nod and a wink? Or the full-on gambit?"

"Oh, definitely the full-on gambit for this one," she said. This arrogant Falleen would be offended—and curious—if he thought his powerful pheromones weren't working on her.

Vos's eyes danced. "Be my guest." He stepped back, merging seamlessly with the shadows and the hunched shapes of the regulars. Ventress stood for a moment, letting the Black Sun Falleen's gaze come to her first. When their eyes met, she walked slowly to the bar and slipped into the seat beside him.

"Hello there, soldier."

He smirked. "Hello yourself, gorgeous. Can I get a pretty lady like you something to drink?"

Ventress licked her lips, keeping her gaze locked with his. "I'm not thirsty. Not for alcohol, anyway." She leaned closer and whispered, "It's hard to . . . *talk* in here." She ducked her head, running a hand through her short fair hair—the signal they had agreed upon that first time she and Vos had tried this together, on their hunt for the pirate's wandering lover. Out of the corner of her eye, she saw a figure slip out of the room.

The Black Sun guard was so proud of himself and his oh-so-irresistible pheromones. This was going to be fun.

"Yeah, it is hard to . . . *talk*," he replied.

"Then let's get out of here."

He almost knocked the stool over getting to his feet. Ventress winked at him and took him by the hand, leading him through the cluster of sorrowful drunkards down a dark corridor toward the restroom.

The guard didn't waste much time, shoving the door open and kicking it closed behind him. "Come here, pretty lady." He grabbed Ventress by the shoulders, pushed her against the wall, and leaned in for a kiss.

Ventress's hand was on his chest. She chuckled throatily.

"Not so fast, buddy. Didn't we leave the barroom because we wanted to talk? Give a girl some conversation first."

He pulled back, his grin widening as he looked her up and down. "You're a tough one, aren't you?"

"You have *no* idea" came a cheerful male voice.

The guard, taken completely by surprise, grunted "Huh?" as he turned to stare at Vos, who had been awaiting their arrival concealed in one of the stalls. Watching as Vos slammed his lower left arm into the Falleen's throat, Ventress had to wonder if the Black Sun syndicate was losing its edge. The guard choked slightly, but recovered enough to strike. It was a swift blow, but Vos ducked it with those almost unnaturally fast reflexes of his, his booted foot crunching into the Falleen's knee. The guard doubled in pain, and Vos flipped him over the rest of the way so he ended up sprawled on the sticky floor with Vos's knee on his throat. For good measure, Vos grabbed the guard's arm and bent it back at a clearly painful angle.

Vos looked up at Ventress and grinned. She let herself return the smile as she sank down beside the guard, her gaze on him as cold now as it had been inviting before.

"Who are you?" the guard demanded, his eyes flitting back and forth from one to the other.

Ventress ignored the query. "Where are the Pyke hostages?"

"H-Hostages?" He tried to look innocent. It didn't suit him.

She sighed. "Come on, honey. Don't make this more difficult." As if on cue, Vos leaned a *little* forward on the Black Sun guard's neck, pulled a *little* back on his arm, and the Falleen broke just that fast.

"They're in the main holding cell. At the house."

"We're going to need more than that," Vos said.

"No, I can't, they'll kill me!"

Patience had never been Ventress's strong suit. The Black Sun guard represented the sort of person she despised most—the kind of swaggering thug who had no passion, no drive, for anything but his own base pleasure. She drew her lightsaber and activated it with a *snap-hiss*. "Yes, you can, or *we'll* kill you."

"Okay, okay!" Vos eased up on the Falleen's throat. The guard coughed, then spoke. "Upper level, left-hand side. The doors are all rigged with defenses, and there are twelve guards on duty at all times. Six above and six below."

Ventress smiled, extinguished her blade, and patted his cheek. "There, was that so difficult?"

Even now, the guard looked hopeful. Ventress shook her head in disbelief, made a fist, and punched him in his overlarge jaw. His eyes rolled back in his head and he went limp. She had originally wanted to kill him, but Vos had convinced her that they didn't want to have Black Sun after them for murder if it could be avoided. And really, all they needed was to keep the guard out of the way long enough for them to get in, get Krim's mate and children, and get out.

"Don't worry," Vos said as he dragged the guard into the end stall. "He won't be waking up anytime soon. Not from one of your trademark punches." He paused, then, on a whim, arranged the unconscious Falleen in an undignified position.

Ventress didn't want to smile, but she couldn't help it. "Come on. We've got a fortress to infiltrate."

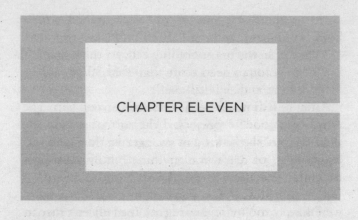

CHAPTER ELEVEN

It occurred to Vos, as he stared up—and up—at the ominous structure, that he was putting an awful lot of time and effort into doing things that really weren't even close to completing the mission. Take this Black Sun fortress, for instance. The thing towered over the mining facility and the ramshackle houses like an enthroned giant, and it was almost a town unto itself. The guard had referred to a "house," as if the area were an ordinary dwelling place. This house, though, was perched high inside the massive tower that was the centerpiece of the fortress. Lights shone like eyes, and the whole thing reeked of power and the willingness to use it.

He and Ventress had tethered their fleas at the edge of the town and had picked their careful way to the outlying area of the fortress, where they took up position on a storage building. Using a pair of electrobinoculars, he made a slow sweep of the area.

"There are the guards, just like he said," Vos murmured.

Ventress peered through her own goggles, touching them with a long finger to magnify.

"It's a fairly fortified compound, but nothing I haven't broken into before," she replied. From anyone else, the words would have been a boast. Vos knew that from this woman, it was a simple statement of fact, and she had uttered it as such.

After spending so much time in her company, he now understood why Kenobi held her in such respect, even though she had been an enemy. Was, still, an enemy. Sort of. Or was she? He mentally shook his head and refocused on the task at hand. Even with a Jedi and a powerful Force-user like Ventress, there were simply too many guards at the main entrance to either take out or try to sneak past.

"Your would-be boyfriend said they were in the main holding cell in the house. Top section, left-hand side."

Vos looked upward along the "house" itself, and his eyes fell on an area of the roof that wasn't sheer wall. *Aha!*

"I see our entry point. Come on."

Swiftly, silently, they moved across the open area. As they circled around to the side of the huge tower, the flat stone of the courtyard area gave way to jagged black rock.

Vos peered upward. "That looks like the base of an overhanging balcony," he said. He fired his liquid cable launcher, and it found a secure purchase. "Grab hold," he said to Ventress.

She gave Vos a quick glance, then pointedly reached for her bow, sending up her own plasma cable instead. For an instant, he simply stared as she quickly ascended, pulled up by the retracting cable. Vos found himself unexpectedly stung by the gesture. It hadn't been necessary. What was he going to do, try to steal a kiss in midair? She knew better than that. Fresh concern about ever really gaining her trust washed over him, but he banished it and followed his partner—if she really could be called one.

Ventress had reached the balcony first, and had used her lightsaber to cut a circular entrance through several of the metal railings. The railings made the whole area look like a cage—which, of course, it was. Vos slipped through the opening onto the balcony, carefully avoiding the orange, nearly molten metal around the entrance Ventress had made and landing lightly. "Jackpot," she said, "but it seems awfully convenient."

She indicated a series of diamond-shaped, grated openings that served as windows. Vos heard the humming of an energy field. Carefully, he peered inside and beheld two small, huddled shapes clinging to each other. It was a welcome sight.

"It does," Vos agreed. "We need to move quickly. It could be a trap."

Ventress stepped to the side next to a set of controls. She plunged her still-activated lightsaber into an open terminal beneath the controls, overloading the shield generator. Vos slipped easily through the now-open window. The children's heads whipped up, but Vos crouched down and lifted a finger to his lips.

"Shhh," he said, projecting calmness at them in the Force. He smiled. "We're going to get you out of here. You just have to trust us and keep as quiet as possible, okay?"

Trembling, they nodded. Ventress speared the control panel next to the door with her lightsaber, locking it. She turned, her blue eyes taking in the children and then scanning the room.

"Where is she?"

Vos started to ask *Who*, but stopped as realization dawned. The mother wasn't here.

"What's your name, little guy?" he asked the boy.

The child wiped his face with his hand and tried to look brave.

"I'm Vram," he said. He indicated his younger sister. "This is Laalee."

"Where's your mother, Vram?"

Laalee started to cry. Vram swallowed hard. "They took her away from us when we were captured. I heard them say they were worried that Father might send someone to find us."

Vos put all his sincerity into his words. "Those guards were right, and we're that 'someone.' We'll find her. Don't worry."

He rose and went to Ventress, his back to the younglings. Quietly he said, "Well, this complicates things."

Ventress's eyes were narrowed in anger. "I guess the guard at the bar wasn't that stupid after all. He double-crossed—"

She was interrupted by the shrill *whoop-whoop* of an alarm. The children gasped, huddling together and looking at Vos and Ventress with wide, frightened eyes as their would-be rescuers ran to the window and looked down. Guards were flooding into the tower.

Ventress slipped on her goggles and zoomed in on the chaos. "There he is," she muttered.

"Your boyfriend from the bar?"

"Oh, please," said Ventress in a scathing voice. Vos recalled the position in which he'd left the Falleen, and despite the direness of the situation, he couldn't suppress a small chuckle.

"Guess you should've hit him harder," he said.

Ventress started to retort but fell silent as the guards started banging on the door.

"So what's it going to be? Lava flow or guards?" Vos asked.

"Normally I'd say the guards. But we have baggage to protect." She waved in annoyance at the children.

"Okay, lava flow it is! Hop on!" Vos said cheerily. Vram and Laalee, however, looked at him skeptically when he knelt in front of them.

Ventress also knelt, barking at the children, "Come on, we don't have all day."

The brother and sister exchanged glances, then clambered atop their rescuers' backs. At the feel of Vram's small body quivering with fear, Vos's heart abruptly surged. He and Ventress *were* going to get these two innocents—*and* their mother—back to their father. As if he could feel Vos's emotion, Vram tightened his grip and his shaking stopped. Vos straightened. At that moment, the unmistakable sound of blasterfire joined the steady sound of the alarm.

"Guess they got tired of knocking," Vos said. He threw a quick glance back to the door and saw a thin crack at its base. They'd be inside shortly.

He jumped out onto the balcony, whistled loudly, reaching out with the Force, and felt the lava fleas respond. He glanced over at Ventress. Their eyes met, and she nodded. They leapt gracefully down onto a lower level, the children screaming as they hung on. Blaster bolts whizzed past Vos's ear, letting him know that the guards had broken into the room above and were none too pleased about finding it empty.

"Hang on," he heard Ventress shout, and she disappeared over the balcony railing. For a moment, Vos watched as she plummeted, little Laalee, silent as death, looking up at him from Ventress's back. Blaster bolts zipped by, too close for comfort. The moment he saw Ventress land nimbly on the rocks below, Vos leapt, little Vram's arms tight around his neck. When he landed, Ventress was already leaping from boulder to boulder, and up onto an abutment, which she continued to run along. Vos caught movement and looked past Ventress to see the lava fleas bounding to meet her. As the first one drew near, Ventress flipped up and out in a graceful arc, making a perfect landing in the saddle.

"Wow!" exclaimed Vram, his fear forgotten for the moment.

"Kid, you've not seen anything yet," Vos assured him, and prepared to make his own jump. "Watch *this*."

His flea was almost beneath his perch on the abutment. He grinned, looking down, knowing he had timed it perfectly, and then he leapt. This kid would have a story—

Sudden pain seared his shoulder. A blaster bolt! Caught off guard, Vos grunted and jerked. Instead of landing perfectly astride the flea, he struck it hard and bounced off, hurtling toward the waiting lava below.

He twisted, trying to adjust his trajectory, and at the same time stretched out his hand to use the Force to cushion the impact. Vos landed on his feet on a jutting rock, but Vram lost his grip. The boy cried out as he fell and then rolled toward the roiling orange flow.

Vos, his body racked with pain, leapt for Vram, stretching out his hand, willing it to catch the sobbing child. Vram was too far away. Narrowing his eyes in intense concentration, Vos reached out to Vram. Suddenly the boy's fall ceased, and his body hung suspended above the lava—just long enough for Vos to grab him by the arm.

"Come on!"

Vram flung his arms around his rescuer's neck, his sharp little elbow digging into the blaster burn. Vos gritted his teeth and looked up to see Ventress, mounted on her own flea and holding the reins to his in one hand while she expertly batted away blaster bolts with her other. With an effort, Vos hurried to climb back up the boulders. When he reached Ventress, he hoisted himself and Vram into the saddle. The boy was wailing in terror, but mere moments later, as the tower that had held them prisoner shrank in the distance, both children began to cheer.

It hurt. Of course it hurt, it was a blaster burn. Vos sat in the hold with the children, who regarded him from as far away as possible. When Vos realized they were staring at his blackened, bloody shoulder, he adjusted his position so the wound was out of their line of vision. Unfortunately, he could do nothing about the reek of burned human flesh. He heard the clank of Ventress's boots on the metal rungs of the ladder and turned to smile at her, but he could feel that it was barely a ghost of his usual cocky grin.

She was holding a medpac and knelt beside him. A flicker of concern rippled over her features.

"It's not as bad as you think," Vos lied.

Ventress glared. "It's every bit as bad as I think, because I've seen them before and I know *exactly* what to think. I—"

He jerked his head slightly toward the children and raised his eyebrows. She fell silent and began to treat the wound.

Vos watched her work. Her hands were capable and cool, strangely gentle as she positioned his arm to tend every patch of blackened flesh. She sterilized the wound and applied bacta-treated bandages. The pain ceased, but Vos found himself still staring at her long, slender fingers. They wielded a lightsaber with deadly skill, controlled the Force, piloted a ship, landed one hell of a punch. For Ventress, her hands were weapons, tools. But now they touched him, for the first time, with care.

"This," she said as she packed away the equipment, "is why I don't have a partner."

The words came before Vos even realized he'd thought them. "No," he said quietly. "This is why you *need* a partner."

He reached out his good arm to touch her hand with his own, noting that the darker brown of his skin made her own seem even paler.

She froze. Vos looked up to find her ice-blue gaze fixed on him. Her expression was unreadable. He swallowed, suddenly and for the first time in his adult life utterly unsure of himself.

"We need to find the mother." Ventress's voice was flat. She rose, sliding her hand out from under his, and without another word marched back to the cockpit.

What just happened? Vos had no idea. So confused was he that at first he didn't even notice the soft sound of music coming from the corner where Laalee and Vram were huddled. Vos shook his head, clearing it.

"Hey, Laalee," he called genially, "what have you got there?"

Laalee gasped and inadequately hid something behind her back. "N-nothing," she stammered.

Vos held out his hand. "May I see it? Please? I promise I'll give it right back."

Laalee hesitated, then held out a small locket. Vos took it and opened it, revealing a miniature hologram of a Pyke female.

"It's Mommy," Laalee said softly, tears welling in her eyes.

But Vos hardly heard her. As had happened to him countless times before, the world fell away.

"No!" their mother screamed, struggling against the burly Falleen guards who none-too-gently were hauling her away from her children. She looked so fragile, as if they could easily snap one of her slender limbs with a single hand. And yet she fought like a nexu defending her cubs. "No! Laalee! Vram!"

"Mommy!" Laalee shrieked.

"Don't take her away!" shouted Vram.

The guard laughed nastily. It was the Falleen from The Last Resort—the one whom Vos and Ventress had tricked into revealing the location of the hostages. "Don't worry, Ziton will take good care of her at the palace!"

The vision cleared as abruptly as it had appeared. Dazed, Vos pushed painfully to his feet and stumbled toward the cockpit. Without preamble, he blurted, "We need to go back to the fortress. The mother's in Ziton's palace."

Ventress turned to regard him. "Really," she said. "And how would you know that?" Her gaze fell to the locket he still clutched in his hand.

"Laalee told me." It wasn't entirely a lie. She had handed him the locket, and *that* had told him.

Her gaze didn't waver. "Neither of those kids seemed to know anything before."

Vos mustered his old grin. "Well, I guess they felt like they could trust me. I'm good with kids."

"You behave like their *peer,*" Ventress said. "I am unsurprised." She looked at him for a moment longer. Unbidden, the memory of how her cool hands on his skin had felt returned to Vos. Then she said, "Okay. Let's go."

Vos glanced back at the two children in the hold. "What about them?"

"What *about* them?"

"We can't just let them run around the ship—they're kids. They'll have this thing reduced to scrap metal. And what if they wander off?"

"I'll take care of it."

CHAPTER TWELVE

Fifteen minutes later, they had landed their ship in the courtyard, in full view of the tower and the guards stationed there. Ventress snapped down the shoulder harnesses on the containment chairs while Vram and Laalee yelped in protest.

"Wow," Vos said unhappily. "You sure they're going to be okay in there?"

Ventress looked at him, confused. "What? These restraining chairs lock down the baddest villains in the galaxy. I think they can hold a couple of kids."

"That . . . wasn't what I meant. But all right."

"Vos!" Laalee whimpered, reaching out a small three-fingered hand.

"Sorry, kid, it's her ship." He gave them a shrug and lifted his arms in a what-can-you-do? gesture. "Hang tight, and we'll be back with your mother before you know it."

He patted Laalee on the head and grinned at Vram. He turned to face Ventress, and his smile faded. She stood with her arms folded in front of her—a defensive gesture, and he wished he knew what she was thinking.

"Just so we're clear," she said, "I'll keep them occupied while you find the mother." She reached for the door controls.

Unable to help himself, Vos called out softly, "Hey . . ."

She turned. "What?" Her voice wasn't chilly, but neither was it warm or inviting.

What had he been going to say? He wasn't sure, and now, beneath her scrutiny, he couldn't think of anything. Finally, he said, "Try not to get yourself killed."

Ventress smirked, as he had known she would, but just before she opened the door and descended the ramp, Vos thought her expression melted for a moment into a genuine smile.

He took a deep breath. *Get your head in the game,* he told himself, and waited until the guards' attention was fully on Ventress before he slipped quietly down the ramp himself.

Ziton Moj was not happy.

He had not been happy when Marg Krim had unexpectedly rejected the very lucrative offer of combining the Pyke Syndicate with Black Sun. Ziton was even unhappier that he was therefore compelled to kidnap Krim's entire family. And he was extremely unhappy indeed to have learned that a scant twenty minutes earlier, two of his three hostages had been rescued.

Ziton looked up at Kurg Utal as the aide approached, knowing immediately that Utal was about to make Ziton the unhappiest yet.

"Master Ziton," Utal said, and he came perilously close to wringing his hands, "we have been unable to find the renegades who took the children."

Ziton sighed. "Pity. Marg Krim knew what the penalty would be if he attempted a rescue. Prepare to execute his wife."

"Yes, my mas—" Utal began, but he was interrupted by the sight of his guards marching up, escorting a female with short, silver-blond hair.

"My lord," the head guard said, "an envoy from the Pykes is here to negotiate the release of the hostages."

Utal and Ziton exchanged glances, and Ziton turned to examine the newcomer. Her timing was remarkably coincidental—and Ziton was not one to believe in coincidences. She was clearly not a Pyke, and in fact did not even look like she was anything as impressively named as an "envoy." Her leather clothing was well worn, and she had the air of a warrior rather than an unctuous diplomat.

"Interesting," he mused, settling back in his chair with an inviting smile. "I'd very much like to hear what you have to offer."

"Sorry," the "envoy" said, "first things first. I want to see the children and the wife to make sure they're still . . ." She made a show of searching for the right word. "Breathing."

"One thing at a time. I can show you the wife, but the children will have to wait."

He beckoned for Kurg to lean in and whispered, "Go forward with our plan, but bring the wife here. I will send this envoy, if such she truly is, with Tezzka Krim's head and an eyewitness account of me severing it from her body myself."

"And if she is not truly an envoy?"

"No matter. Tezzka must die regardless, and this stranger will soon follow her."

Kurg smiled thinly, his eyes twinkling with admiration for his master, and bowed. As he left the room, he gave the envoy a scornful glance. She met him stare for stare.

Ziton smiled again at his visitor. "Tell me," he mused, stroking his beard, "do you think I am a fool?"

Her blue eyes narrowed. "Why, particularly, do you ask?"

"I know you took the children."

She looked convincingly surprised—and angry. "What? Are you saying you don't *have* them?"

He growled, softly, deep in his throat. The guards standing beside the envoy tensed, slightly. They knew the signs of their master's encroaching anger.

"How long are we going to play this game?"

She was unmoved. "Do you really think I'd be here right now if I had taken them? You clearly don't know how good I am at my job."

He had opened his mouth to retort when the door to the cells slid open. Tezzka Krim stood in the doorway, her blue eyes wide and darting about. Ziton smiled. This was going to be a pleasure. "Well, there she is."

"And here *I* am," came a voice. A human male, dark of skin and hair and sporting a strange yellow tattoo across his face, stepped in front of the Pyke, grinning broadly.

Surprise caused Ziton to hesitate for a fraction of a second, but then he dived for his weapon. Before he could fire it, the stranger with the yellow tattoo shot it out of his hand.

The blond woman had already dispatched one of the burly Falleen guards and was now snapping the other's arm with frightening casualness. Blaster bolts sang as the dark human, dodging attacks with lithe grace, shot the blasters from the hands of the guards. Ziton stared, aghast, as the intruder almost cheerfully made a show of whirling his own blasters around his fingers before holstering them, then charged the nearest guard.

So intent on Yellow Tattoo was Ziton that he failed to notice the envoy until she was but a meter away. With an angry bellow, he exploded from his chair and met her head-on. He took a swing at her, but struck only air. Then he was stumbling backward, his head swimming and his jaw aching from a well-placed kick. One foot struck the base of his throne and he collapsed into it.

In the moment the woman took to whirl around and smash in the face of a guard who was getting too close, Ziton was up again and charging her. He was well versed in a variety of martial arts and expert in mixing styles up in such a way that his enemy could not anticipate what he might do next.

This one somehow did.

Almost as if the fight had been choreographed, she blocked his every blow, from the Strike of the Nexu to the Kick of the Bantha, with almost disinterested ease. The sounds of thuds and groans from his guards told him that her compatriot was easily handling three, probably four attackers at once. Who *were* these people?

As if she had tired of playing with him, the envoy ceased simply defending herself and moved in for the kill. Her punches and kicks became a blur, and panic started to rise in Ziton's throat. *Dodge—parry—block—strike—*

A left hook made the world turn gray for a moment, and then she was clutching his throat. No . . . wait—she was standing nearly two meters away from him. Her arm was extended, her fingers curled, miming the gesture of crushing his windpipe, and yet he felt it—

Then he was lifted up in the air. Ziton kicked and squirmed, reached up to claw invisible, incorporeal fingers from his throat as the woman spoke in a low, chilling tone.

"I have a message from the Pykes. Don't *ever* put family in the middle of this again."

She hurled him with such force into his throne that it toppled over. Ziton lay on the floor, gasping, and then finally the pressure around his throat disappeared. He got to his feet. Not only were the envoy and Yellow Tattoo nowhere to be seen, but neither was Tezzka Krim. Fury erased fear—fury, and embarrassment.

Massaging his throat, he said, coughing, "Stop them! Guards! Guards!"

He could hear more blasterfire as the guards stationed outside doubtless tried to halt the escaping trio. Surely, the two rescuers would be tired from the fight against so many in the throne room. He heard a strange noise and, rising, caught a glimpse of a blur of light off which his guards' blaster bolts seemed to be ricocheting back at them. A lightsaber?

He charged out in time to see the envoy gripping Tezzka's arm and rushing her up the ramp of a waiting ship. The blaster bolts struck the ramp mere centimeters from their running feet, then the two women disappeared inside.

The guards turned all their focus onto Yellow Tattoo. He responded by grabbing a guard and thrusting the unfortunate Falleen in front of him, using him as a shield. Then the stranger hurled the massive body at the other guards—and Ziton—who were closing in on him. As the two guards stumbled, knocked off balance, the stranger sprinted for the ship. It was already lifting off, and the stranger was forced to leap to catch ahold of the retracting ramp.

Ziton seized a blaster from one of the fallen guards and took aim. Blaster bolts whizzed past the intruder, who somehow managed to clamber up the ramp to the safety of the ship in the nick of time.

The last Ziton saw of him, as the ramp closed and the ship took off, was a cocky wave.

After the excitement of the narrow escape came a joyous and tear-filled reunion. Ventress could hear small voices shouting, "Mommy! Mommy!" and the soft, murmured sobs as Tezzka doubtless hugged her children tight.

"I love happy endings," Vos, who was seated behind her, said. She could tell he was smiling by the warmth in his voice. "And you, Asajj Ventress, were fantastic back there with Ziton. That guy was *up*set."

Normally, after a successful mission, Ventress eased comfortably into conversation with Vos. But this time, something felt different. There was tension between them now, and she was at a loss.

As she had told Vos at the outset, she didn't mix business with pleasure. While it was true that her life was mostly business, pleasure did happen occasionally. But never anything that lasted beyond the single encounter. And never, *ever,* with someone she worked with and respected.

Ventress had no idea how to process the utterly alien emotions his hand on hers had created. She was alone, and she was strong that way. There would be no mate, no children such as Tezzka now embraced tightly.

So she simply did not reply. Vos tried again to strike up a conversation, but eventually fell silent.

They stayed that way for the entire trip.

* * *

When the *Banshee* settled down on Oba Diah's landing platform, Vos told her to go in without him. He would stay behind, he said, and prep the ship for their departure while she got their credits. The younglings begged him to come with them, but he just smiled and hugged them good-bye.

That wasn't like the Quinlan Vos whom Ventress had come to know. Something was definitely amiss. She awkwardly accepted Marg Krim's thanks and, much less awkwardly, the extremely large pile of credits he gave her.

"We'll need to refuel shortly," Vos told her when she returned. "And I could use a drink after all that running around in a hot place." He sounded like his old self, and he grinned, but the humor didn't reach his eyes. So, that was how he was going to play it. Fine with her.

"Catch," she said, and tossed a bag containing half the credits his way.

He deftly obeyed, then frowned. "This is too much."

"Marg Krim was pleased. In his excitement, he doubled our payment."

"Great," Vos said. "More to spend at the bar. Shall we get going?" His enthusiasm sounded forced.

Ventress frowned, but didn't push. She never liked it when someone hounded her, so she extended the same courtesy to Vos. Silently she laid in the coordinates for a nearby planet.

They had just left atmosphere when about a dozen ships came out of hyperspace. Ventress's eyes widened. The vessels were a collection of fighters and *Interceptor*-class frigates—all bearing the stark, ugly symbol of a spiked sun with a circle in the center like an all-seeing eye.

Black Sun.

"No," said Vos, his voice a broken moan. *"No . . ."*

Ventress saw in her mind's eye the children hugging Vos, felt for just a moment Laalee's soft little hands wrapped around her neck and shoulders as she ran.

Then, because there was nothing else she could do, Ventress flipped the controls and the *Banshee* went into hyperspace.

They headed for the bar first. Vos ordered in a flat voice, knocked back a shot, and asked for another.

Ventress sipped her own drink in silence. While she said nothing, he knew she was watching him. He kept his face expressionless, which cost him, and behind the mask he suffered. Had Black Sun followed—no, they knew where the Krim family lived: They'd abducted Tezzka, Laalee, and Vram easily enough. They had simply come to finish the job. Vos knew in his heart what would happen. Black Sun would execute them, and leave Marg Krim to behold their bloody bodies while at the same time trying to fight for his own life.

His fist hurt. Blinking, he looked down to see he'd slammed it on the bar. Slowly he raised his head. Everyone was staring at them. Suddenly, he couldn't stand being in the crowd of people. He downed another shot, the burn of the liquor almost painful as it trickled its way to his stomach, tossed some credits on the bar, and turned to Ventress.

"Let's walk," he said. She raised an eyebrow, but accompanied him.

Dawn was breaking on this world, and the streets were largely deserted. In the forgiving light of the first rays of the sun, everything looked new, even the things that were battered, broken, and dirty.

But Vram and Laalee wouldn't see another sunrise.

Impulsively, he grabbed the small pouch that he kept in his shirt. Tugging it out, he thrust it at Ventress. "Here. You earned this."

Ventress scrutinized him, not taking the money. "Don't bail on me now, Vos," she said quietly. "We're just starting to make a good team."

"But we *aren't* a team," he said. He hadn't known what he intended to say, but the words spilled out of him in a rush, as if they had been dammed too long and were eager for freedom. "For a team to work, there's got to be trust. And—I haven't been truthful with you about who I am."

He took a deep breath. "Asajj . . . I'm a Jedi."

CHAPTER THIRTEEN

"I know," Ventress replied.

That, Vos hadn't expected. It threw him utterly. "Y-you *do*? How?"

She gave him a little smile that was much gentler than her usual smirk. "I'm not a fool. I see what you can do. Those cat-quick reflexes of yours. Your fall back on Mustafar? That should have killed you and Vram."

"Oh," Vos managed weakly.

"Why?"

He closed his eyes for a moment, deciding how much he should tell her. The answer came, clear and true: *Everything.*

"The Jedi Council has ordered me to kill Count Dooku. They thought the best way to do that was through you."

She folded her arms, but she looked more curious than anything else. "Elaborate."

He did. He told her that the Jedi Council, and now he, knew that Dooku had cast her aside and tried to kill her. That she knew Dooku better than anyone. That she had tried, alone, to kill her former Master, and failed both times. That Master Yoda thought that, together, she and Vos would succeed.

Ventress listened without interrupting. When Vos fell silent, she said, "I'm surprised that the Jedi Council would take such action—not that I disapprove of it, mind you. But it's a big step from Jedi to assassin. I've watched you struggle with some of the things we've done, Vos. And trust me, you've only seen a very sanitized version of what goes down in a usual bounty hunt." She shook her head. "Your Council doesn't fully appreciate what it will take to accomplish this goal."

"I'll do it. Whatever it takes."

"I respect your confidence," she said, a hint of a smile playing around her full lips. "And," she added more seriously, "your honesty. I don't normally encounter someone with both. You're a rare breed, Vos. But Dooku . . . I'm not sure you're ready for that kind of fight."

"Then *make* me ready. That's what the Council sent me to you for."

She started to turn away. "You don't understand what you're asking."

Impulsively he caught her arm. Ventress glanced from his hand to his face, almost wary. "Then tell me. Make me understand."

She faced him then, her eyes searching his. "It will require you to forsake nearly everything that it means to be a Jedi. But you have already begun down that path, I think. Your grief over the deaths of the Krim family does not speak of nonattachment."

He frowned. "Jedi aren't without emotion. We're allowed to grieve."

"Perhaps," Ventress allowed, "but somehow I don't think most Jedi try to drown the pain with alcohol and slam their fists on the table."

"No," Vos admitted. Her words were truer than he dared let her know. But one truth he could speak. "I . . . Ventress, this war . . ." He shook his head. "The Council's right. All our resources are being poured into it, and it's a bottomless pit. A victory here, a loss there—we're too busy simply reacting to the next crisis. We're Jedi, not generals. We should be fighting organizations like Black Sun, doing things that make a difference. Dooku *is* the war. When he dies, it's over. With him gone, the Jedi could really *help* people again, really do something that makes a lasting difference. More than just a single rescue here and there that in the end doesn't . . ."

Vos swallowed hard. He realized his fingers were digging into her arm. Ventress didn't seem concerned, but he forced himself to loosen his grip slightly and took a breath.

"So—*yes*. I want Dooku dead now. His death will fix everything."

Ventress placed a hand on his chest. His heart sped up beneath her fingers and he knew she could feel it. Gently, she said, "You will have to harden that soft heart of yours."

"Whatever I have to do, whatever I have to become—I'll do it. I'll *be* it."

She regarded him steadily, then said, "We shall see."

Seated in the dim shadows of the 1313 bar, Obi-Wan Kenobi resisted the urge to check the time again. He knew Vos was late; he didn't need to know exactly how late. The information would serve nothing except to make Kenobi more irritated than he already was.

In many ways, Vos was the perfect choice for this

mission. He had a knack for quickly and thoroughly ingratiating himself with anyone.

But Asajj Ventress wasn't just anyone. She was, in fact, that rare thing—an enemy Kenobi admired. And, if all went according to plan, a soon-to-be ally.

He took a deep breath, reaching gently into the Force to place a layer of calm on his irritation, like oil upon water. It helped, and eventually, a familiar figure stepped into the bar and made his way to Kenobi's table.

"You're late," Kenobi said without preamble, adding pointedly, "again."

Vos shot him his usual grin. "Hey, at least I'm consistent."

He dropped into the chair, put his booted feet on the table, and placed his hands behind his head, looking utterly at home.

"How is your mission progressing?"

"I've made some real progress. As expected." With the tip of his boot, he gently tapped his empty glass and lifted his eyebrows in query. Kenobi sighed lightly, and reached across the table.

"No trouble with our new 'friend'?" he inquired, filling Vos's cup.

"None at all. In fact, she's been quite helpful. Says she's got contacts within the Separatist Alliance that are indebted to her. They'll contact her when one of them knows where Dooku will be next."

Kenobi slid the glass across the table. Vos caught it just as it was about to tip over. "And you trust her?"

Vos drained the drink and wiped his mouth with the back of his hand. Something prickled in Kenobi, a sense that things were not right. Vos was taking just a little too long in replying. Only a Jedi—and one who knew Vos well, at that—would have noticed.

"Yes," Vos said firmly, "I do." He slid the glass back over to Kenobi for a refill.

Obi-Wan searched his friend's face. Beneath the expression of absolute confidence, he looked . . . vulnerable. In a kind voice, he said, "Have caution, Quinlan. Ventress is nothing if not manipulative. She won't hesitate to use your trust against you the instant it serves her own selfish purposes."

Back the glass slid across the table. Vos caught it and looked Kenobi right in the eye. "She's been faithful to me."

That's a curious choice of words, Kenobi thought, and the unease stirred inside him again. But there was nothing to be done. He had warned Vos, and he could do no more. The other Jedi, after all, was a fellow Master, and one who had been in this sort of duplicitous situation many more times than Kenobi had.

He contented himself with saying, "For now." They clinked their glasses and drank. Kenobi placed his down on the table and rose, donning his helmet and clapping Vos on the shoulder.

But even as he left, he couldn't shake the peculiar sense of foreboding.

Ventress set the coordinates for a world to which she had never desired to return, but she knew in her heart it was the right place to begin Vos's training.

He clearly sensed her need for silence and respected it, though knowing him, he was probably bursting with curiosity. When they came out of hyperspace and the red planet filled the viewport, Ventress felt a dull, sick ache—a sensation she knew would only grow sharper with what was about to unfold.

She brought the *Banshee* in for a landing beneath

the curving, blackened trunks of what had once been eighty-meter-high trees. A few had escaped the flames, and some of them still bore poignant, precious fruit. Ventress sat for a moment in the cockpit, opening to the pain, letting it slice her soul like a knife across an open palm, her grief, hatred, and guilt dripping out like blood. It had been less than a year since the slaughter, and the wound was still fresh and raw.

Without a word to Vos, she rose, went to the door, and tapped the controls to open it and extend the ramp. He followed as she descended, looking first at her, then gazing upon the red-tinted, mist-wreathed world. He stiffened abruptly. Ventress suspected he was sensing the grip the dark side had upon her birthplace; how strong it was, and how deep it went.

"Do you remember sharing Lassa Rhayme's whiskey that night?" Ventress asked quietly. He nodded. "I asked you what your story was, and you said you didn't have one. Do you recall what I said when you asked me that question?"

"You said you had quite a few of them, but none of them ended well," Vos replied, quietly.

"I'm going to share one of those stories with you now," Ventress said, her voice huskier than usual with emotion. "About a sisterhood. And a girl who was taken from it, and came back home."

She walked among the faint shadows of the trees and heard Vos's swift intake of breath as, now, he saw the skeletons of more than a forest. None remained intact; the scavengers had done their jobs, but here and there was the unmistakable shape of a human skull.

"When I was an infant, my clan was forced to surrender me to a criminal. I became his slave, but he was a surprisingly kind master. He was killed when I was still quite young during an attack by Weequay raiders. I was rescued by a Jedi Knight named Ky Narec, who sensed that I was strong in the Force. He was stranded on Rattatak, and he took me under his wing. I became his Padawan."

"You were trained by a Jedi?" Vos stared openly at her.

Ventress nodded and clenched her teeth for a moment. Sorrow gripped her heart, and she let it. "For ten years, we helped the people of Rattatak. We became heroes—to most. But to some, we were the enemy."

"The Jedi are always enemies to some," Vos said.

"Narec died in front of my eyes. He, too, was killed by Weequay," Ventress continued. Speaking the words opened the gates even more, and she felt a flare of the old, never-quite-gone pain . . . and the comfort, cold but real, of hatred. "You may have noticed I dislike them. I vowed vengeance, and I got it. Soon, the warlords were dead, and I ruled in their place. It was on Rattatak that Dooku found me, and I him." She shrugged. "I hated the Jedi for abandoning my Master, and Dooku wanted an apprentice as filled with hatred as he was. It was a good match."

"So . . . what changed?"

Her lip curled in a snarl as she recalled Dooku's words. "He abandoned me without warning. He said I had failed him for the last time, and left me for dead. But I survived, and I vowed to kill him. I knew I would need allies if I were to succeed. And so I came home." She gestured to the place in which they stood. "Home to the Nightsisters, where I was made welcome, and our clan leader, Mother Talzin, helped me plot my revenge. Twice, I attempted to assassinate Dooku. Twice, I failed."

Ventress turned to regard Vos intently. She could

tell he sensed the deep anguish of the place. His gaze fell to the ground, lingering on the broken remains of a Nightsister's bow.

"Dathomir is where you got your bow, isn't it?" Wordlessly, Ventress nodded. "No wonder it is so important to you." He bent, picked up the bow respectfully . . .

. . . and gasped. Sweat broke out on his forehead and his body went taut. His eyes widened, seeing not what was here now, but what had been here then—

The bow tumbled from his shaking fingers and he stepped back from it. Recovering, he said, "I'm sorry, I—my talent, my psychometry . . . When I hold an object and focus on it, sometimes I can see and hear things that have happened during its history. And sometimes . . . sometimes I can *feel* what happened."

"Then you know that Dooku ordered the massacre," Ventress said quietly. "It happened the same night that I undertook the ritual to become a true Nightsister. Dooku sent General Grievous here with an army. We responded with the same. We used our magicks . . . and we summoned the dead."

She gestured to an area of trees that had managed to escape the fire, and pointed to the large sacks that hung like giant teardrops.

"These contain the bodies of my sisters," Ventress said. She reached to caress the smooth casing. "When one dies, so I was told, we perform a ritual to honor her. We bathe her in a sacred pool, then enclose her in this pod. In this way, a sister never truly leaves us. She is dead, but she is nestled inside something vibrant and alive. She is suspended between sky and soil, because she is truly of neither. She is always near, always part of the clan. I was taught that our dead sisters can share our celebrations of joy, and our ceremonies of grief. And that one night—they shared our fight."

Ventress gestured to the skeletons around them. For a moment, her voice caught. "But . . . I do not know the secret of preserving the fallen, and no one else was left to tend to them . . ."

"Asajj . . ." Vos spoke with great tenderness as he reached to touch her arm gently. "I am so, so very sorry."

For the briefest of instants, the simple sincerity of his words and gesture almost undid her. Ventress slammed the door down on the feeling at once, before she was overwhelmed. She had brought Vos here to teach him of hatred, to make him strong enough to face Dooku, not to comfort her. It was the only way. She knew without knowing how she knew it that Dooku would only be killed by someone with hatred in her—or his—heart. So she disengaged herself and turned to face Vos.

"Don't be. That's a weakness. Stretch out your feelings even more, Vos. Don't hold back. Feel the presence of my sisters—their fear, their anguish, their hatred . . . It is this you must learn to focus on if we are to succeed."

Sensing the presence of a living thing, she turned to one of the burned branches. A black snake about half a meter long twined lazily about it, flicking out its forked tongue to smell her. Unafraid, she touched its mind and called it to her. It obeyed, climbing up her left arm to her neck. Its tongue tickled as it touched below her ear.

"My hatred?" Vos laughed uneasily. "That's not exactly the Jedi way."

Ventress didn't answer at once. She watched the snake make its way across the back of her neck and halfway down her other arm. It lifted its head and turned to meet her gaze. Stonily, her eyes locked with its slitted ones.

"As I warned you . . . to defeat Dooku, we cannot do things the Jedi way."

Ventress lifted her right hand, and the snake obligingly coiled its first few centimeters about it. Ventress raised the creature so it was only a few centimeters from her face.

Hatred.

The snake hissed, and then began to thrash. Vos started to interrupt, but Ventress lifted her left hand to stop him.

"When Ky Narec was killed, I allowed my hatred to take over." At the words, the snake's struggle intensified. Ventress drank in its panic, closing her free hand on empty air as the Force throttled the animal for her. "Hatred gave me access to abilities the Jedi think are too unnatural. But the Sith know that the path to hatred is the path to ultimate power."

The snake went limp. She let it fall from her hand to the ground, dead. Vos stared at it for a long moment. Then, not taking his eyes from the creature, he began to speak.

"I . . . I understand your feelings. I also lost my Master. He was killed early on in the war. It was hard to suppress my emotions—the rage I felt at his passing. And I understand your guilt, too."

He paused for a moment, pressing his lips together, as if not wanting to speak the words. "I was supposed to be his partner that day. But instead, the Council sent me on a separate mission." His eyes darkened and his body tensed as he spoke. "I always felt that if I had been there, I could have saved Master Tholme."

Still savoring the snake's torment, Ventress noted the hatred building in Vos. "I remember that battle," she said, sending him encouragement to dive still deeper into his emotions.

His head whipped up and he stared at her. "You were *there*?"

Too late, Ventress realized her misstep. Fear, usually a stranger, suddenly welled in her heart. If Vos knew, he would— No. She could fix this; she could use Vos's feelings for her to do so.

"No," she lied smoothly. "Dooku bragged about it to me. It was he who killed your Master. He even kept Tholme's lightsaber as a *trophy*."

Vos winced. His faith in her words did not waver, and Ventress felt a surge of relief at the fresh spurt of anger she felt from him.

"I never knew," he said. "The *Council* never saw fit to tell me."

Ventress realized that she had cemented his trust in her, given him a personal vendetta against Dooku, and sparked resentment toward the Council, all with a few well-chosen words.

Such was the treacherous power of the dark side.

She lowered her voice till it was a husky purr. "Let that anger guide you," she said. "Your feelings for the loss of your Master."

When Vos spoke, staring straight ahead, his voice was unsteady. "I was trained to not use those emotions."

"Because you *were* a Jedi," Ventress said.

He winced at the inflection of her words. "But . . . I am still . . ."

Ventress stepped in front of him. Their gazes locked. Vos was trembling. To her astonishment, Ventress realized she was, too, but with what emotion, she could not tell. She stroked his cheek with unsteady fingers, strangely hypersensitive to the rough scrape of stubble, and he closed his eyes and leaned into her hand. His warm, quick breath fanned her wrist.

"There are other emotions the Jedi taught you not to use," she whispered. "Do you deny them, as well?"

Vos opened his eyes, rich and warm and brown. He stared at her for a long moment. Then, with a sound of both desire and anguish, as if something had broken within him, he pulled her into his arms and kissed her.

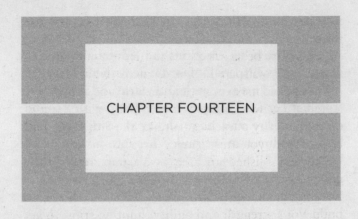

CHAPTER FOURTEEN

Vos's head and heart were awhirl with emotions as the days unfolded. Ventress was opening him to a new level of being—a plane of intensity, depth, and sharp sensation. She had awakened in him a hunger he had never suspected, though he now realized that other Jedi had known of it. Vos had grown used to being called "unorthodox" and "maverick" for the simple delight he took in his Force abilities. No wonder the Jedi Order had preached against attachment, or exploring the depths of one's feelings. For who, having once tasted what Vos now shared with Asajj Ventress, would turn away from it?

He reveled in their passion, cherished the sweetness of simply being able to reach out and stroke her cheek knowing she savored the gesture. He realized the emotions to which he was joyously giving full rein had been dormant within him for a long time, perhaps as soon as he had met her on that exciting, frustrating, *fun* chase for the Volpai. Certainly since she had tended his wounds after they had rescued the Krim family. Now and then, when he held her in his arms, he believed she shared them, too.

When it came to training to face Dooku, Ventress informed him that she would train him as a Night-sister would be trained. "I had conversations with Karis and Naa'leth. They told me of what they underwent. Nightsisters know the dark side better than anyone. We grow up steeped in it, but we can use it as a tool and stay ourselves—unlike the Sith. That balance is what you must learn."

They established an area as a camp, respectfully gathering the remains of Ventress's fallen sisters and burying them with care. They went on climbs to build Vos's strength and agility; hunting trips, to get him comfortable with killing for food; and long runs to build his endurance. It was on one such run that Vos was permitted a brief glimpse of Ventress's home.

He had seen the large, red mountain in the distance, but Ventress had been taking him on runs in the opposite direction. One morning, though, they ran toward it.

The mountain's peak loomed larger as they approached, but huge trees concealed the base until they were almost upon it. Here, the damage to the forest was even greater than where Ventress had set the *Banshee* down. Vos could feel the temperature drop, and faint echoes of the pain the Nightsisters had suffered brushed his thoughts.

Ventress had been in the lead, but now she slowed. Taking his hand, she led him through the trees and to a clearing.

Vos stared in astonishment. It was not simply a mountain—it was a fortress hewn out of one. Massive statues of women had been carved into the mountain's face, their arms extending upward, appearing to be supporting the weight of the entire vast edifice on the palms of their hands. There had to be row upon row of them, vanishing into the darkness

of the artificial cavern's shadows. Some of the statuary lay broken on the ground, mute evidence of the
attack that had claimed Ventress's clan. Not a few
skeletons still lay here, but they were not alone; parts
of droids were scattered about, as well.

The statues were exquisite creations, but it was the
enormous carving on the side of the mountain fortress that took Vos's breath away. It was the stylized
face of a woman, her mouth open to the heart of the
great stone . . . structure? Natural formation? The
carving was in such harmony with the land that it
was hard to tell where nature ended and artistry
began.

"What—" His voice was rough with wonder. He
cleared his throat. "What's inside?"

Ventress stood, staring quietly. "My village," she
said. Her eyes were dry, but her pain was all but pal-
pable. Vos squeezed her hand reassuringly, but she
shook her head.

"No," she said. "No sympathy. Only the knowledge that Dooku destroyed everything that was precious to me. You are not ready yet to go inside. But
when you do"—she looked up at him with eyes gone
cold and hard—"you had better make sure you come
out."

Ventress was quiet on the run back, and distant from
him the rest of the day. Vos wasn't surprised. She'd
made certain they had not come to the fortress before
now for her own reasons—surely one of which was
that it would inflict fresh pain upon her.

Vos had known some of the basics of Ventress's
history—the parts that the Jedi cared about knowing, at least. But there was so much more to this
astonishing woman than her life as first Dooku's ap-

prentice and later his most passionate enemy. In her unguarded moments, he could see glimpses of the innocent child she had once been, and in those moments of trust Vos fell deeper into . . . whatever this feeling truly was.

When they returned to their encampment near the *Banshee*, she told him she would go alone to hunt their dinner. He spent the time waiting for her cleaning and checking their weaponry, and had a fire going when she returned carrying two medium-sized veekas. A few moments later, the red-plumed birds were plucked and spitted, and an appetizing scent filled the night air.

Ventress's distant mood was still upon her as they finished and cleaned up. They leaned against a fallen, blackened tree trunk, close but not touching. Vos waited patiently, and at last Ventress spoke.

"Do you remember our first day here?" Ventress asked, turning to look at him. The firelight was reflected in her eyes.

"I'll never forget it." Vos reached to touch her cheek gently. Ventress caught his hand and brought it down, firmly but not ungently.

"I was referring to the snake."

Vos released her hand and nodded. He would never forget *that,* either; the sight of Ventress summoning the snake to her, and then Force-choking it as it whipped and writhed in an invisible grip. He also remembered speaking of his Master's death—and Ventress's revelation that Dooku had been the one to murder Tholme.

He felt the anger gather in the pit of his stomach, a knot that was both icy and scalding. Ventress sensed it and nodded her approval.

"Good, Vos. You can now touch the dark side at will. But it's one thing to feel those emotions—rage, hate, anguish—and quite another to use them. You must let go of your compassion, and focus on your hatred."

"And . . . use them on a living creature."

"Precisely."

Ventress extended a hand and made a beckoning motion. Vos saw the glitter of firelight on two small, cold eyes, and then the reptile Ventress had summoned slithered into view. It coiled in on itself, its eyes fixed on the Jedi. Vos regarded it sadly. While he had fully and eagerly embraced the emotions that surged through him for Ventress, willingly drowning in the sensations of passion and deep connection, this was something different. Even had he not been a Jedi, Vos knew he would have recoiled from such senseless killing. And this was as senseless as it got, it seemed to him: killing an animal, a being that was inherently part of the Force and utterly innocent of good or evil, who at the moment had posed no threat at all, simply to go farther down a dark path.

But this was the job he had been sent to do, was it not? This had never been about capturing Count Dooku, or facing him in a fair fight. This mission had, from the outset, been all about assassination. He understood that millions of innocents would survive who would otherwise die if this abominable war continued much longer.

Innocents like Tezzka, Vram, and Laalee.

For the greater good, he thought, and lifted a hand.

Sensing Vos's intent, the snake reacted immediately. It reared and hissed, exposing sharp fangs.

Ventress's voice, strong and soothing, floated to his ears through his concentration. "No, gently . . . you want it to come to you willingly."

That was worse than a simple attack, but Vos nodded, shifting his energy and his focus. The serpent

responded, closing its mouth. Its tongue still flickered, smelling him, but it was curious, not hostile.

"Good," Ventress said. "Now draw him in. Lower
his guard . . ."

Vos's hands moved in a flowing motion. In his
mind, he saw the snake willingly approach, and a
heartbeat later the creature moved over rock and soil,
its powerful muscles squeezing and releasing as it
propelled itself toward Vos.

Ventress's voice was almost more felt than heard
when she spoke again. "*Feel* the dark side. It gives
you power. You are in command—in control. You
can bend things to your will."

She was right. From time to time, Vos had used the
Force to make "suggestions" to those whose minds
weren't strong enough to resist. His interaction with
the serpent reminded Vos of those times, except increased by a thousandfold. The snake was not merely
biddable—it was enthralled.

Vos shivered as Ventress's lips brushed his ear.
"Now . . . use that power. *Kill it.*"

Kill it. Kill Dooku. It was what he had been sent to
do, what he must do.

Vos took a deep breath, trying to drop deeper
into his connection with the enraptured snake. He
closed his fingers slowly, visualizing the snake in his
hand, his forefinger and thumb in a circle beneath the
creature's head, throttling—

"Aaah!"

Searing pain shot through him as the snake bit
deep. Vos jerked his hand back and the snake, its will
once again its own, slithered away with astonishing
rapidity.

He clutched the wrist of his bitten left hand with
his right one, looking up at Ventress. Her face was

harder than he had seen it in weeks, her beautiful eyes once more as cold as ice chips.

"You are not yet ready to face Dooku. But you will be."

It was not the response he had expected. He looked down at his hand, which was beginning to swell.

"Poisonous?" Vos managed through gritted teeth. He knew the answer even as he spoke. The pain was increasing, and he felt as if he'd plunged his hand into boiling water. At the same time, he shivered. Vos realized he was going into shock.

"The venom isn't lethal, but it has its uses."

Dizziness and nausea swept over Vos, and before he knew what had happened he had dropped to his knees. *It has its uses?* What did she mean by that? Wasn't she going to treat it? Impossibly, the pain increased. He looked up at her. Her form was shifting, blurring, and her voice sounded hollow and distorted.

"The pain will let you access your rage. Accept it— as punishment for your failure."

As if her words had been instructions to the venom, torment, exquisite in its intensity, spread through his body. It was as if his heart pumped liquid fire, not blood, and Vos could no longer bite back a howl of agony. He fell to the ground, its hard surface unforgiving, the rocks jutting into his skin releasing fresh waves of pain so sharp he couldn't believe he was still conscious.

He writhed, screaming, and Ventress stared down at him, her face a shifting mask of implacable aloofness.

And that was a pain far worse than the venom.

CHAPTER FIFTEEN

Vos dreamed the dreams of the tortured. Nightmare after nightmare crested over him, visions of shadows and slaughter and pain, both caused and received. Through them all danced Asajj Ventress, on her beautiful face every expression he had beheld there and some he had not. But the last dream was not of pain, but of ecstasy, of the tender brush of her fingers on his face, of her whispered words . . .

The touch became cooler, still smooth but textured. Vos opened his eyes to discover a serpent twining about his body, its triangular head slithering beneath his chin. He yelped and sprang back, adrenaline surging through him. The snake, disinterested, slithered away, and Vos forced his breath to slow.

The scalding agony was gone. In its place was sluggishness, as if he were swimming through mud. Mist hung low on the ground, obscuring his vision—or was it the lingering effects of the snake's bite? No, he could feel moist air clinging damply to his skin. He became aware of a slight rustling behind him. Turning, he was greeted by the sight of yet another snake—this one as thick as his arm and three meters long. He got to his feet and stumbled away from it, moving far too slowly and with too much exertion. The snake was also averse to confrontation, and slithered off in search of its breakfast.

"Time to test your Jedi training, my sweet."

Vos realized his lightsaber had been placed within easy reach. He had, of course, hidden it from Ventress during their early days together, but once on Dathomir there had been no reason not to make use of it during their hunts. He was certain, though, that he had not had it on him last night. Now he picked it up with clumsy fingers.

Ventress's voice seemed to come from everywhere. Vos's thinking was still torpid, and he looked around, trying to spot her, wondering what new lesson she had in store. He heard the *snap-hiss* of a lightsaber and awkwardly activated his own as she leapt on him from above.

Thanks to the lingering effects of the venom—and simple disbelief—Vos registered that she was deadly serious barely in time to step back and parry her strike. Ventress sprang adroitly over his head and Vos turned, again nearly moving too slowly to prevent her from slicing him in half.

Their blades clashed and sizzled, and she moved forward, her face mere centimeters from his. A cruel smile curved her full lips. "Very good, Vos," she said, almost mockingly. "At least you know how to fight back."

She executed a backward flip, landing in a crouch atop a large boulder.

"But can you finish the job?" And with a quick leap, Ventress vanished into the fog.

What was she talking about? They were partners— more than partners. Vos knew Ventress cared for him. He could feel it in her touch, sense it in the Force. As for what he felt, he—

Her laughter, cold and cruel, chilled Vos more than the increasingly thick mist. He stepped forward, moving toward where he had last seen her, reaching out in the Force to try to locate her. His head was starting to clear, and irritation replaced confusion. Whatever she was doing, it wasn't necessary, and it was starting to make him angry. They were wasting time in a foolish—

A second time, the hum of her lightsaber alerted Vos to Ventress's presence, and he again whirled to parry her attack from behind. Her beautiful face was contorted in a snarl, and she came at him full force. Ventress rained blows upon him, not holding back, pushing in for the kill. Unwilling to harm her, Vos took one step back, then another, concentrating on blocking her attack. The damp air muffled the sizzle of lightsabers clashing in deadly earnest.

Still Ventress pressed the attack. Something inside Vos snapped. A furious cry escaped his lips and he moved onto the offensive. This time, it was she who was forced to give ground as he advanced on her, swinging his lightsaber so swiftly it was little more than a green blur. As she drew back to strike again, his hand shot forward and closed on her throat, his fingers digging into warm flesh, lifting her easily into the air and hurling her to the ground.

Ventress hit hard, sprawling with an utter lack of her usual controlled grace. She coughed, one hand massaging her throat. Vos found himself standing over her, lightsaber raised for the next blow, but instead a smile touched her lips.

"You see?" she said, her voice rough, the faint shadows of a bruise already starting to form on her pale throat. "Your anger has made you powerful!"

He lowered the lightsaber and switched it off. The red rage that had colored his thoughts was fading. So it really *had* been a test, and nothing more. Vos frowned. He did not like being toyed with.

But before he could say anything, Ventress had leapt to her feet and was again racing into the mist. What now? His lips pressed together in a tight line and he pursued. This game had gone far enough.

And a game it was. Over and over again, Ventress allowed him to glimpse her just long enough to keep her in sight. They leapt over fallen tree trunks, ducked beneath chunks of stone. Vos realized that Ventress's path was taking them to the mountain fortress. He recalled what she had said to him the first time they had beheld it together: *You are not ready to go inside. But when you do . . . you had better make sure you come out.*

He was ready. He knew it. He could take anything Ventress could throw at him.

Ventress raced into the open now, her slender, long legs bearing her easily across the stone to the gaping mouth of the cavern. She vanished into darkness. Vos ran behind her, slowing as he felt the cool fingers of a shadow caress him. He held his lightsaber before him and moved cautiously, reaching out into the Force to try to sense her.

Vos walked between the statuary pillars and emerged into an interior space of both darkness and beauty. When Ventress had said "village," Vos had expected something small and primitive. But this cavern was gargantuan, and what it housed was vast and compelling in its scope and strange loveliness.

Most of the illumination came from pools of water that glowed a soft, mesmeric shade of blue. Here and there, thin streams of water poured from above, their source so high as to be shrouded in darkness. The dim lighting revealed that, as with the exterior, those who had constructed this place had worked in tandem with nature. Here, in the village of Ventress's sisters, was no forced architecture; nothing, at least at this first glance, that looked like it had ever been created in a factory. Towering stalagmites jutted from the cerulean pools, their peaks so high that they vanished into the darkness above. Into these natural formations had been carved doors, windows, stairways, and overlooks at several levels. Specks of what looked to be phosphorescent stone augmented the azure light. No doubt, once, there had been torches, as well.

Vos stepped forward into a wide-open area of flat stone. Here and there he saw remnants of ordinary life: overturned pitchers and vases, braziers, bowls.

It would have been one of the most beautiful places Vos had ever beheld, if it had not been so steeped in the dark side. It was strong here; controlled, directed. At the far side of the open area, he saw an altar, and wondered what sorts of horrors it had borne witness to. Perhaps once, this had been no more than a cavern, a neutral place, eventually permeated by the energy left over from centuries of dark work. Or perhaps it had always dwelled on the edge of darkness.

It didn't matter. All Vos understood was that Ventress knew the twists and turns of her village intimately, he was a stranger, and she was hunting him.

He sensed her presence, but the location was muddied, difficult to pinpoint. Moving silently, Vos made his way to a smaller stalagmite and sprang out from behind it with a grunt, his lightsaber swinging.

But Ventress wasn't there. She was behind him, screaming as she swung her glowing yellow blade. Vos was forced to dodge. Swift as a thought, Ventress raced past and whirled to face him.

"You are strong," she said, and to his surprise she stepped back and extinguished her lightsaber. Uncertain as to her intent, Vos hesitated. "Don't worry, Quinlan. This part of the test is over."

He nodded and switched off his own lightsaber. "I can't say I'm sorry. What now?"

Ventress turned and looked out over the blue pools. "A major component of Nightsister magicks is a fluid that we call the Water of Life," she said.

"From these lakes?" Vos guessed.

"Not exactly. The Water of Life is . . . harvested."

Vos's dark brows knit. "I'm not following you."

"The depths of these pools have never been plumbed. All we know is that they are very deep indeed, and they are home to many creatures. There is one that the Nightsisters called the Sleeper. To fully be accepted as an adult, a young woman of my clan underwent a rite of passage. Using her Force abilities, she would awaken the Sleeper, dominate it, and force it to remove a piece of its body."

"A trophy?" Vos was repelled.

"No. An ingredient. That piece of the Sleeper is boiled with water from the pool and other items to create the Water of Life. I was told the Sleeper was very strong-willed. To lose control over it, even for a moment, would mean the initiate's death."

Vos gazed out on the luminous water. "How often was the rite successful?"

"I never asked."

"What's the catch? Simply controlling an animal, even a strong-willed one, is fairly easy for a Jedi."

"It would be—*if* this creature were just an animal, and if you only needed to use the light side of the Force," Ventress said. "Quinlan—it's *the* Sleeper, not *a* Sleeper. It's ancient. The stories about it go back to the earliest days of my clan. You can sense how strong the dark side is here. Everything, even the wildlife, has been touched by it in some way. The Sleeper can only be awakened and controlled if someone thoroughly subjugates it with dark side power."

"I see," Vos said. He looked back over the water. "Well, let's get on with it."

She placed a hand on his arm. "Not yet. I know little enough about the Sleeper, but I will share with you what I do know." Ventress smiled a little. "Now you know why I wanted you to build up your endurance. Your next exercise will require swimming—and holding your breath."

CHAPTER SIXTEEN

"I do have an aquata breather, but I'd recommend training both with and without it," she told him as they ate that night. "The pools in the cavern are opaque, so your vision will be limited. You might also want a pair of goggles that will let you see beyond the visible spectrum."

Vos thought about it as he carved off a chunk of a small lizard turning on the spit, then shook his head. "No. That doesn't feel right. The whole point of this test, as I understand it, is for me to dominate it with my ability in the Force, not with technology."

"Your ability wielding the *dark* side of the Force," Ventress reminded him.

He nodded and bit into the chunk of mild-tasting flesh. "So, what else can you tell me?"

Ventress looked frustrated. "Less than I'd like. I know it's large, terrifying to look at, and physically powerful. And as I've said, its will is impressive."

"You mentioned swimming and holding my breath," Vos said. "I take it I'll be fighting it underwater?"

"Ideally, no," Ventress replied. "The Sleeper can be

lured onto land, and of course you'd have the advantage there. But you need to be prepared for anything."

"So . . . what does this thing *look* like?" Vos asked. He forced himself to eat more than usual. He would shortly be burning thousands of calories a day in training.

"It varies from person to person," she said. "Karis claimed it was the same hue as the water. Luce said it was pure white. Talia told me the Sleeper had enormous eyes and pincers. Naa'leth said no, it had tentacles. The one thing everyone agrees on is that they were terrified. It seems if you don't control it quickly and get dragged into the water—presumably by pincers or tentacles—you risk coming into contact with the substance you're trying to harvest. That can cause hallucinations." She looked down. "Talia watched her twin simply freeze. She was paralyzed with fear. The Sleeper dragged her down with it."

"Hey," Vos said, reaching out to squeeze her shoulder. "I have a lot of respect for the Nightsisters and their Force abilities. But I'm not a youngling, I'm an adult with the skills and training of a Jedi Master. And," he added, hoping to lighten her mood, "I've got the best coach in the universe who has a vested interest in seeing I survive."

Ventress looked at him, her eyes searching his. She reached to touch his face, her fingers stroking his lips. He shivered and bit down, gently.

Chuckling softly, she pulled her hand away and tapped him on the nose. "Don't forget that, Idiot."

"Never," he said, and kissed her.

Dathomir was not without its oceans, and Vos soon grew intimately familiar with them. They began with simple submersion. Vos's Jedi training gave him excellent control over both his mind and his body, which would be the key to his success. If he stayed calm throughout, his heart rate would remain slow and his body would not burn more oxygen than was absolutely necessary. Well aware that if he didn't establish and keep control over the Sleeper at the outset he would certainly be involved in combat, he practiced fighting creatures underwater, as well.

"Your training is coming along well," Ventress said one evening as they ate stew prepared with a burra fish Vos had killed that day.

"I am glad you think so," he said. He hesitated, then asked, "What about . . . after?"

She eyed him as she helped herself to more stew. "What *about* after?"

"When we've killed Dooku."

Ventress looked back to the pot of stew bubbling cheerfully on the fire. She lowered her head so he couldn't see her face in the flickering light. She had no desire to think about what would happen afterward. This time together was precious—and forbidden. The Jedi would never accept one of their own with a . . . companion, let alone one who was a former Sith. When Dooku died, so would their connection. Vos would leave her, and she would be alone. Again.

But she understood that. Ventress knew how to be alone, and she had always known that even this brief time with Vos was a gift.

She kept her tone conversational. "It will be hard for you to go back to the Jedi, but it's possible."

"Asajj."

She stilled. Vos took her bowl, set it aside, and gathered her hands in his. He looked at her strong fingers, her callused, scarred palms, then pressed his lips to each one in turn.

"I don't want to go back," he stated. Ventress

closed her eyes, scarcely daring to believe the words. "I want to be with you."

Now she did risk a look at him. His face shone with intensity, his warm eyes catching the firelight above the yellow stripe that adorned his features. "I can't walk away from this, and I don't want to. Do you?"

For a moment Ventress couldn't speak.

"No," she managed. "I don't want to, either. But Quinlan . . . be sure. It's all you've ever known."

"I know *you* now," Vos replied, squeezing her hands for emphasis. "And if being Jedi means I can't be with you . . . I also know what I choose."

He released her hands and unbuckled his bracer, placing it on the ground. She watched, a brow arched in confusion. He found a rock, tossed it in the air, and caught it.

Vos looked at her solemnly. "It starts now." And he brought the stone smashing down on the holocomm button, severing contact with the Jedi for now, and—forever? Could he really do so? Ventress stared at the broken piece of equipment, then lifted her gaze to his.

Vos smiled at her, fully, freely. No shadow of regret lay upon him, only a calm certainty. An emotion surged through Ventress that was so alien she almost didn't recognize it as joy. The name of another feeling, richer and deeper, hovered unspoken between them, danced on her lips—perhaps on his, as well. They had a bond, real and vibrant and strong, that seemed to her to be unbreakable.

"Together," he said, emotion making his voice husky.

Ventress didn't trust herself to speak. She showed him instead, pulling him toward her and kissing him passionately. Vos responded at once, returning the kiss with a fierceness that heightened her desire. Every sense was alert, expectant, and every touch had the intensity of something more than physical. He got to his feet, taking her with him, kissed her hard, and then swung her up in his arms and strode toward the ship.

A small, blinking red light appeared in the darkness. Ventress closed her eyes and growled. Vos laughed ruefully, his warm breath stirring her hair as he kissed the top of her head and set her down.

"You should get that."

"The timing could have been better," Ventress said, and pulled out her holocomm. A small figure appeared, squat and wrinkled. It jabbered excitedly. *"Kuck chi sol ildi."*

Ventress felt a lurch in her gut. So soon? Her gaze flickered to Vos, who raised an eyebrow in curiosity. Apparently, Gossam was not a language he understood.

"I see," Ventress said to the holographic image. "You have done well, Sumdin. And the location of this gathering?"

Sumdin lifted a graceless, three-fingered hand and operated something Ventress couldn't see. In the Gossam's place now swirled the hologram of a pleasant-looking green-and-blue planet.

And then Vos understood. "You found Dooku!"

Ventress gazed at the tiny world for a moment longer, than deactivated the holocomm. "He'll be on Raxus. I know the day and time."

Vos grimaced slightly. "His home turf." Raxus was the capital of the Confederacy of Independent Systems. Security was bound to be excessive. "But if you've found him—we've got to go."

Ventress didn't reply. His brow knit in confusion. "Well?"

"Quinlan . . . I'm concerned that you're not ready. You've barely begun to explore the dark side, let alone master the ability to walk the knife's edge. You've not called the Sleeper, and if you can't do that—if we leave now, you could be in jeopardy."

He gave her a lopsided smile. "More than I am already?"

"More than you can possibly realize."

"I understand your concern. But we can't afford to miss this opportunity."

Ventress didn't reply at once. She had expected to have more time. More time for Vos to train, to master the mercurial and untrustworthy nature of the dark side; more time for them to be together before they faced an unspeakably dangerous foe . . . and more time for her to gather her courage and tell him the truth about his Master. But she couldn't, not at this juncture. She would tell him afterward, when they had slain Dooku and truly left their pasts behind. When they were together, and things were calmer.

Even if he did understand and forgive her, it would be a shock to him, at least at first. To succeed in their mission, she needed Quinlan Vos at his best and most focused . . . and the personalized hatred she had falsely instilled in him toward the count could only help.

Also—he was right. There was no telling when they would get a second chance. The count was slippery as a Mon Calamari eel.

He placed his hands on her shoulders and gazed down at her. "Asajj—I admit it. The dark side has made me powerful. You've opened my eyes to so many things. But it hasn't hurt me. All it's done is make me believe we can succeed."

Ventress smiled sadly. "That's the danger."

He sighed. "Let me prove it to you. I know I'm ready to call the Sleeper—and defeat it."

Ventress did not share his confidence. It wasn't his

ability to use the Force that was in question. It was his ability to use *only* the dark side of it. Vos was a good man. She was worried that even now, he might still be too good.

She closed her eyes and took a breath. "All right," she said. "Let's go."

CHAPTER SEVENTEEN

The two were silent as they made their way to the caverns. Vos felt the caress of the dark side as they entered the open area, and his thoughts were myriad and chaotic.

Ventress paused as they approached the blue water of one of the cavern lakes. "What is it?" Vos asked.

They stood near an artificial pool that had been created on the open, flat-stoned area near the altar. Its water was neither clear nor blue, but a rich inky black. Ventress pressed her lips together. "This was where I truly left being a Sith behind. Where I became a Nightsister. I was too old and experienced to call the Sleeper, so my initiation was somewhat . . . different."

"What happened?"

She looked up at him, and there was a hint of peace along with pain on her features. "I was reborn," she said. "I went into the waters a Sith . . . and emerged a Nightsister."

"By using magicks?"

"Some. But mostly by choosing to leave it behind, and being willing to accept the love of my sisters."

Vos touched her cheek gently. "You never cease to amaze me."

"Well," she said, attempting lightness, "this time, you get to amaze *me*."

He squared his shoulders. "Right. So, the sooner this is over with, the sooner we get to go after the count. And once that's done . . ." He kissed her forehead lightly, then stepped back. He held out his lightsaber to her and she took it. The Nightsisters had no weapons when they faced the Sleeper; neither would Vos. This was a battle of the mind. "Take care of this for, oh, the next few minutes, because I'm going to want it back."

"Don't worry. It'll be waiting for you, I promise."

He nodded, then turned and stepped toward the edge of the pool.

"Quinlan," she called. He turned to look at her. "Don't rush this. Make sure you're ready when you call it."

Vos nodded. He had not asked Ventress if she would aid him if he got in trouble, and she had not volunteered. He wasn't sure he wanted to know the answer, and he had no plans to find out. He began with adjusting his breathing; slow, deep, and rhythmic. Vos felt oxygen saturating his blood and being pumped through his heart, gaining the control that Ventress had assured him was vital to his victory over this mysterious, and apparently horrifying, Sleeper. He opened to the darkness, felt it almost physically curling around him.

Vos inserted the aquata breather into his mouth and reached out with his mind. There were many life-forms in this water, from tiny single-celled organisms to moderately sized fish and crustaceans. They were simple, uncomplicated, and he brushed their consciousnesses gently and continued searching. Down his mind went, into the depths of the blue-murk waters. Some things hid in caverns. Some swam freely. But Vos sensed one life-form that was more complex than the rest; more complex, and very . . . old.

Ancient.

It dreamed. Vos understood as he brushed it with the Force that it had been dreaming for some time, undisturbed. He wanted to send it calmness and peace, and let it rest, but he could not. Vos steeled himself and, still willing his body to remain calm, allowed his mind to gradually open to the Sleeper. He felt it stir unhappily, resisting him with surprising strength even in this state.

Awaken.

It would not. Vos lifted a hand and spread his fingers, calling out to the unseen beast.

Awaken! he demanded. And the Sleeper's consciousness snapped into full presence. It was not sullen or sluggish, but alert and focused, and that focus was on Vos. Vos grunted slightly with the effort, knowing that he could not lose the upper hand even for a moment. He harnessed his concern, and twisted it into anger and resentment.

Rise. I will have it so.

And it did. He felt this impossibly old creature stir from its cavern, where it had rested and dreamed dreams unimaginable, and slowly, balefully, move upward. A bubble rose to the surface of the thick blue water, popping with a sludgy wet noise. A second bubble followed, then another.

Two huge lavender eyes, each the size of Vos's head, emerged from the water. They swiveled on narrow stalks, seeming to look in every direction at once, then locked onto Vos standing at the edge of the pool. A wave of resentment that was so powerful it was almost physical buffeted Vos. He didn't hesitate. He harnessed the hatred and hurled it right back at the Sleeper, who shuddered.

I said rise! All the way! Obey me and come onto the land!

For a terrible instant, Vos was certain he had failed. The Sleeper did not move. Then, slowly, fighting his command all the way, it did. It reared up, and up, seven meters long if it was a centimeter, revealing a long, carapace-covered body, quivering antennae, and two—no, four—appendages. The first pair appeared to be sickles as long as it was, tapering to spearlike points. The other limbs were narrow where they attached to its body, expanding into large clubs at the end. This set of legs the Sleeper kept tightly curled.

Vos noted all this in a heartbeat, but what astounded him most was how beautiful it was. Its limbs and eyes must have seemed ghastly to a child who had never ventured beyond her own world, but Vos had seen more frightening things. No, it was the kaleidoscope of colors that made the Sleeper so visibly remarkable. Every hue Vos could dream—or have nightmares of—adorned it. He had known other species to have eyes similar to the Sleeper's, which could see five or ten more colors than he could. But the Sleeper's eyes were even more complex, and Vos briefly wondered if this creature was so difficult to subdue because it might be able to actually see the Force.

It was an effort to keep his attention focused, but Vos managed. His anger hot but his body calm, Vos stepped backward, not knowing how much room the thing would take up once it had clambered onto land. Just as it reached the place where he had stood a moment ago, its sickle-legs shot out with astonishing speed, impaled themselves into the surface so hard the stone cracked, and heaved its bulk onto land.

Vos had assumed the creature was a sort of crustacean, but once it was wholly out of the water, he realized that its lower appendages were not legs, but tentacles, long and shiny and every shade of blue that the eponymous protocol droid from Sheb's black-market shop had known and probably more. So astonished was he that for just a moment, Vos felt his control waver.

The Sleeper felt it, too, and gathered itself for an attack. Immediately Vos lifted both his hands and Force-shoved it so it slid along the rocky surface, smashing into braziers and pottery. Hatred, cold and pure, wrapped around Vos, and he met it.

You. Will. Obey!

It fought him for a moment, its massive body rocking back and forth, tentacles and legs flailing.

Stop.

The cold hatred brightened with a sharp sensation of pain. Vos's will was hurting the beast. He strengthened his power in the Force, cruel and harsh, and the creature subsided. It tucked its limbs in close to its body, and its tentacles ceased wriggling.

Vos took a deep breath but didn't lessen his intense control. He'd done it. And he hadn't even needed the aquata breather. He pulled it out so he could speak. "Ventress," he called out, not taking his eyes from the enormous, almost pixilated ones of the Sleeper, "I don't need to make it cut off a limb, do I?"

"No." Her voice was strangely heavy with regret. "Vos . . . listen to me, but don't let your attention waver."

He felt a flicker of unease. The creature's tentacles undulated, sensing it, waiting to exploit any crack in his will. "Okay," he said. "I'm listening."

"You have to kill it."

Vos's shock lasted only a fraction of a second, but it was enough. With a blast of triumphant loathing, one of the Sleeper's tentacles whipped around Vos. Together they tumbled beneath the pool's surface.

Vos's face struck the water hard, and his aquata breather flew from his hand. The tentacle's pressure against his chest compressed his ribs, forcing him to expel air in a rush of bubbles that meant life. His empty lungs clamored for breath, and his internal organs felt like they were being slowly squeezed to pulp. One arm was trapped, immobilized at his side. He could barely see in the milky-blue depths, and panic made his heart race.

Through sheer will, Vos slowed its beating as he had practiced. Abruptly he was hauled through the water again, to come to a stop less than a meter away from the Sleeper's face. Two flat, teardrop-shaped scales beneath its eyes turned from sickly green to a pulsing, angry red. Vos realized that the change signaled an imminent attack. Without thinking, only trusting completely in the Force, he shoved his free hand toward the second set of clublike legs with enough power that the trajectory of the blow was altered.

The strike was faster than he could see. Suddenly the water around Vos was boiling from the intensity of the shock wave, clouding the blue water with black liquid and ragged chunks of the Sleeper's own tentacles. The spots that had been red before now were the color of an angry bruise; it had struck itself, not Vos, with pulverizing force. An earsplitting rumble of pain assaulted Vos's ears. He fought to keep from wasting his rapidly dwindling supply of air in his own agonized cry as the bubbling, boiling water scalded his flesh.

Taking advantage of the Sleeper's distraction, Vos used the Force to propel himself upward, gasping for air as his head broke the surface and he struck out for the safety of land. Pain shot through him; the Sleeper had struck him a glancing blow with one of its razor-sharp sickles, and he could feel it growing maddened from the sudden flow of his blood in the water.

He sensed another tentacle reaching for him and whirled, Force-grabbing the appendage and squeezing it tight. Again, the Sleeper rumbled in pain, its focus on him broken. Vos used the few seconds of respite to clamber onto the stone, then turned and seized the creature in the Force. He closed his eyes and directed a command with every bit of strength he had, and the Sleeper grew still. It was no longer angry, or bloodthirsty, or filled with hatred.

The Sleeper was terrified.

Vos drew in great, ragged gulps of air, his body straining with tension. He heard Ventress's voice shouting at him, "What are you waiting for? Kill it, Vos!"

And yet, even now, after the battle, he hesitated. The Sleeper had no evil in it. It was a simple creature, innocent of knowing wrong from right. It only wanted to be left undisturbed, and when threatened, it had protected itself. What would this unnecessary killing prove?

"Ventress," he called, still controlling the Sleeper, "it may be the last of its kind!"

"Yes, and if it dies, a great secret of my clan dies with it. That doesn't matter. We both have to make a sacrifice. You have to do this!"

"It's obeyed me twice! Why do I need to kill it?"

"Because you were sent to *kill* Dooku, in cold blood if you have to. If you can't use the dark side to kill now, can you do so later, when it truly matters?

Or will you let your Jedi compassion destroy everything?"

Tears stung his eyes; tears, as she had just accused, of compassion. Vos desperately wanted to send the Sleeper back to its peaceful burrow, to let it rest and heal from its wounds. Ventress would be disappointed and angry, but he would find another way to convince her that they could kill Dooku without him going to the dark side. It gave him power, true, but at what cost?

But in his heart, he understood the distinction Ventress had made. The Jedi had fought Dooku before, and the possibility had always existed that the count could be slain in such a struggle. What Vos had been ordered to do wasn't just killing. It was assassination; it was murder.

And now, Ventress wished him to snuff out the life of a simple beast that didn't have to die.

The moment stretched, taut, each passing second draining Vos further. He could delay no longer.

He made his choice.

He focused on his earlier fear: the helplessness he had felt, and his anger at it. He narrowed his eyes, calling up the hatred and rage, feeling them burst into him, white-hot and so very powerful.

This was an enemy. This was Count Dooku. Vos extended his hand, slowly, deliberately, taking the time to truly experience the emotions as they translated from thought to action.

Die.

The Sleeper's head snapped back. Puzzlement flowed through it, then cold, primal, simple fear. So pure. So strong. So—*liberating.*

Vos lifted the Sleeper from the water, continuing to manifest his emotions into a Force energy while simultaneously suffocating it.

It suffered as it died. Vos cleared his mind of everything but this moment, as it writhed in agony, its powerful punches and spearlike limbs striking only air. With a final spasm, the great beast crumpled. Vos released it. It splashed into the water, sinking for a moment, then floated, partially submerged.

Vos stared at it. His body was tingling. His heart raced, but not with fear—with exultation. So engrossed was he in the sensation of unleashing such power that he didn't hear Ventress approach until her voice said, right beside him, "Quinlan?"

He whirled, his hand raised for an instant before his mind cleared and he let his arm fall, alarmed at his reaction and reeling from what he'd just done. Ventress appeared to understand, looking at him with pride and not a little awe.

"Quinlan," she went on, laying a hand on his arm, "I know that was difficult for you, but it was necessary. You've come so far in such a short time. I'm impressed."

Words crowded his mouth, but he spoke none of them. Not about the sharp delight he had taken in brutally asphyxiating an innocent creature. Not about the desire to do it again, and to harness that power and unleash it any way he chose. He couldn't speak, either, of the wrenching sadness that permeated him as he realized that something in him had broken, or the delight at having been freed of its shackles.

He didn't need to. He could sense Ventress, proud and pleased, her desire for him only the stronger for the ordeal through which she had put him. She knew what he was feeling.

So Vos said just, "The Jedi have always taught that the dark side is a quick and easy path."

"You must be cautious how far down that quick

and easy path you go," she warned. "Now that you have tapped into it, it can consume you. It is a delicate balance to strike—being free enough to feed from it, but remaining your own master."

"Like you did."

"I fought my way back. I almost didn't make it." Her eyes grew sad and she slipped into his arms. "I regret that this is a path you must tread. But it must be done, if we are to defeat Dooku."

Vos stroked her short, pale-blond hair. The recollection of his actions unnerved him, and her words were sobering. He stepped back, his hands on her shoulders, and looked her in the eye.

"Dooku *is* strong. But *we* will be stronger." He caressed her cheek. "Together."

Her face softened into a smile that had nothing of the darkness about it, an expression that, Vos knew, few had ever been permitted to glimpse.

"Together," she agreed, and kissed him.

CHAPTER EIGHTEEN

Vos was late. Again. Kenobi settled in to wait at the bar on Level 1313. One of these days, he mused, Vos would show up on time. Kenobi wondered if his heart could bear the shock.

The minutes ticked by. Still no Vos. When two hours had crawled past and Kenobi had been forced to consume more alcohol than he had really desired and what passed for a meal to go along with it, he finally gave up. He activated his comlink.

"Master Obi-Wan, to hear from you, surprised I am."

"Master Yoda . . . I am . . . troubled by something, and I wish to speak privately with you."

"To the Temple, return, and speak, we shall."

When Kenobi entered Yoda's quarters, he found the Jedi Master sitting in meditation next to a small fountain designed with crystals known as "singing stones." They emitted soft sounds, something between a chime and a stringed instrument, as water flowed over them. Kenobi usually found the resulting music deeply soothing, as was the scent of special oils heated over small flames, but today even their influence did not dispel his sense of worry.

Yoda did not open his eyes. "Welcome, you are, Obi-Wan. Across from me, please sit."

Kenobi obeyed, and managed to calm his thoughts at least somewhat. A few moments later, Yoda spoke again.

"Clouds your heart, this concern does. Speak of it, you will?"

Obi-Wan bit his lip. "Master Vos did not show up for our appointed meeting. I fear that something has . . . happened."

"Sense something in the Force, do you? A vision, you have had?"

Obi-Wan shook his head. "No. But there was something off about him the last time we met. He was guarded. I could sense it, although he behaved like his usual self. And he used words that . . ." He paused, searching. "At the time, I simply thought that the challenge of the mission was starting to wear on him, but in retrospect . . . Master Yoda, he may have placed too much trust in Ventress. She may have discovered who he really is."

Yoda's ears curled in slight surprise. "Gone on many undercover missions, Quinlan Vos has. Carefree, he is, but careless, he is not. Possible it is that attached, he has grown. Always a risk, there is."

"Vos? He never has before."

"When one trusts another with his life, forged a bond is. In this position, neither Vos nor Ventress has been."

"He did say they were working well as a team," Kenobi said. "And I have always known that Ventress lets us see just what she wishes us to. She is a complex individual. I can only imagine what it must be like to be in such constant contact with her as Vos has been."

"And now, contact *him,* you cannot."

Kenobi nodded. "I probably should have come to you the moment I had concerns, or else just voiced them to Vos. But it seemed so ludicrous, to be worried about word choices and a vague sense of unease. Vos isn't a Padawan, he's a Master. He didn't deserve to have suspicion fall on him for such trivial things."

"More to say, you have, but not on this subject."

Kenobi frowned, then nodded. "Yes. I had misgivings from the beginning about this entire enterprise. I still believe that sending a Jedi to assassinate a man was wrong. And I fear that I will likely lose not only a fellow Jedi Master, but someone I consider a friend, and we will have nothing to show for such a loss."

Yoda rose, picked up his cane, and went to his friend. Gently, he laid a small hand on Obi-Wan's shoulder. "Disagree with you, I do not. But now, in motion things are, and stopped, they cannot be. All must proceed as the Force wills it. Sometimes it is a dark path we must tread so that long more for the light, we shall."

Kenobi placed his own hand over Yoda's. He did not ask if it was Vos or the Jedi Order that was treading the dark path—because in his heart, he didn't want to know the answer.

"May the Force be with him" was all he said.

"Here we go." Ventress hit the controls and the *Banshee* dropped out of hyperspace. "Keep your eye on the comm channels."

"On it," Vos replied. "I hope Sumdin's clearance code is accurate, or this could get very interesting very quickly."

"It will be. Sumdin is thorough. Transmitting now."

Ventress angled the vessel to merge smoothly with a moderately heavy flow of space traffic heading toward Raxus. Up ahead was the checkpoint—a blockade of massive vessels. Vos kept his eyes on the comm channel as they passed close by one of the enormous ships.

"We're cleared," he said. "One potential disaster averted. All we need to do now is get into the event, find Dooku, and kill him. Piece of cake." He rose from his seat behind her and leaned against her chair.

"One more thing to do before all of that," Ventress said. "We need to make a quick stop in Tamwith Bay."

"Tamwith Bay? I thought Dooku's party was being held in Raxulon."

"It is. We have to purchase clothing first," Ventress said. "Tamwith Bay is still a major city, but it's quite a distance from Raxulon. There will be less security."

"I wouldn't have pegged you for the shopping type."

She leaned out of her chair to give him a withering look. "Were you planning on our just walking into a twenty-thousand-credit-a-plate gala event looking like this?"

Vos whistled. "That much? I hope we have time for dinner. Just don't ask for my opinion on footwear."

"Don't worry. You have the fashion sense of a Wookiee."

Vos glanced down at the well-worn leather outfit he'd worn since . . . forever. Whenever he wasn't in his Jedi robes, this was what he reached for. It offered decent protection, he could move freely in it, and it didn't draw undue attention. In his usual circles, at least. "But . . . black goes with everything."

Ventress snorted. "Leave it to me."

She took them to an establishment that catered to the sort of people who would be attending the ludicrously priced gala. In short order, Vos was fitted with black trousers, comfortable leather boots, and a white tunic with bold golden stripes.

"The contrast with your skin coloring is most striking," the tailor assured Vos, finally letting him see himself in the mirror.

His dark skin seemed to glow against the hues of the tunic. Its crisp, tailored line and the knife-sharp creases of the trousers accentuated his long legs, broad shoulders, and narrow waist.

"Huh," he said. "Not bad."

"Agreed," said Ventress. She eyed him in a manner that made his heart skip a beat, and he grinned at her.

"Well, if my lady likes it, I'll take it." To Ventress, he said, "What about you?"

She held up a bag. "I already found something while you were getting the trousers fitted. Let's go."

"Let me see," he said.

"We don't have time for dolly dress-up," she retorted, and Vos knew better than to argue.

The flight from Tamwith Bay to Raxulon was quick. Vos didn't even have time to get his new outfit dirty. As the sun set over the beautiful capital of Raxus, casting warm rose and lilac hues on the tall spires, Ventress vectored them in to dock not at the main port, but at a smaller, lesser-used one. It was efficient enough—the droids that rolled up to begin refueling and cleaning the *Banshee* looked like fairly new models, and the place was clean. It was, however, obviously a local landing pad, not one meant for the rich, famous, and powerful, and Ventress and Vos were the only ones currently making use of it.

Vos stepped outside and took a careful look around, just to make sure. A few moments later he heard the *clack-clack* of heels. He turned around. "So let's see this . . ."

He fell into a stunned silence. Vos thought he had seen Asajj Ventress in all her guises. He'd seen the efficient warrior, the cold rager, the temptress practicing both the wink and the nod and the full-on gambit. And, most beautiful and most amazing of all, he'd seen her by starlight, just her, lying in his arms.

But this was something else again.

She wore a two-piece, sleeveless bodice of rich ebony-hued fabric, with hints of a subtle swirling pattern of dark-purple embroidery. Lacing of the same deep purple cinched it closed. The top section enclosed her breasts and revealed a small patch of her taut stomach. The bottom section flared over her hips. A midnight-black skirt, slit in front and back, fell to the floor. She had just finished concealing her lightsaber in a band around one slender but powerful thigh. As she straightened, their eyes met.

The outfit was elegant and subtle, and the woman in it was vibrant and strong. The overall effect made Vos like a falcon poised in that exquisite instant between free fall and flight, and for a moment he couldn't breathe.

He gulped air and said, "I . . . you look . . ."

Emotions flitted across Ventress's face. Annoyance, pleasure, and something he'd never thought to see there—embarrassment.

"Go ahead, spit it out," she muttered.

"You look . . ."

Like a goddess of love and war and hope and ecstasy. Like a glimmering star that I have somehow been blessed to hold.

Like the rest of my life.

". . . nice." He wanted to kick himself.

Ventress rolled her eyes. "No wonder you Jedi are so frustrated," she said. "As I said earlier, this unfortunate outfit is necessary for our mission."

Vos tried and failed to wipe the grin off his face as she descended the ramp. He pulled her into his arms and murmured against her long, slender neck, "I'm liking this mission more and more."

Before Ventress could deliver a no-doubt scathing retort, she turned her head sharply. Vos followed her gaze, but he saw nothing.

"You expecting someone?"

"Sumdin." At the sound of her name, the Gossam stepped out of the shadows. Ventress went to meet her, kneeling in front of the much shorter saurian.

Sumdin looked at Vos for a moment, then Ventress. "*Qwaazzz zuck chi cho wazz?*" she inquired.

Ventress nodded. "Yes, everything has gone smoothly so far. Where are the passes?"

Sumdin held up two small, engraved cards. "*Cho chuck chuck zoo zum.*"

"I'm sure it wasn't easy," Ventress agreed. She smiled. "You've done well. Thank you. Your loyalty will not be forgotten."

She leaned forward and placed her left hand on Sumdin's shoulder, squeezing gently. A sudden blur, a familiar *snap-hiss,* and Sumdin crumpled without a sound. There was a smoking hole in her torso. Ventress's face was calm as she extinguished her lightsaber and rose.

The murder had happened so fast that Vos had barely had time to register it, let alone stop it.

"What are you *doing*?" he cried. "She *helped* us!"

Ventress's voice was cold. "Remember what I taught you, Vos. No compassion. No loose ends. She doesn't matter. All that matters is what we came here to do. There must be nothing—absolutely *nothing*—to stand in our way now. We've come too far."

Still reeling, Vos looked down at the tiny, crumpled form. Sumdin had been, no doubt, a professional informant—selling her knowledge to the highest bidder. But she had also been a person. She didn't deserve to be summarily executed when she had done everything she had promised.

But had the Mahran refugees deserved to be blown to bits in space? Did any of Dooku's unwilling subjects deserve slow, painful deaths of starvation, or random murder at the whim of someone they had displeased? What if Sumdin had been playing both sides?

Anguished, Vos closed his eyes for a moment. It tore him up inside, but Ventress was right. They needed to ruthlessly eliminate anything that might prevent them from carrying out their mission. Dooku must die. He hoped that Sumdin's would be the final death that could be laid at the evil count's feet. Wordlessly, he picked up the body, thinking that Sumdin weighed no more than little Vram had. And that thought made him angry.

He held on to that anger as they headed to the gala, letting it fuel him for what lay ahead.

CHAPTER NINETEEN

"I'm afraid I must check you for weapons," the beefy human guard said as they handed him their passes.

Ventress eyed him up and down and smiled. "Where would I possibly conceal a weapon in this dress?" she said, hands indicating her garment.

The guard chuckled. "Where could you possibly be concealing a weapon in that dress? Go ahead, little lady."

She winked and stepped forward. Vos planted a similar suggestion and he, too, was admitted. "Dooku needs better security," he muttered to Ventress as he slipped her arm through his.

"His arrogance will not permit the concept of a Force-user coming after him here," she replied.

Vos glanced at the well-dressed crowd milling about and making idle conversation in the square. He had never had any difficulty adapting to his environment. He could make himself at home in a barren wasteland, in a den of crime bosses, in a seedy bar, in front of the Jedi Council. This gathering, however, set him on edge. He was still rattled from Ventress's efficient murder of her contact, though not as rattled as he once would have been. And within the hour, he knew, he and Ventress would either have slain Count Dooku, eliminating his threat forever—or else be dead themselves.

Or maybe it was just his clothing. He restrained himself from tugging at the high collar of his tunic and decided he'd tell himself the unease he felt was that, and nothing more.

Ventress, however, moved as if she had never known anything other than the high heels and elegant, flowing dress. She had even put on perfume to complete the performance. It made his nose twitch, but he had to admit she not only looked and moved as if she belonged, now she even smelled like it. Vos found it difficult to take his eyes off her, but he forced himself to do so. They had a job to do.

They strolled, arm in arm, through the throng of obviously well-to-do guests gathered in the plaza square. The crowd was tight but not claustrophobic; combat droids were doing a superlative job of managing the multitudes, and besides, Vos guessed, the guests didn't want to muss their hair. Or feathers, or tentacles.

The wave of beings flowed slowly and in an orderly fashion toward a building at the far end of the square. Vos wasn't sure what the place was, but it had that official, government-building stolidity to it that seemed to be the rule everywhere he'd ever been. It sported a walkway and a balcony, and all faces were either turned upward toward it or else gazing expectantly at a large dais in the square's paved center.

A thought occurred to him. "You know," he said, "you didn't tell me—what kind of celebration is this, anyway?"

Ventress rolled her eyes. Pitching her voice low, she leaned in and murmured, "The Confederacy of Independent Systems is honoring Count Dooku with the Raxian Humanitarian Award."

Vos snorted in amused disbelief, quickly turning it into a cough at her glare.

The crowd had been chattering in anticipation, but now a murmur rippled through the square. Several battle droids had just emerged onto the balcony, taking up sentry positions. Vos felt his pulse quicken. He took a breath to calm himself and slow its racing. Focus was the only way to properly control the Force—either side of it.

"Showtime," Ventress said.

And Count Dooku, clad in full military regalia, stepped onto the balcony.

The crowd went wild, applauding and cheering, hooting and making all manner of other sounds of excitement. Dooku, looking every bit the benevolent patrician leader, waved and smiled warmly. Down in the square, symbolically "among the people," his three-meter-high hologram did the same thing.

Vos thought about Master Tholme. How Ventress had told him he'd died, sliced into two pieces by Dooku's crimson lightsaber. Once, Vos would have banished the hot rush of emotion, but now he embraced it, let it flow through him, settling in his center like a coiled snake ready to strike.

Dooku was not alone. General Grievous, the cyborg commander of the count's vast droid army, stood a few steps behind his lord. With his four arms, skull-like mask, and clawed feet, Grievous was like something one would expect to see in spice-induced nightmares, rather than in reality. He was more machine than living creature, but there was a terrible malice in the slitted eyes that peered through the white mask.

"Looks like Dooku brought his sidekick," Vos murmured.

Still smiling, Dooku raised his hands in a gesture for silence, then began to speak.

"It is an honor to stand here before you, for you represent the freedom and the future of our galaxy. The once-great Republic and Jedi Order have become victims of their own ambitions, and the Supreme Chancellor is no more than a pawn of corporate monopolies."

Vos folded his arms, listening. Ventress appeared to be doing the same, but out of the corner of his eye, Vos observed her unobtrusively watching the crowd.

"As a people you called out for change, you called out for leadership, and I humbly answered that call," Dooku continued. His voice, as always, was sonorous and strong. "Together we challenged the system. We asked for equality. And how were we met? With war! The Jedi secret army of clones was revealed, and their treachery was far greater than we could have imagined!"

Angry muttering, shaking fists, and low booing rippled through the crowd. Dooku looked to be filled with righteous fury as he continued.

"Countless living beings—these clones the Jedi created—have been sent to their deaths, while we sacrifice mainly droids."

Vos grimaced slightly and said to Ventress, "He makes a good point." She gave him a sidelong look that conveyed exactly how unimpressed she was.

"Our soldiers of flesh and blood are willing participants! They are your fathers and sons, mothers and daughters, who fight not because they were grown and designed to do so, but because they know in their hearts that they are fighting for a just and noble cause!"

More cheering. Vos glanced around at the faces, alight with excitement and adoration. It was unnerving to realize how beloved Count Dooku, monster and murderer, was among these people. Ventress's gaze was not focused on Dooku, and though she did a good job of keeping her expression composed, Vos knew her well enough to see through the act to the loathing that simmered just beneath the surface. She squeezed his arm and inclined her head to the colonnades to their right. They began threading their way through the square while Dooku finished his speech.

"It is not a simple thing to be your leader during this unfortunate war, but I shall receive this humanitarian honor, and take it as a sign that my leadership has met with your approval."

Like trained pets responding to a command word, the crowd erupted in applause. Beaming, Dooku spread his arms in an avuncular fashion, enveloping everyone in the gesture. "Let the celebration begin!"

The crowd applauded for a long while, then began to drift toward another set of wide-open doors at the far end of the colonnade. "Grievous being here complicates things," Ventress said without preamble. "Think you can handle him?"

Vos nodded. "Shouldn't be a problem. I just have to detain him, to make sure we get to face Dooku alone."

"According to the invitation, there will be some drinking and socializing, and then the banquet will be starting. I'll head inside and pay the count a visit. He'll most likely contact Grievous then. Make sure you're in position."

Vos gave her his cockiest grin. "Hey," he said, feigning affront, "have I *ever* let you down?"

His words, meant to lighten the mood, somehow had the opposite effect. She looked at him for a moment, touched his cheek lightly, then turned and fell in step with the rest of the banquet attendees. Confused, he gazed after her for a moment, then headed off to find Grievous.

Head high, walking at a casual pace, Ventress entered the vast dining room. It was enormous, almost cavernous. Statues posed in the corners; the busts of famous politicians stared blankly at the guests. The walls were a deep, warm red, hung with paintings of vibrant starscapes, portraits, and still-life works of art. In the center of the room, beneath ten ornate chandeliers, several tables were arranged. Some guests were already seated, while others milled about. Droids bearing trays of appetizers and beverages maneuvered deftly through the press of beings. Ventress's despised gown was the perfect costume; any attention she attracted was from those who had eyes only for her physical appeal.

She smoothed its folds, and her mind went back to Vos's reaction earlier. Ventress was accustomed to scrutiny from men; she made use of it when it suited her goals. It was, as she had told Vos, simply one more tool. But the look in his eyes was one she had never seen before. It had made her feel . . . vulnerable. Not merely desired, but truly *seen*. Known. Cherished.

Vos had shown her that he was prepared to leave his old life behind when this was all over. Was it possible she could do the same? What was it he had said once? *Do you ever take your mind off the job?*

The answer had always been no. It was her identity, her way of interacting with the world. Ventress used her "tools"—lies, lightsaber, the full-on gambit, the

Force—to become whatever was needed for whatever task was at hand: a killer, a seductress, a deceiver.

Who would she be without a lightsaber or a false face? Would there be anything left of Asajj Ventress if she were to truly let go of hatred and instead accept what had shone in Vos's eyes—that she was loved for simply *being*?

Something surged through her, and she did not know if it was longing—or terror.

A server droid, with metallic bobbed hair and a short red dress, extended a tray of cocktails. Ventress snapped out of her reverie, cursing herself for her wandering thoughts, snared a beverage, and sipped at it as she scanned the room.

As she had expected, Dooku was in the center. People milled about him. But they were not acting like an eager throng surrounding a holofilm star. No, these beings affected a casualness that bordered on indifference. Ventress had observed this behavior of the rich and powerful from the shadows; now she strode into their midst.

A burst of loathing swelled in her chest as she made an indirect path toward the count. It was all she could do not to whip out her lightsaber and attack, then and there. But he had trained her, and her past defeats had proved that she alone could not bring him down. She thought of Karis and Naa'leth, and their first attempt to slay Dooku. Mother Talzin had assured Ventress that the two women were the finest warriors of the Nightsisters, and they had proven excellent. But even numbering three, and even with dark magicks that obscured them to Dooku's vision, they had failed. A second time, Ventress, with Mother Talzin's aid, had tried to kill the count. This time Ventress took the Nightbrother Zabrak named Savage Opress and trained him in a brutal manner, forcing the dark side upon him with Mother Talzin's rituals and torturing him when he disappointed her in training. He was her thing, her creation, but when the time had come, Opress had turned against both Ventress and Dooku.

With Vos, it was different. He was with her willingly, as Karis and Naa'leth had been, and like Opress he had tasted the dark side and trained for the task. But he was his own man. He had been strong enough to pass all the tests she had given him. With that training—and with her lie about who had really killed Master Tholme fueling his hatred—together they were strong enough to defeat Count Dooku.

His words just now had saddened her, and of course he had not understood why. Indeed, he had never let her down. She had let *him* down with her lies. But once this was finally over with . . .

She drew closer. Dooku's back was to her, and he was chatting away, his smooth voice hateful to her ears. Suddenly he stiffened. He looked about the room in a seemingly casual manner, but Ventress knew him, knew every one of his movements, and she realized he'd sensed her.

Good.

She took the final step and whispered in his ear, "Hello . . . *Master.*"

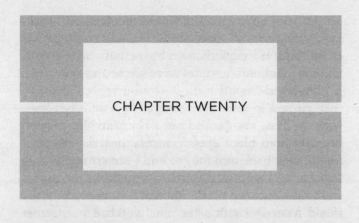

CHAPTER TWENTY

The count was silent for a moment. Ventress found herself utterly calm as they faced each other, looking to all the various dignitaries and power players as if nothing in the universe were amiss.

Dooku sighed. "It was an unfortunate decision to return, my dear. I will make sure to tie off this loose end this time."

The same words she had said to Vos, or close enough; Ventress wondered if she had picked up the phrase from her old teacher. She made a *tsk-tsk* sound.

"My, my, that's not very *humanitarian* of you, is it? Besides, you won't kill me here, not so publicly." She knew she was right, and that the words would only irritate him further.

His mellifluous voice was sharp as he snapped, "What is it that you want?"

"I'm done chasing you. I want a fair fight, nothing more. Tonight, meet me on the overlook. Let's end it, one way or another."

"End it I most certainly—ah, Governor, thank you for attending."

"It is such an honor!" enthused the Aqualish, shaking Dooku's hand vigorously. He was dressed in a crisp uniform weighed down by medals and epaulets, and his arachnidlike tusks were white and polished.

"The honor is all mine," Dooku replied politely, then turned to greet the governor's wife. Overcome with shyness, she ducked her bald head and averted her enormous black eyes. Ventress took the opportunity to melt back into the crowd. A conveniently large Falleen, who reminded Ventress strongly of the guards she'd fought at the Black Sun fortress, proved a good shield from Dooku's sight. She watched her former Master closely as he finally extricated himself from his admirers long enough to remove a comlink and speak into it.

Ventress didn't bother to hide her smile of victory as she glided out of the room.

"General?"

The voice belonged to Count Dooku. From his perch on an overhang, Vos muttered a triumphant, "Yes!"

Grievous's unique, raspy voice replied, "Yes, my lord?" It hadn't been difficult for Vos to determine where the center security hub was, and it had been even easier for him to eliminate the droid guards at either end of the hall.

"The betrayer Ventress is here. Meet me on the overlook."

"Yes, Master!" Grievous replied instantly and, a second later, "Let's move!"

The clones sometimes called enemy droids "clankers," and Vos thought it a particularly apt term as Grievous and three battle droids *clank*ed out of the security room.

Vos somersaulted down, drawing his lightsaber as he landed on his feet. He slashed at the door controls, sending sparks flying as he sealed the door shut. A blaster bolt whizzed past him; he sensed it coming and dodged, whirling to parry the next round of fire. He let the momentum carry him forward, slicing off the head of a battle droid. It issued a squeaking cry of surprise, firing harmlessly upward, then toppled to the floor.

Vos maneuvered so that Grievous was between him and the remaining two droids, who looked at each other, trying to decide if they could get off a clear shot without harming their commander. While they hesitated, Vos shot out his hand, fingers splayed hard. Even as Grievous reached for the two lightsabers at his waist, they flew into Vos's grip.

"You won't be needing these," Vos said pleasantly.

Grievous, who had a deplorable lack of a sense of humor, bellowed and charged, as Vos had anticipated. Almost leisurely, Vos stepped to the side and sliced upward with his lightsaber, severing the general's left hand at the wrist. The mechanical limb dropped to the floor, comlink still clutched in its metal fingers.

"Sorry," Vos said, picking up the comlink and waggling it at the infuriated Grievous. "Need this, too. Can't have you contacting the count, now, can we?"

Like an insect rearing up, Grievous spread all four arms wide, then charged. Vos met him halfway. The two clashed in midair. Grievous was the heavier, and his momentum carried them back toward the wall. Laughing sadistically, Grievous closed both right hands around Vos's throat. He threw Vos hard, intending to slam him down into the unyielding stone of the walkway. Grievous's mistake was in letting

Vos out of his grasp, and Vos landed in an easy crouch.

Springing up, he turned. "I'd stay and kill you," he told the cyborg, "but I'm short on time today."

Realizing they had a clear shot, the battle droids opened fire with renewed enthusiasm. Vos batted away the screaming red bolts, giving Grievous a cheery wave as he slammed his hand into the controls of the last door. He slipped through just as it closed, and then ensured it would remain so by frying the controls on the opposite side.

He paused to enjoy the pleasant sound of Grievous bellowing and banging on the walls, and lingered long enough to hear one of the battle droids, obviously trying to open the door, say, "Uh-oh . . ."

The entire fight had lasted less than sixty seconds.

Mission one accomplished. Now . . . for Dooku.

Ventress leaned on the overlook's stone railing, where earlier Dooku had given his effusively hypocritical acceptance speech. Night had fallen, but the sky was far from dark. Lavish fireworks cast illuminations of every hue imaginable, their booms echoing.

As the count had sensed her earlier, so Ventress sensed him now as he approached: a cold darkness, not inviting as the night was, but sinister and ugly. Not for the first time, Ventress wondered how it was that she had all but worshiped this man.

She continued to stare upward at the bursting fireworks, the night air stirring the long skirt of her dress and her pale, short hair.

"Care for a drink?" Surprised, she turned and saw that Dooku held two glasses. He extended one to her. "Alderaanian wine. An excellent vintage—and rather hard to come by these days."

Ventress didn't even dignify the offer with a response. Rare vintage or not, the sleemo had probably poisoned it, and even if he hadn't, she would die before sharing a drink with him. She turned away again and he shrugged, sipping from the glass he had offered her and placing the second one on the railing.

"Such a pity, you and I," he mused, looking up at the fireworks as he swirled the wine absently in one hand. "We had the entire galaxy before us. But it was just not meant to be, my failed apprentice."

Ventress was done with condescending banter. She was more than ready to fight with her lightsaber, not her sharp tongue. "You destroyed my life," she snarled. "My *people*!"

A little half smile parted his beard. "Even now, you display why you failed time and again. It was foolish for you to have come alone. *I* would never have made such a grave error."

He clicked his comlink, smirking as he said, "General."

Silence.

Yes. The readiness was tightly wound within Ventress, about to burst free into the most fiercely joyous fight of her life.

"General?" A worried note had crept into Dooku's voice. Ventress smiled slowly, savoring it. Behind them came the unmistakable sound of a lightsaber humming to life.

Dooku whirled. Turning toward him, Ventress saw with a satisfaction as deep as space that the color had drained from his face.

"Looks like I learned something after all," she drawled.

"A Jedi?"

Oh, this moment was truly to be relished. Ventress

didn't think she'd ever seen Dooku so nonplussed. Then, even more incredulously: *"Vos?"*

Vos gave a laconic shrug. "I'm a little surprised about it myself, Count."

Dooku looked from him to Ventress and then, strangely it seemed to her, affected a look of utter unconcern. "You will never take me alive." And then he actually sipped his wine.

Vos was still smiling. It wasn't a pleasant smile, but Ventress's heart soared to see it. She took a step away from the railing and brushed back her skirt with one hand, reaching for her lightsaber while Dooku's attention was on her partner.

"*We* aren't planning to," Vos said, and he charged.

Dooku, still trying to comprehend the situation, was taken aback, but only for an instant. He found time to carefully set down his glass of Alderaanian wine while drawing his lightsaber. Ventress swung, but the count ducked.

He leapt between the two of them, kicking out at Vos while blocking Ventress's strike with his crimson lightsaber, almost dancing between his two enemies so that they had to guard against injuring each other as they sought to slay him. Ventress cursed under her breath, executing a backflip while kicking off the ridiculous high heels. With the connection they had forged, Vos immediately picked up on her tactic, moving for a better position from which to press the attack.

As he did so, Dooku struck him. It was only a glancing blow across Vos's left side, but he jerked, and in the blue light of the exploding fireworks Ventress saw his face contort first with pain, then harden into hatred.

Pain, she mused, *makes us strong.* And she knew much of pain.

Snarling, Ventress charged at Dooku, reveling in the strength of her muscles as she dealt strike after strike. Her old Master parried expertly, but she forced him back. He dodged to one side. Just as Ventress realized she had overextended, Dooku's left hand clamped down on her right wrist and he brought up his own lightsaber. It was Ventress's turn to seize his arm and hold the scarlet blade at bay. For an instant, the two, their faces only centimeters apart, stared into each other's eyes in a mockery of lovers. Then Dooku heaved her up and sent her sprawling. Unable to catch herself in time, Ventress landed heavily with a grunt.

Enraged, Vos charged Dooku from behind. The Sith Lord whirled, catching Vos's strike with his own weapon and twisting his wrist to parry. Vos countered with a feint that caused Dooku's chest to be unguarded, and dived for the kill. Dooku twisted out of the lightsaber's path, but for the first time since the fight began, Ventress saw awkwardness.

"You fight well for a Jedi, Vos," Dooku said.

"I had a good teacher," Vos retorted. He jerked his chin in Ventress's direction as she got to her feet and began to circle Dooku. Even as he spoke the words, Ventress realized what a mistake it was.

"Ventress?" Dooku's brows rose as he eyed her. "I . . . see."

She adjusted her grip on her lightsaber. "Vos," she warned, shouting over the explosions in the sky. "Focus! Remember what I told you!"

Ventress didn't dare be more specific. The less Dooku knew, the better. Vos's brown eyes narrowed, and with an incoherent cry, he charged. But the dynamic had shifted; Ventress could feel it. Dooku no longer appeared the least bit unsettled. He looked like a man who had drawn a winning card in a sabacc game. Ventress felt a chill that had nothing to do with the crisp night air or the light gown she wore.

He stood tall, imposing, and as Vos raced toward him, Dooku didn't flinch. He lowered his sword and extended his hand. Vos rose in the air and then Dooku shoved, sending the Jedi slamming into one of the pillars. The count turned, almost nonchalantly performing the same maneuver with Ventress. The wind was knocked out of her and she couldn't breathe. Stubbornly, using her hate the way she had told Vos to do, she summoned energy to push herself up to a kneeling position, still clutching her lightsaber.

Dooku's lip curled in a manner that might have been a smile or a snarl. Abruptly Ventress found herself dangling in the air as he whirled her around behind him and then threw her down like a spoiled child discarding a disliked toy.

The pain was excruciating, but Ventress remained conscious long enough to see that Dooku wasn't yet done. She could only watch helplessly as she slid, headfirst, into the unyielding stone of a meticulously carved bench. The world went white, and she knew nothing more.

CHAPTER TWENTY-ONE

Asajj!

Grief and fear flooded Vos. He wanted to rush to her, help her, but that would do nothing other than give Dooku a chance to kill him. In the space of half a heartbeat Vos recalled Ventress's lesson with the Sleeper. It had been crushing his ribs, and primal fear had surged through him. He'd used that fear then—turned it to hatred, and slain the Sleeper with it. Now Vos again harnessed and directed his own terror at the thought of Ventress's possible death.

His mind cleared, to be filled with one cold purpose: *Kill Dooku.*

Dooku smiled, as if pleased. "So," he mused. "She has given you a taste of the dark side . . . and perhaps other things as well, I gather. Tell me Vos, how many Jedi vows have you broken to destroy me?"

Vos twitched as if stung. In Ventress's company, it had been easy to think about what he had gained, not what he had given up—and would give up forever, if he were to remain with her.

For a heartbeat he stood frozen. Then, with a roar, he attacked. Never had his blows been as strong as now, when he was fueled with white-hot fury. His lightsaber was a blur as he struck. Dooku retreated under the assault, but to Vos it seemed as though the count didn't have much trouble parrying the blows.

"He's . . . manipulating you" came Ventress's voice, weak but determined. "Don't listen to him!"

She was alive! With renewed will, he struck again, but his green blade was caught by Dooku's red one as Dooku countered and leaned in. Colors from the glowing lightsabers and the fireworks reaching a crescendo in the air above cast dancing, eerie light on the count's face. They were so close that Vos could smell the floral scent of wine on Dooku's breath.

"I can sense the dark side is already strong in you," Dooku said. "Stronger than it *ever* was in Ventress!"

Vos, surprised, cast a quick glance at Ventress. She was on her feet now. Her short, fair hair was matted with blood, but she held her lightsaber firmly.

The count was lying, and Vos would have none of it. "You can't deceive me, Sith!" He leapt over Dooku, landing on his feet behind this man, who was the only thing that stood between him and his future with Ventress. He lashed out with a blow that should have removed Dooku's head, but the count dodged the lightsaber easily.

"Oh, no, Master Vos. I am not deceiving you. But *Ventress* is!"

Vos shook his head wildly, but the faintest tendril of doubt had already crept in. She had insisted he not progress further—why? Why wouldn't she want to use every tool they had at their disposal to bring down Count Dooku?

"She's using you," Dooku stated. He struck again, and Vos was forced to back up against the wall, parrying desperately. "She has not taught you your true potential. Not as *I* can!"

"Quinlan!"

The usage of his first name jolted Vos. Ventress rarely used it, nor did he often call her Asajj. He whirled away just in time to see her charging—

Grievous! How had the general—

Vos planted his boot in Dooku's stomach, taking the count by surprise, then shifted his weight and kicked Grievous with his other leg. The cyborg tumbled, bellowing, over the railing. Too late, Vos realized that Grievous had a firm grip on Ventress's arm. He watched, horrified, as the two fell together.

"Asajj!" he cried. Instinctively he moved toward the railing. At the same moment, out of the corner of his eye, he saw Dooku bringing his lightsaber down.

If he's killed her . . .

Vos reached for the final layer of darkness that had slumbered inside him until this moment. Ventress had warned against using it, but why? He *needed* it!

Fresh strength surged through Vos, an inferno of shadows fueled by the poison of his raw, unchecked emotions. He released it all. For a second, Dooku looked alarmed at the renewed attack. Vos dived and leapt, darted and struck—

—like a snake—

—leaping onto the railings and kicking Dooku square in the face with his boot. The count's head snapped backward, and for one wild, glorious instant Vos thought had broken Dooku's neck. But then Dooku rallied and pressed the attack. He was smiling broadly, his eyes gleaming with approval.

"Yes, use your anger! Surely Ventress told you that it is the only way you can defeat me!"

Ventress. A burst of fear filled Vos's chest. He grabbed it and bent it to his will. His throat was raw from primal cries as he went after Dooku with everything he had.

And this time, Dooku went down.

He scuttled backward, still parrying blows from the ground, but the sight gladdened Vos's heart. All he needed to do now was to get past the old man's blade.

A quick feint to the chest, a twist of his wrist, and Dooku's lightsaber went flying.

The green blade was a centimeter away from Dooku's throat, and the count froze, staring up at his adversary. Vos took a deep breath and lifted the blade over his head. He wanted to execute Dooku deliberately—not just kill him in a fight. He wanted to see those eyes go wide with terror as the count saw death approach.

He should have been prepared for Dooku's next move, but he wasn't. The man who had a second before been cowering now seized Vos's wrist as the green lightsaber descended. A sharp tug, and the roles were reversed. Now it was Vos who sprawled on the ground. Dooku had a knee planted firmly in Vos's back, using the Force to augment his own not-inconsiderable strength. Vos couldn't move. The count twisted the arm with which Vos still clutched his humming lightsaber, squeezing down with inhuman strength on the webbing between thumb and forefinger. Vos willed his hand to obey, but it was useless. The lightsaber fell, and the green glow vanished.

Devastated, Vos watched it roll to the edge, between the rails of the balcony, teeter there for a moment, then tumble out of sight.

Ventress's lightsaber flew out of her hand as she and Grievous plunged downward. She struck the ledge of a lower level hard, her head hanging over the edge. Grievous was atop her, his slitted golden eyes hungry for blood as he growled down at her, his foot on her throat. He seized her with his four hands and hurled her down to the level below them. She slammed against the wall beside one of the elegant windows and crumpled to the ledge.

She was taking a bad beating, she realized in some distant part of her mind. The earlier blow to her skull should have killed her. As it was, it had knocked her out for at least a couple of moments, and her head now ached violently. Her vision was untrustworthy, and as she got to her feet a wave of dizziness overcame her.

She had no time to indulge it. She looked up and saw Grievous leaping toward her, issuing a guttural sound that was intended as a triumphant laugh, and she rolled to the right. Ventress was wounded, disoriented, and had lost her lightsaber. There was nothing to do but give up or fight—and Ventress was not *about* to give up.

She snarled and charged at Grievous, executing a kick with her bare feet that still managed to send the larger and heavier cyborg staggering backward. He growled, clearly surprised.

Blasterfire whizzed past her and Ventress leapt clear, taking cover beneath a metal support beam. As she heard the marching battle droids come closer, she glanced up. She would not be trapped here. Summoning the Force to lift her, she crouched, then sprang upward, balancing delicately. Movement caught her eye.

Vos's lightsaber.

She reached out in the Force and seized it. It sped toward her, still warm from Vos's grip. Ventress refused to think about what was happening to him. If she didn't eliminate the threat here, Dooku and Grievous would come after both of them.

She leapt to the lower level and began reducing the battle droids to scrap metal. She batted the blasts back directly toward one, sliced through a second, and kicked a third off the ledge. She turned toward Grievous, her face bathed in a green glow.

Grievous reached down for his own lightsabers—and growled in frustration to find them missing. "Detain her while I go help the count!"

"Roger!" came a chorus of high voices from the droids. There were ten of them.

"I have no time for this," Ventress muttered, and surged forward.

It was over, and Vos knew that he had failed.

He heard the tramping of at least half a dozen battle droids as they formed a semi-circle around him. Dooku, having retrieved his lightsaber, stood holding it as he gazed down at Vos's prone figure.

"Go ahead," Vos said through clenched teeth. "Finish it!"

But Dooku shook his head. "Oh, no, Master Vos," he protested. "I'm actually rather impressed. I now have other plans for you."

His hand shot out. Blue streaks sprang from his fingers and danced over and through Vos's body. The pain was like nothing Vos had ever experienced. It simultaneously burned and froze him. Every muscle tensed and cramped, his body spasmed uncontrollably, and his heart tried to burst from his chest. He heard someone screaming, as if from a long distance, and it took him a moment to recognize his own voice.

After a second, or a thousand years, the torment ended. His body sprawled limply on the stone, and he could offer no resistance as metallic hands closed on his arms and began to drag him away.

"Quinlan! *No!*"

Ventress was still alive! Summoning the last re-serves of his strength, Vos craned his neck to see her.

He tried to shout her name, but it came out as a dry whisper. More droids surged past him, all firing on her. Willing himself to stay conscious, Vos struggled feebly, his gaze on Ventress.

She stayed and fought. For a while. But there were too many, even for Asajj Ventress. The last thing that Quinlan Vos saw was the woman he was falling in love with turn and flee—abandoning him to the mer-cies of Count Dooku. It was only then that Vos real-ized that the necklace about her long, slender throat had been crafted to look like a snake.

Ventress huddled in the sewers. Above, she heard the distinctive voices of battle droids.

"Nothing," one of the droids reported. "There has been no sign of the intruder."

"Orders are to keep looking," another replied. "Move on to sixty-six through ninety-nine."

"Roger."

When she could no longer hear them, Ventress re-laxed. Her whole body ached. She needed to tend her injuries, and rest. But for a moment she didn't move. Ventress held Vos's lightsaber, looking at it, seeing it again in his hands, remembered when he had given it to her on Dathomir.

Take care of this . . . because I'm going to want it back.

Don't worry. It'll be waiting for you, I promise.

She had kept it safe for him then; she would do so again.

Pain that had nothing to do with her physical wounds threatened to overcome her. For a wild moment, Ventress thought about contacting Obi-Wan Kenobi. Vos had told her that they were good friends, and that Kenobi had been the one to suggest involving her in the first place. Ventress even knew which bar hosted the Jedi's meetings. The Jedi would . . .

. . . not believe her. Not even Obi-Wan Kenobi would entertain the notion that she had never planned for this to happen.

Who else? Ventress couldn't do this alone. But she was too drained to think clearly now. She had to get to safety. And then . . .

Fiercely, she whispered, "Quinlan . . . I won't give up. I won't let him have you. By the blood of my sisters, I swear it."

CHAPTER TWENTY-TWO

There was no way for Vos to reckon the passage of time in the cell. It could have been a few days, or a month. The lights were always on. Meals, when they came, were at irregular intervals. Droids monitored his sleep patterns to ensure that he was jolted awake in agony during the REM stage.

Vos was no stranger to torture. In the past, his mastery of the Force had enabled him to focus his mind and distract himself from the pain. Hitherto, however, those who would see him suffer were strangers to the Force, and had been after specific information.

Neither was the case with Dooku.

The count came when he pleased, in silence; sometimes to observe Vos simply hanging, suspended, while a torture droid went about its programming. Other times, Dooku entered the cell, casually blasting Vos with Force lightning so that the former Jedi Master was reduced to screaming and writhing helplessly.

Each time, Vos tried to get him to talk, to find out what Dooku wanted. The count liked to gloat, and it was possible that he might let something slip that might be of help—some reference to the layout of this place, perhaps, or an unguarded comment on troop movements.

It was a futile effort. Vos was nothing more than an animal tormented for no apparent reason save Dooku's whim. And Vos knew, despite his training, both in the light and, now, the dark side of the Force, if that went on long enough . . . that was what he would eventually become.

So when Vos heard Dooku's footfalls over the hum of the torture device that bathed him in erratic pulses of energy designed to target nerve endings, he was not hopeful. But he refused to give up.

For the tenth, or perhaps the thousandth time, Vos lifted his head. He twitched as another agonizing pulse seared him but bit back a cry. Dooku, as always, was smiling, as if he were a kindly grandparent watching a child at play.

For the thousandth, or perhaps tenth time, Vos asked in a voice raw from screaming, "Why not just kill me and be done with it?"

"Tell me," Dooku said, "what did you hope to gain by teaming up with Asajj Ventress?"

All this time of silence, and he asked this? Vos was so surprised that the pain receded for a moment. The droid monitoring his reactions gave a passable impression of a frown and upped the level. Vos couldn't entirely smother a hiss of agony.

"I think that's . . . obvious enough," he said through the pain. "I was . . . s-sent to eliminate you."

Dooku stroked his beard thoughtfully. "It seems a desperate strike by the Jedi Council, not to rely solely on their vaunted Jedi Knights for such a task. Has the Order become so weak in my absence?"

Vos rallied as best he could. Looking Dooku square in the eye, he managed a chuckle. "Look around,

Dooku. On every front, the Republic is winning the war."

"I'm so glad you think so. But you are changing the subject." He shook a chiding finger at Vos. "I was not asking you about the war. I was speaking of Ventress."

Instantly Vos was on alert. He had been in so much pain when he had been captured, he wasn't sure what, exactly, had happened. Had Ventress abandoned him by choice? Or had they forced her off? His memories of that night were so fuzzy . . .

"Ventress has no sense of charity," Dooku went on. "She would not help you unless she had something to gain."

"She sure hates you," Vos offered.

"Of course she does," Dooku replied. "But she never works with anyone she can't control."

A sick jolt went through Vos. He thought about the previous attempts Ventress had made on Dooku's life. Then, she was in the company of her sisters, or else had—quite literally—created and shaped what she had thought would be the perfect co-assassin.

Had she been creating and shaping him as well?

Have caution, Quinlan, Kenobi had warned him. *Ventress is nothing if not manipulative. She won't hesitate to use your trust against you the instant it serves her own selfish purposes.*

"Well," Vos said, forcing his voice to be confident, "maybe you don't know her like I do."

Dooku arched an eyebrow, suddenly keenly attentive. "No," the count mused. "Perhaps I do not. But I see you *do* know her. Quite intimately, in fact, hmm?"

Vos didn't reply.

Dooku stepped closer. "I sense much fear in you, Vos."

Vos seized the chance. He would control the fear,

turn it to anger; anger turns to hate, and hate made him strong. "You're wrong," he scoffed. "I'm not afraid of you!"

"No, I don't believe you are," Dooku agreed. "But you *are* afraid."

Vos tried to redirect his thoughts, to focus on the loathing he felt for the man standing so smugly, so certain of his power, before him. But he was so weary and weak, and the pain kept directing his thoughts from strength to fear.

"Your thoughts betray you," Dooku said, and despairing, Vos knew it was true. "Ventress was teaching you. Well, well . . . this explains much."

"You're wrong. There's nothing she could teach me!"

Dooku shook his head and sighed. "You do yourself no favors by lying to me. You yourself said that you had a good teacher. Don't you remember?"

Vos struggled to keep his face from revealing the stab of anguish as he realized that, indeed, he *had* forgotten. What else was he not remembering?

"I left the Jedi because I had grown beyond them," Dooku continued. "But I see now that you and I, Vos, have much in common."

Vos rallied at the abhorrent words. "You and I are nothing alike. You're a traitor!"

"And what are you?" Dooku's normally modulated voice cracked like a whip. "You were raised in the Jedi Temple, but now you *reek* of the dark side! Soon enough, you will stop denying the truth of so very many things. And you will understand that I am not a traitor, but a visionary! Fear leads to anger, anger leads to hate, hatred leads to suffering."

The count nodded to the torture droid. This time, Vos convulsed in the grip of the blue crackle of electricity.

"But what the Jedi failed to teach you, what I have learned, is how to persevere, to pass *through* the suffering, and achieve ultimate power!"

Dooku nodded again. The pain stopped. Sweat ran down Vos's face. His heart was racing, his body quivering in remembered agony.

"Do not worry, my apprentice. The lessons that Ventress began—*I* shall now complete."

He waved a dismissive hand to the droid, and Vos tensed in anticipation of the next wave of electricity that would jolt through his body. Dooku turned.

Vos's screams followed him down the hall.

Akar-Deshu fell into step with Obi-Wan Kenobi as the Jedi Master strode toward the Council Chamber. He said nothing, merely kept pace with the human, and Kenobi sighed.

"Desh," he said quietly, "you know I cannot say anything about Master Vos or his assignment."

"I know, Master Kenobi," Desh said quietly. "You do not need to speak for me to know that something's gone wrong."

Kenobi gave the smaller Jedi an irritated glance. "There are times when I wish that certain Jedi were not quite as Force-sensitive as they are. And yes, I know precisely how that sounds."

"I said it last time and I will say it every time," Desh said, "if there is anything I can do to help—"

"You are rather too attached to Vos, Desh," Kenobi snapped.

"So are you," Desh added, "Master. Admit it—Vos does have a way of getting under one's skin."

"So does a tick or a splinter," Kenobi muttered. Nonetheless, he put a hand on the Mahran's shoulder and gave him a troubled smile as he entered the Council Chamber.

Yoda, Windu, Ki-Adi-Mundi, Saesee Tiin, and Plo Koon were present. All eyes turned to Kenobi as he entered and bowed to Master Yoda.

Yoda's expression was hopeful, but almost immediately he looked down and his ears drooped. "No word have you had from Master Vos," he said heavily.

"None," Kenobi said. "No word *from*, and no word *of*. It's as if he's completely vanished. As we discussed, I've continued to show up at our prearranged meeting place and time."

"Perhaps Ventress discovered his identity," Plo Koon said. "And killed him for deceiving her."

"I think not," Kenobi said. "If such had been the case, Ventress would have made sure that word of her displeasure with the Council reached us." He did not elaborate on the various grisly ways she might have done so.

"Asajj Ventress is a known Sith," Ki-Adi-Mundi said.

"Former Sith," Kenobi corrected, marveling not for the first time that he was now in the curious position of defending Ventress's honor.

"Is anyone even *capable* of being a 'former' Sith?" Windu demanded. "It's possible she's tricked Master Vos into going down a dark path with her and now we have a rogue Jedi on our hands."

"Possible," Kenobi agreed, "provided any of you really think that Quinlan Vos is so weak-willed that he'd forsake everything he's known his entire life. The man was *raised* in the Temple."

"A powerful allure, is that which is forbidden," Yoda said.

"Until we know something—anything—for certain, it is unwise to speculate," Kenobi said.

"We don't even know if he's still alive!" Mace's eyes were dark.

"This could be part of the plan."

"It could be," Mace said. "Or he could be dead. The point is we don't know—and we should, Master Kenobi. We *should*."

Ventress stood for a moment in the doorway of the Mos Eisley Cantina, letting her eyes adjust to the darkness from the blazing sunslight of Tatooine. This was not the path she would have preferred to tread, but she could think of no other option.

It felt like eons ago when she had entered it for the first time. Then, too, she had been reeling with a devastating sense of loss after Grievous had slain her entire clan. But then, she had been stumbling, directionless. Now Asajj Ventress had but one laser-keen sense of purpose.

She scanned the crowd and her gaze fell upon a familiar green, reptilian face above a bright-yellow flight suit. Familiar, too, was the perky young woman with bright orange pigtails and lavender skin. And— yes, *he* was there, too.

Ventress steeled herself and headed for them. Bossk spotted her and his face grew even sourer with a grimace. Ventress hadn't realized such a thing was possible. He leaned into a booth to talk to an unseen occupant. A moment later, two attractive Twi'lek girls slipped out of the booth, throwing Ventress wary glances.

"Hey!" called a voice Ventress remembered, boyish and intense. "I'm not paying for all of you!"

Bossk folded his arms and glared at her as she approached. In no mood for banter, Ventress stared him down. After a second or two, he threw up his hands in a hey-all-right-I'm-backing-off gesture, stepped back, and she slid into the booth across from Boba Fett.

His eyes widened in shock, then he scowled. "No Name," he said, "you've got a lot of guts coming here."

Ventress ignored the comment. She leaned in and said, quietly and with sincerity, "I need your help."

Boba Fett's double take was priceless. Then he cupped a hand exaggeratedly to his ear. "I'm sorry?"

Ventress choked down the urge to strike him. "You heard me."

He smirked. "No, I don't think I did. Say it again."

For some reason, the irritation bled out of her. All she felt was exhaustion, and a hopelessness that needed to be shut down, right now, lest it run over her completely. She repeated, in the same calm voice, "I need your help."

He scoffed, shaking his head in disbelief. "After what you did to me on Quarzite?" As she had suspected, Fett, indeed, had not gotten over being insulted, Force-choked, bound, gagged, and tossed into a trunk. Even if Ventress *had* left everyone their fair share of payment.

He got up to leave, disgusted. Ventress shot her hand across the table, shoving him back into his seat. "Sit," she snapped, stabbing a finger at him.

"Why should I?"

"Because I need your help."

Latts Razzi and Bossk, hovering just outside the booth, exchanged glances. Latts shook her head in disbelief.

"And," Ventress said, including the two of them in the conversation, "I'm willing to pay. I want to hire you and your syndicate."

That got everyone's attention, even Boba's. He

looked unconvinced as he replied, "That's going to be expensive. *If* I even decide to bother with you."

"I have the money."

His brows drew together. "Credits won't square you and me." He took a swig of his drink and drew his sleeve across his mouth.

"Not even a hundred thousand credits?" Ventress asked.

Latts's eyes grew large as saucers, and Bossk's jaw closed in astonishment. Boba looked at Ventress evenly.

"No. Not even *two* hundred thousand credits."

Ventress had underestimated how badly she had wounded the boy's pride. It was proving to be an expensive mistake.

"Two hundred fifty."

That got him. Boba's mouth hung open for three full seconds before he closed it. Latts and Bossk glanced at each other, and then, in perfect step, they moved forward.

"We'll take the job," Bossk said.

"Absolutely!" Latts agreed immediately.

Boba stared at them. "But—you don't even know what it is!"

Latts shrugged. "For two hundred fifty thousand credits, I don't care!"

Boba looked at Ventress, then at his bounty hunters. He threw up his hands in surrender. "Fine!" He sank back sullenly. "But the Syndicate gets its cut. You guys have fun." Fett took another long pull at his drink. He looked profoundly irritated with all of them.

"No deal," Ventress said bluntly. "I want the whole team." She counted them out on her fingers. "Bossk. Latts. Highsinger. Embo. *And* Boba Fett."

Boba narrowed his eyes. He looked at her in silence

for a long moment. Then he leaned back and asked, "What's the job?"

Ventress had planned out exactly what she was going to say. "A rescue mission. One man, on Serenno. We get in, we get out—you get paid."

Boba considered. "You know the layout of where we're going? The defenses, the weak points?"

"As if I lived there," she replied smoothly.

Boba suddenly slammed down his drink and leaned in to her. "It can't be that easy. There's more to this than you're saying, I know it."

Ventress knew something, too—how to play Fett. "There are always variables. Any *experienced* hunter knows that." She put exactly the right amount of inflection into the word, and sure enough Boba fairly bristled at the implied slight. He grabbed his helmet, having obviously had enough of the conversation.

"We get paid up front, or no deal. Transfer the credits today."

Ventress inclined her head. She'd been expecting this demand, just as she'd expected to have to up her initial offer. The sum represented almost everything she had saved up during her time as a bounty hunter. But if they could do it—if they could get Vos out of that hellhole where Dooku was doubtless torturing him—Ventress wouldn't care if she earned another credit as long as she lived.

Latts and Bossk looked like children who'd just been given presents. "Yessss!" hissed Bossk gleefully. Latts, grinning from ear to ear, playfully punched his breastplate in a show of solidarity.

Boba still looked as if he had taken a bite of something particularly nasty. "Go get Highsinger and Embo ready. We'll run through the basic layout of the mission in one hour." They nodded and practically skipped off. He watched them go, then turned back to Ventress.

"For the record—" Ventress looked up to find his blaster three centimeters from her face. This, she *hadn't* expected. "—I know you're going to betray us at some point. They might not see it, but *I* do."

She gazed at him evenly, hiding her surprise.

"And also, just for the record," he continued pleasantly, "I'm not the kid you left behind on Quarzite. You double-cross me again—you'll pay for it."

He twirled the blaster around his finger before holstering it, then shoved his helm on his head and followed Bossk and Latts.

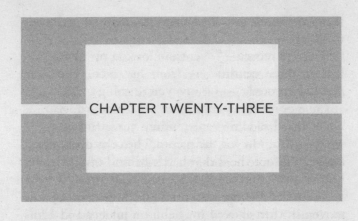

CHAPTER TWENTY-THREE

More time passed. More torture, more screams, more nightmares in the few moments when Vos passed out long enough to have them. He dreamed of darkness and blood, of fear of danger known, which was bad, and danger imagined, which was worse.

The worst dreams of all were of Ventress. Sometimes she was his torturer, sneering as she blasted him with Force lightning, reveling in his pain. She told him that everything she had said, everything they had shared together, was a lie, and reveled in the fact that this hurt him far more than physical pain.

But the dreams Vos dreaded even more than those were the ones where he held Ventress in his arms. When she told him she loved him, and he knew it to be true.

His senses had grown dull. He had no taste or hunger for food, no sensitivity to anything but the agony of the various methods the droid used to inflame his nerves or lacerate and then heal his body. Vos alternated between numb and sluggish and excruciatingly alive with torment. He ate only because some part of him knew he needed to keep up what little strength he had left. He, Dooku, and the droid had been performing this dance for enough time that Vos's muscles were beginning to weaken, except for those that screamed constantly from being placed in positions they were never designed to execute.

The dreams this time had been particularly bad, so when the droid came to awaken him, Vos actually welcomed it. He was surprised when the droid deactivated the force field that had held him suspended by his arms. Unable to catch himself, he fell awkwardly as he dropped a meter to the floor. Stiff from lack of movement for so very long, his shoulders and arms were on fire, and Vos bit back a scream. It felt like the snake venom that had coursed through his system on Dathomir, which led back to thoughts of Ventress.

"Get up," the droid ordered. When Vos failed to comply, the droid signaled. Two battle droids appeared and snapped to attention. The torture droid deactivated the force field and the battle droids stepped inside. They wrenched Vos's arms behind his back and snapped on a pair of binders, then each took one of his arms. As they dragged him out of the cell, the agony in his arms increased a thousandfold, and once again blackness descended.

Vos came to when he was tossed to the ground. He lay there for a moment, then became aware of the smells. Roasted meats, the tang of freshly cut fruits, the sweet fragrance of just-baked pastries—*real* food, not the tasteless stuff he had been forced to consume. Moisture flooded his mouth, and for the first time since the hideous ordeal began, his stomach rumbled. Slowly, hissing, he pushed himself up to a kneeling position and took in his surroundings.

The room was large and lavish. Fine art from a variety of worlds hung on the walls. The carpeting beneath Vos was thick and comfortable. Soft music came from somewhere, and a large, ornately carved cabinet hung on the wall. All these things, Vos noticed only fleetingly. His eyes were riveted on the display before him, which was both inviting and obscene. There were, quite literally, dozens of foodstuffs on a dining table that could easily have seated sixteen.

And at the head of it, pouring effervescent wine into a fluted glass, sat Count Dooku.

He lifted the glass in a toast to Vos. "Welcome," he said, and drank.

This was perhaps the worst torture yet, but Vos steeled himself. If Dooku thought to see him beg for table scraps, the count would be sorely disappointed.

Vos swallowed so he could speak. "Well, look at you and your pampered life." His voice dripped contempt. "Your servants, your feast, your palace. It must have been so easy for you to turn your back on the Jedi Order."

Dooku cut another bite from the thick, rare steak and lifted it to his mouth. Juices dripped onto the plate. He chewed with obvious enjoyment, dabbed at his lips with the napkin, and then replied.

"Yes," he agreed, "I live a privileged existence now. But like you, Vos, I too was taken from my home as an infant and raised in the Jedi Temple. It was only later in my life that I discovered my true heritage—a legacy of power and pedigree that was far too intimidating for the Council to accept."

A plate was set at the far end of the table. Food was within easy reach of it, and the flute of wine had been filled. Clearly, Vos would be welcome to dine with the count—if he requested it. Vos tried to decide which was the smarter course of action—refusing to give Dooku the satisfaction of eating, or taking the chance to consume some real food that would increase his strength.

"Pedigree," he scoffed. "Like an animal. You could have done so much, helped so many people. Instead you used that legacy to spread your evil throughout the galaxy." The fragrance of the freshly baked bread in front of him almost broke him.

Dooku rose from his seat, setting down his napkin and picking up his glass of wine. He walked to the entrance of a large, open balcony and pulled back the gently billowing curtains. For the first time since he had been taken, Vos had a sense of time. It was night, here on whatever world he was on, and the stars glittered serenely, teasing him with a freedom he didn't have.

"Evil?" Dooku chuckled. "What a childish notion. Unworthy of you, Vos. Today's lesson begins with this." He turned and regarded Vos, the glass still in hand. "There is no good or evil. Only those with power, and those without it."

Vos grunted in disgust. He had decided against eating. If he started, he wasn't sure he could stop, and he refused to let Dooku see just how famished he was.

"Your Master Tholme understood this." Dooku tossed out this verbal grenade with utter casualness.

For a moment a sheet of red darkened Vos's vision, and he was so outraged he couldn't breathe.

"How dare you speak his name! You *murdered* him!"

Dooku looked convincingly surprised, and then almost sad. "Ah . . . so that's what she said. Given your, er, relationship with Ventress, I wondered if you knew the truth. It was she who killed your Master, not I."

"You lie!" shouted Vos, trying to rise. The droids shoved him back down.

"No, Quinlan. I don't have to lie." Dooku shook his head. He stepped into the hall and motioned. A moment later, a squat technical droid rolled into the room. Dooku went to it and tapped a few controls as he spoke.

"One of the many advantages of having a droid army in the field is the ability to study the battle recording. Win or lose, I always find the holorecord . . . illuminating."

A final tap, and Dooku straightened. The droid chirped and then began to project the scene of a battle on a planet Vos couldn't identify. He could make out the figures of what seemed like countless battle droids locked in combat with hundreds of clones. A major conflict, then. Vos's throat tightened, dreading what he would see.

"Magnify," ordered Dooku. The hologram shifted, then narrowed its focus to a handful of combatants.

One of them was Master Tholme. Despite himself, Vos gasped slightly. He was surprised at how painful it was to behold an image of his Master. Tholme's gray-streaked black hair was held back in a long ponytail. He stood his ground, his lightsaber, green as Vos's own, a blur as he shouted out orders and cut down battle droids.

Suddenly there came two flashes of red. A woman— bald, pale as the stars, clad in black leather and expertly wielding twin lightsabers, appeared.

Asajj Ventress.

The Jedi and the Sith acolyte engaged in a heated fight. Ventress's lightsabers had unusually curved hilts, so that she needed to wield them in a slightly different manner from the standard, straight lightsabers. Vos watched, forgetting to breathe, horrified but unable to tear his gaze away from the brutal spectacle. Then, so swiftly Vos couldn't even see what happened, Ventress had gotten the upper hand.

Tholme's lightsaber went flying. Ventress pointed both her weapons at Tholme. He raised his hands and knelt before her. Surrendering.

Ventress ran him through.

One glowing blade pierced Tholme's heart. The other gutted him. Vos's beloved Master fell to the ground.

"Freeze" came Dooku's voice, as if from far away. Vos's blood thundered in his ears. He stared at the miniature Tholme, dead, and at the tiny Ventress, standing before the treacherously slain Jedi and grinning in triumph.

"Ventress was a fair apprentice," Dooku continued. "However, as she became more powerful, her lust for bloodshed could not be sated. She grew ever more violent and unpredictable."

Vos stared, his gaze roving the face he had caressed, the lips he had kissed.

"She slaughtered Master Tholme, against my orders. We had the battle won, there was no reason to justify the death of an old friend." Dooku's voice, bizarrely, was kind, like that of a father comforting a devastated son.

"But—why would she do this? Keep this from me?" Vos's voice sounded shattered, even to him.

"Ventress has a hunger for power. That is what she truly desires, and she would do anything, lie to anyone, to get what she wants."

Dazed, Vos shook his head. His whole body ached from the motion. "No. No, not to me."

Dooku stepped closer, staring down at Vos. "Especially to you. I know. You thought you knew her, as I did. You thought she cared for you, but she was doing nothing but spinning a web of lies. Lies that I can free you from, as I freed myself!"

Vos didn't answer. His gaze was fixed on the droid that had shown him such a horrible truth.

Or . . . had it?

He blinked. There was something about Dooku and recordings . . . what was it? And then he remembered. Now Vos stared up at the count, his mind clear and focused once again, his voice strong.

"You falsified this recording," Vos snarled. "You erased yourself and put Ventress in your place. It's easy to do. You've tried to fool the Jedi with this trick before!"

Dooku looked at him sadly. "You grasp at straws, Vos. I understand why. It is a hard thing to accept, that the world you thought you knew was not the truth. It is difficult to step away from everything, to let go. But do it, Vos. Come away from that false world. Join me!"

"I will *never* join you!"

Dooku turned away, pacing, now and then glancing back at Vos as if trying to make up his mind about something. "I think I must show you the cabinet, after all," he said. "Truly, I would have spared you this, if I could have. Remember that I did try."

"The cabinet," Vos repeated. "What's that, some fun new style of torture?"

"That all depends on you, Quinlan. It will, truly, be in your own hands."

"I think I'd like to go back to my prison cell. I prefer straightforward torment to this preposterous game you're playing. You won't break me, Dooku."

"You know, I believe I won't," agreed the count, surprising Vos. "But you will break all the same. And it will be your choice to do so."

Dooku walked toward the end of the room and stood before the cabinet. Vos tensed, not knowing what new horror Dooku would subject him to this time.

"Your proof is in here," Dooku said.

"You think if your little holoshow didn't convince me, something else will?" Vos sneered.

"I do," the count replied with complete confidence. A chill shivered through Vos. Dooku seemed so certain. Vos felt sweat break out on his forehead and beneath his arms. What the hell was in that deceptively ordinary-looking cabinet? With one final, almost regretful glance at Vos, Dooku opened the cabinet's double doors.

Mounted with great care, resplendent against a padded background of blue velvet, hung at least twenty lightsabers. A portion of the case was bare; Dooku had left room for the collection to expand.

Vos swallowed hard, fighting nausea, unable to tear his eyes away. "Whenever Grievous or Ventress cut down a Jedi, they brought me these little souvenirs of the battle," Dooku said in a casual tone. "They make for quite the handsome display, don't you think?"

I remember that battle.

You were there?

No. Dooku bragged about it to me. It was he who killed your Master. He even kept Tholme's lightsaber as a trophy.

Blood thundered in Vos's ears. The hilts were crafted of metal, or wood, or even gems, each as unique as the Jedi who had made it. With a soft sound Vos closed his eyes and turned his head.

"Make him look," Dooku ordered sharply, and there was steel in his voice. A battle droid dug its metal fingers into Vos's hair and yanked his head back.

"I believe in the old adage *Know your enemy,*"

Dooku said. "I've spent a considerable amount of time studying the Jedi Masters. I know their strengths, their weaknesses—and their unique skills. For instance, I know that you, Quinlan Vos, have the rare gift of psychometry."

And with a sickening realization, Vos suddenly knew what Dooku was about to do.

"Free his hands," Dooku said to the droids. Vos stayed completely still as the droids obeyed their master. He flexed his wrists, ignoring the sensation of numb limbs tingling to life, and got to his feet, stumbling awkwardly.

"I'm certain you'll want to determine the truth in a way it is impossible for you to deny," Dooku continued. A thought seemed to occur to him. "Although . . . I imagine it will be more than a trifle unpleasant. Isn't it true that, in addition to seeing and hearing things regarding the object you touch, you will also *experience* what its owner felt? Hmm?"

Count Dooku smiled, and held out Tholme's lightsaber.

For a long moment, Vos simply stared at the weapon. Then, uttering a wordless cry, he launched himself at Dooku. The count did not appear to have been expecting this, and Vos was able to wrap his hands around the other man's neck and squeeze, using the Force to increase the pressure. But even so, he was much weaker than the count, and Dooku broke the chokehold and sent Force lightning throughout Vos's body.

While Vos writhed on the floor, Dooku got to his feet and ordered the droids, "Take him back to the cell. But do not restrain him. And," he added, handing one of them Tholme's weapon, "take this with you."

The droids each took one of Vos's arms and hauled him up. Panting, Vos lifted his head.

"You can make me touch it," Vos gasped, "but you can't force me to read it!"

"I know," Dooku said mildly. "But you will, Vos. Eventually, you will."

CHAPTER TWENTY-FOUR

Ventress felt a mingled stab of worry and nostalgia as *Slave I* landed at Serenno's spaceport. Her most recent visits to this world had been her two failed assassination attempts. Now she couldn't care less about Dooku. Her hatred and burning desire for revenge was easily put aside for something so much more important. Funny how one's priorities could shift so completely in the most unexpected of ways.

Her boots clanked on the metal of the ramp as she, Latts, Bossk, Highsinger, and Boba descended. Embo disembarked from his own saucer-shaped *Guillotine,* but not alone; his anooba Marrok, trotting down the ramp from his own private entrance, fell into step with his master. Ventress had worked with all of them but Embo. He was a Kyuzo, swift and agile. He had one of the more interesting tools she'd run across—a hat that did triple duty as accessory, shield, and weapon. C-21 Highsinger, as far as she knew, was that rare thing—a unique droid.

The spires of Dooku's fortress towered, catching the morning sunlight. They were beautiful, elegant, and refined. The place looked both too lyrical to be a prison where unspeakable torment was performed, and too beautiful to be the home of such a wretched creature as Dooku.

We're coming, Vos.

Ventress pointed at it, her body as calm and poised as her thoughts and emotions were roiling. "There's the palace."

"And you're certain this Count Dooku won't be there?" Latts pressed.

Ventress gave the younger woman a scornful glance. Lying smoothly, she replied, "He has an entire *war* to manage. He's got greater things to worry about and better places to be."

Fett gnawed his lower lip, gazing at the spires. "I don't like it. What did your friend do to get himself imprisoned by a man like Dooku, anyway?"

She'd known the question would be asked and replied with the simple truth. "Honestly? He tried to kill him."

Latts whistled. The bounty hunters, all with raised eyebrows, looked at one another. Clearly they were kicking themselves for not asking this question sooner.

"*Un*-believable," said Fett. "So this is why you agreed to pay us in advance!"

Ventress planted her hands on her hips. "Look. The plan is simple. You're running a distraction. That's it. I'll do the hard part and break into the prison. Just hold the guards' attention. Think you can manage that?"

Boba bristled. "Easily," Bossk said. "They're most likely just droids."

"Dlaaa beerrkkkk," protested Highsinger.

Bossk ducked his scaly green head. "Sorry, pal, no offense."

"Hurrkkk!" Highsinger was obviously not entirely mollified.

"Try to make it look like you're stealing a starship," Ventress said. "We don't want to tip our hand that this is a rescue attempt."

Latts laughed. "Why stop at the 'look like' part? Let's just steal the thing!"

"Yep. Bonus!" Bossk agreed.

At Ventress's expression, Fett laughed out loud. "Don't forget, you asked for our help."

"I'm having second thoughts," she murmured as they set off for the palace.

Ventress had lived here long enough to know how Dooku liked things to run. She remembered exactly where and at what time supplies were delivered to the palace. Tucked away out of sight behind the opulence of the palace's imposing entrance was a delivery area where encroaching trees had been cleared away so that shuttles could land. It would be easy to ambush the droids tasked with off-loading the supplies; the trees not far from the landing area offered plenty of cover. It was so obvious that, for a brief moment, Ventress wondered why an attack such as the one they were planning had not been attempted before; then she realized that any sane person would balk at simply walking up to Dooku's battle-droid-protected palace, rear entry though it might be.

She checked her chrono. "Any minute now," she told her companions.

"How many shuttles will there be?" asked Latts.

Ventress shrugged her thin shoulders. "It depends on the size of the delivery. There's room for anywhere from one to five to land in this area."

"Great," muttered Latts.

"Quiet," Fett said. They waited. Within five minutes, they could all hear the sound of approaching ships. Ventress listened closely—more than one, certainly. Perhaps three? Not as bad as it could be, but it would certainly present Fett's team with a challenge.

They waited for the signal from Boba. The young bounty hunter leaned against a tree trunk, his face hidden by his helmet. One of the shuttles settled down, followed by two others. Boba slowly raised his hand, and when the first shuttle extended a ramp and two battle droids trundled out carrying a large box between them, Boba gave the signal for his team to move forward.

Carefully, quietly, they each took their position. Ventress had never felt more alive. Her body was calm, under her absolute control, and her focus was laser-sharp. The killing machine she could become when needed was fueled now by the heat of her anger toward Dooku—and another warm emotion she was too afraid to name.

She would get Vos out. She refused to even consider any other outcome.

A disk-shaped metal object came out of nowhere and clipped one of the battle droids in the head. It stumbled and fell, its head smashed beyond repair.

"Hey!" its partner objected, turning to see who had thrown the projectile. The droid was cleanly decapitated by the disk as it circled back toward its owner, and its head toppled off its shoulders.

Embo extended a hand and snatched his flat, broad-brimmed hat. "Nesta nesta balotelli," he said smugly.

Latts Razzi had positioned herself near the second ship. As the droids emerged, she cracked her grappling boa. In her expert hands, the boa coiled around a hapless, squeaking droid like the snake for which it was named. In a series of moves that looked more like a dance than a fight, Latts snared one, whipped it around her, and deposited it at the feet of Highsinger. The bounty hunter cheerfully crushed the enemy droid beneath his metal feet.

The air was filled with multicolored bolts. Fett took out a pair of other droids while Bossk scrambled atop one of the shuttles. He fired a repeating blaster, laughing gleefully as he mowed down battle droids and finally targeted one of the shuttles. It exploded in a very satisfactory manner, leaping flames and oily tendrils of black smoke climbing into the air.

Even the battle droids would notice that, Ventress thought, and sure enough, at least a dozen of them scurried out of the entrance to the palace's lower levels.

"It's clear," Ventress called to Fett. "I'm going in."

"We'll hold the droids here," Fett shouted back. "But you've only got fifteen minutes, understand?"

"I'll be quick," Ventress said. She sprinted for the open doors.

"Fifteen minutes!" Fett yelled after her.

Silently, swiftly, Ventress hastened through the dimly lit hallways. Here, deep inside the well-fortified heart of Dooku's palace, was where the count kept his prisoners. She remembered precisely where the cells were—and what went on inside them. There had been a time when she herself had participated in "interrogations" that were, in the end, merely an excuse to inflict pain. No one was ever released, whether or not they provided useful information. She could only hope that Vos was still alive.

The sound of metallic feet marching reached her ears. Ventress leapt straight up. Using the shadows in the corners as cover, she found hand- and footholds, and waited. Six armed droids hurried through the corridor, doubtless alerted to the ruckus outside.

Ventress dropped directly on top of one, ripped off its head, and flung it at one of its companions. Deftly she executed a handspring and came up kicking out with both feet, using the Force to empower the strike. The droids slammed into the walls and collapsed like puppets with their strings cut.

Activating her lightsaber—*no, Vos's lightsaber*—Ventress turned to the remaining three. One had recovered enough to fire at her, but she batted back the bolts as if she were swatting an annoying insect. In one smooth motion, she sprang, sliced, and three heads went rolling.

Ventress dropped to a crouch, listened, and moved on.

Turning left at the next corridor junction, she raced down the long hall. At the end was a huge metal door, flanked by controls. This was the entry to the cell area. Ventress paused for a heartbeat to steady herself, then pushed the button.

The door slid open just as two droids turned the corner to enter the hallway.

"Hey!" said one of them. "You're not supposed—"

Ventress nocked one arrow, let it fly, and loosed a second. The droids didn't even have a chance to open fire.

She pressed on. Two more droids approached, carrying battle staves. Ventress didn't even slow her pace, running straight toward them as they charged at her, brandishing and whirling their staves. At the last moment she veered, ran up the wall, flipped in midair, and seized one of the staves. For a moment, Ventress balanced atop it with one hand, sizing up the droid's positions. Then she dropped with precise control, flipping so she held the weapon in both hands.

The droid that was still armed began to attack.

With a single quick motion, Ventress sent its stave flying and slammed her own first into one droid, then the other. Pieces of them clanged to the ground. Ventress dropped the weapon and entered the cell section.

The cells were all empty. Dooku must have finished with the prisoners she remembered and not replenished his stock. *Except for Vos.* She ran down the hallways, glancing left and right into each cell, rounding the corner—

He knelt, his back to her. His back was bowed and his body shook, as if with sobs.

"Vos!" Ventress cried brokenly, slamming the controls with her palm and deactivating the force field.

He froze, but didn't turn around. A lump rose in her throat. Slowly, Ventress stepped forward, reaching out to touch his shoulder. "It's me, Vos. I came back for—"

Still without turning, Vos lifted a hand and clenched his fist. Ventress shot into the air. Invisible fingers strangled her. Blood pounded in her ears as she clawed futilely at her throat, struggling to force words out.

"Quinlan . . . no . . ."

"You," he said, "are a liar . . . and a murderer."

CHAPTER TWENTY-FIVE

Ventress had feared for his life, but now a fresh terror surged through her. Vos knew the truth—Dooku had revealed it to him. She had vowed to tell him herself, when this was all over, but for Vos to have heard it from *Dooku*—

"Quinlan," Ventress rasped. Her vision was starting to go dark around the edges. "Listen . . . to me . . ."

"Shut. Up." Now Vos rose, his back still toward her. Every line of his body was taut with tension. "I am done with listening to your *lies*!"

"I warned . . . about this!" A moment longer, and she would black out. If he didn't crush her windpipe first. Ventress struggled to get the words out while she still could. "You need to . . . tap into the darkness but not . . . let it consume you!"

"Like you let it consume *you* when you *killed my Master*?"

Vos flung her away from him, hard. She slammed into the stone floor and slid, coughing and gasping for breath. As quickly as she could, Ventress got to her feet—and her heart shattered inside her chest.

Vos's eyes were no longer a warm, rich brown. They were a blood-rimmed shade of yellow.

"I trusted you." His voice shook as he raged. "I *believed* you. And everything you said—everything you promised me, everything I thought I meant to you and believed we could have together—it was all a lie!"

"No!" The word was almost a sob. "I—"

Vos extended a hand. Across his palm lay a lightsaber hilt.

Ventress recognized it. Despair and horror filled her as she realized what it meant, both for herself, and for him. Vos now knew, beyond the shadow of a doubt, that Ventress had coldly executed his Master. But Dooku hadn't told him. The count, in the depths of his cruelty, had made Vos find it out for himself.

Vos had told her how his psychometry affected him. He received input from sight, sound—and emotions. The Order did not approve of Jedi using such a skill to handle weapons of violence, as the wielder's feelings could be sensed—and those emotions could lay a Jedi bare to the power of the dark side.

"Oh, Quinlan," she said, brokenly, aching with compassion.

"Don't you *dare* lie to me now, Asajj Ventress," Vos snarled. She looked up at his Sith-yellow eyes again, and this time she saw tears on his cheek. Impulsively, she reached out to him, stepping forward.

With a *snap-hiss,* Tholme's lightsaber sprang to life, and Vos charged.

Ventress was barely able to activate her own lightsaber and bring it up in time to prevent him from slicing her head off. Faster than she had ever seen him move before, even when she had pressed him on Dathomir, Vos twisted, and her blade slid off his. He rained blow after blow, his teeth bared in a snarl, forcing Ventress back down the corridor.

Vos had been a Jedi Master, and while she had defeated such before, the battle was never easily won. Now those skills were augmented by a dark side that had greedily feasted on his pain and rage. It seemed to her that his blows were effortless, and he did not tire.

Ventress had to reach him, somehow. Vos was drunk with this new power, unfettered, as she was, by the thought of striking a lethal blow. While she was only attempting to either knock him out or seize his lightsaber, he wanted her dead.

"You *used* me!" he shrieked. Left, right, left he struck, and she parried, feeling the jarring up her arm. Their blades sizzled, the two green blades striking sparks off each other.

"You came to *me*!" Ventress reminded him. "You asked for *my* help! The Council—"

Vos bellowed, springing back and shoving hard with his left hand. Ventress was hurled backward, slamming into the unforgiving stone wall.

"They all warned me you were out for yourself. And you were. You didn't care about me at all!"

Her head was ringing, but Ventress got to her feet. She leapt toward Vos, landing behind him and kicking at the back of his knee. He hadn't been expecting it and stumbled. She seized the arm that held the lightsaber and yanked it back, trying to force him to drop it.

"If that were true," Ventress said, pleading, "if I didn't care, then why am I here? Why did I risk my life to come back for you?"

For a moment a faint shadow of doubt flickered across his features, and he ceased struggling. Then his face grew hard. "Because you needed me. You hated Dooku, and when I came along, you took advantage of it. You couldn't do it alone, but with me, you might have managed to kill your hated Master. I was never anything to you but a means to an end."

The bitterness in his voice stabbed like a dagger. Her own eyes stung with tears. And in that moment, Ventress hated the dark side for what it—and Dooku's torture—had done to this man.

"Vos, you were *everything*! This is the pain and the dark side speaking! This isn't who you are!"

With a roar, Vos lunged forward, hurling Ventress over his head. He wrenched his arm free and whipped his lightsaber around. The tip grazed Ventress's midsection as she tried to roll away, and she cried out in pain.

"It *is* who I am! It's who I want to be! *You* gave me this cup, Ventress. *You* made me drink from it."

It was the truth. She had pushed him, in the caverns. She had forced him to kill the Sleeper in cold blood. And it seemed he had learned that lesson all too well.

"But you can control it! You're strong, Vos, stronger than it is! Don't let it win. Let's leave everything—Dooku, the Jedi, everything. We can go away together, just like we planned. Just you and me!"

"Run away with someone who lied to me?" The words were harsh, but Vos wasn't fighting, wasn't charging her. Even so, he held his lightsaber ready as he asked, "Why did you do it?"

Hope, nearly burned to ashes, surged within her at the anguish in his tone. For this moment, there was more pain than rage in him. And the pain might just listen to her.

Slowly, Ventress lowered her weapon. She was ready to defend herself, but Vos didn't move to attack. She licked her lips, took a deep breath, and spoke.

"I did lie to you. And I lied to you because I was afraid."

His eyes narrowed. "You've never been afraid of anything, Asajj Ventress."

She shook her head. "You're wrong. I was terrified."

"Of what?" Vos scoffed.

"Of losing you." She let the words hang there for a moment, and when Vos still appeared to be listening, she continued. "I've been lying for so long. It's second nature to me. We learned to trust each other, but what I felt . . . I was so scared. I was afraid to tell you about Tholme because I thought you'd hate me. I'd only just learned how to trust and care about someone again, and I . . . I couldn't bear the thought that if you really knew me, knew what I had done, you'd despise me."

Her voice broke. Vos's body posture eased. His eyes were glued to her face. "You should have trusted me," he said softly.

Ventress nodded. "You're right. I should have. And even if you had left me, I'd have done the right thing. But I was too afraid. *I was wrong.* I am so very, very sorry."

Tears stung her eyes. Ventress let them fall. She had not wept since the slaughter of her sisters, and even then she had grieved in solitude. Never had Ventress spoken so to another living being, not even her beloved Jedi Master. She stood, her heart wide open, her soul naked before him. Surely, he would see it, even through the darkness that clouded his mind. Surely, he would understand what this meant. Quinlan Vos knew her in a way no one else ever had. He would see, and understand.

The yellow hue faded from his eyes and he blinked. "Asajj?" he whispered.

"I brought your lightsaber back to you," she said. "Yours. I kept it safe for you, just like I did on Dathomir. Don't let Dooku use Tholme to divide us. I wish I could, but I can't change the past. I just want a future—with you."

It was the wrong thing to say. Vos looked down at the blade he held, and his beloved face turned ugly with hatred. The awful yellow hue returned to his eyes as he looked back up at her.

"That," Vos growled, "is the worst lie of all."

Shattered, Ventress rolled out of the way as he leapt at her, bringing up her blade in a frantic parry as he forced her around the corner. She called his name, again and again, but Vos was now deaf to any plea she might utter. Ventress realized that he would not stop until he had killed her. And for one brief moment, she wanted him to. It would be easier than living without him, knowing that this was where she had unwittingly led him.

No. She would not give up. She would *not* let Dooku and the dark side have him.

With his fury-fueled attacks Vos forced her to retreat, back toward the exit, and Ventress let him do so. She understood now that he was too far gone to be talked into accompanying her willingly, but if she could bring the fight back out into the open, she might be able to maneuver him toward Fett and the others. The aid of even one of the bounty hunters might be enough to subdue Vos and drag him onto one of the ships.

Even though she retreated deliberately, Vos's attack demanded every bit of her focus. He seemed to grow stronger, his attacks more powerful, while Ventress had to draw on everything she had simply to stay alive.

Vos barely even seemed to need to breathe, and he threw everything he had at the woman that, Ventress knew in her heart, he had once cared for so deeply. As they turned another corner, Ventress nearly stumbled over the debris of a battle droid she had torn apart but a few moments before. Vos shot out a hand. Several pieces of broken metal rose in the air. Grunting, Vos gestured, and they all launched themselves at Ventress.

She sliced a torso in half with her lightsaber, used the Force to deflect various limbs, and dived out of the path of two severed heads. Ventress landed on her feet and immediately brought up her weapon to deflect the blur of Tholme's lightsaber. She used the Force to shove it and Vos back, and kept retreating.

It seemed like an eternity before Ventress saw that the dimness of the corridors was growing brighter. Hope surged in her as she realized that they were close to the exit. The emotion made her careless; she found herself suddenly lifted and flung backward out the door.

Ventress sailed through the air for several meters, landing hard and awkwardly, and for a wild moment was unable to rise. Then someone grabbed her arm and hauled her to her feet.

"Where's your friend?" Fett demanded.

Ventress turned back to the doorway. Quinlan Vos stood there, his cruel face illuminated by the glow of a dead man's lightsaber. Behind him followed a host of battle droids.

Ventress pointed at Vos. "There," she said brokenly.

"*That's* your friend?"

Suddenly Vos's head whipped to the side. Following his gaze, Ventress saw something thoroughly unexpected—Count Dooku, trapped in some sort of webbing, lying on the ground with Bossk's blaster aimed at his head.

Vos threw Ventress one final, hate-filled glance, then turned and raced to Dooku. The droids followed Vos obediently, firing at the bounty hunters.

"Go!" Fett shouted, gesticulating toward one of the shuttles. They needed no second urging. Bossk turned his head as he ran, snapping at Dooku over his shoulder in frustration, but followed Embo, Highsinger, and Latts up the ramp of the nearest shuttle. Embo motioned to Fett and Ventress to hurry up.

"Come on, No Name!" Fett cried.

"I . . . I can't leave . . ." Her gaze was riveted on Vos, who had freed Dooku from the netting and was now helping him up. He glanced up, perhaps feeling her gaze, and said something to Dooku. They stood side by side, a team . . . a Master and an apprentice. The sight was so devastating that Ventress barely registered that six battle droids were now racing toward them.

Vos smiled.

"We have to go!" Boba yelled. He seized her hand and started running, dragging Ventress along with him. Together they raced up the ramp, which started to close the second they set foot on it. The shuttle had already lifted off as Ventress and Fett flung themselves inside.

Ventress went to the viewport, hoping against hope to see some signal from Vos that told her that he was only pretending; that this was all some kind of bizarre act. All she saw was the two former Jedi Masters, once so different, but now united by the darkness, staring impassively up at the departing ship.

Ventress looked away, no longer able to bear the

sight. Her gaze fell on Fett, who removed his helmet and dragged a hand across his sweating face.

"You could have left me behind," she said quietly.

He nodded. "Yeah, I could have. But I'm not you."

The words cut Ventress in ways Fett couldn't even imagine.

It was an hour and forty-seven minutes past the appointed meeting time. Obi-Wan Kenobi did not truly expect to see Quinlan Vos, but he held to the ritual of showing up, clad in his bounty hunter disguise, hoping against hope that *this* time, for *this* meeting, Vos would be there. Each time Kenobi was forced to depart alone, and that flicker of hope grew dimmer. He debated leaving early, but he was too stubborn. Kenobi would give his old friend the courtesy of waiting the two hours he always had before giving up and returning to the Temple.

The server droid zipped up to him and put another bottle on the table. She gave him a metal-lidded wink. "You're becoming quite a regular," she chirped.

Kenobi gave her a wan smile, and as she rolled away he pulled his nondescript, ragged hood farther over his face. A shadow fell over the table and he looked up, smiling with relief, but the words of greeting died on his lips.

Before him stood Asajj Ventress—but not the Ventress with whom he had crossed lightsabers on so many occasions.

She now had short, pale-blond hair, and she looked like she had aged ten years. Her ice-blue eyes were bloodshot and there were deep circles under them. She had changed more than physically; emanating from her was a bleak resignation that failed to entirely mask a deep-set ache.

Apprehension rose in Kenobi, but not for anything he thought she would do. He suddenly, desperately hoped she would not speak.

For a long moment, Ventress was indeed silent, her gaze lowered. Then she took a long, shuddering breath and lifted her eyes to his. When she spoke, it was in the same husky voice he remembered. But it was not filled with fury or cruel amusement. It was the voice of someone adrift . . . and bereft.

"He's not coming back. He belongs to Dooku now."

Kenobi's eyes widened. *No* . . . , he thought. Not him. Not the ebullient, eternally playful Quinlan. *No.*

Wordlessly, he reached for the second cup he always ordered, hoping Vos would show up to drink from it. Now Kenobi filled it and slid it across the table. Ventress stared at it, then at him, and finally eased herself into the chair slowly, as if even simple movement hurt.

She took a slow sip.

They sat there, together, for a long time.

CHAPTER TWENTY-SIX

Asajj Ventress had spent a lifetime living in the moment. She was a woman who had no patience for regrets or what-ifs. She moved resolutely in a single direction—forward.

Except now. Now her dreams were filled with the images of Quinlan Vos with yellow eyes; Quinlan Vos wordlessly pleading as she watched him be . . . *let* him be . . . dragged away in torment by two of Dooku's battle droids. Could she have pressed the attack and freed him then? Could she have acted more swiftly, said something to reach him? Regret, hitherto a stranger, now dogged her tracks as constantly as her own shadow.

Though she had never been one who drank to get drunk, she discovered that drinking helped. She had exhausted both her credits and any meager sense of goodwill she'd had with Fett and his syndicate on the rescue attempt that had gone so sickeningly wrong. Ventress took on jobs as they came her way, channeling the guilt and pain into action unleashed on whatever hapless bounty she was after on any given day. Most of the credits were spent on alcohol. Sometimes, if she drank enough, she would have a dreamless sleep. Sometimes.

Ventress lost count as the days merged into weeks, then months. She had a bad shock early on, when she was knocking back a fourth shot of something strong and green and a holovid had come on with first Count Dooku's face, and then Quinlan's. They didn't know who he was, but the vidcasters referred to him as "this unknown new right hand of Count Dooku." Ventress had managed to get out before snapping and destroying the holoprojector with her lightsaber.

Quinlan's lightsaber.

Since then, she'd avoided bars with holovids, but she couldn't escape the war entirely. Soon "Dooku's mystery man" was "Dooku's new admiral," complete with a colorful nickname already: "Admiral Enigma," and people were gossiping about him as often as not. Ventress was dimly aware that at least one battle had been won by the former Jedi Master, but she left before the number of casualties had been revealed.

Sometimes, when she had been drinking extra heavily, Ventress grew paranoid. She became convinced that Vos was sending people after her, to finish the job of executing the murderous woman who had so hatefully deceived him. Ventress would begin watching the shadows, and more than once she had inadvertently terrorized an innocent passerby.

Tonight, Ventress hadn't been drinking hard—well, not yet—and she was still getting the sensation that she was being watched. She frowned into her beverage, tossed some credits onto the bar, then looked around with feigned casualness. No one stood out particularly; then again, if this being were good at his/her/its job, she wouldn't immediately notice. Ventress rose, taking care to wobble the precise amount that would suggest that she'd had a little too much to drink without overdoing it, and left the bar with an exaggeratedly careful stride.

Days and nights down here on 1313 were dark, but there was always someone out on the streets. Most beings gave her a wide berth. As she faux-stumbled down the alley behind the bar, dodging piles of refuse and snoring drunks, Ventress listened carefully. She heard nothing out of the ordinary, but she couldn't shake the feeling. She turned the corner, pressed herself into the side of the building, and waited.

A few seconds later, a shape emerged. Ventress reached out in the Force, seized her stalker, raised him up into the air and slammed him down. An instant later she had a knee on his chest, and the glow of the lightsaber a few centimeters from his throat revealed the large, startled eyes and furry muzzle of a Mahran. He made no move to resist her.

"Give me one reason I shouldn't kill you," Ventress demanded.

"We have a mutual friend," the Mahran replied.

"I don't have friends." She brought the sizzling green blade closer, singeing the fur along his neck.

He stayed motionless. "I have a weapon at my waist. Take it."

Ventress reached with her free hand, still keeping the lightsaber a centimeter from his throat. Her hand closed on something cylindrical and made of cool metal, and her eyes widened as she looked at the lightsaber.

Slowly, Ventress sat back, removing her weapon but not extinguishing it. She kept his lightsaber.

"Start talking."

"They didn't tell me you were quite so fast," said the Mahran, relief in his voice. He sat up, slowly and carefully lest she change her mind.

"I can be even faster. What do the Jedi want with me?" she asked, adding bitterly, "This time?"

"My name is Desh, and the Jedi don't know I'm here. I'm . . . Quinlan Vos was one of my best friends."

Surprising, how much hearing his name still hurt. "Jedi aren't supposed to have best friends."

"Since when was Vos a typical Jedi?"

"You have a point. Go on."

Desh looked somber. "We know about what happened. With Dooku. And . . . with you."

"And what, exactly, do the Jedi think they know about me?"

"Master Kenobi said he spoke with you. You came to him, and told him what happened to Vos." He was avoiding the question. "Some of us wanted to go after him. We've been overruled. So far."

Now she understood. "And you thought that if I were involved, I could help."

Desh bared his teeth in what was clearly a sheepish grin rather than a threat, and scratched behind one vulpine ear. "Um . . . well, yes. I thought that if I could talk to you, I could . . . well . . ." His large golden eyes met hers. "Convince you to come back to the Temple with me."

"Kenobi sent you?"

"Like I said, the Jedi don't know I'm here. But I am willing to bet that if he did know, Master Kenobi would be glad. Sometimes it's better to ask forgiveness than permission."

"How do I know this isn't a trap?"

"You don't. And I won't force you to come with me. But if you walk away from this . . . Vos won't stand a chance."

Ventress appraised him. Desh did seem like the sort of being that Vos would have gravitated toward. It wasn't anything she could put a name to, but she could picture them getting into scrapes together. She reached into the Force, and sensed from the Mahran only genuine concern.

She thought back on the existence she'd led for the last few months, and her stomach soured. If there was even a chance the Jedi were, indeed, willing to help—

Ventress stood. "What are you waiting for? Let's go."

Ventress, Desh, Obi-Wan Kenobi, and a clearly unhappy Anakin Skywalker entered the Council chambers just in time for bad news. The Council members were watching a holofeed of a terrible battle. Republic and Separatist fighters and attack cruisers were engaged in combat. As Kenobi watched, a dreadnought came into view, targeting a cruiser. The Republic vessel cracked in half under the onslaught. Fire, fed by the ship's own supply of oxygen, roiled upward.

Yoda eyed Ventress with mild surprise and pressed a button, pausing the holo. Others reacted in a much more vigorous manner. Mace Windu got to his feet, one hand going to his lightsaber. Ki-Adi-Mundi, Shaak Ti, and Plo Koon, also present, did the same.

"Asajj Ventress," Windu snapped, "thank you for making the job of arresting you so much easier."

Ventress threw Kenobi a shocked and furious glance. Kenobi lifted a hand. "No, Master Windu," he said calmly. "Ventress came here in good faith and of her own free will to offer what help she could. I have given her my word that she would come to no harm within the Temple walls, and I will keep that promise."

Everyone turned to Yoda. The ancient Jedi Master regarded Ventress steadily, assessing her. Ventress straightened and did not shirk the scrutiny. Kenobi recalled that the last time the two had met, Ventress had used lies and deception in an attempt to kill Yoda, but the head of the Council was his usual calm self. Finally, he nodded.

"Asajj Ventress," he greeted her. "A liar of Master Kenobi, we will not make. Grateful we are for your help. Questions for you, we have."

"Get on with it," Ventress replied, crossing her arms.

"You will speak to Master Yoda with respect," Windu said.

"I will speak my truth however I please."

"If it is, indeed, truth," said Plo Koon.

"Please, Masters," said Kenobi. "Let's just get to the business at hand, shall we?"

"Fine," Windu said. "You and Vos were close, weren't you?"

"You could say that," Ventress said, her expression revealing nothing. "We were working well as a team."

"So, it was a professional relationship, then?" asked Kenobi.

Ventress rolled her eyes. "Just spit it out, Kenobi."

He took a deep breath. "Very well. Did you become lovers?"

She had to have been expecting this, but couldn't hide her reaction. A pained look flitted across her strong features, and her body hitched, ever so slightly.

"Yes," she said, quietly. Everyone exchanged glances.

Kenobi had suspected as much. He felt a stab of pity for the woman standing before them. There had been a time when he would have rejected such a statement as a flat-out impossibility, but he knew she told the truth.

"Did you teach Master Vos the ways of the Sith?" asked Plo Koon.

Ventress closed her eyes and inhaled deeply, pressing her lips into a thin line. Kenobi hoped she would deny it, but feared he knew better.

"Not . . . as such."

"What is that supposed to mean?" Anakin snapped. Kenobi lifted his hand and Anakin fell silent.

"Continue, you may," Yoda said, not unkindly.

Ventress spoke to Yoda directly. "Sometimes, you must fight fire with fire. Vos wasn't ready to take on Dooku. Managed correctly, the dark side would give him the edge so that we could complete the mission. I know the danger of even the smallest misstep."

"You tried to 'manage' the dark side?" Kenobi asked, incredulously. "Knowing the danger you were putting him in?"

Ventress regarded him steadily, coldly. "It was a calculated risk."

"But you pushed him, didn't you?" said Mace. "You pushed him too far."

Her jaw tightened. When she spoke, her voice was icy with controlled anger. "I was trying to protect him in the only way I knew how!"

"By leading him by the hand straight into hell?"

Ventress clenched her fists, clearly struggling not to leap at Windu. Equally clear to Obi-Wan was the fact that the Jedi Master might have welcomed the excuse to attack her. Ventress's breath came in quick, angry gasps as she spoke.

"I will remind you all that it was you who assigned him this mission. It was you who led him to me. Everyone in this room knew who and what I was from the beginning, Windu. Don't fool yourself—the blame isn't mine alone to bear."

It was a brutal truth, but truth it was nonetheless,

and the Council knew it. An uncomfortable silence fell.

"Care for him still, do you?" asked Yoda gently.

Ventress looked as though she sensed a trap, but knew better than to lie to so many Jedi Masters. She didn't look at anyone as she spoke. "Yes."

"Enough to become Sith again yourself?" Kenobi asked the obvious question before Windu could.

Ventress took a long time in replying. Finally, she lifted her head and looked at Yoda. "No."

Yoda nodded. "Further questions, has the Council?" No one spoke. "Jedi Knights Desh and Skywalker, outside with Ventress you will wait. Speak with the Council alone, I must."

CHAPTER TWENTY-SEVEN

Ventress looked wary, but she accompanied Desh and Anakin outside into the corridor. When the doors closed, Yoda looked around at the Council.

"Cooperative, has she been."

"As much as someone like her can be, yes," Kenobi agreed.

"Truth has she spoken, within this chamber. Loves Vos still, she does, and lead us to him, she will."

"And when we find him? What then?" Ki-Adi-Mundi asked. "We have seen what 'Admiral Enigma' has done already. If we do not successfully capture him and he escapes, then we have turned another Sith Lord out into the galaxy."

"If we can take him, we can turn him back," Kenobi said.

"You cannot save everyone, Master Kenobi," Plo Koon said, not without sympathy.

Yoda nodded. "Save themselves, they must."

"I understand that, Master Yoda," Kenobi said. "But if given permission to mount a recovery, I will take responsibility for Vos myself. I was his supervisor for the original mission. I alone will see it through."

"Even if we do manage to capture him successfully, how do we know we can trust him? He was introduced to the dark side by that woman, and is now Dooku's pet," Mace pointed out. "Those roots go deep."

"With respect, Master Windu, I believe that Ventress was right. We bear more than a little accountability for what has happened to Vos. He was raised in the Temple, so there is no excuse for him not being properly prepared to face this sort of challenge."

"To which 'challenge' do you refer, Master Kenobi," Mace inquired caustically, "Dooku or Ventress?"

"Both," Kenobi said. "Ventress is at fault, yes, and of course Dooku. But this, Masters . . . this one is *our* responsibility. We owe Vos the chance to choose again, and, with our help, wisely."

"Then I believe that Ventress should not be part of the rescue mission," Mace asserted.

Yoda shook his head, looking pensive. "Key to this, she is," he said. "Need her, we will. Master Kenobi—permission you have, to recover Quinlan Vos. But not alone will you be. Jedi Skywalker and Ventress both, you will take."

"I do not understand, Master Yoda," Windu said, his voice betraying his exasperation. "I yield to your wisdom. But I think we all must be aware of the disaster we are courting if we're wrong."

"Believe me," Kenobi said, "I am more than aware."

A small light built into the curve of Yoda's chair began to flash. "A message, we have," Yoda murmured, and pressed the button.

A holographic image of Admiral Wulf Yularen appeared in the middle of the room. "Master Yoda," he said in his clipped, elegant voice, "we have received new intel on Count Dooku and his Admiral Enigma."

"Bring in Ventress!" Yoda snapped. Kenobi ushered Ventress, Anakin, and Desh into the chamber. Ventress started to object and jerk her arm away, but Kenobi hushed her with a gesture.

"Proceed, Admiral," Yoda said.

"We have a sighting that places Enigma on a *Providence*-class dreadnought," Yularen continued. "We're currently investigating rumors that this ship is about to attack Taris."

"Ventress," said Kenobi, turning to her and smiling mildly, "are you up for a trip?"

Ventress looked from Admiral Yularen, to Yoda, and then back to Kenobi. "You've got to be joking."

"You know as well as I do that there is still hope for him."

"I don't know that," she said bluntly. Kenobi was surprised. Mace Windu frowned, leaning forward. "You weren't there. You didn't see his face. You don't know how hard it is to come back from—"

"You did it," Kenobi interrupted quietly.

Ventress paused in midsentence, her eyes looking piercingly into his. He could sense how stunned she was by his recognition of what she had done. Some of the heat had gone from her voice as she replied, "Just barely."

"But still," Kenobi pressed, "you understand what it takes. There may be a chance for him yet, but we have to stop him before he goes any farther down that path, or it might indeed be too late."

Ventress glanced around at the Masters regarding her, her gaze lingering upon each one. Her chin lifted slightly at Windu's open disapproval.

"I'll do it, but how do I know you won't arrest me upon our return?"

"Well," Kenobi hedged.

"A pardon, the Council will offer." Everyone turned to look at the diminutive Master. He was smiling gently, his eyes kind. "A clean slate, Asajj Ventress shall have, if help us, she will."

Anakin shifted his weight. "That's . . . quite the deal, Master Yoda," he said.

"A Jedi Master recovered, and to the light returned? Little enough, it is, for so great a deed."

Ventress looked as if she couldn't believe what she was hearing, and if the truth were to be told, Kenobi could scarcely believe it himself. But he found that he agreed.

"Accept, do you?" Yoda asked.

Ventress nodded. "I do. But you're going to have to trust me."

Anakin, of course, didn't trust Ventress as far as he could Force-throw her. Kenobi did—to an extent. He trusted Ventress to not do something that would get them all killed, and . . . he trusted what he believed she felt for Vos. It remained to be seen, of course, if Vos returned her sentiments, and if so, that would have to be dealt with. But all that could wait until they had brought the Jedi Master safely back home.

Anakin fidgeted. Kenobi could hardly blame him. It was not a place he had ever dreamed he'd willingly be, yet here they both were in the *Banshee*'s cockpit.

"And you're certain the ship's cloaking device is active?" Anakin asked uneasily. "I don't want to be hurtling out of hyperspace unprotected into the path of a dozen Separatist cruisers . . ."

Ventress smiled a little. "I'm as sure as I'm going to be. Have a little faith, Skywalker."

"Faith? In *you*?"

"I'm the only chance you've got right now, so yes, you'd better have faith. Here goes nothing. Fingers crossed, boys." She pressed the button with a long forefinger, and they dropped out of hyperspace into the very center of a crowded flow of dozens of Separatist vessels, everything from starfighters to frigates to Dooku's looming flagship.

"Oh, boy," muttered Anakin.

"It isn't . . . too bad," Kenobi said, sounding unconvincing even in his own ears. He and Anakin exchanged tense glances.

Ventress stretched, catlike, in the chair. "And nobody seems to notice us. How about that?"

While Anakin scowled at Ventress, whose smirk only grew, Kenobi put in, "Well, it would be nice if we actually had a plan."

Ventress's stony look returned, and she ceased toying with Anakin. "I believe the plan was to get Vos off that ship."

She pointed at the enormous *Providence*-class dreadnought that was leading the fleet. Ventress slowed and allowed the *Banshee* to drop back, carefully maneuvering out of the path of any of the other ships—which were, thankfully, clearly unaware of their presence. Obi-Wan could see the ship's hangar. The doors were open, but of course there would be a particle shield erected to prevent anyone or anything from entering or departing without permission.

"And exactly how do you intend to do that?" Anakin asked.

"I worked with the Separatists once, remember? They have a finite number of channels and codes that vary depending on the sector and the name of the operation's flagship. Given that, I think it should be . . ." She touched the controls.

"—permission to depart" came a voice.

Obi-Wan and Anakin exchanged glances. The elder Jedi was impressed

"Code?"

"AYF-47562."

"Permission granted," said the voice. And while the fighter eased out to join its fellows, Ventress brought the cloaked *Banshee* smoothly inside. She landed it gently, any noise it might have made covered by the sound of the fighter's departure. There was a slight shimmering around the entrance to the hangar as the force field was reactivated. The lights inside the hangar dimmed, indicating that attention was no longer on the area. Ventress did a quick scan for droids or life-forms.

"We're clear," she said, and lowered the ramp.

"Okay," Anakin said grudgingly, "that was . . . um . . . not too shabby. Now we just have to figure out where Vos would be."

"Well," Kenobi said, lifting a hand and casually using the Force to short out the security cams, "since he is apparently an admiral, he's bound to be on the bridge."

"What about Dooku?" asked Ventress.

Anakin's face hardened. "I'll take care of him. Looks like we might get two for one today—Dooku's death and Vos's return."

"May the Force be with us," Kenobi murmured, and they began the hunt.

CHAPTER TWENTY-EIGHT

Ventress wished they could simply charge through the ship, destroying anything and anyone that got in their way. But while she was passionate, she was also practical. Stealth had gotten them into the ship; stealth would have to get them to the bridge.

Only once before had she worked in a similar manner with so many fellow Force users: when she, Karis, and Naa'leth had attempted to kill Dooku. She had to admit that both Skywalker and Kenobi were stronger in the Force than her sisters had been. Together they were extremely powerful. It was a pity that the three of them and Vos could not team up against Dooku. The sleemo wouldn't stand a chance.

Vos. Ventress felt again the stab of doubt. It had been impossible to entirely escape the images of his face on the HoloNet. And she'd seen the telltale yellow of his eyes in Dooku's prison. But there had been that moment—when she had fully owned her lies and laid herself open to his judgment—when Vos had hesitated, and Ventress had seen the true Vos still inside. He had understood how hard it had been for her, if only fleetingly. Was it really possible that she could reach him again? Or had Dooku so dominated him that there was nothing left of the man she . . .

Well. If he was lost, she would do what was necessary without a second thought. It would be what the real Vos, the Jedi, would want her to do. Ventress recalled the difficulty with which Vos had finally reconciled himself to killing a simple, nonsentient creature. That man would be horrified to be used by Dooku to kill thousands of innocent beings.

With what felt like agonizing slowness, they made their way through the ship, hiding from wandering patrols of droids, and shorting out any security cams before they could be detected.

They paused at the end of the hallway. "There's a corridor directly below us," Ventress said. "We go down that and the set of doors at the end opens onto the bridge."

"You're sure?" asked Kenobi.

"I've spent a great deal of time on this ship," Ventress said. "The bridge is three levels. The captain's chair is on the first level, facing forward. There will be eight computer stations, each operated by a droid. Possibly, there will be other droids on the bridge."

"So, ten, maybe twelve," Anakin said. "No problem."

"Where will Vos be?"

"In the captain's chair," Ventress said grimly. "We can take either the ladder"—she pointed to a narrow set of rungs to one side—"or the lift. The ladder's safer. We'll be able to spot any droids in the corridor before we come across them. If we take the lift, we can't control what it would open up on."

"Agreed," said Kenobi. "I'll go first. Anakin, you bring up the rear." Ventress stifled her irritation. Even now, they didn't trust her.

Kenobi climbed quickly and quietly down the ladder, pausing to listen and extend his senses with the Force before dropping down. Ventress and Anakin followed.

Ventress pointed to the far end of the corridor. "Those are the doors to the bridge. They're motion-sensitive, so they'll open automatically. We'll—"

There was a soft ding behind them and the lift doors opened. They whirled. A single, very puzzled-looking battle droid peered at them, then summoned the presence of mind to yelp into its comlink, "Intruder alert!"

"Not so fast!" Obi-Wan punched the droid in the face and it staggered back. Kenobi closed the door on it, ignited his lightsaber, and melted the controls. "Let's go!" The three of them raced down the hall and flung themselves through the door onto the bridge.

The figure in the captain's chair had risen. His lightsaber was in his hand but not yet activated. His brows were drawn together in a thunderous scowl as he shouted, his voice dripping loathing, *"Jedi!"*

"Dooku!" exclaimed Kenobi, surprised. "You weren't the fellow we were looking for, but since you're here—"

Skywalker, however, wasted no time in banter. He leapt at once for Dooku. Blue and red lightsabers clashed and sizzled. The droids had begun firing, and Kenobi batted the bolts back with practiced ease, doing his best to angle the shots so they returned to the droid that fired them.

Ventress paid neither Dooku nor the battle droids any heed. She vaulted down to the third, lowest level. Still crouching, she thrust out both hands, Force-grabbed a droid in each one, flung them behind her. Both droids hurtled toward the lightsaber combatants. Dooku glanced up and sprang down to the second level. Anakin followed him.

Two droids approached Kenobi, firing at him simultaneously. The Jedi Master leapt upward, clinging briefly to the ceiling as the droids realized, too late, that they were now firing at each other.

"He's not here!" Ventress shouted over her shoulder to Obi-Wan. She sliced the head off of one battle droid, Force-threw another against the bulkhead. Six remained.

"Get back up here and cover me!" Kenobi shouted, fighting his way over to one of the consoles on the first level. Ventress leapt across the bridge and positioned herself between Kenobi, who was checking the ship's computer in an attempt to locate Vos, and the droids who were firing on him. She spared a glance for Dooku, one level down. The fight between him and Anakin was close and constantly shifting. Ventress felt a brief flash of amusement as she realized that for the first time, she was actually rooting for Skywalker.

Dooku made claws of his hands, and Force lightning crackled in the space between him and Anakin. Skywalker got his lightsaber up and held his own, slitting his eyes against the blue glare and flying sparks. Still sending Force lightning with one hand, Dooku reached out with the other. A dismembered droid torso shot up in the air, hovered there, and then Dooku flung it at Anakin. The Jedi leapt down to the third level, and the count followed him.

With their master otherwise occupied on the other side of the bridge, the remaining droids opened fire freely. Dozens of bolts streaked toward Ventress and Kenobi. Calmly, Ventress batted back some with her lightsaber; the others she simply redirected using the

Force. Three more droids fell, twitching and sparking.

"I've got him!" Kenobi shouted to be heard over the noise of combat. "Ventress, he's not on the bridge because he's in the brig! He's still a captive! Do you realize what this means? There *is* no 'Admiral Enigma.' Dooku's been using Vos as a tool to lower Jedi morale!"

Ventress was flooded by joy so intense that she almost couldn't breathe. Renewed energy filled her and she reached out, grabbed a protesting droid in the Force, and smashed him down.

"You two go on!" called Anakin. He dodged a strike from Dooku's red lightsaber that whizzed past the top of his head and brought his own blade up for a counterstrike. "I'll take care of *him*!"

"Insolent whelp," snapped Dooku, parrying Skywalker's strike.

Together Ventress and Kenobi cut down the remaining droids. Debris toppled everywhere, legs and arms, heads and parts of torsos. When they reached the door and raced through it, Ventress took a moment to pierce the controls with her lightsaber.

"Anakin's still in there," Kenobi said.

"So is Dooku," she retorted. "And this way, he can't summon droids to improve his odds."

"Excellent point," Kenobi conceded. "The brig is—"

"On the level below us," Ventress said. "Come on!"

Vos hung, naked to the waist, from glowing shackles. His back was toward Kenobi, and Obi-Wan felt a pang of empathetic pain at the sight. Dooku, it seemed, had decided to forgo more elaborate methods of torture in favor of the basic ones. Vos's broad back was a ribbon of older scars and newer welts; some were scabbed over, and not a few were still bleeding. His once-muscular but sleek frame was emaciated and pale, as if he had not seen the sunlight in months. He appeared to be unconscious.

"Vos!" Kenobi rushed forward. He cradled Vos's brutalized body in one arm while he slashed with his lightsaber at the shackles. Vos cried out sharply as his arms shifted from the position they had been forced to maintain for who knew how long. Obi-Wan eased him to the floor.

"Obi-Wan? Is it really you?" Vos's voice was ragged.

"Yes, it's me, old friend."

"Is Ventress . . . ?" Vos looked around and his face lit up. "Asajj!" Wincing at the pain the motion cost him, he reached out to her. But strangely, she hung back, reminding Obi-Wan of a wild animal about to bolt. Vos appeared not to notice. "I dreamed of you. I'm so glad you're here, so glad . . ."

"Can you walk?" Kenobi asked.

"Yes, I think so . . ." With Kenobi's help, Vos awkwardly got to his feet. His gaze was fixed on Ventress, and his smile faded at the look on her face. "Asajj?"

Vos moved toward her. She took a step back, narrowing her eyes. "I'm so sorry I attacked you. I had to."

She scoffed. "Forgive me if I find that hard to believe."

"You know Dooku." Even speaking seemed to tire Vos. "He records everything. There were devices in my cell, and I had to let him think he'd turned me. But I—I couldn't keep up the act."

Again, Vos reached out for her. "He suspected I

hadn't turned and put me back here. He comes and tells me all the things that I've done as his 'admiral.' Ventress, I—"

"Stop it!" she shouted. "Kenobi—we're too late!"

"What?" Kenobi was shocked.

"I saw his eyes then, and I can feel the fury inside him now. He's just itching to break our necks!" Ventress activated her lightsaber and brought it in front of her, holding it with both hands and poised to attack. The green light illuminated the glitter of unshed tears in her eyes.

"Now, hang on a moment, Ventress—" Kenobi said soothingly, trying to calm her through the Force.

"Asajj, how can you say that? It's still me." Vos put a hand on his chest, which was also bleeding from recent lacerations. "It's still your Quinlan. I've not changed, I swear. I'm the same."

"The same as you were when you tried to cut my head off with your Master's lightsaber?"

"Wait, what?" Kenobi looked at Vos searchingly. The other Jedi turned to him, pleading. Kenobi reached into the Force and tried to sense what Ventress claimed to feel. Vos was physically weakened, disoriented, and in pain both physically and emotionally, but any darkness Kenobi could pick up on was that of simple despair.

"I don't sense anything sinister, Ventress," Kenobi said slowly. "I think perhaps your emotions are clouding your judgment."

She looked at him as if he had suggested they sprout wings and fly. "My emotions allow me to see the *truth*! This is a trick! How can you not sense it? The hatred is seeping out of his pores!" Ventress looked back at Vos, shifting her weight on the balls of her feet. "My connection to the dark side was tenuous at best, and even I could barely pull away from its grasp." She swallowed hard. "Vos . . . has been consumed."

Shock rippled through the Force as Vos stared at her, stunned. "Ventress—"

"Shut up!" she screamed. "I can't listen to your lies any longer. I . . ." Again, the tears glittered in her eyes. When she spoke, it was in a broken whisper.

"I am so sorry. This is the only way you can be free."

And she brought the lightsaber sweeping down.

CHAPTER TWENTY-NINE

Obi-Wan sprang in front of Ventress, his lightsaber hissing and crackling against hers. He pushed her back, shouting her name, but she was beyond reason. She leapt over him, landing in front of Vos. The Jedi fell to his knees, throwing up his hands to Force-shove her backward. He was so weak that even this attack to save his own life merely pushed Ventress back a few steps. That was enough for Kenobi to land a flying kick to Ventress's hip and she stumbled, turning the fall into a flip and landing facing Kenobi.

"Why can't you feel it?" she cried, and her sincerity and pain were so real that Kenobi felt a rush of pity.

"Ventress, think for a moment! This place is steeped in dark side energy! And Vos is in terrible pain!"

Ventress didn't pause. She was a righteous angel, intent on destroying the thing she believed Vos to have become, and for a fleeting instant Kenobi wondered if he ever appeared that way to those he was forced to slay. Then all thought needed to be focused on preventing Ventress from murdering the very man they had come to rescue.

"Get out of the way!" Kenobi shouted to Vos. Vos

obliged, supporting himself by leaning on the wall as he put distance between the two combatants.

"You don't understand," Ventress cried. "You weren't *there*!" She whirled, targeting Kenobi now instead of Vos. Her green lightsaber was a blur and Kenobi was hard-pressed to parry.

"You know," he said, slipping his blade alongside hers then twisting it to throw her off balance, "I rather think fighting you was easier when I was trying to kill you."

Vos leaned against the wall, panting, his torso slick with blood and sweat. From his position he could see down the next corridor. "We've got company!" he shouted, and sure enough, Kenobi could hear the clatter of metallic feet.

Ventress abruptly dodged Kenobi's blow and returned her focus to Vos. By this point Obi-Wan was not just alarmed by Ventress's single-minded and inexplicable distrust of Vos, but growing profoundly exasperated.

"Ventress, by all that is good in this galaxy, can we *please* settle this later?" He reached out in the Force, lifted her up, and plunked her a few meters farther down the corridor the way they had come. "Go!" he shouted.

In their many previous encounters, Kenobi had taunted Ventress by reminding her how good she was at running away. But this time, for one terrible moment, Kenobi was afraid Ventress was willing to sacrifice them all if it would ensure Vos's destruction. Fortunately, her survival instinct kicked in and with a frustrated growl, she sprinted off.

The droids were closing on them. Blasts ricocheted off the curving metal walls and illuminated the hallway with red light. Kenobi pulled the weaponless Vos in front of him, supporting the weakened man with one hand while partially turning around to bat back the blasterfire.

Abruptly Ventress skidded to a halt. Vos and Kenobi almost ran into her. A fraction of an instant later a circular chunk of the corridor's ceiling crashed straight down in front of them. Standing in the center of the metallic circle was Anakin Skywalker. His lightsaber was still lit, and the circle's molten rim was orange.

"Hi, Vos," Anakin said. "Nice to see you again."

"Nice to see you too, Anakin," Vos said, peering up, baffled, through the hole Anakin had just cut in the ceiling. Blasterfire pelted down, and the four of them leapt forward, heading toward the hangar and escape.

Droids dropped through the hole, some of them landing atop their fellows that had pursued the group from Vos's cell. Squeaks of "Hey, watch it!" and "Ow!" ensued from the hapless droids, but soon enough the clankers were again in pursuit—and firing.

The Jedi and Ventress made it to the hangar and raced up the ramp to the *Banshee*. Vos all but fell into one of the seats in the hold, fumbling at the straps. Kenobi stilled his hands and began to secure his friend while Ventress began to fire up the ship.

"Come on," she muttered under her breath, then cursed. "They've changed the code for the shield! I'll have to try to figure it out again."

"And now they're closing the doors," Anakin said. Kenobi looked up from Vos to see that Anakin was right.

"Can you get us free?" Kenobi asked.

Ventress's fingers flew over the controls. "Maybe," she said, "but that door is closing fast and the droids will be here any minute!"

Vos looked up. "I know where both sets of controls are," he said. Before Kenobi could stop him, the injured Jedi had risen and was opening the ramp.

"No!" shouted Ventress. She sprang from the pilot's chair and jumped down into the hold, trying to tackle him. Kenobi grabbed her arm. Startled, she wrenched it free, but Vos had already jumped to the ground and raced out of sight.

"You let him get away!" Ventress snarled. "Don't you see? He's not coming back!"

She drew back her fist, but Anakin's hand shot out to grab it. "Settle down, Ventress," Anakin snapped. "We don't know anything for sure!"

"*I* do!" Ventress stabbed at her chest with a forefinger so hard that Kenobi thought the gesture would leave a bruise. "*I* know he's fallen! And I know he can't be brought back."

"Um . . . Ventress?" Anakin pointed, and Ventress looked through the viewport. The hangar doors had stopped closing, and then a heartbeat later, they began to reopen.

"Check the controls!" Kenobi said. "Is the shield deactivated?"

Ventress was already back in her seat. "We're free," she said, confusion in her voice.

"And here comes Vos," Kenobi said, unable to keep the triumph out of his voice as he waved his friend forward. Ventress turned to look, emotions warring on her face. Blasterfire screamed, and it seemed impossible that Vos wouldn't be struck by it.

"Go! Go! Go!" Vos shouted, leaping for the ramp. He struck it clumsily, crying out with pain, clambering aboard as it retracted. Ventress didn't give him a second glance—all of her attention was on getting them out of there. They were out of the hangar just as the ramp door closed, with the droids' blasters catching the stern of the ship.

"Great job, Vos!" Anakin enthused. "It's good to have you back." Vos had his eyes closed, gritting his teeth against the pain. Some of his wounds had reopened and were weeping blood.

"Strap yourselves in," Ventress called back to them, "we're not out of trouble yet!"

Ventress's warning had come just in time. Dooku had launched fighters after them. Kenobi's spirits sank even farther when he realized that these were droid tri-fighters, so called because of their trio of arms, each fitted with a light laser cannon. The arms surrounded a gyroscopic ball in which its droid pilot was seated. The core was equipped with a large laser cannon. Devoid of sentient, living beings, the tri-fighters were not only flown by an integrated droid brain, but dispatched discord missiles bearing buzz droids—small droids that attached themselves to the target and set about disabling it. Everything hinged on Ventress's skills now.

"How fast can you jump to hyperspace?" Anakin asked.

"Not fast enough," Ventress said. "Skywalker, I need you on the triple blaster. Kenobi, you're on one of the laser cannons."

"What about me?" Vos asked her.

"You stay put."

"Ventress, this is foolish, I know this ship like the back of—"

Kenobi's stomach dropped out as Ventress plunged, darting beneath one of the tri-fighters, then soared upward in a loop, coming perilously close to another one.

"Ventress, what are you doing?" shouted Anakin

as he lurched into the cockpit. "Are you trying to get us all killed?"

"I'm trying . . . to do the . . . exact opposite," Ventress grunted. The ship veered hard to port, then lurched up again. Kenobi understood her tactics. Ventress was flying like a madwoman because that was the one thing the droids could not counter— irrationality. They expected their enemy to behave in a logical fashion. For instance, Ventress's present tactic of flying straight at them—

"Damn it, Ventress, let me help!" shouted Vos.

It was obvious Ventress wanted Vos to touch nothing on the ship, but Kenobi had an idea. "Vos," he called as he fired the laser cannon at one of the enemy vessels, "keep an eye out for the buzz droids! If you see them coming, use the Force to send them back to their ships!"

"Whoa!" exclaimed Anakin as the ship turned upside down—and kept flying that way.

"Here we go!" shouted Ventress. And just as one of the droid ships directed a blossom of laserfire at them, Kenobi saw the welcome sight of the stars appearing to turn into streaks of light as they made the jump, at last, into hyperspace.

Everybody leaned backward, indulging in relief. "Now then," Kenobi said briskly, unfastening Vos's shoulder harness and locating a medpac, "let's see about your injuries, Vos."

"I'm fine," Vos replied.

"No, you're not," Skywalker said, "and I bet Ventress doesn't want blood on her containment chair."

Vos tensed at the mention of her name. Kenobi shot his former apprentice a glare. Too late, Anakin realized his faux pas and mouthed, *Oops, sorry.*

Vos's wounds were sterilized and bandaged in awkward silence. There were so very *many* of them,

Kenobi thought. He stepped forward when Anakin was done.

"I brought an extra cloak," Kenobi told Vos. "Here." Vos accepted it, shaking his head as Obi-Wan tried to assist him. He paled slightly as the rough brown fabric touched his brutalized torso, but made no word of complaint. For a moment, Vos seemed lost in thought, then he rose. He ascended the ladder to the cockpit slowly, lips tightly closed against any utterance of pain. Kenobi and Anakin exchanged uncomfortable glances; they were close enough to the cockpit so they'd hear everything the two said. Which was, honestly, the last thing Kenobi wanted.

"Ventress," Vos said quietly, "I never meant . . ." His voice trailed off. Kenobi thought that would be the end of it, but Vos tried again.

"I thought for sure you would understand what I was doing. You know how Dooku thinks. Did you believe that there would be a minute when I wasn't under surveillance? I never meant to hurt you. I was just playing a part. We—"

"There is no 'we' anymore." Ventress's voice was pure acid. Kenobi sensed the underlying anguish that turned it so very bitter. "The Quinlan Vos I knew is dead."

Kenobi could feel how the words bit. "Please . . . ," Vos began.

"Stay out of my way, or I will kill you."

Even Anakin winced at that one. A moment later Vos made his painful way down the ladder and slumped back in his seat. He looked as if all the pain of the entire galaxy had descended upon his lacerated shoulders.

The three Jedi sat in awkward silence. Anakin and Kenobi couldn't pretend they hadn't overheard. Although Vos was clearly distressed by Ventress's cutting words, in the long run a Jedi could not have attachments. Vos would, one day—soon, Kenobi hoped—be grateful to Ventress for not prolonging what could not be. Even so, he found himself wanting to offer words of comfort. He was surprised when Anakin beat him to it.

"She'll come around," Anakin said kindly. "We know it's really you who's come back to us."

"Yes," Kenobi said. "She'll realize the truth soon enough."

Vos looked at them with anguished dark eyes, then buried his face in his hands.

It was a long trip home.

CHAPTER THIRTY

Desh stood just outside the Jedi Council Chamber. His muzzle was split with a huge grin, revealing sharp white teeth. "You're late," he said. "As usual."

Ventress watched as Vos's eyes lit up and he extended his hand to his friend. Desh moved as if to clap Vos's shoulder, then paused as he noticed the cloak—and a glimpse of the bandaged flesh it hid. His ebullience faded and he said, "I'll save the welcome-home roughhousing for later."

"I'd appreciate that," Vos said. He gave a tired smile.

How could none of them feel it? Ventress wondered. Vos's eyes hadn't changed color, not once, but the dark side wrapped his soul as the cloak wrapped his body. Her heart broke every time she tried to second-guess herself and opened to the Force. She hadn't lied to him. Vos—*her* Vos—was dead. Murdered by Dooku . . . and, Ventress had to acknowledge, by her. She'd thought she was strengthening Vos by lying to him about Tholme, but instead she had handed Dooku the perfect weapon.

He also hadn't been ready for the Sleeper. She'd

pushed too hard, too fast. He had needed more time—time to work with both the dark and the light, to understand the balancing point between the two so that he could do what was needed and still stay himself.

Perhaps it would have been better if they had died, together, fighting the count, never knowing what pain lay in store.

"Ventress?" Skywalker said, in a tone of voice that indicated it wasn't the first time he'd spoken her name. Ventress snapped out of her bleak reverie and followed them into the Council Chamber. The wary looks cast in her direction did not escape her notice, nor did the fact that every Jedi present, with the exception of Vos and Yoda, had a hand on his or her lightsaber.

"Master Quinlan Vos," Yoda said, his voice warm with affection. "Happy you are back, we are."

"Thank you, Master Yoda. It's good to be back."

"A difficult time, you have had. Yet strong, you have stayed."

"Most would have broken under Dooku's . . . tutoring," Mace Windu said. "Master Kenobi and Jedi Skywalker have assured us that is not the case."

Ventress bit her lip, hard. She'd tried to warn them. If she protested now, they wouldn't believe her. She could only hope that Vos would give himself away at some point. It was not her job to save the Jedi from their own blindness.

"Asajj Ventress," Yoda said. She looked up, meeting his eyes evenly. "Return something that was lost, you have. Grateful, we are."

"To show our appreciation for your aid in the rescue of Master Quinlan Vos," Windu said stiffly, "the Council honors its promise to grant you an official pardon for *all* of your past misdeeds. From this moment forward, consider yourself an unmarked woman."

Ventress felt Vos's gaze on her. She refused to look at him. She shrugged, uncomfortable for about a thousand reasons with the words Windu spoke. "Thank you for your . . . generosity," she managed. Her voice sounded strangled to her own ears, and by their expressions, to theirs as well. She didn't care. She just wanted to be out of this room.

Away from the monster that wore a lover's face.

"May the Force be with you," Yoda said.

Ventress bowed perfunctorily, turned on her heel, and headed out—away from the Council Chamber, away from the Jedi, and away from Vos. As she passed Desh, he asked, "Hey, are you all right?"

Ventress paused. "No," she said, "and neither is he."

Desh looked at her, confused. Ventress continued down the hall, struggling not to break into a run. She was no longer a criminal; she had no need to flee. She heard footsteps behind her and grimaced. She probably shouldn't have said anything to the Mahran.

"Desh," Ventress said, turning, and the words died in her throat.

It was Vos. "Please," he said, "let me talk to you."

Ventress turned away quickly, continuing to stride down the hallway. "Not interested. Clearly."

"Just for a moment?" He hurried ahead of her, blocking her path. Pain at the movement rolled off him, but not the choking darkness she had sensed before. Ventress came to a stop, and her eyes searched his. There was no hint of ugly yellow or blood red in them, only the warm brown depths in which she had once lost herself.

Against her better judgment, she nodded. He jerked his head in the direction of an alcove, and Ventress followed. Vos stared at her, apparently unable to find words now that she had agreed to listen to him.

"Well?" she snapped.

"I'm so sorry."

Ventress rolled her eyes. "Not this again." She made to shove past him.

"Hey," he said, and grabbed her arm.

Cold fury shot through her and she whirled. "Take your hands off me," she demanded.

Vos obeyed at once, holding both hands up in a placating gesture. "Please," he said, "I'm . . . I'm begging you. Just hear me out."

Ventress did not try to pass him again, but neither did she look at him. Vos took a deep breath, and she sensed him still struggling for the right words. It was important to him—but she did not know whether it was because he was truly sorry, or because he was still trying to trick her. The thought knifed her.

"I made the wrong decision. I should have just seized the chance to escape when you came for me. But I thought if I stayed, I could complete the mission. I never for a moment thought you'd really believe I'd turned. If I've lost you, it wasn't worth it. *Nothing* would be worth it. I can only hope you can find your way to forgiving me, as I forgave you when you lied to me."

She had, hadn't she? Deliberately, and selfishly. Ventress knew in her heart that she could tell herself all she liked that she'd done it for the mission, but that, too, would be a lie.

"Asajj . . . Everything we had was real. It still is. My feelings for you haven't changed."

Despite herself, Ventress's heart leapt. Now she did permit herself to look at him. It was true. She could feel it in the Force. Had she been mistaken?

Then her gaze fell on the brown cloak Obi-Wan

Kenobi had placed around Vos's shoulders. She had watched the Jedi Council welcome him back. He had said nothing to *them* about his feelings for her. So, in the end, even if it were true, it meant nothing.

Ventress reached out and fingered the coarse brown fabric. "But that is not the Jedi way, is it? You've chosen your path."

She could feel his eyes as she walked away. Tears filled her own. But she didn't look back.

Anakin was able to leave the Temple and sneak into Padmé's apartments at something resembling a reasonable hour. Vos's arrival had thrown everyone into a state, and Anakin was glad of the reprieve. He marched into their living room, where Padmé was preparing a light supper for herself, and swept his petite wife into his arms for a long, passionate kiss.

"Anakin!" Her eyes sparkled with pleasure as he gently placed her down. He grinned. His name, when spoken by her lips, was the sweetest music in the galaxy.

"Were you expecting someone else?" he teased.

Padmé punched his chest playfully. "I was expecting my husband, but not so early. I'm glad."

He poured them both a glass of wine and they sat on the couch while Anakin filled her in on what had happened with Vos. He took creative license with the part about Vos being sent to assassinate Dooku. He was pretty sure a senator would not approve of such an action, and so modified "assassinate" to "capture." Chancellor Palpatine had not been informed, either; the mission was deemed to be Jedi business. Anakin wasn't sure that was the right call. It felt wrong to him for the Jedi Order to keep secrets from the Chancellor, but the decision, like so many others, was out of his hands. Padmé had met Vos on occasion, but she was not as familiar with him as she was with some of the other Jedi, so the whole story was new to her.

She listened raptly, her brown eyes wide, and when he had finished, she sighed sadly. "What do you think about all this?"

"It's a mess," Anakin said, shaking his head. "I was against the idea of Ventress being involved at all, but nobody asked my opinion."

"But you said neither you nor Obi-Wan sensed that he had gone dark. Why do you think Ventress did?"

"It's pretty clear she seduced him," Anakin said. "She's . . . kind of like that."

"And how would you know?" Padmé tried to look serious, but couldn't quite hide a smile. Anakin loved that expression of playfulness, so rarely on his serious wife's face. He brushed back a lock of her brown hair.

"Rumor has it," he said, unable to resist adding, "You should see how she flirts with Obi-Wan when they're swinging lightsabers at each other." His humor faded. "If Vos did go to the dark side, I'm pretty sure it's her fault. She as much as admitted that she wanted him to be stronger. But he couldn't handle it. Vos should never have gotten involved with her."

"You said Ventress seemed genuinely upset."

"She was. First time I've seen a real emotion out of her that didn't involve removing someone's body parts. But it doesn't matter. A Jedi isn't supposed to . . . um . . ."

Anakin's flow of words slowed as he realized how hypocritical he sounded. Padmé was watching him with a slightly wry smile, but her eyes were kind. "We're different," he said. "*We're* in love."

Padmé ran a small hand along his cheek. "Yes, we are," she said. "And maybe they are, too."

"Ventress isn't capable of anything as selfless as love," Anakin scoffed. "And Vos couldn't possibly have cared about a murderess like her. Besides, she's the one who took him to the dark side in the first place."

Padmé shrugged. "Stranger things have happened," she said. "And maybe, if she loves him, she's his way back from it."

Anakin found he had no response to that.

CHAPTER THIRTY-ONE

"Big day today for Quinlan," Desh said, falling into step with Obi-Wan Kenobi and Anakin Skywalker.

"Indeed," Kenobi said. "But I'm not terribly concerned about it. Vos has performed well on the smaller assignments the Council has given him. I've no doubt they'll pronounce him fit to take on more important ones."

Desh nodded, but he looked somewhat troubled. "Something on your mind, Jedi Akar?" Kenobi asked.

The Mahran hesitated, then said, "When she left, Ventress seemed to think that there was something wrong with Master Vos. And he's been avoiding me, I can tell."

Kenobi sighed. "It doesn't surprise me to learn that Vos might be avoiding people he'd been particularly close with, having realized the damage attachment can cause. I'm sure it's nothing you've done. As for Ventress . . . she and Vos were, ah, *entangled*. I think she was disappointed that he chose the Jedi and not her. She kept insisting that Dooku had turned him, but no one—not I, not Anakin, nor anyone on the

Council, has seen or sensed anything that leads us to believe she was correct. Ventress's emotions colored her perception, that's all."

"Or else she's just flat-out lying," Anakin put in. "I mean, come on. This *is* Asajj Ventress we're talking about."

"I prefer to give her the benefit of the doubt," Kenobi said.

"You always take the high road, Master Kenobi," said Desh. He looked relieved. "Well, I will miss knocking back drinks with Vos and reminiscing about old times, but if the trade-off is that we have him back, alive and well, there's no question that it's a minor price to pay."

"Anakin, you and Desh can wait outside if you wish. I think this is one Council meeting that won't take particularly long." Even as he had gently chided Desh for his affection toward Vos, Kenobi knew that he, himself, had not been impartial. It was difficult not to like Vos, even when one wished to strangle him. He reminded himself that he would have done the same for any Jedi.

"Master Kenobi," Yoda greeted him. "A happy duty to discharge, we do. Tell us of Master Vos, if you will."

"With pleasure, Master Yoda. I sent you all the 2-1B's reports on Vos's physical condition. He will have scars, but over the last month he has healed physically."

"And otherwise?" asked Plo Koon. "Dooku has broken others ere now. A former Jedi Master would understand our weaknesses better than any other enemy."

"I cannot deny the truth of your statement," Kenobi admitted. "Vos was . . . wounded in spirit, as well. It was for this reason that I've spent so much time in his company, and been the one to supervise his missions. But I doubt if any of us could say any differently had *we* been in Dooku's prison cell. I've seen nothing that makes me think that Quinlan Vos succumbed to the pull of the dark side—if, indeed, he ever really ventured there at all."

"It is our understanding that Asajj Ventress felt that he did," Mace Windu said.

Kenobi hesitated. Vos had never spoken of Ventress to him, except when directly asked. He was loath to place doubt if no one else knew what he did, but Kenobi felt that total honesty was the only way to truly restore Vos's reputation. Kenobi told Windu what he had said to Desh a few moments before— that he suspected the Jedi Master and the former Sith had been involved, but that it was clear that Vos had chosen the Jedi over Ventress, and she had mistaken his rejection of her for a descent into the darkness.

Most of the other Masters nodded as he spoke, but Windu frowned. "Asajj Ventress isn't a good person to develop feelings for. Are we certain she didn't just turn him over to Dooku?"

"Vos says no," Kenobi replied. "During their joint attack on Dooku, they were forced to fight both him and Grievous, as well as dozens of droids. In the end, they were simply outnumbered. I will remind the Council that Ventress even attempted a rescue mission at a later point, but failed to recover Vos."

"Because Vos didn't want to go with her," said Mace.

"Master Vos has explained what happened several times," Kenobi replied. "He's not hiding anything. He stumbled, yes, but he did not fall."

"Made his choice now, he has, and a wise one, it is," Yoda said. "Painful though it was. Satisfied, I am, with what I am hearing."

The others echoed Yoda's words, all except for Windu. "I would prefer we give him another month. Just to be certain."

"With all due respect, Master Windu," Kenobi said, "Vos has been in a unique position. For a time, he convinced Dooku that he was on the count's side—that he could be trusted. He's learned so much, and reported it all to us. Going forward, we can use that knowledge as we strategize."

"I agree, but Vos doesn't have to be in the field."

"But if he *is* there, he will be able to react immediately with any knowledge he has that we don't," Shaak Ti said. "I feel he is ready to be sent on a more delicate mission."

Windu looked troubled, but he bowed his head. "I yield to the will of the Council. Send for him."

A few moments later, Master Quinlan Vos appeared before the Jedi Council. Kenobi thought of how he had looked a few short weeks ago: malnourished, pale, bleeding, and brokenhearted. His healthy color had returned, and he now moved without any hint of pain. Quinlan Vos looked every bit the Jedi Master he was. Perhaps, mused Kenobi, this ordeal had, in a perverse way, been exactly what Vos needed to temper his occasional excessive enthusiasm.

"Performed well, you have, Master Vos," Yoda said.

"Thank you, Master Yoda," Vos said, bowing. "I want you all to know I understand why you have been so hesitant about putting me back in the field. I'd have done the same thing to anyone who'd spent months in the tender loving care of Count Dooku."

"Satisfied, we are," Yoda said. "A task for you, we have."

"I will serve you with all my ability," Vos said.

Mace Windu pressed a button on his chair. The hologram of an asteroid appeared in the center of the room. "We've gotten a tip on the location of a Separatist supply storage base."

Vos tried, and failed, not to look disappointed. "Of course. As the Council wishes."

"This is no little matter, Master Vos," Ki-Adi-Mundi said. "The base is massive and concealed in the interior of this asteroid. Our intel says it contains medications, arms, ship repair materials, and foodstuffs. If we can take this base, we can get vital supplies to worlds that are in desperate need."

"And deny them to the Separatists," Mace added. "Did Dooku mention anything like this to you, Vos?"

Vos thought for a minute. "He did say something about a supply base once, but I thought it was on a planet. Maybe Toola?"

"We're pretty certain it's here," Windu said.

"I'm sure there's more than one such base," Vos conceded.

"Master Kenobi, Master Vos, you two will lead this mission," Windu continued. "Take two other Jedi with you, and as many clones as you think necessary to transport the supplies. It looks like any defense you will encounter will be sparse; I think Dooku was relying on the obscurity of the location to keep it secret, but you should go in prepared for a fight just in case this hidden base has some hidden fighters."

"Understood," Kenobi said. "With the Council's permission, I'd like to take Skywalker and Akar-Deshu with us."

"Of course," Windu said. He addressed both Kenobi and Vos, but Obi-Wan noticed his gaze lingered on the other Jedi. "Gentlemen, these supplies could potentially help us save thousands of lives. It's not a glamorous assignment, but it's a vital one. May the Force be with you."

*   *   *

"I can see why Dooku thought no one would spot this as a base," Anakin said. "It looks just like a big rock."

"That's pretty much what an asteroid is, yes," Desh said. He, Anakin, Kenobi, and Vos were all in their own Eta-2 *Actis*-class interceptors, heading toward the asteroid. Certain materials in the asteroid's composition had rendered it impossible for sensors to detect whether anything—or anyone—was inside it, so a visual inspection was necessary.

"All right, everyone ready for our first pass?" Kenobi asked.

"Let's do this!" Vos exclaimed, clearly happy to be, as he had said to Kenobi, "sprung from his cage."

"More than ready," Desh said.

At that moment half a dozen droid starfighters emerged from the asteroid's interior. "Oh, hey, look at that," Anakin said. "I think we've found the right place."

"We're outnumbered two to one," Desh said. "This'll be easy." Even as he spoke, Anakin had swooped down on one of the starfighters, scoring a hit. The damaged ship spiraled out of control and then exploded. Kenobi jigged and jagged as two latched on to his tail.

"I'm on it," Vos said, coming up behind the two. Kenobi pulled up and back, executing a loop and firing while upside down. He struck his target squarely, and Vos took care of the second one.

"Three down, three to go!" said Anakin. "Watch this."

"Anakin—" Kenobi cautioned, then added under his breath, "Why do I even bother?"

Anakin flew over two of the ships and fired on each

one, then came around beneath the third. He fired on it, as well. Like anoobas that had spotted a jakrab, the three fighters set off in hot pursuit. Kenobi, Vos, and Desh brought up the rear and picked off the last three.

"That was not *nearly* enough fun," Anakin lamented.

"Let's just be glad it was only six and not a dozen or more," Vos said.

"Master Vos, you disappoint me," Anakin chided. "You're as dull as Master Kenobi."

"Now, now, let's not exaggerate," Kenobi said, permitting himself a small smile. "I think we're safe now. Fall into single-file formation and we'll fly over it, slowly and carefully."

Somewhat to his surprise, they obeyed, and then, in the shadows of a concavity, Kenobi saw the entrance. It was large enough to admit a medium-sized transport, and the single-person interceptors had no trouble negotiating it. The tunnel was long and curving, but it widened as the Jedi maneuvered around a bend and entered an enormous cavern. Abruptly, the chamber flooded with light. Kenobi realized that they had probably passed through an environmental field, and the grotto would therefore be able to suit humanoid life. The light illuminated crate after crate of various supplies, and caught the gleaming curves of metallic ship parts.

Anakin whistled. "Okay, Master Windu had good intel. You lost this round, Master Vos."

"I'm delighted to be wrong," Vos replied. "*Look* at all this!"

"We're going to have to requisition more transports, but I think that's a problem we're grateful to have," Kenobi said.

They brought their ships down onto a vast landing pad that would easily accommodate the three transports they had brought and had room for several more. The four Jedi hopped out of their vessels and paused for a moment to simply take it all in.

"This is going to help a lot of people," Vos said.

"And," put in Desh, "make Dooku gnash his teeth when word gets out that we now have control of it."

"Enough patting ourselves on the back," Kenobi said. "Let's get to work."

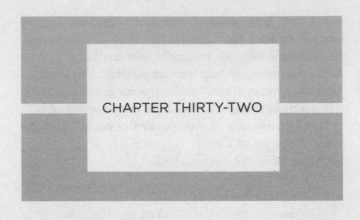

CHAPTER THIRTY-TWO

Desh returned to the Jedi light cruiser to inform the clones that they could bring in the transports. Kenobi, Vos, and Anakin looked around, and then at one another.

"I hardly know where to begin," Anakin said.

Kenobi stroked his beard. "It *is* rather intimidating. Fortunately, it's not our task to catalog or distribute the items. All we have to do is assist the clones in getting the supplies onto the transports."

"If I may," Vos said, "I'll leave you two in charge of that. I'd like to have a look around. I've got a hunch that there might be something more valuable here than food, a few blasters, and spare parts."

"Something that Dooku might have stashed here for safekeeping?" guessed Skywalker.

"Got it in one."

"And you're the one to recognize something like that when you see it," Kenobi said, nodding in approval. "All I have to say to that request is, good hunting."

"I'll find the end of . . . all this and work my way back. I'll let you know how deep the cavern extends."

"I think you just want to get out of doing the grunt work," Anakin grumbled.

"You're giving all the right answers today, Anakin." Vos grinned. Kenobi watched for a moment as the other Master paused, then shrugged and picked a direction, vanishing through one of the narrow spaces between the tightly packed crates and equipment.

"What now?" Anakin asked.

"We move crates."

"I was afraid you'd say that."

They set to work. Vos checked in after a few moments, letting them know that he was already about a thousand meters in with no end yet in sight. Desh returned, followed by the three transports. Clone Commander Cody, Kenobi's clone marshal commander, jumped out of the first one. "This will be much less exciting than a battle, I fear, Commander," Kenobi told the clone leader.

"That's as may be, sir, but I reckon that we can do with less excitement if it means more lives saved," Cody said. "Come on, boys, let's get to it. How far back does this stretch anyway, sir?"

"Master Vos reports the distance at nearly a thousand meters—so far."

Rex, the clone trooper captain who served under Skywalker, whistled. "We've got our work cut out for us, then."

"We'll be able to help with the heavier items," Kenobi said. He gestured to a deck cannon, then closed his eyes and settled himself, feeling for the essence of the weapon in the Force. When he found it, he visualized it rising, light as a feather, as air, as nothing at all. He extended his arms in front of him and raised them, palms up. When he opened his eyes, the cannon hovered in midair. Smiling softly, Kenobi moved his right hand, maneuvering the cannon to settle in the transport hold.

"Well, sir," Cody said, "looks like we can knock off and let you Jedi handle this."

"Not quite," Desh said. "Many hands make light work."

"But *Jedi* hands make work light," another clone trooper, Jesse, said, eliciting a groaning laugh from some of the other clones even as he set to work with Cody to begin moving crates into the transport.

Kenobi's comlink chirped. "Vos, what's your status? Find anyth—"

"Kenobi!" Vos's voice was taut with tension. "Get the men on the transports and get them out of here. The rest of you, too. Right now!"

"What's going on?" Kenobi was calm, alert.

"Bombs," Vos replied. "They've rigged this whole place to blow!"

"Vos," Desh said, "how many? Any chance we could disarm them?"

"Negative," Vos said. "I spotted at least six of them, and they're all set to detonate in about three minutes. Go! *Now!*"

"How is that possible?" Anakin asked. "They didn't know we were coming!"

"The droids must have set them before they attacked," Kenobi said. "They probably thought they'd deal with whatever was out there and then disarm them upon their return."

"And if they *didn't* return," Desh said grimly, "the items wouldn't fall into enemy hands."

"We can worry about the hows and the whys later," Vos said, "but right now *you need to get the hell off this asteroid!*"

At a nod from Kenobi, Cody started shouting to his men. They hurried back and jumped into the transports. The first one to close its doors lifted off and flew back down the tunnel to open space and safety.

"All right, one—no, two—transports are on their way out," Kenobi said to Vos. To Desh and Anakin, he said, "Get in your interceptors."

"But—" Desh began.

"That is an order, Jedi Akar! You too, Anakin. Go!"

The two cast a last worried look over their shoulders, then sprinted for their vessels. The final transport had lifted off and had disappeared down the tunnel toward open space.

"You too, Kenobi," came Vos's voice.

"I'll just stretch my legs till you get here."

"Damn it, Obi-Wan, you've only got about a minute!"

"Then you'd best hurry, hadn't you?"

"Obi-Wan—"

"Stop talking and focus on running!"

Kenobi jumped into his interceptor, prepped it for immediate takeoff, and settled in to wait. The seconds ticked by. Fifty seconds . . . forty . . . thirty-five . . .

The figure of Quinlan Vos hurtled over a pile of crates marked as ammunition. Relief surged through Kenobi. He touched the controls and the Eta Interceptor lifted off. Glancing back, he saw Vos's ship do the same.

. . . *twenty-two* . . .

The Jedi took the curves of the tunnel at top speed. Kenobi reached out into the Force, sensing the walls and the path ahead and leaning his body and his ship into them. He shot out of the tunnel with Vos barely a ship's length behind him. He did not slow, but kept going at top speed, putting as much distance between him and the asteroid before it—

Kenobi squinted as a bright yellow-orange fireball rolled out of the tunnel, casting stark shadows through the cockpit viewport. When he could see clearly again, he realized that the asteroid was still intact, though obscured by black smoke billowing out from the entrance. While he was grateful that there had been no loss of life, the sight pained him nonetheless. All those supplies—food, weaponry, medical equipment—up, quite literally, in smoke. Well, perhaps not all . . .

"Jedi Akar," Kenobi said, "I'd like for you to keep a single transport here and supervise the loading of any salvageable debris. Since the explosion didn't crack the asteroid, it's possible that much of it is still contained in the cavern."

"Yes, Master Kenobi," Desh replied, though Obi-Wan detected a note of resignation in the Mahran's voice. "Let's hope there's something left of use."

"Indeed. Vos, Anakin, let's head back to Coruscant."

Ventress sat at a bar in Pantora's spaceport district, swirling her glass. She had known from the minute she walked in that coming back here, to the same bar where she and Vos had embarked on their partnership, had been a bad idea. She could kick herself now for yielding to the impulse. Somehow, she'd talked herself into thinking that seeing the place again would strip it of the power it had over her and become just another bar; the opposite had been the case. But now that she was here, Ventress figured she could at least try to drown her pain in the thick, bitter liquid and then sleep it off . . . somewhere.

She tossed back the shot and gestured to the bartender for a refill. Then, she stiffened. Surely, it was just the memory that was making her think that . . .

"Ventress?"

She pressed her lips tightly together. "So now you're stalking me."

Vos slid into the seat in front of her. He looked more subdued than she had ever seen him. It wasn't a good look on him. "I came here for, I think, the same reason you did."

She laughed humorlessly. "To try to erase me from your memory?"

"No." His voice was quiet, without the desperate pleading she'd heard from him before. He waited, as if expecting her to order him away again, but Ventress was too soul-weary of it all to fight with him. Vos signaled to the bartender. "I'll have what she's having."

"You won't like it," Ventress assured him.

The bartender plunked a glass and a bottle in front of him. Vos poured a shot and downed it. Immediately, he began to cough.

"When you're right," he wheezed, tears coming out of his eyes, "you're right." His cough turned into a choking laugh.

For an instant, Ventress caught a glimpse of the Vos she had grown to care for so deeply. "I'm always right," she said. Why was she smiling into her glass?

"Not always," he said. Ventress froze, abruptly realizing that she was not sensing the dark side pouring off him anymore. Why?

I can't trust him. I can't trust this . . . "No," she said. "I was right about you. Wasn't I?"

She looked him dead in the eye, extending her feelings into the Force. There was still darkness in him, but it was different. It was . . . *human*. What she would expect from anyone who had been tortured, emotionally and physically.

What she would expect from someone whose heart was breaking.

Vos didn't answer at once. He frowned into the empty glass, turning it in his fingers. He didn't look at her when he answered, "Yes, you were."

She shoved the chair back and stood. "I'm done here."

Vos peered up at her. "*Were.*"

"And I suppose you're all better now?"

"No." It was the truth. Ventress could tell. Vos continued. "When you came back for me—it was right after I had held Tholme's lightsaber."

"Right after you experienced me murdering him." Ventress stated it bluntly.

He nodded. "I was reeling. I'd been starved, beaten, deprived of sleep, injected with things that . . . Asajj, you were my anchor. Thoughts of you, of *us,* kept me sane. But when I felt Tholme—" Vos couldn't bring himself to say the word. "After that, I thought that everything between us had been a lie. So yes, I let the dark side in. And that's what you saw in my eyes."

Vos again looked down into his glass. Slowly, Ventress resumed her seat and waited.

"For a while, I admit it, I did help Dooku. But then I began to understand what it must have been like for you as his apprentice; the kind of lessons you were learning from him. He was trying to teach me those same lessons. But you decided you didn't want to be like him. And . . . I wasn't angry at you anymore."

"Just like that? You saw and *felt* me gut a man who had surrendered to me—the Jedi who was your beloved Master—and then suddenly it's all right?"

Vos shook his head. "No, not suddenly. But it did happen. It helped me shore up my resolve to not give in to the darkness anymore. I wanted what we had. What we were *going* to have. Together. We had a future."

"*Had* being the operative word." Her own anger and pain were returning.

"We could still have it."

Ventress shook her head. She downed another shot of the bitter drink, letting it fuel her. "Impossible. Not after everything that's happened."

"I forgave you. For killing Tholme, and for lying to me. And you will forgive me too, one day, Asajj Ventress." He hesitated, and took a breath. "That's what you do for . . . for the one you love."

He wasn't lying. Ventress could feel it in the Force. Quinlan Vos was, truly, in love with her. Joy and pain bombarded her simultaneously. For a moment, Ventress was so stunned she couldn't respond. Why had he said this, now, when—

"Love," she said, having difficulty speaking the word, "is not a part of your world anymore. You're back with the Jedi now, and they would never allow it."

Vos leaned forward. All the earnestness, the . . . *hope* . . . that had been absent just a few moments before returned in full force. "When you turned me away, I did go back to them, yes. I tried to be a Jedi again, I really did. But I don't belong there anymore, Asajj, I belong with *you*."

"Are you telling me that you're willing to leave the Order?" She had to hear it, explicitly, to believe it. It had been one thing, when they were alone together on Dathomir, to talk about leaving the Jedi. Vos's life with them had been so far away, and it would have been easy for the two of them to simply disappear. But he had been welcomed back with relief and, Ventress had to admit, affection.

His gaze was locked with hers. "Yes. I am. There are a few more things I can do to help them destroy Dooku. I think I owe them that much. But once that's done, I'm yours. If you'll have me."

For answer, Ventress stretched out her hand. Vos took it in both of his, kissed it, and pressed it to his heart.

CHAPTER THIRTY-THREE

"Master Vos," said Yoda, "for your actions, grateful, we are. Saved many lives, you have."

"Thank you, Master Yoda," Vos replied, "but it was what any Jedi would have done. It's Jedi Akar who deserves your thanks—he's the one who gets to sort through the mess."

Amusement rippled through the gathering. Kenobi noted that the tension was gone. The nearly imperceptible aura of mistrust that had filled the Council Chamber every time Quinlan Vos was present now seemed conspicuous in its absence.

"The Council believes that you are ready to once again fight against the Separatists," Windu said to Vos. "Though that is not the primary purpose of this mission. Our intel indicates that Count Dooku has placed a listening station on Vanqor."

Kenobi made a sour face. He and Anakin had once been stranded there while in pursuit of Dooku. Anakin had been unfortunate enough to have a second bad experience there, when he and Windu had been trapped beneath the rubble of a crashed ship. Both events had involved the huge, four-armed predators known as gundarks, and Kenobi was none too keen to return. All eyes turned to the hologram of the blue-gray, rocky world.

"Vanqor," mused Kenobi. "Charming place. Delightful fauna. Did Dooku ever tell you anything about this station, Vos?"

Vos frowned, thinking. "The count kept his cards pretty close to his vest," he said. "He never did trust me entirely. But I do recall something about a listening post in that sector. If you're confident on your intel, I'd say that this is the one Dooku was talking about."

"Then, Master Vos, Master Kenobi—your job is to take it out," said Windu. "Depending on how key this site is, you may be met with a large welcoming party. Plan accordingly."

As Vos and Kenobi left the chamber, Anakin joined them. "Why do you always assume you're on the same mission we are?" Vos asked.

"Because I always am," Anakin replied.

"Sadly, there is no countering that argument," Vos said wryly.

"Now that that's settled," Anakin continued, "what's our mission?"

"To destroy a listening post," Vos said. "We should be prepared to be fired upon."

Anakin looked at Kenobi, confused. "Our listening posts don't have a lot of defenses," he reminded them. "They rely on the fleet coming the second the all-clear signal stops being transmitted."

"That's because *we* put lives on the line," Vos said. "For us, the best allocation of resources works out to the fewest men at the station, with plenty of help on call in a real emergency. Dooku has more than enough droids to have them provide adequate defense at all times."

"Droids only?" Kenobi inquired.

"There will be a few people stationed there to supervise and make gut-check judgment calls," Vos said. "But the defense will almost certainly be droids. We should be prepared for a good fight. I know I'm itching for one."

"Sounds like everything's back to normal with you, Vos," Anakin said. "I'm glad."

"So am I, Anakin," Vos said. "So am I."

Kenobi, Vos, and Anakin were in their interceptors when the *Vigilance* came out of hyperspace and the hangar doors opened. They, along with two dozen of the heavily armed ARC-170s starfighters—the initial wave—launched at once, soaring out into space ready for battle. There was not a single fighter present to offer resistance. As they descended toward Vanqor and their target, they remained unchallenged.

"Kinda quiet here," Anakin said over his comlink. "You know. The peaceful silence of space. With nothing happening. At all."

"I agree," Kenobi said. Where was the defense Vos had warned them about? Dooku's forces should have launched their attack immediately.

"Do you suppose it's a trap?" Anakin asked. "Think they're waiting for us to penetrate the atmosphere and launch a ground attack?"

"That seems a very poor tactic if it's so," Kenobi said, "but nevertheless, something's not right here." Tapping the controls, he zoomed in on the planet's surface. "Master Windu's intel was spot-on about the listening post, however." He opened a channel to the attack cruiser. "Admiral Block, we're going to go ahead and descend. We're prepared to encounter resistance from the ground."

"Of course, General Kenobi," the admiral said. "Do you wish the second wave to launch?"

"Yes, go ahead," Kenobi said. "Better safe than sorry." He changed the comm channel to address his team. "It's far too still for my liking. There may indeed be a trap. We go in expecting hostile fire."

"*That's* more like it," said Anakin. As usual, the boy was all on fire to be out in front and in the thick of the action. The Force, Kenobi mused, *had* to be protecting him. Otherwise, Anakin's impulsiveness would have gotten him killed a thousand times over.

"Remember," Kenobi said, "there's no room for rash decisions. Stay the course. That means you, Anakin. No fancy maneuvers."

In response, Skywalker's ship suddenly dropped and executed a loop. "Sorry, Master Kenobi, you're breaking up! I think something might be wrong with my comlink."

"Anakin!"

"Some say I'm reckless, others would say I have guts. It's subjective," Anakin—who clearly had nothing at all wrong with his comlink—said.

"It's really not."

Vos laughed. "You two kids never change."

More elegantly than his former apprentice, Kenobi tilted the nose of his Interceptor down. The surface rushed up to meet them. He glanced at his readout, then used his own eyes and the Force.

Listening posts were precious things. The Republic had a fleet ready to defend them at a moment's notice, and, according to Vos, Dooku kept sufficient defense on site. The design was similar to the Republic's— a simple station with a large tower to which a dish was affixed. Unlike Republic stations, which had a single, rather small landing pad, the area around this post was clearly designed to accommodate several vessels. Vos was right—there should have been at least a few dozen fighters to safeguard the post. And yet—it looked . . .

"It's abandoned," Vos said. "Not a single ship."

"It does look that way," Kenobi said. "But we should be cautious nonetheless. Let's try a strafing run and see if we can flush any hiding jakrabs."

The three Jedi brought their vessels into formation. Anakin actually cooperated by taking his place on Kenobi's left and letting Obi-Wan have the lead. The clones fell in behind them in their ARC-170s. Obi-Wan, Vos, and Anakin all fired their laser cannons simultaneously. A fireball wrapped in black smoke plumed upward. The mammoth dish cracked and tumbled in pieces to the ground. The clones followed with a second attack. Blue laserfire screamed, and this time the tower itself crumbled beneath the assault. The group veered upward and came about for another pass.

"Hold your fire, everyone," Kenobi said. "Let's see what reaction we get." They flew over again, but there was no movement on the ground. No ships, no vehicles, no people, not even droids. Nothing.

"Scans indicate no life-forms," Anakin said, adding, "Well, none larger than a literal jakrab. Hey, no gundarks this time."

"Master Kenobi? I'd like to go down there and see what we can find" came Vos's voice.

"We . . . kind of just obliterated it with laser cannons, Vos," said Anakin. "Not a whole lot left that would be of any use to us."

"Not to you," Vos said, "but maybe *I* can get some answers."

A few moments later, they and the clones were on the ground. "Commander Cody," Obi-Wan ordered, "have your squadron break down into teams and do some scouting. This place looks empty, but it may not be."

"Yes, sir," Cody said. Over his shoulder he shouted, "Come on, you lot, you heard the general." He began giving instructions.

"Well," said Kenobi, "as Anakin pointed out, the tower itself is demolished at this point. Let's see if we can find some barracks that are still somewhat intact."

The three Jedi leapt easily over the major chunks of rubble blocking the path to the station's operations center and living quarters. As they stepped carefully amid the debris, Anakin said, "While I'm always pleased to not see bodies, I kinda miss the droid parts."

Vos picked up a small chunk of blasted console and closed his eyes. A few seconds later, he opened them, looking irritated.

"This is useless," he said. "It's all been too damaged, and too many people have touched it. We need something more personal and mostly intact."

"I'm guessing the living quarters are located belowground," Kenobi said. He tapped his bracer to activate his comlink. "Commander? Have any of your squad members located another entrance?"

"Yes, sir, we did indeed." Cody gave them the coordinates. The entrance was several meters from the tower, well hidden by the boulders that were a common feature in the area. A quick scan revealed that the structural integrity of the tunnels was still intact. The Jedi activated their lightsabers as a precaution against any possible remaining droids, illuminating the metal corridors with soft blue-green radiance. A series of doors lined the path. At each one, they cut their way in and peered about.

"Storage," said Kenobi. Most of the rooms were

bare, save for the occasional small piece of equipment or an empty crate. "This place looks like it could have been abandoned for years."

"No." Vos bent over and picked up a curved piece of metal. "This is a repair part for a B3. Whatever happened here, it's recent." After a time, the path sloped upward and they came to a sealed metal door. Kenobi cut through it, and the three Jedi emerged into an area that had six beds and very little else.

"Well," Anakin said, "I think this is the best we're going to find. Can you get anything off a bedpost, Vos?"

"I've got something better," Vos replied. Grinning, he held up a comb. "Nothing too exciting, but it'll do." He wrapped his fingers around the item, closed his eyes for a moment, then opened them.

"That's it?" Anakin asked.

"That's it," Vos said. He looked annoyed. "They bugged out about two weeks ago. Dooku wasn't about to take chances that I'd lead you here, and sent orders to abandon the post."

"I don't suppose someone happened to mention where the new post would be located?"

Vos shook his head. "I think anything useful went up with the tower. Important orders wouldn't be discussed in the barracks. I can try everything here, if you'd like."

Kenobi clapped his friend on the back. "Don't worry, Vos. This was bound to happen."

Vos's shook his head, still irritated. "Well, it means that pretty much any information I learned while I was . . . with Dooku is now moot."

"Hey—we've got you back," Anakin said. "That's more important."

Kenobi rubbed his chin thoughtfully. "I wonder," he said, "if that's all that's going on here."

"What do you mean?" Vos asked.

"Well, it does make sense that Dooku would change things up a bit. Anything you knew could indeed be used against him. But it does seem strange that this has happened twice in a row. I can't help but wonder if we might have a leak."

Vos frowned. "A leak? You think there's someone feeding the Separatists information?"

"I wouldn't say that's too far out of the realm of possibility," Anakin said. "It's happened before, unfortunately. Whatever it is, we'll deal with it back at the Temple. Master Yoda will know what to do."

"It's certainly an unsettling thought," Kenobi said. "We have to hope that this is simple coincidence. Anything else you can get from the comb?" he asked Vos.

"Well," Vos replied, "its owner used to flex in the mirror when he thought no one was watching."

CHAPTER THIRTY-FOUR

Kenobi requested a private audience with the two people he could absolutely trust—Yoda and Mace Windu. He outlined the circumstances of both missions and put forth his concerns. "There's nothing that decisively points to a leak," he finished. "It could be coincidence, or a simple and predictable result of Vos turning his back on Dooku."

"Examine everything, we must," Yoda said. "Correct to bring this to us, you were, Obi-Wan."

"This doesn't feel right to me," Windu said. "I think there's more going on here than coincidence." He grimaced. "I think there's a chance that Vos isn't fully rehabilitated. I *did* express my concern that we might be putting him back in the field too quickly."

"Vos?" Kenobi exclaimed. "With respect, Master Windu, I think you may be jumping to some rather unfounded conclusions. I've seen or felt nothing that indicated that, and I've known him well for years."

"With respect, Master Kenobi," Windu snapped, "it's precisely because you've known him so long that

I worry your judgment is clouded by your friendship."

"I saw firsthand what Dooku did to him," Kenobi said, bridling slightly. "Don't you think I was alert for any signs?"

"Let's look at the facts. Nothing like this has happened for quite some time until his very first mission directly against the Separatists, when suddenly a tremendous amount of valuable supplies blow up."

"It's a logical thing for the Separatists to have done," Kenobi pointed out.

"Saved your lives, Vos did, with his warning," Yoda added. "Escape in time, he himself almost did not." Kenobi nodded his thanks to Yoda.

"All that is true," Windu agreed. "What is also true is that Vos was the one who, very conveniently, spotted the bombs. Today we attack a Separatist listening post to discover that it's been abandoned. And the only one who can tell us exactly why those orders were issued happens to be . . . Quinlan Vos."

"Come now, Mace," Kenobi protested. "This is all a bit far-fetched and overly dramatic, don't you think? If Vos is indeed a traitor, why is he not leading us into ambushes? He could destroy thousands of the 'enemy' at one go."

"So obvious, a well-positioned traitor would not be," Yoda said thoughtfully. "Too much attention, it would draw."

Kenobi turned to Yoda, his heart sinking. "You, too, Master Yoda? We need proof! We can't call a man a traitor just because we don't like what we're seeing!"

"Speaks the truth, Master Kenobi does," Yoda said. "Evidence, we must find."

"Now I wish we had looked harder at the listening post debris," Kenobi said.

"Why?" Windu asked. "If Vos is indeed a traitor, he will make sure that anything you find corroborates what he wants us to think."

"Return to that site, we could," Yoda said. "But eyes we have on another one already."

"The asteroid," said Kenobi. "I've been checking in with Desh, but thus far he's reported nothing out of the ordinary." With some trepidation, he activated his holocomm, and a small image of Desh appeared.

"Master Kenobi." Desh bowed slightly, adding hopefully, "I don't suppose you're reassigning me?"

"We need you right where you are, Desh," Kenobi said. "I'm with Master Yoda and Master Windu in the Council Chamber. What I'm about to tell you must remain confidential."

"Of course," Desh replied, though his ears twitched in concern.

"It's possible—even likely—that we have a leak."

"A leak? Not a Jedi?" Desh's ears flattened.

"A Jedi," Kenobi confirmed, adding, "or another party who is privy to sensitive information. We're gathering evidence at the moment. Have you run across anything unusual in your sorting through the debris?"

Kenobi's heart sank at Desh's hesitation. "Well, sir, now that you mention it, there *was* something," Desh said. "We didn't think much of it at the time."

Kenobi looked at his fellow Masters bleakly as he asked, "What is it?"

"There were some Republic-made items among the debris. It's not unknown for Separatists to use whatever they can find. But . . we're pretty sure that the bombs were not Confederacy-issue, which means they got their hands on some of ours."

Kenobi felt the blood draining from his face.

"And you didn't see fit to report this?" snapped Windu. Yoda lifted a calming hand.

"My apologies, Master Windu," said Desh. "As I say—this happens in war. We do it, too. A blaster's a blaster and a bomb's a bomb, after all. One is the same as another."

Except when it isn't, Kenobi thought, sickened. "Thank you, Desh. We'll be in touch."

"So," Windu said. "Now we know. Vos planted those bombs!"

"We don't *know* anything yet," Kenobi retorted. "If we're going to brand a man a traitor and destroy his life, it must hinge on what we can prove!"

"Correct, Master Kenobi is," Yoda said solemnly. "Another line of inquiry, I alone will pursue. But if proof we find . . . a painful task, we will have before us."

When, two days later, Obi-Wan received a summons to Yoda's private quarters, he steeled himself to not give in to either hope or despair. He mentally repeated the Jedi Code to calm himself:

There is no emotion, there is peace.
There is no ignorance, there is knowledge.
There is no passion, there is serenity.
There is no chaos, there is harmony.
There is no death, there is the Force.

It helped. He was in control of his emotions by the time he reached Yoda's door and entered. Yoda was, as usual, seated by the fountain crafted of singing stones. The familiar scents of the heated oils teased

Kenobi's nostrils as he sank down beside his old Master.

"You summoned me, Master Yoda?" he asked quietly. "Is this regarding Quinlan? Is . . . is there news?"

Yoda had not been meditating, but he had been regarding the fountain's flow. Now he turned to Kenobi. He did not need to say anything further. The answer was in his wonderful, warm eyes, now filled with sorrow and a deep compassion.

"Oh, no," Kenobi breathed.

Gently, Yoda reached and placed a small hand on Kenobi's. "Vos, saw I today. Acknowledged his aid through his unique skill, I did. Touched I his hand, through which flows the Force. Able at times, I am, to see that which is hidden. The Force was with me this day. The truth to me has been granted. Taken by the dark side, Quinlan Vos has been, though conceal it well, he does." Yoda hesitated. "Lost to us, I fear he is."

Kenobi sagged. "She was right," he whispered, thinking of Ventress; of her grief and pain, of her determination to "free" Vos. How blind they had been, all of them—except for her. Asajj Ventress, she who had danced so long with the dark side, had been the only one to recognize it when it contaminated one Kenobi now believed she had truly loved. "She was right all along."

"Dull the senses, attachment does, but open the eyes, betrayal can," Yoda continued, his voice still so very kind, so understanding. "Open now, they are, and act, we must."

A few moments later an emergency meeting was quietly convened. Yoda, Mace Windu, Obi-Wan Kenobi, Plo Koon, and Ki-Adi-Mundi—all the Council members who were on site—assembled in the Council Chamber. Kenobi found himself too restless to sit; he chose to stand, looking out the vast windows as the business of Coruscant swirled past. Although he knew he must appear distracted, he listened intently to the conversation.

Yoda went over everything they knew: How long Vos had been in Dooku's power. That Ventress had claimed he had fallen to the dark side. That Republic-crafted bombs, small enough to be hidden in the voluminous robes of a Jedi and "discovered" by Vos, had destroyed the supply base on the asteroid. That a key listening outpost had been abandoned, and that the only information as to why was, again, discovered by Vos in a way that only he could verify.

"In his heart, darkness I found," Yoda said sadly. "Deep, secret, powerful. The history of items, does the Force permit Vos to understand. The history of a soul, does the Force permit *me* to understand. Unacceptable in a court of law, it is, but of lying, no Jedi will accuse me." The comment was so inarguably true that no one felt the need to voice agreement. Taken with everything else, Yoda's statement painted a damning picture. "Meet now, we do, to discuss his punishment."

"If he has been in communication with Dooku this entire time," Ki-Adi-Mundi said, "then we must assume that Dooku knows everything Vos does. And that is, unfortunately, a very great deal."

Kenobi closed his eyes briefly. *There is no emotion . . .*

"This is by far the greatest breach of trust the Jedi have seen since Count Dooku himself betrayed us," Mace sad. "Even General Krell's deception did less damage. Vos isn't just a Jedi, he's a Jedi Master with unique skills. And he is a Jedi Master in wartime who has worked side by side with Dooku. This is going to have massive repercussions."

"We all appreciate how serious this is, Master Windu," Kenobi said, a touch sharply.

"Do *you*, Master Kenobi? For my part, I think we need to seriously entertain the possibility of execution."

"*What?*" Kenobi turned to stare at him, aghast.

Ki-Adi-Mundi nodded. "I agree," he said, his voice solemn. "Many lives will be lost because of what Quinlan Vos has done. Yet again, the Order has been shaken to its core at a time when we can ill afford anything but solidarity and faith in one another. We weathered a storm such as this poorly with the treachery of Barriss Offee. None of us could have imagined such a seemingly ideal Padawan turning into a Separatist terrorist. Now that it has happened again, it must be dealt with in the firmest manner possible."

"Execution?" Utterly disbelieving, Kenobi looked from one face to the next, finding only cold resolution. "You can't be serious!"

"Can't we?" Mace said flatly.

Kenobi turned to Yoda. In the Jedi Master's wrinkled face, Obi-Wan did not see the same merciless expression the others shared. Even so, Yoda was not dismissing the idea. He looked at Kenobi for a long moment before saying, with reluctance, "Everything, we must consider."

"But . . . but this is madness!" Kenobi protested. "We are not Sith—we do not deal in absolutes. And few things are more absolute than death. An eye for an eye isn't our way. Nothing that Vos has done has cost lives!"

"That we know of. We still don't know what he was responsible for as Dooku's 'Admiral Enigma.' But going forward, it *will* cost lives." Windu was relentless. "Once Dooku realizes that we're on to Vos, he'll stop holding back. He'll exploit every bit of knowledge that traitor has given him. We'll be seeing more than our share of ambushes and destruction, Kenobi, and all of it can be placed at the feet of Quinlan Vos!"

"But don't you see?" Kenobi pleaded. "He's as much a victim as anyone! You know what Dooku did to him. The man was *tortured,* forced to the dark side! He can't be held completely responsible for what he's done."

"Others have fought the sway of the count—and won," Mace said. "Even your friend Ventress."

"What else would you suggest?" Plo Koon said.

Kenobi didn't know. He was so shocked by the turn of the discussion it was hard to gather his thoughts. He took a deep breath. "We could banish him. Send him to the Outer Rim. Maybe even beyond." Even as he spoke the words, he realized how impossible such a solution was.

"With all due respect, Master Kenobi," Ki-Adi-Mundi said, not unkindly, "we are dealing with a highly trained Jedi Master who has turned to the dark side. Because of his actions, albeit indirectly, thousands will die to appease his Sith Master's thirst for bloodshed. Coming back from such a dark place is difficult, even for the strongest of Jedi. He is too dangerous to be unleashed upon the galaxy."

"Imprisoned, then," Kenobi tried desperately.

"He has *fallen* to the *dark side,*" Mace said, as if trying to explain something to a youngling. "He will be looking to escape—and Dooku will be looking to get him back. How long do you think we could hold him?"

Come on, Kenobi, think . . . "What if he's given the chance to turn on Dooku?"

"What do you mean?" Windu asked.

Kenobi worked it out as he spoke. "We sent him to kill Count Dooku. Perhaps if Vos sees the count again, and has the chance to assassinate him, he'll be able to resist the dark side. He could redeem himself—come back from it. Isn't that what we really want? Or are we all just looking for sport?"

"That is untrue and you know it, Master Kenobi," chided Plo Koon.

"I do, and I apologize," Obi-Wan said. "But this is Vos's *life* we're talking about."

The three who had called for execution exchanged glances. Yoda's gaze was fixed on Kenobi, and Obi-Wan could tell he was pleased.

"Go on," said Mace.

"Vos is completely unaware that we know of his transition to the dark side. So—we set a trap to test his allegiance. We'll send him after Dooku. If Vos sides with him, then we'll know."

"I fail to see how giving Vos back to Dooku is a good thing," Mace said.

"You misunderstand. We'll follow him, and watch his every move."

Windu considered this. "You will stay close to him."

"Absolutely."

"Should Vos fail to execute Dooku, you will need to intervene. Do you understand, Master Kenobi?"

Kenobi took a deep breath. "I believe I do, Master Windu."

"Cloud your judgment, your feelings must not," Yoda said. "Do what you must, you will."

"I shall. Thank you, Master Yoda. This test will allow us to see Vos's true colors. And," he added, "his true heart."

Yoda nodded. "Reveal himself to us, Quinlan Vos will. And his own fate, he himself will decide."

CHAPTER THIRTY-FIVE

They had taken to meeting in one of the popular floating parks that hovered above the surface of Coruscant. A little under two thousand square kilometers, it boasted meadows, forests, and even an artificially created mountain and several lakes. Nonthreatening wildlife had been brought in from various worlds, and the lakes were stocked with fish. When Vos had first suggested it, Ventress felt exposed. She was a creature of the dark skies of space and the dim light of a cockpit; of shadowy alleyways and bars with out-of-the-way alcoves. Even on her homeworld of Dathomir, which was not crowded with beings, the Nightsisters had preferred the confines of the artificially lit cavern to the open.

The two had been meeting nearly every day, as often as Vos could sneak away from the Temple. "Think about it," he said once, as they walked hand in hand on a trail beneath towering trees. "This is what our new life could be like. Not having to hide who we are, and how we feel." He nodded pleasantly to a pair of Nautolans who passed them by, also holding hands. "Here, we're just like they are."

Ventress had thought the idea was like the park itself—a beautiful but imaginary escape, nothing more. But as time passed, she felt it shift to become her new reality. This could indeed, she realized, be who they were—just two lovers, nothing more and, assuredly, nothing less.

Vos was late today. It didn't bother her at first. He was nearly always late, and it was not unpleasant to sit on a bench by the lake with her face turned up to the sun and wait. But time crept past, and worry crept upon her. Had the Jedi discovered their plans to escape?

Then Ventress sensed him behind her, his presence warm and strong and welcome. His hands came down on her shoulders, thumbs working to ease the knots, and she smiled as she leaned back. He kissed the top of her head, then jumped over the bench to sit beside her.

Her pleasure abated as she saw the furrow on his forehead. "What's wrong?"

"You're not going to believe it," he said.

"Try me."

Vos draped an arm around her as he spoke, and she leaned into him. "The Jedi," he said, "have assigned me a new mission. Or, rather, asked me to complete an old one."

Ventress stiffened and pulled back, her eyes searching his. "You're joking. They want you to try to kill Dooku? Again? Vos, you almost didn't make it out the last time!"

"I know. But I'm much stronger now."

"Are you sure you're ready to confront him again?"

He nodded firmly. "I'm ready. I now know exactly what he'll try to do, and I'm prepared for it." Vos tilted up her chin and kissed her softly, lingering for a moment before drawing back to smile at her. "You don't need to worry about me."

Ventress trailed her fingers over his face, tracing the yellow tattoo, the curve of his jaw. Alarm bells were going off inside her. This wasn't a good idea.

"Leave the Order. Let's get out of here. Now." Her voice was low and urgent.

He laughed softly, his breath stirring her hair. "Temptress," he growled playfully, then leaned back and sighed. "I can't."

"Why not?" Vos didn't answer right away. He took her right hand in his left, intertwining their fingers. The alarm bells clanged louder now, shrill and insistent, and Ventress's heartbeat quickened. Had he changed his mind about leaving the Jedi?

"I didn't realize it until they assigned me this task, but . . . Asajj, you and I . . . we're not free of Dooku. Not really. Not yet, and not ever, until he's dead."

"I don't believe that," Ventress said. "I don't *care* whether he lives or dies, I don't *care* about making him pay. Not anymore. I don't need it. The Jedi will get him, or they won't. But someone will. It doesn't have to be me. Or you. Quinlan . . . the only thing that matters to me now is being with you."

"That's exactly why I have to do this," Vos said. "How can we possibly find the life we want if we're always looking over our shoulders? That man casts a very long shadow."

"Please." The word came hard for Ventress, and he knew it. Surprise flickered over his face. He closed his eyes for a moment.

"Asajj," he said, "I have to. It's the only way I can find peace. You and I met because I had this task. Now I have a second chance to truly end the threat he poses. And that will give us our chance to be together."

Together. Ventress remembered when Vos first, quite literally, leapt into her life, tackling Moregi on Pantora. How he had kept pushing for them to work together until she agreed. It was a word he loved to use, a word that always made him smile, just as he did now.

"Then let's do it. I'm coming with you," Ventress stated.

"No," Vos said. "Absolutely not. I'm *not* going to risk losing you. Not now."

"But you expect *me* to simply sit by, wring my hands, and hope you come home in one piece? Not a chance!"

Vos frowned and started to protest. Ventress wrapped her arms around his neck and kissed him deeply. She felt the tension in his body dissolve as he pulled her closer. She melted into the kiss, putting all the things she felt but couldn't say, not yet, into it. All too soon, Vos drew back. Both of them were trembling.

Vos pressed his forehead to hers. "I should have known better than to think I could talk you into staying behind," he whispered, smiling.

Ventress chuckled warmly. "Yes, you should have."

"Together?"

"Together."

Ventress had allowed herself to hope that she had seen the last of the Jedi Temple, so she was not at all pleased to be following Vos inside not just the Temple, but to the Jedi Situation Room. Each of the Temple's towers had one, Vos told her, and it filled an entire level. She stood next to Vos as they ascended the turbolift in silence, shifting uneasily. Even though she had been given a full pardon, she knew what she and Vos were planning, and she was on edge. When the blast doors opened to admit them, Ventress saw that the room was as imposing as Vos had intimated. The walls were covered with tactical displays, and in the center of the room, standing around a huge holotable, were several Jedi Masters. The expressions on their various faces ranged from Yoda's mild, surprised acceptance, to Kenobi's confusion, to everyone else's outrage.

After the recent weeks of newfound connection, it was hard for Ventress to feign disinterest in Vos. He, however, seemed to have no such difficulty, perhaps because he had already been hiding their relationship from the Jedi on a daily basis.

"What is *she* doing here?" Mace Windu demanded. "This is a highly sensitive area, Master Vos!"

"Master Windu," Vos said, "the Council asked me to research and prepare for my mission to assassinate Count Dooku. I consider Asajj Ventress the ultimate resource for that task, and I will remind the Council that it ordered me specifically to seek her out the first time." His manner was calm, but his voice was strong.

"So we did," Ki-Adi-Mundi said, his voice laden with regret. "And she was indeed granted a full pardon."

"You should have cleared this with the Council first," Windu continued.

"With respect, I've learned something from young Skywalker," Vos said. "Sometimes it's easier to ask forgiveness than permission."

"Ventress," said Windu, giving her a withering glance. "May I inquire as to whether Vos asked you here solely as a resource? Or did he invite you to tag along?"

Before Ventress could answer, Vos stepped in

smoothly. "Ventress and I came very close to achieving the goal last time," he said. "We've learned from the errors we made then. We worked well as a team, and I'm sure we will do so again."

"But—" Ki-Adi-Mundi began.

"Must I remind the Council of its own actions a second time?" Vos said. "You pardoned her, remember?" For a moment, Ventress was certain that they were about to have her forcibly ejected from the Situation Room. Then Master Yoda spoke up.

"Pardon her, we did," Yoda agreed. "Trust her, we do." To her surprise, Ventress felt a flush of . . . was it shame? . . . under his kind gaze. She did not like this, any of it, and the sooner she and Vos were well away from here, the easier she would be.

"It's settled, then," Kenobi said before anyone else could utter another protest. "This is the most up-to-date information we have on Separatist activity." He activated a button on the holotable's side, and images of several different worlds appeared.

Ventress walked slowly around the table, examining the holographic worlds, quickly analyzing and dismissing options. She did not miss the questioning look that Kenobi threw Vos, nor Quinlan's calm nod of reassurance. She paused in front of one of the translucent blue orbs.

"Here," she said. "Christophsis." She touched the hologram and it zoomed in on a city, not small, but not obviously key, either. "Grievous will be here."

"This battle?" Windu asked. "It's so . . . irrelevant."

Ventress smiled thinly at him. "Not to Dooku. He has his own vendettas. And Grievous's boss will be . . ." She zoomed in further, then drew her hand upward. The view changed from looking down at the city to up at the skies above it. She expanded outward again, then yet again, and pointed a slender finger triumphantly at a Separatist dreadnought.

". . . right here," she purred.

"You're certain?" Kenobi asked dubiously.

Ventress narrowed her eyes. "Why," she said, "after everything that Dooku has done to me, would I possibly lie to you about this?"

"A point, Ventress has, hmm?" Yoda commented. To Vos, he said, "Full circle, you will have come, when complete this task is. May the Force be with you."

Vos bowed, then turned to leave. As she followed him, Ventress muttered under her breath, "Yeah, yeah."

"You did great," Vos said to her as they approached the *Banshee*. It was sitting in the middle of a row of Jedi vessels. Ventress thought it was an accurate reflection of her own recent position.

"You weren't so bad yourself," Ventress said. "No wonder it took me a little while to catch you out. You're good at this."

"*We're* good at this. *We.*"

He grinned at her. She smiled back. And for a moment, it was just like old times. Then Ventress stiffened. Vos caught it at once. "What is it?" he asked.

She paused and looked around the landing platform. "Are you sure this is a solo mission? They seemed kind of jumpy in there . . . I wonder if we're being followed."

"Actually," Vos said, "I'm counting on it."

Ventress eyed him narrowly. "What sort of game are you playing, Vos?"

"No game, I assure you," he said. "Well . . . perhaps gambling. But it's a risk I have to take."

"I don't like this," she warned him.

"I know, and I promise you, everything will soon become clear."

"There was a handsome idiot who told me once that for a team to work, there has to be trust."

Pain showed in his brown eyes. Vos placed his hands on her shoulders. "Hey," he said. "Sometimes secrets have to be kept for a little while. That doesn't mean you can't trust me."

"Not from me, Quinlan," Ventress said. "You shouldn't keep secrets from *me*."

"I could say something really cruel right now about Master Tholme, but I'm not going to. You could say something cruel right back. Or," Vos said, lifting her chin with his forefinger, "you can trust me. Or at least trust in what I feel for you."

Ventress still felt uneasy, but she nodded. That was one thing she was sure of. It would have to be enough.

"Come on," she said. "Let's go kill a count."

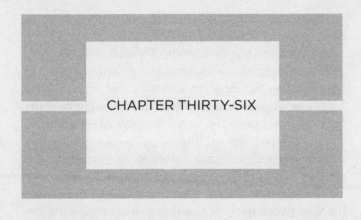

CHAPTER THIRTY-SIX

The *Banshee* came out of hyperspace near Christoph-sis. "Wow," Vos said, peering out at the fleet of battleships in the distance. "I don't even know what this vendetta is about. Do you?"

"Don't know," Ventress said drily, "don't care." She touched the controls. "Well, well, it pays to arrive when a battle is in progress. The doors are open and all hangar shields are deactivated so the ships can get in and out as needed."

"Asajj," Vos said quietly.

Ventress froze at the tone in his voice and looked up at him. "Don't you dare," she said, her own voice a warning.

"There's no way we can hide this ship in the hangar. And . . . this is my battle. You yourself said you didn't need to see Dooku dead. I still have to. I want to do it for me, and I want to do it because I know what good it will do the galaxy."

"You want me to just hang around and drive the getaway speeder, is that it?"

Vos knelt beside her chair. "I want you to be safe," he said, taking her hand, "and wait for me. Because I am coming back to you when this job is done. I promise."

Ventress's eyes searched his. Then she reached out, grabbed the front of his robe, and pulled him toward her, bending her head to kiss him. He returned the kiss eagerly, almost desperately, one hand cupping the back of her head, the other around her shoulders. Then Ventress released him.

"You better," she said. "Because if you don't, I'm coming in after you. That's *my* promise."

"Deal," he said, and rose. She watched him make his way to the back of the ship and take position beside the door, and then she turned to the controls. Gently, she moved the cloaked ship beside Dooku's massive dreadnought, taking it slowly and carefully toward the open hangar doors. Vos was right—a single person might be able to slip in unnoticed, but her ship would not.

"Opening the doors," she called, and suited action to word.

"Almost, almost . . . ," Vos said. "Just a little closer."

Ventress dropped deep into herself, using her awareness of her surroundings in the Force to bring the door close enough for Vos to leap to safety, but not so close that she would slam into the hangar. She closed her eyes, moving her fingers on the controls, then opened them. She was there.

Ventress turned to look at him. "Now!" she cried.

Their eyes met. Vos gave her a confident grin, and leapt.

The shuttle had been Anakin's idea. Naturally.

They had brought a commandeered Separatist shuttle aboard the *Vigilance,* complete with two defunct battle droids Anakin had reprogrammed to be operated remotely. Hidden behind the two droid "pilots" seated in the cockpit, Kenobi and Anakin were pressed tightly together in the cramped space.

"Anakin," Kenobi said, maneuvering the handheld controls, "this plan, like most of your plans, is completely insane."

"Try not to be a downer. Just for once. For me." Anakin spoke into a jury-rigged comlink, and his voice now issued through the droid's metallic mouth. He shot Obi-Wan a triumphant look.

"You're going too fast. They're going to know something's wrong," Kenobi warned. Unlike Anakin, he chose not to speak through the makeshift comm.

Anakin's droid hit Obi-Wan's in the arm with a touch too much enjoyment. "Lighten up, will you? Okay. Our intel shows that Ventress and Vos have split up, and Vos is inside that cruiser. That must be where Dooku is."

"And clearly, you just plan on waltzing in."

"Roger, roger," Anakin said, and grinned.

The reprogrammed droids continued to be useful even after the trick enabled the Jedi to, as Obi-Wan had said, waltz in. Now on foot and following a good distance behind the clankers, Anakin and Kenobi sent them up ahead into corridors, seeing what the droids saw. At one point, Kenobi said, "We need to find out where Dooku is. I'd say on the bridge."

"Hold that thought," Anakin said. He marched his droid up a corridor toward a group of blaster-holding battle droids.

"Anakin—"

"Shhh," Anakin said. His fingers tapped the controls, and his droid pointed to its own throat. "My vocabulator's broken," he said.

"Wow, you sound terrible. Better get that repaired," one of the other battle droids said.

"Roger. I have information for Count Dooku. Where is he located?" the Anakin-droid asked.

"He's on the bridge, but he's heading to the observation room now. I'd change your voice first, though," the other one advised.

"Roger, roger," Anakin's droid said, and marched on.

Kenobi turned and said with reluctant admiration, "Well done, Anakin."

"Roger, r—"

"No," Kenobi interrupted. "Let's get to the observation deck before Dooku does."

They continued to utilize their droids for recon, finally "parking them" in an out-of-the-way corner. The droids would be discovered at some point, but the Jedi hoped to have their business concluded by then and be on their way back to Coruscant . . . one way or another. Even taking an indirect route, they did arrive before the ship's master, though with only a few moments to spare. They glanced around, chagrined.

"Why does Dooku have to be so . . . *tidy,*" Anakin muttered. There was only one place to hide, and it was painfully obvious: beneath the large, curving desk off to one side.

"Cluttered room, cluttered mind," murmured Kenobi absently. "Well, at least it's not a difficult choice. We can both fit under there if we try. But we'd better hurry." Kenobi was right on both counts. He and Anakin had just settled themselves into a position where, if they were careful, they could peer around the edge of the desk when the door slid open.

Count Dooku entered alone, and for a moment Kenobi thought he had sensed them. The count paused, frowning, his gaze moving about the room.

Both Kenobi and Anakin ducked back, gripping their lightsaber hilts. Dooku was actually walking toward the desk when the door opened again.

Standing in the doorway, flanked by a group of battle droids, was Quinlan Vos—but one who looked nothing like the cheerful Jedi whom Kenobi had known for years. This man looked cold, arrogant . . . evil. Beside Kenobi, Anakin made a soft, angry sound and started to rise. Obi-Wan laid a hand on his arm and mouthed the word, *Wait*.

"We brought him here, sir, just like you asked," one of the battle droids said.

"Vos," Dooku said. "Were you successful?"

"I'm here, aren't I?" Vos answered. His voice was as icy as his expression.

Dooku chuckled, looking the other man up and down appraisingly. "You seem . . . unburdened. I sense a greater strength in you."

"I agree," Vos said. "I am calmer. More focused. Stronger than before." In the blink of an eye, he seized and activated his lightsaber. Its green glow bathed his face as he smiled. "Strong enough to kill you."

This time looking relieved, Anakin moved to get up. Again, Kenobi held him back. "Let this play out," he whispered. "We must be absolutely certain."

Dooku's own lightsaber was activated now, and the two men regarded each other. Dooku sighed. "Must we do this yet again? This time I shall make certain to swat this pesky *fly*!"

The count went from standing perfectly still to a blur, but Vos was faster. He leapt up and over Dooku, just in time to prevent the red blade from severing his legs. Dooku whirled as Vos's blade slashed down and caught it on his own. Vos kicked out in a long swipe, angling his body to force his enemy's blade down.

Dooku let himself fall, seizing Vos in the Force and hurling him across the room. The count extended his arm, and Force lightning leapt from his hand.

But Vos wasn't there. He stretched out his own hand and Dooku's lightsaber flew into his open palm. Vos smiled, a cruel, satisfied smile. Dooku appeared unrattled, blasting another round of Force lightning. While Vos crossed both green and red lightsabers in front of him in a protective X, Dooku made a pulling motion with his other hand, and Vos was flipped backward. The red lightsaber returned to its owner, and the fight continued.

Both Jedi watching were prepared to act if need be. Indeed, Anakin was more than eager to do so. But, truth be told, Vos seemed to be holding his own against Dooku. He leapt, sprang, ducked, and tumbled. Dooku might have been a master of technique, but Vos's characteristic unpredictability—quite possibly even to himself—often gave him the edge.

As it did now. Vos all but danced around Dooku, forcing the older man to whirl, strike, and block from every side. And then—there it was. Dooku overextended—only a trifle—and the next thing Kenobi knew the count's lightsaber was across the room and the count himself was on his back.

Vos smiled down at the defeated Sith. The tip of his lightsaber was a centimeter away from Dooku's throat.

Even now, Kenobi waited. Why wasn't Vos taking the final step?

Dooku, defiant to the last, spoke up. "What can you possibly think you'd gain from my death?" he sneered. "A sense of satisfaction? A badge of honor?"

Vos leaned closer, his gaze locked with Dooku's.

"A new Master," he said.

"What's he doing?" Anakin hissed.

Dooku, too, seemed startled. "Impossible!" he snapped.

Vos calmly grabbed Dooku by the hair and slammed his head violently against the floor. "Is it?" he asked. "After all of your betrayals? Your mistakes? You think your lord would be so quick to deny me?"

"Sidious will kill you as soon as he lays eyes upon you! Do *you* think he accepts just *anyone* as an apprentice? A mediocre Jedi, no less?"

"Mediocre? Who's got the lightsaber?" Again, Vos slammed Dooku's head against the unyielding metal of the deck, this time with his hand around the older man's throat. Vos's fingers tightened.

"You need . . . an introduction . . . ," Dooku choked out.

"Obi-Wan," Anakin said in a low, urgent voice. Kenobi held up a hand. He sensed there was more to learn before they intervened—perhaps even the identity of this second Sith Lord.

"You're lying," said Vos, but Kenobi noticed that he had relaxed his grip so that Dooku could speak more easily.

"Am I? Go then. Find him. See what happens. Or you could join with me again. We will defeat Sidious together!"

"I won't be your apprentice!" Vos started to choke Dooku again.

"No, no!" Dooku wheezed. "A team. Equals."

"Sith don't work that way."

"Are you and I ordinary Sith?"

Vos still looked skeptical. "You know where he is? And do *not* lie to me!"

"Of course I know. I'm the only one he trusts!"

There was a long, tense minute. Kenobi hoped desperately that Vos wouldn't take that final step, that one that would doom him. *Don't let him go, old friend . . .*

Vos released Dooku. "Then let's go find—"

As one, Anakin and Obi-Wan sprang from their place of concealment. Dooku leapt up, hissing, "*Jedi!*"

Obi-Wan was too devastated to speak. He lunged for Dooku, kicking the count's legs out from underneath him, then thrust out his hand. Dooku's lightsaber flew toward him from the corner of the room where it had rolled. Obi-Wan ignited it and placed the tip a hair's breadth away from Dooku's chest.

Anakin had targeted Vos, head-butting him and snatching up Vos's lightsaber. He stood over Vos, pain and anger warring on his face as he spoke. "I am happy to say that this little unholy alliance you two have formed is officially *over*!"

"Count Dooku, Quinlan Vos," Kenobi said, surprised at how strong and steady his voice sounded, "you are both under arrest on charges of treason."

"Obi-Wan," Vos began, staring with a shocked expression at his old friend.

"You had your chance," Kenobi snapped. "More than one. Come on."

CHAPTER THIRTY-SEVEN

The darkness of the *Vigilance*'s war room suited the somberness of the news. The only light came from the multicolored small screens on the various black consoles, and from the cool blue of Master Kenobi's grim-visaged hologram. Beside the Mahran, Kav Bayons, a Chagrian Jedi Knight, stood in shock, his mouth slightly open. Even Commander Cody looked stunned.

"There . . . there must be some mistake," Desh stammered.

"I wish there were," Kenobi said. He looked . . . old, and sadder than Desh had ever seen him. "The only good news is, we now also have Count Dooku in custody. General Skywalker and I will be rendez-vousing with you shortly with the prisoners." Kenobi hesitated. "Bayons, Desh . . . you should know that my orders from the Council originally stipulated ex-ecution. It may yet come to that, and we may be the ones asked to perform it."

"Execution? *Both of them?*" *This can't possibly be happening . . .*

"Both of them," Kenobi repeated heavily. "I'll be

checking in with the Council immediately upon my arrival, and I hope they will be open to reconsidering the sentence. I wanted you both to understand the full import of this situation. Please meet us in the hangar—and bring enough men to properly provide escort for the prisoners to the brig."

"Yes, Master Kenobi," Desh said automatically. Kenobi's image flickered and disappeared. Desh stood for a moment, dazed.

Cody looked at him with a mixture of pity, compassion, and resolve. Bayons had a sympathetic look on his light-blue face. Tall, younger than Desh, he had distinguished himself in battle, but the Mahran suspected this was the Chagrian's first encounter with the true power of the dark side. Truth be told, it was Desh's, too, and it was more devastating than he ever could have imagined.

"Desh, I'm so sorry," Bayons said. "I know you and Master Vos were friends."

"Yes, I—I've known Quinlan for most of my life. I can't believe it."

"It's always a shocker when one of your own betrays you," Cody said. "We clones had a similar situation a couple years back. One of our men, Slick, turned against us. He was working with the enemy. Said he loved his brothers, but he was selling information to Ventress and sabotaging our supplies . . . doing things that could end up getting a lot of those brothers killed. Funny way of showing love, if you ask me."

He shook his head. "I hope you'll forgive me saying this, sir, but—I'd almost rather have my mate seduced by the dark side than be a simple turncoat."

"No forgiveness needed," Desh said. "But either way, it's a tragedy." He squared his narrow shoulders and gathered himself. They had a job to do. "Com-

mander," he said, "how many men should we bring
to the hangar?"

Cody chuckled humorlessly. "For Count Dooku
and Quinlan Vos? Two hundred ought to do it."

It was considerably fewer than two hundred, but a
full two dozen armed clones, handpicked by Cody,
assembled in the *Vigilance*'s cavernous hangar to
await the arrival of the infamous prisoners. Even
with advance warning, Desh wasn't prepared to see
his old friend being marched out of the Jedi shuttle in
stun cuffs alongside the infamous Count Dooku.
General Skywalker looked as if he wished he could
lop off Vos's head then and there. Master Kenobi also
wore a grim, angry look, but there was pain there,
too.

Desh reached into the Force and calmed himself.
He could see it now, he realized: the flat, cold expression in Vos's eyes. The cruel set of his mouth, so much
like Dooku's. Doubtless feeling his gaze, Vos turned
to regard his old friend Desh. There was no flicker
of remorse, or pleading, or anything other than cold
hate on those familiar features. Desh swallowed hard.
This was going to be the most difficult thing he'd ever
done.

"Sir," said Cody, "we've brought two dozen of our
finest men to serve as escort, and I've stationed clones
every couple of meters between here and the brig."

Skywalker was practically shoving Vos toward
Desh as Kenobi said, "Good job, Commander." The
Jedi Master transferred Dooku to Bayons with more
decorum, though no less distaste. Desh noticed that
Kenobi seemed unable to bring himself even to look
at Vos. "These two have a tendency to slip away."

"Not on my watch, sir."

"Let's go tell the Council, Anakin," Kenobi said. With a final glare at both Dooku and Vos, Skywalker turned and followed Kenobi.

And then Desh was face-to-face with Vos. He found himself baring his sharp white teeth in a silent snarl. Wordlessly, he nodded to the clones. Four of them—including Cody, who made straight for Dooku—stepped up to grasp the prisoners' arms and march the captives to the hold.

"Desh, you're making a mistake," Vos said.

"*You* already made one," Desh snapped. The hackles on his neck rose and his nostrils flared as he drew breath to calm himself. "And now you might have to die for it."

He knew he shouldn't say anything more. He should be calm, remind himself of the Jedi Code. Remain nonattached. It simply wasn't possible.

"What the hell were you thinking, Vos?" Desh's voice cracked slightly. "Why did you *do* this?"

"His reasons are his own," Dooku said smoothly.

"*You* be quiet," Bayons snapped.

The group continued in silence. The four clones flanking the prisoners kept a tight hold on manacled arms. A dozen clones walked in front of them. The Jedi followed behind, and the rest of the clones brought up the rear. Somewhat to Desh's surprise, neither Vos nor Dooku offered resistance.

Abruptly, Vos stopped and turned to Desh. "You want to know why I did it?" he asked, and Desh couldn't read his expression.

"Don't bother pleading," said the clone on Vos's right, yanking his arm.

"Sir," warned Cody, "do *not* listen to him."

Desh held up a hand. "No, wait. It's all right, Commander. I want to hear this." He stepped directly in front of Vos and folded his arms, his ears flat against his head. "Go ahead."

"Jedi don't understand," Vos said, his voice dripping contempt. "You can't grasp the full power of the dark side. You're too afraid to wield it. You're not prepared to make the sacrifices necessary. You're weak, Desh. *Weak*. And pathetic. And I'm—"

Desh's lightsaber flew into Vos's hands.

"—sorry," Vos finished, violently Force-shoving the shocked Jedi into the clones behind him. They went flying.

Desh sprang to his feet just in time to see Vos slice through Dooku's bonds. The count emulated his ally, seizing Bayons's lightsaber. In rapid succession Dooku cut down one clone escort, Force-threw Cody down the corridor and against the bulkhead, freed Vos, then blasted everyone in front of him, including Bayons, with Force lightning. The Chagrian and the four clones went down, writhing in agony.

Holding Desh's blue lightsaber, Vos charged at him. Their eyes met. Desh growled and started toward his old friend, but just as he reached out to grab Vos in the Force, the former Jedi Master soared over the heads of both the Mahran and the clones and continued running down the hall back toward the hangar. Dooku followed him.

Desh glanced over his shoulder. All but one of the clones lay at such unnatural angles that it was clear they would never rise again. Cody seemed to be injured, but alive. Bayons was a little dazed, but he quickly shook his head and joined Desh in giving chase.

The few clones still on their feet were firing at the escaped prisoners. Vos whirled, batting back the blasts and shouting to Dooku, "Take them out!"

"With pleasure," Dooku purred. He paused, shot

both hands out in front of him, and raised his clenched fists. The clones were lifted in the Force, dropping their blasters as their hands went to their necks to pry off invisible hands. Desh heard an awful crunch, and they both went limp. Sneering, Dooku hurled the corpses directly at Bayons and Desh. The two Jedi dodged, and kept coming.

There was only one thought in Desh's mind as he summoned the Force to him and used it to leap at a man he had considered a great friend: *Stop Vos*. It was clear to Desh now that the only way to do that was to kill him.

To kill him . . . and to die with him.

The Mahran snapped his right wrist as he sprang, splaying his hand. A six-centimeter shard of bone, slick with black venom, emerged directly below his palm. The action of exposing the stinger released its toxin into Desh's bloodstream. It was not painful . . . not yet. Just as his leap was about to bring him crashing down atop Vos, the Sith apprentice—for such Desh now knew him to be—shot out a hand. Desh was suddenly whipped around. To his horror, Vos had hurled him straight at Bayons.

Desperately, Desh tried to twist to the side, to angle his stinger away from his fellow Jedi, but it was too late. The lethal tip grazed the Chagrian's blue face, drawing a thin line of blood. The surrounding flesh began to swell immediately. Bayons's eyes went wide as he stared, shocked, at Desh. He lurched to the side, catching himself on the wall.

Venom pumped more freely now throughout Desh's body. He lay where he had fallen, shaking with agony as his blood turned to liquid fire, scalding him with every beat of his heart. He bit back a howl, and froth dripped from his muzzle. His vision was starting to deteriorate. In a few moments, he would be completely blind, but for now, he could dimly make out the figure standing over him.

Vos knew about the Mahran birthright. And he knew that death, while inevitable, could sometimes take as long as ten minutes and would be an excruciating torment.

So it was that, when Vos lifted Desh's own lightsaber and brought it sweeping down, Desh was unsure if Vos meant the death blow as a cruelty, or a kindness.

Kenobi took a deep breath. There was no point in putting this off any longer. He pressed a button on the holographic table in the war room and an image of the Jedi Council appeared. He looked to Yoda first, who regarded him solemnly.

"Fallen, Vos has." It was a statement, not a question.

"Yes, Master Yoda," Kenobi replied. Even to his own ears, his voice sounded disheartened. "We have taken both Vos and Dooku into custody." He gave them a brief summary of events.

"I am truly sorry things worked out this way, Master Kenobi," Windu said. "But . . . I think we can all agree that this matter has been resolved. Quinlan Vos has signed his own death warrant."

The entire Council looked dismayed, even Windu. There was no doubt in Kenobi's mind that the other Master would have preferred to be wrong.

Yoda nodded sadly. "Signed it, he has."

"We, ah . . . can take care of the matter here, if you wish." *Bloodless words for a bloody deed,* Kenobi thought as he spoke them.

Yoda shook his head. "Anticipate a capture of both, we did not. To the Temple you will bring them.

If information from them we obtain, saved, lives can be. But in the end . . . executions, must we have."

"Yes, Master Yoda." Kenobi pressed a button and the hologram disappeared. He placed both hands on the table and bowed his head for a moment.

"Hey," said Anakin, "this isn't your fault."

Kenobi gave him a humorless chuckle. "Isn't it? I'm the one who suggested him for the mission in the first place."

"You couldn't possibly have—"

"General Kenobi! General Skywalker!" Cody's voice issuing from Kenobi's comlink was frantic. "They've escaped! Looks like my men are all dead. They got Desh and Bayons, too. They're heading down the corridor now, back to the hangar."

"Can you give chase?" Kenobi asked. As he spoke, he and Anakin had already activated their lightsabers and were heading to the door.

"Sorry, sir, that's a negative, my leg's been snapped like a twig."

"We'll get you patched up, Cody, don't you worry," Anakin said, muttering, "Those slippery, slimy . . ."

"Save your breath," said Kenobi, "and run."

"Ventress?"

Ventress closed her eyes in relief. "Vos? Is it done?"

"I'm sending you the coordinates of our location." His voice was tense.

"Coordinates? *Our?* Who's with you?"

"I'll explain later."

"You'll explain *now.*"

"Now is *really* not the time." His voice was rising and he sounded distracted.

Again, the alarm bells sounded in her mind. "Fine. I'm on my way. But I don't like this, Vos."

She entered the coordinates and her eyes widened. Vos was on a Jedi cruiser! For a moment, Ventress hesitated. Something had clearly gone wrong. But Vos wasn't dark. The Jedi needed to know that. Perhaps she should reach out to Kenobi—

Even as she had the thought Ventress dismissed it. No. Better to rescue Vos and disappear immediately. Let the Jedi think what they would. Their opinion would no longer matter.

Ventress brought her ship beside the hangar door just as it opened. Activating the door to the *Banshee,* she heard two thumps as Vos and his unknown companion jumped inside. She hit the controls, slamming the door shut and sped off, entering random coordinates to confound pursuit, then unbuckled herself and strode back to greet Vos.

"I see you're still in one . . ." Her voice trailed off. *Dooku!* Standing in the hold and peering up at her, the count seemed almost as shocked as she was. White-hot anger shot through Ventress and she whirled on Vos. "What have you *done?*"

"It's not what you—" Vos began.

"It's not what I think? How is this *possibly* not what I think? Dooku? In the flesh? Still *alive?*"

"Our escape plans hinged on her?" Dooku exclaimed almost at the same moment, his lip curling. "The most abysmal assassin of all time?"

Vos's face went hard and he shoved Dooku. "Watch your mouth!"

"I don't trust her!"

"Well, I *do,* and you're free because of me. We had a deal. Understand?" Contempt and resignation flickered over Dooku's patrician face, then he nodded. "Good. Now strap yourself in."

"Vos," Ventress said, barely reining in her anger, "we need to talk. Now." She jerked her head toward the cockpit. Vos nodded and quickly climbed the ladder. Glancing back at the hold, Ventress whispered, "What the *hell* is going on?"

"I will tell you. I promise."

"Yes, you will," Ventress agreed. "Right now."

"Right now, we've got a Jedi cruiser on our tail. Let's get somewhere safe first, and then I'll tell you everything."

"Where is 'safe'?"

"Christophsis. We'll rendezvous with a Separatist cruiser there that's expecting us."

While he was speaking, his gaze wandered to the hold and his eyes narrowed. Ventress looked at him incredulously for a moment. She searched his face, seeking answers there. He was right. They were fleeing, and Dooku absolutely needed to be watched every minute.

"All right," she agreed. "But I don't know of anything you can say that can convince me that bringing him along isn't a huge mistake—one that might get us killed."

CHAPTER THIRTY-EIGHT

Skywalker and Kenobi stood on the bridge of the *Vigilance*, which was closing the distance fast. "Obi-Wan," Anakin said, watching the *Banshee* head straight for a Separatist dreadnought, "we can't allow them to escape again. We've got to fire on them."

"And risk killing all on board?" Kenobi shook his head. "No. We must take them back to the Temple alive. There's too much they know that we need to find out." *Yes*, he thought bitterly, *by all means, let's make sure we keep them alive, only to kill them in the end anyway.*

"Just a graze. I promise," Anakin insisted. "It'll damage their ship, and they'll be forced to land. It's far better than the alternative of them getting away."

Kenobi stroked his beard, pondering. Ventress's ship was closing the gap. "All right," he said.

Anakin turned to Threepwood, the clone at the weapons station. "Fire when ready. Bring them down!"

"Aye, sir!"

*   *   *

They had almost reached the waiting dreadnought. Ventress was all too keenly aware of the Jedi cruiser behind them. She was torn between taking evasive maneuvers and getting the *Banshee* into the hangar as soon as possible. She reached into the Force—

"Hang on!" she cried. Ventress pulled the ship hard to port, but not in time to evade the Jedi's attack. The *Banshee* rocked violently. Smoke began to fill the cabin as the controls went haywire. Frantically, Ventress tried to keep the *Banshee* heading toward the open hangar, but like a rancor set on charging, the ship would no longer obey her. She couldn't make it to the ship, but maybe she could land it on Christophsis. There was no question at this point but that they were going to crash. The question was, how hard.

"Hang on!" she shouted. "Strap in and brace yourselves, I'm going to try to set us down!"

They hurtled through the atmosphere, the unforgiving crystalline ground rushing up as if eager to meet them. Ventress struggled with the controls, trying desperately to slow the fall, get the nose up—

She let go of the controls and tapped into her fear and anger, commanding the Force. She would *not* die in a ridiculous crash. There were questions she needed answers to. She poured forth all her will, insisting, *demanding,* that the *Banshee* slow, slow, even out, and—

They slammed into the surface.

Obi-Wan piloted the Jedi shuttle to the crash site and hovered over it. He and Anakin stared at it silently. It had been easy to locate; Ventress had left a trail of sheared-off blue-green crystal in what was obviously a barely controlled approach.

"You assured me it would be just a graze," Obi-Wan said.

"Sorry, sir," said Threepwood. "They veered at the last minute."

"Let us hope there are survivors," Kenobi said. "Prepare to take on injured."

As he settled the shuttle down on a flat area near the wreckage, Obi-Wan wasn't optimistic. The crash was bad. The clone had been right. Probably using her Force sensitivity, Ventress had indeed made a sudden move at the last minute. What was intended to be a graze had ended up being a solid strike at the ship's stern, and the engines had been damaged. Christophsis was a bad planet on which to crash, and the *Banshee* had not landed gently. Bits of debris were strewn everywhere.

The two Jedi, lightsabers ignited, and Threepwood, Tracker, and Boil, the clones who had accompanied them, made a silent circle about the downed vessel. Anakin signaled for the others to stay back as he stepped forward to cut a hole in the ship's door with his lightsaber. Using the Force, he pulled out the circular chunk of metal and placed it down. Smoke billowed out. He stuck his head inside, then turned to look at Kenobi. His face was contorted in anger.

"They're not here!"

"Sir," Tracker called out to them, "there's blood here. I think they kicked their way out of the forward viewport in the cockpit."

Kenobi looked. There was indeed blood—quite a lot of it. "Well," he said, "someone's been injured. They can't have gone far, then. Start searching the forest."

Anger, Ventress thought sourly, was good for so many things. Right now it was doing a superb job of keeping her on her feet, even moving with a fair approximation of speed, although her left knee and shoulder had been gouged by the shattered controls when they slammed into the unforgiving ground. They were heading for a tower where, Dooku assured them, they would find ships waiting to take them offworld to their next destination. She had no idea where that would be, of course. No one was telling her anything.

Vos had some bruises, but otherwise appeared to have escaped unscathed. Dooku was the most severely injured of the three. He hadn't been properly strapped down in the ship's hold when the Jedi had fired on the ship, and he was paying the price. He had one arm slung around Vos for support as they made their way through huge, jutting hexagons that comprised what served Christophsis for a forest.

As if on cue, she heard that smooth-as-silk voice, tense now with pain, pant, "I . . . have to stop."

"Ventress, hold up," Vos said. He lowered Dooku to the ground, propping him up against a tall, blue-green natural obelisk. The count winced and put a hand to his side.

Ventress gritted her teeth. "Of course, the one we came to kill is going to get us *all* killed." Shaking her head, she limped up to Vos and shoved him, hard. "You promised me that it would be over!"

Her words made Dooku chuckle, though he winced slightly at the pain. "Over? My dear Ventress, quite the opposite. It's only begun."

A cold finger of apprehension traced its way along her spine. "Vos," she said slowly, "what's he talking about? *What aren't you telling me?*"

Vos jerked his head at Dooku, then took her elbow and attempted to steer her out of hearing range. She wrenched her arm free, but accompanied him.

"I have something better in store for us," Vos said in a low voice. "You have to trust me on this one, Asajj, okay?" His eyes were pleading.

"This isn't about you," she said. "This plan was about *us. Together.* Remember?"

"It *is* about us, I promise!"

"You've been making promises an awful lot in the last hour," Ventress said. If he were anyone else, she'd simply strike off on her own at this point. But where could she go? She'd helped Vos escape, with *Count Dooku* himself in tow, no less. Somehow, she didn't think the Jedi would offer her a pardon a second time. And . . . she could still sense Vos's feelings for her. Whatever this "plan" was, he really was doing what he thought was best for the two of them. She had to keep trusting him, at least for now. This time, when he touched her face hesitantly, mindful of her turning away from him as she had earlier, she sighed and leaned her cheek into his hand.

"If you two lovebirds are done with your nauseating display," came the count's unwelcome voice, "we should probably keep moving."

Ventress turned to him, not bothering to hide her loathing. "You were the one who asked us to stop," she reminded him. At that moment her comlink began to blink. She looked at it in surprise, then started to thumb it off.

"No," Vos said. "Go over there. Take it."

She nodded. She limped a meter or two away from them, leaned against a chunk of stone, and answered. A hologram of Obi-Wan Kenobi popped up. He lifted his hands pleadingly. "Ventress," he said, "don't disconnect, please. Hear me out."

In a whisper, she said, "I don't have time for this, Kenobi."

"I'll be brief. Master Yoda has sensed that Vos has

turned to the dark side. He has entered into a partnership with Count Dooku. You must convince him to surrender, or we'll be forced to execute him!"

She inhaled swiftly. Execute? First Dooku, now Vos . . . she had never expected this from the Jedi. Then the other words the Jedi had said sank in.

No. It wasn't possible. She'd been able to sense the darkness in Vos before, but that was gone. He'd come back from it, as she had . . . but—no matter how much she believed Vos loved her, he *had* insisted on bringing Dooku, and he was definitely keeping something from her. Ventress looked over at the two men. Both were watching her, but neither could hear what she or Kenobi was saying. Keeping her voice low, she whispered, "You're wrong, Kenobi. He's going to complete his mission. You must give us time!"

Ventress clicked it off and took a deep breath. Vos stepped up to her. "What did he say?" he asked quietly, not wanting Dooku to overhear.

She spoke bluntly. "Obi-Wan told me you've turned to the dark side. He says they're going to kill us all unless you surrender."

Vos's eyes widened at the word *kill,* but he shook his head firmly. "Surrender? Now? No way. Not when we're this close."

"Close to what?"

His expression softened. He cupped her bone-white face in his dark hands. "Close to the end. Close to being utterly and completely free." He bent and kissed her tenderly, and Ventress returned his kiss almost desperately, hoping with all that was in her that he was right.

"She's blinded by love," Anakin said, not without sympathy.

Kenobi didn't disagree. All he said was, "We've got to find them."

His comlink chirped again and he answered quickly, hoping it was Ventress. Instead, the image of a grim-faced Mace Windu appeared.

"What's your status, Master Kenobi?"

"We were in pursuit of the vessel and brought it down to the surface. It looks like all aboard survived and, unfortunately, managed to escape. We're following them now. At least one appears to be injured." Obi-Wan hesitated. "We spoke briefly with Ventress, but she said very little. She doesn't believe Vos has turned. She says he is close to completing his mission . . ." He hated how uncertain his voice sounded.

Mace, however, was decidedly not uncertain in his response. "If he was close, it should have already been completed. The time for action is now. Trying to bring them in alive was clearly a mistake. Find the fugitives, and execute them."

A still, small voice inside Obi-Wan Kenobi said: *This is wrong.*

"*All* of them?" he asked in disbelief.

"Anyone who gets in your way," Mace replied.

CHAPTER THIRTY-NINE

Ventress, Vos, and Dooku pressed on. At first the promised tower appeared to be nothing more than another one of the beautiful, gigantic natural formations that adorned the planet's surface. But as they drew closer, Ventress saw that what once had indeed been nothing more than simply another crystal—albeit a particularly emormous one—had been cunningly hollowed out. It gleamed in the sunlight, but some of that gleam was on windows and weapons. It was indeed a tower, a place where death and deceit were conducted, and Ventress felt a peculiar, hot rush of hatred at the violation of something that had once been both extraordinary and innocent. They were close enough so that they walked in the tower's shadow, but before their arrival was detected, Dooku requested another stop.

"What now?" Ventress demanded.

"I mustn't look weak," he said. "Most of those we encounter will be droids, but there are a few organics among them. Vos—help me—"

Ventress folded her arms and watched. She had hoped Dooku would bleed out on the journey. She and Vos could return to the Jedi, having completed the mission. Once things had settled down, then, at last, they would leave as they had planned. Unfortunately, Dooku was as determined about this as he was about many things, and he insisted on clinging to life. As Vos assisted him in cutting loose the bloodiest part of his shirt and draping the outer fabric so that it concealed the wound, Ventress bit back a scathing comment.

Vos, you'd better be right about whatever it is you're planning.

"That's better," Dooku said.

"No *thank you?*" Ventress couldn't help it. The count gave her a disdainful look, straightened himself, and strode forward. Ventress had to admit, he gave away nothing. He was indeed a master of deceit.

Hundreds of droids clustered at the base of the tower, more hexagonal formations hitherto serving as concealment. It was a disconcerting feeling to have so many weapons pointed at one simultaneously. "Hold your fire!" Dooku shouted, striding out of the crystal forest into the open area with his hands raised in a commanding gesture. "It is I, your lord!"

"Count Dooku!" There was a clatter as every droid lowered its weapon in perfect unison.

"There, that's a better way to greet your master. Now take me to the command room."

"And them?" One of the droids peered at Dooku's companions. Ventress tensed. Against so many droids, the outcome was certain, but she'd go down fighting. If Dooku was going to betray them, now would be an ideal moment, when they were completely at his mercy.

"Yes, they are with me," Dooku said smoothly. Ventress relaxed, ever so slightly.

"Roger that. Right this way, sire."

* * *

Ventress's skin crawled at being in the very heart of a Separatist site. She had to stifle the urge to cut every droid she saw in half. By the time . . . whatever this was . . . was done, she knew she would be utterly drained. But then, she and Vos would be together and away from all of this—the Jedi, the Separatists, Dooku, everything. And that was worth adrenal depletion now.

They followed Dooku into a lift that took them up to one of the top stories, and stepped into a large room. Presumably one-way glass wrapped around the room floor-to-ceiling, providing a 270-degree view. Even the naked eye could see for kilometers, and, listening to the hum and whir of various displays and consoles, Ventress realized that from here, the Separatists could also monitor nearly everything on Christophsis. The planet's unique composition had provided Dooku the ultimate camouflage for a key base.

The room had been buzzing with high-pitched droid chatter, which fell silent when Dooku entered. Vos and Ventress hung back slightly. She glanced at Vos, but his gaze was locked on Dooku. Ventress wondered if he was starting to have second thoughts. She hoped so.

"Sir," one of the droids piped up, "Darth Sidious has been trying to contact you. He says it's urgent!"

"Urgent? Really?" Dooku asked. "I wonder what he could want. Reach out to him immediately." He eyed Ventress and Vos. "You two will wait here." The count turned and stepped into a side door on the right of the lift. Vos immediately slipped in behind him with no glance at Ventress. Furious with both of them, she followed just as the doors were closing.

The chamber was dark, the only light coming from a single holotable in its center.

Dooku turned, irritated. "I told you to wait outside!"

"No way," Vos said. "You said something about an introduction, if I recall." He faded back into the shadows near the door, gesturing Ventress to move to the other side of the holotable. She pressed back into the corner, hiding most of her noticeable white face with one arm in case for any reason Sidious turned around. The other gripped her lightsaber hilt.

The count seemed to want to protest, but at that moment a hologram appeared. Dooku fell to his knees, his head bowed. Ventress had seen Darth Sidious before, but had never beheld his face. Nor would she likely see it now. He wore the same heavy robes and dark cowl that he always had, concealing his features even now, when he assumed he would only be talking to Dooku.

"Darth Tyranus," intoned Count Dooku's Master. Even though he wasn't physically present, the simple sound of his voice—rasping, papery somehow, like the rustling of ancient parchment—sent a shiver through Ventress. This man was steeped in the dark side of the Force, saturated with it, in a way that she was certain Vos, perhaps even Dooku, had never been. She tightened her grip on her lightsaber.

"Master," Dooku replied, his voice laced with a tone Ventress had never heard in it: subservience.

"You seem to have disappeared for quite a while."

"My apologies, my lord. I was briefly detained by Republic forces, but have managed to evade them."

The cloaked figure turned his head. "Who is there with you? In the shadows?"

Vos stepped forward. "This . . . this is my new . . .

assassin," Dooku replied, his poised demeanor slipping slightly.

"Assassin?" The papery voice had dropped to a lower timbre, simmering with disapproval and warning. "You know my feelings about the kind of help you are wont to employ."

"He'll be no trouble," Dooku assured him quickly.

"I'm sure he won't." Darth Sidious's tone was a dangerous purr.

Dooku quickly changed the subject. "Master, we are too exposed here on Christophsis. We must find a safe haven. Perhaps you could send a ship?"

There was a pause. Then, "Perhaps," Darth Sidious said. His hologram disappeared. Ventress exhaled slowly.

"Your *assassin*?" Vos snapped.

Dooku, once again haughty and contemptuous, replied, "What would you have me say? *Your rival?*"

Before Vos could retort, there came a thundering *crack* and the entire tower shivered. "What was that?" Dooku exclaimed, stumbling to his feet and lurching out the door. It opened onto shambles. The windows that enclosed three-fourths of the space had been blasted away, along with the consoles on that side. Incongrously beautiful chunks of crystal covered the floor. Tongues of flame licked upward, and the room was starting to fill with acrid smoke. Droids were firing, futilely, and as Ventress watched, the Jedi shuttle came around for a second pass.

"Down!" Vos shouted, and Ventress and Dooku obeyed, dropping to the floor. Ventress propped herself up on one elbow, deflecting debris with her other hand. The tower trembled, again, and then lurched violently.

"Where are the stairs?" Vos demanded, shaking Dooku.

"This way!" Dooku got to his feet and went through the door on the opposite side of the lift. Though not narrow, the carved, gleaming stairs were winding, and Ventress knew at once that running down them would take too long. Steeling herself for the pain her wounded leg would experience on impact, she Force-leapt to a spot below. She bit back a cry, noting with satisfaction that Dooku was unable to stifle his. Again and again, the three leapt, following the spiral downward. Ventress only hoped they would make it to the ground before the Jedi brought the whole tower crumbling on top of them.

This is wrong.

The still, small voice would not let Obi-Wan be. It kept brushing his thoughts, gentle but persistent. *Which part?* he wondered. *Killing all three of them, even Ventress, who tried to help? Executing Vos without a trial?*

Sending Vos to assassinate Dooku?

Above, the shuttle and the ARC-170s Kenobi had ordered for reinforcement continued their aerial attack while dozens of troops had joined him and Anakin on the ground. "Fire!" Anakin shouted. The clones obeyed, launching a slew of grenades at the droids clustered at the base of the tower. The attack dropped most of the battle droids, and the cannons blasted a huge hole in the magnificent chunk of crystal. Orange flames sent black smoke spiraling into the incongruously blue, cloud-dotted sky.

"We need more firepower!" Anakin shouted. "Send in the walkers!"

This is wrong.

Abruptly, Obi-Wan was unable to withstand the

mild prodding. "Anakin," he called, "we need to back off. They won't survive this if we keep firing."

Anakin gave him a look of surprise. "You heard what Master Windu said. Kill anyone who gets in our way!"

"I know what he said," Kenobi replied, "but I think if it's a possibility, we should still try to get them out of here unharmed. I'm telling you to pull back!"

Anakin's golden brows drew together in a frown. "I'm not going against Master Windu's orders. Especially not for Dooku, a traitor and a—"

His words were drowned out by the roar of the walkers, all firing simultaneously at a single spot on the tower. A deafening *crack* rose above even the cacophony of the tanks. As cleanly as if it had been snapped in two by an unseen giant, the tower broke. The top portion, a good two-thirds of the obelisk, toppled slowly but inevitably. The firing continued, this time at the exposed interior. Smoke plumed upward, joined by sparkling crystal powder, and smaller fires began breaking out.

"We've got to find them!" Kenobi shouted, coughing from the dust that made his throat as dry as Tatooine. "They're still inside!"

CHAPTER FORTY

Ventress came to in darkness. Something heavy was pressing down on her, and her eyelids were sealed shut with a sticky substance. She tried to lift a hand to wipe off whatever was covering them, but pain shot through her at the movement and she almost lost consciousness a second time. The last thing she remembered was being in mid-jump. A sound like nothing she had ever heard had thundered in her ears, and then—

The tower. It had shattered. Vos . . . was he . . .

"Ventress!" Despite the physical agony, relief washed through Ventress. He was still alive. Maybe the tower had taken Dooku with it to both their demises.

"*Ventress!*"

She tried to call out to him, but her torso was squeezed so tightly she could barely breathe. "Vos," she whispered.

"We've got to get out of here." Dooku's voice, ragged but imperious as always. "They'll storm through here in a matter of minutes. Leave her!" Ventress couldn't see Vos's reaction, but she heard a sharp growl of anger. She found herself smiling. Even when he could reasonably expect her to be dead or beyond help, even when his own life was at risk, Vos would not abandon her.

"Ventress!" He was closer now, and she tried again. A groan escaped her lips; faint, but sufficient. She heard grating sounds above her and forced her eyes open, tearing off some lashes in the process. Light, awhirl with glittering dust, met her gaze. And then, the beloved face. He'd suffered a head injury, and a trickle of scarlet contrasted vividly with both his dark skin and his bright-yellow tattoo. Ventress didn't know yet the extent of her injuries, but by his expression, she knew they were serious. He knelt beside her.

"Put your arms around my neck," he said. She tried to do so, but she suspected that one arm was broken. The other was heavy, so heavy. Ventress made a sound of frustration, and he soothed her, "That's all right, I've got you. I've got you. Come on, we're going to get out of here to someplace safe."

He slid his arm around her shoulders and she bit back a cry. Dooku was glaring at them; doubtless he wished he'd put his lightsaber through both of them at an earlier opportunity. He, too, had been injured in the collapse of the tower. The crystal chunk that had sliced along his chest must have had an edge as sharp as a finely honed blade. Blood oozed out from a tear in both fabric and skin.

A too-familiar sound caught their attention—that of booted feet running toward them. "Jedi and their clones," growled Dooku.

Vos tossed the count his lightsaber. "You'll need it," he said, slipping his other arm beneath Ventress's knees. "This'll hurt," he said to her, "and I'm sorry."

A scream tore from her throat. The pain increased when Vos broke into a jog, bearing her out of the ruined building and following Dooku toward a large crystal boulder, a camouflaged outlying building. Ventress felt a flicker of hope that they would be able to buy enough time for Sidious's ship to reach them.

If Sidious, whoever he was, was indeed sending a ship.

If they all survived their injuries.

If . . .

Droids clattered dutifully behind them, some of them stopping to fire on the approaching clones. Ventress could see red and blue blasterfire streaking through the air, and the occasional flash of green and light blue that denoted the Jedi's lightsabers. It all became a blur, and she closed her eyes.

Vos flung himself to the right, sending searing pain through Ventress's whole body. Her eyes snapped open to see blue fire missing her by a few centimeters, and then they were inside the crystalline building. Another blaster bolt, and this time, it hit. Dooku had just made it to the threshold when he suddenly arched in pain and collapsed. Vos placed Ventress down as quickly as he could and hauled Dooku's limp form inside with one hand, fending off the blaster bolts with his lightsaber. The doors closed, but Ventress could still hear the sound of the continued onslaught. Outside, the droids strove to protect them. The crystal this time was not part of the building, but merely a second protective layer. The inside looked like someone had gone to great effort to design either the ultimate prison, or the ultimate refuge.

Ventress chuckled weakly as she stared at Dooku's

body. "It's taken a few tries," she murmured, "but finally someone got him."

Vos knelt beside Dooku, pressing a finger to his throat. "No, he's still alive, just unconscious," he said.

Ventress closed her eyes, scowling. "Damn."

Vos inspected the wound, then rolled Dooku's limp form over. "There's nothing we can do now about the blaster burn, but this injury from the crash has re-opened." Gently, Vos picked Ventress up and laid her down beside the unconscious Dooku. He took her good arm and placed it on Dooku's injury. "Keep pressure on it," he said.

Ventress snatched her hand away, not caring that the sudden gesture sent waves of pain through her. "No!" she snapped. "Let him bleed. This is what we want. This is what we *need*. He must die!"

Vos shook his head. "No! I need him alive. Keep the pressure steady." He pressed his lips together. "This place is pretty impregnable. The only weakness is that door. I'm going to go help the droids even the odds—buy us time for the rescue ship to get here."

"But—"

He kissed her, hard, then raced out to the front of the building. Both worried and angry, Ventress watched him go, then heard the sounds of blasterfire and the hum of his lightsaber.

"Why are *you* so desperate to save me?" Dooku's voice was weak, but as always, the sound of it angered her.

She turned back to her former Master. "Awake now, are you? Actually, I'd rather watch you rot."

He smirked. "I doubt that will be happening anytime soon. Vos is a Dark Lord, as I am, and he knows better than to turn against his kind."

Ventress stiffened. "A Dark Lord?" Could Obi-Wan have been right?

"Oh, yes," Dooku said casually. "He has sworn allegiance to the dark side. He and I will take down Lord Sidious once and for all, and rule the galaxy together." He added, "Hopefully, you'll have been disposed of by then."

Ventress narrowed her eyes and put an unnecessary amount of pressure on his wound. He gasped most satisfactorily. "I've heard that line before. Didn't *we* once have similar plans?"

Through gritted teeth, Dooku said, "No, no. You must have been mistaken. You were never cut out for anything more than grunt work. Vos is different. He was born for the darkness. You"—he smiled cruelly—"you just . . . flirt with it."

Ventress felt doubt creeping into her heart and stole another look at the door. Vos had said he needed Dooku alive. That he had "bigger plans." Was this really what he meant?

Dooku pressed his advantage. "If Vos was going to kill me, why does he protect me? Why wait so long? He's had so many chances . . ."

Ventress narrowed her eyes. This was what Dooku did. It was how he controlled people. He planted doubts in soil he found fertile, and the darkness took root from those doubts. Snarling, she arched up and put all her weight into the wound. "You have no idea what he's planning!"

Again, Dooku winced, but managed, "Apparently, neither do you."

The truth of that bit deep.

"I think they got Dooku," Anakin said, looking through a pair of electrobinoculars. "And I don't see

Ventress. But Vos and the droids are more than holding their own."

He passed the electrobinoculars to Obi-Wan, who unfortunately agreed with him. "This isn't working," Kenobi said with a sigh. "We're able to damage the concealing crystal outer layer, but the one inside is built like a vault. It was likely designed for precisely this purpose."

Anakin gave an unhappy grunt. "I bet Dooku's arranged for someone to get him. If they can fend us off long enough, we might soon find ourselves outnumbered. There's got to be another way!"

Kenobi tugged at his beard, thinking. There seemed to be only one point of weakness—the single entrance. But really, did any well-designed building *not* have more than one entrance?

"A cease-fire," he said.

Anakin stared at him as if he'd suggested they invite Dooku to a party. With tea. And flowers. "*A cease-fire?*"

"You heard me."

Anakin shook his head. "No. No, no, no. We are *not* talking it out with them. The time for discussion is *over*. Vos has had all of the chances he's ever going to."

Kenobi held up a placating hand. "I didn't say anything about talking."

Anakin narrowed his eyes, but his posture eased. "So, what do you propose?"

"You will declare a cease-fire. And then, you and I will sneak around to the back and try to find another way in."

"Sneak around the back," Anakin said, skeptical.

"You're repeating me an awful lot today."

"That's because I'm wondering if you're going crazy. Master, this place is a fortress!"

"And what does a fortress become with only one way in and one way out?" Kenobi asked.

A slow grin spread over Anakin's face. "A trap," he said.

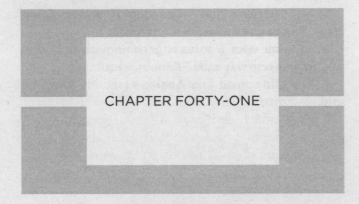

CHAPTER FORTY-ONE

Vos looked pale but determined when he returned. The blood was drying on his face. "I think they've stopped. For now." Ventress was still in a great deal of pain, but she was accustomed to controlling it. Now she willed herself to get to her feet and limp over to Vos. Concerned, he met her halfway. "Ventress, you should—"

"Come with me," she said. He followed her, supporting her, to another room in the shelter. Various supply crates lined the walls, but she had no interest in them. She turned and faced Vos. "Is it true?"

"Is what true?" He looked genuinely confused.

"That you've *joined* Dooku? That you've—you've sworn your allegiance to the dark side?" Despite her effort to speak quietly, her voice rose.

Vos closed his eyes and held up a hand. "Ventress, this isn't the time."

"Oh, yes, this damn well is the time. This is the *only* time. We all may be dead in ten minutes, and after all we've done, all we've *been* through together, all I thought we meant—you're going to tell me the truth. You owe me that much."

Vos looked away. Cold fear clenched at Ventress's heart. Finally, he spoke. "I did it for us."

For a moment she couldn't speak. "For us?" she finally managed. He nodded. She shook her head, stunned. "Vos—you know what he is. He will destroy you the first chance he gets!"

"I can handle him. I know what I'm doing. Asajj, I said we're doing it for us, and I mean that." He took her good hand in his. "You've told me your existence has been nothing but pain and loss. Never feeling secure. Never having a home. You deserve so much, and I can get it for us. The life we'll be able to have together once—"

"What kind of life will that be, Quinlan?" Her voice broke. "The kind where we're slaves to our hatred? Our rage? That's what the dark side made me. That's what it *does*. Nothing is ever enough. You get more, and more, but you're never happy. It's a trap baited with all the things you want most. That life—it's not worth living." She squeezed his hand, imploring. "I already left that behind. You can, too. You have a choice."

All at once, warmth flooded through her. It was as if she were being bathed with soft light. It washed away the pain, and the fear, and the anger, leaving only perfect clarity in its wake. Ventress realized that it was the Force, but it had never felt like this. And it was giving her a gift.

Time slowed to a crawl as a sudden, calm sense of knowing permeated her. She saw, all at once, every possible outcome of the turn of this fraction of a second. Every convolution, every manifestation, every repercussion that would echo far into the future. Death, and life, and new chances lay down one path. The restoration of balance. Fear and disaster, an existence that could never be called *living* but merely crawling about in a shell of flesh that had no spark of joy—that, too, could be the future; burning vengeance that only increased the hunger for more.

She had just told Vos that he had a choice about what path he wished to walk, and the Force was revealing to her the outcome of her own choices, now, this moment, this instant, this breath.

Ventress chose.

Vos saw Ventress's eyes open wide. Her body went taut and she seemed to be staring at something he couldn't see. Fear exploded in him, quivering in the pit of his belly, and he shook her, gently.

"Asajj?"

"No," she whispered, her eyes still unfocused, frighteningly blank. Then, "*No!*"

Violently, she shoved Vos away, putting the Force into the movement so powerfully that he was hurled across the room. As he struck the wall, he heard a terrifyingly familiar sound: the sizzle and crackle of Force lightning.

Dooku stood, his teeth bared in a savage snarl of victory. Ventress was caught in the most violent bolts of Force lightning Vos had ever seen. They danced and crackled about her hungrily, almost like living creatures. Her body spasmed and her face contorted into a mask of absolute agony. Blood trickled from her ears, eyes, and nose.

"*Asajj!*" Vos cried, leaping between Ventress and Dooku. He activated his lightsaber, deflecting the Force lightning back onto Dooku. The count's eyes widened in comprehension a split second before his own weapon turned on him, disloyal, as things of the dark always were. Dooku was flung back and lay on the ground, screaming and trembling, then lying still as the bolts faded.

Ventress lay unmoving on the floor. Her clothes—and her body itself—emitted wisps of smoke. "No," Vos moaned. She was breathing, but her pulse was thready and she was still, so terribly still. "Asajj . . . no . . . *no* . . . !"

Fury, as intense and primal as the bolts that had nearly killed her, shuddered through him, and the world went red. Vos threw back his head and voiced his rage, whirling on the count as he lay, shivering and gasping for breath, on the stone floor.

Three strides brought Vos to Count Dooku. He pressed the humming blade close to Dooku's neck.

"Do . . . it," rasped Dooku. Impossibly, he was smiling. "The lightning wasn't . . . for her. It was for you. She just . . . got in the way. Go on. Take . . . your *revenge*!"

Vos's heart shook his body with its pounding, its aching, its demands. His gaze flickered to Ventress, lying so terrifyingly motionless. His vision blurred. It took him a moment to realize that tears were falling down his face in a river of pain. The dark, rage-filled tide inside him receded, leaving in his heart only the truth of the tears. The count still smiled, still anticipated the final step that would turn Vos irrevocably to the dark side.

"I am not your kind," Vos said, his voice thick. "I do not feed off vengeance." Truth was quiet. It did not need to shout or to demand. It simply existed. "I am a Jedi."

Vos deactivated his lightsaber. Ventress was still alive, and hope, cruel and beautiful and agonizing, flared in his chest as he rushed to her.

"Vos." He didn't turn around at the sound of Kenobi's voice. Somehow, he was unsurprised that

Obi-Wan was here, at this moment. "We'll take him from here."

Vos simply nodded. He might still be executed. He would certainly be taken back to the Council in chains. But none of that mattered. Everything that mattered was here, right before him. He felt raw in this moment—cracked open and laid bare. His senses were heightened and he was almost painfully aware of everything: the smell of blood and scorched flesh; the steady slip of tears down his angular cheekbones, and their salty taste; the coppery tang of blood and fear in his mouth. He saw that strange patterns now decorated Ventress's bone-white skin; traces of darker flesh that looked like lightning bolts. The Force lightning had marked her for its own.

Ventress's breathing grew labored. He wanted to hold her, to keep her alive through the sheer force of his will, but he was afraid touching her would cause her more pain. Her beautiful, ice-blue eyes opened, and she smiled. He tried to return her smile, and failed miserably.

"Hey, handsome," Ventress murmured.

Vos gave a shaky laugh through the tears. "Hey, yourself."

"I won't break, you know." No. She would never break. Not Asajj Ventress. At the invitation, Vos gathered her as gently as possible in his arms. The movement caused her to cough violently. "I'm . . ."

Blood ran from her mouth, soaking his shirt. He bit back a sob. "Don't try to speak."

Ventress gave him a look that was so completely *her,* it tore him apart. "You don't . . . tell me what to do, Idiot."

A small smile surprised him. "Never could," he admitted.

"Damn right." Another bout of coughing racked

her thin frame, and for a devastating, heart-scalding second Vos thought this would take her. But she continued. "I'm proud of you for . . . what you did over there. You chose loving me instead of hating him." Her bloody-frothed lips curved in a smile. "Best choice you've ever made."

Vos wept unashamedly, cradling her, stroking her face. He wanted to memorize its every curve, sear it into his memory, then realized that he had already done so. "It was," he agreed. He swallowed hard. "Asajj . . . you were right. I—I did fall to the dark side. And I've been there this whole time. I just . . . I didn't . . . *know!*"

"You lied to yourself," Ventress whispered. "That's . . . why I couldn't tell."

"I love you, and I've never stopped, not for a moment." Here, at the end, Vos had to make sure she—

"I know," Ventress said. "But you *did* stop lying." She shuddered deeply. Vos felt his heart crack. Her fingers dug into his arm tightly and her gaze bored into his. "Remember . . . you always have a choice to be better. You always have a choice to . . . to pick the right path." She smiled sadly. "Even if that choice comes a little late."

No, it couldn't be too late. Vos still had to tell her everything he'd felt. How his heart had jumped the first time she had touched him tenderly, caring for his injury on the *Banshee*. That seemed like a lifetime ago. When she'd asked him how she looked in the ball gown, he should have told her. And when they had first kissed—Asajj Ventress had changed everything in his world, was still changing it, right this minute. But there was too much to say, and not enough time to say it, and the words crowded his throat and choked him into silence.

With an effort, Ventress reached to touch his face,

tracing the yellow tattoo, lingering over his lips. When she spoke, her voice was so faint that he had to strain to hear it. "And always remember . . . that I loved you, with all of my heart."

He had known it. But he had never before heard it from her lips. Now he found he could speak, the simplest of words. "I will."

Ventress took a shuddering breath. The tension left her body, and she relaxed into his embrace as her eyes began to close.

No.

"Asajj," Vos begged. "Asajj. Please don't go."

Her eyes flickered open, and a corner of her mouth turned up. "I have to, Quinlan. It's my time now. My sisters . . . are waiting."

Fear such as he had never known seized Vos, and he tightened his arms around her, as if by holding on he could somehow prevent death from taking her. "Please . . . please don't . . ."

"You must let me go, my love," Ventress said, her voice so gentle, so tender, and she smiled lovingly. "It's the Jedi way."

And she was gone.

CHAPTER FORTY-TWO

It had been a long, excruciating few months.

Vos had held Ventress in his arms afterward. How long, he did not know, but at some point he heard blasterfire and Obi-Wan Kenobi shouting his name—calling for help. Vos had gone, and the three Jedi fought together as, yet again, Dooku eluded capture. Darth Sidious, whose identity Vos had sacrificed so much to learn, had apparently decided to aid his apprentice after all.

Vos didn't remember the trip back to Coruscant. He suspected he had gone a little mad. Anakin had placed him in the ship's brig. Vos had gone willingly, but when he realized he would be separated from Ventress's body, he had demanded to be with her. Kenobi had assured him Ventress was in stasis, and would be cared for with respect. Somehow, at some point, Vos had slept.

As he had known would happen, he was brought before the Jedi Council, and there, exhausted and soul-sick, confessed every one of his crimes. He told them that he had fallen, but had denied that truth even to himself. His intention had been to use Dooku to get to Darth Sidious, and thus eliminate both Sith Lords once and for all. He accepted full responsibility for the campaign he had led under Dooku's guidance; for planting the bombs in the asteroid; for warning the count about the attack on the listening post. For killing Bayons and the clones aboard the *Vigilance*.

For the murder of his friend Akar-Deshu.

Vos spoke until his voice was hoarse. He had been calm for most of the interrogation, but when they asked him about Asajj Ventress, he shattered.

"She saved me," he wept. "She *saved* me!" They pressed him for more details, but Vos found himself unable to say anything other than those three words. Then, to his surprise, Obi-Wan Kenobi had stepped forward to speak, not just for Vos, but for the woman who had once been numbered among the Jedi's greatest enemies. As it turned out, he and Anakin had borne witness to all that had transpired during Ventress's final moments.

"Asajj Ventress moved Vos out of harm's way, taking the full brunt of Dooku's Force lightning upon herself," Kenobi said. "She sacrificed her life to save him."

"That is commendable," Mace Windu had said. "For her to give up her life for another speaks well of her."

But Kenobi was shaking his auburn head. An odd, unspeakably kind smile was on his face. "You misunderstand, Master Windu. All of you. She didn't just save his life. She saved *Quinlan*. And . . . I believe she may have saved us."

Yoda had silenced the questions and protests, and instructed Kenobi to speak what was in his heart.

"We lost our way," Kenobi had said. "We lost it when we decided to use assassination, a practice so clearly of the dark side, for our own ends, well intentioned though they might have been. All that has happened since—Vos succumbing to the dark side, the deaths he has directly and indirectly caused, the secrets leaked, the worlds placed in jeopardy—*all* of this can be traced back to that single decision. Masters, I submit to you that Vos's fall was of our making. And Asajj Ventress's death is on all our hands. That Vos is here with us today, devastated but on the light path once more, is no credit to us, but to *her*. She died a true friend of the Jedi, and I believe that she deserves to be laid to rest with respect and care, with all gratitude for the life she gave and the life she has restored to us, and this bitter lesson that came at so dear a price. We are Jedi, and we must, all of us, always, remember what that means."

Vos knew he could never repay Kenobi for that, but he had the rest of his life to try.

He worked closely with Yoda for a time, doing all that was required of him. Slowly but steadily, he began to regain the Council's trust. It would never right the terrible wrongs he had done, but Vos was moving into a position to at least begin to atone. Finally, Yoda agreed to release him into Kenobi's care, to take Asajj Ventress on one final journey.

So it was that Vos and Obi-Wan had come to Dathomir.

On a hoverlift between them floated Ventress's coffin. Vos walked with one hand resting atop it. He noticed his friend's reaction to the skeletons strewn about as the two Jedi made their solemn way toward the fortress.

"Dooku slew them all, because they had sided with Ventress," Vos told Kenobi. "And still, she was able to let go of revenge."

Kenobi said nothing, but Vos noticed that he, too,

placed his hand atop the coffin. As they approached the open mouth of the fortress, Kenobi said, "Are you absolutely certain about this, Quinlan? The dark side is very strong within."

"It is," Vos agreed, "but for this moment, the dark side is not our enemy. Can't you sense it?"

He watched as Kenobi took a deep breath, reaching out into the Force. His eyebrows rose as he experienced what Vos could feel. Puzzlement flitted across his bearded face, and he looked at Vos curiously. "Why not?"

"Here, the dark side belongs to the Nightsisters. And we are returning one of their own. I—I don't know how I know it, but I do."

"I believe you," Kenobi said simply. Vos felt a rush of gratitude. They stepped into the cool shadows, walking between pillars carved with the likenesses of strong women. Vos remembered what he had felt the first time he had entered. He had been chasing Ventress with anger in his heart. Now there was only sorrow, an aching sense of loss that he knew would diminish over time, but never completely leave him. And he didn't want it to. Strange as it was, he understood there was grace and strength in this pain; a reminder of what should never be forgotten.

"I never expected to find beauty on Dathomir," Kenobi admitted as they stepped fully into the cavern that had housed the village of Ventress's kin.

"*She* was beautiful," Vos said quietly. They walked to a fissure in the flat stone that contained a dark, still pool. Unlike the luminous blue pools that provided much of the cavern's illumination, the pools that had once housed the ancient Sleeper, the water of this one—if water it truly was—was utterly black. No breath of wind or movement of creature disturbed its mirrorlike surface. Different levels carved into the stone served as steps.

Vos placed both hands on the coffin. Now that it had come time to let her go, he realized that it would take everything in him to do so.

"I can give you some privacy, if you'd like," Kenobi offered.

"Thanks. I—I think I'd like to be alone with her, for a little bit."

Kenobi shifted uncomfortably. "I will have to keep you—"

"In sight, I know," Vos said, "and I understand why. It's all right." He wasn't angry. Leaving him alone in a place steeped in the dark side was not something Kenobi or the Council could permit. Not yet. One day, perhaps. Kenobi nodded and gave a sad smile before striding a few meters away. Vos turned again to the coffin. Then, steeling himself, he opened it.

Ventress had been put into stasis shortly after her death and been prepared respectfully at the Temple. Vos knew that Kenobi had recovered some of Ventress's clothing from the wreckage of the *Banshee,* but he was completely unprepared for what greeted him when he opened the lid.

Asajj Ventress's face was tranquil. Her hair had been washed and combed. Her arms, their injuries repaired, had been folded over her midsection. They still bore the dark tracings of the Force lightning that had claimed her life, but the marks were oddly beautiful, spidery and graceful. Her body was clothed in the elegant black evening gown she had worn on that night when he—

"I'm so sorry," Vos said, knowing how inadequate the words were but needing to say them anyway. "I'd give anything to go back. If I could I'd—" A rueful, bitter chuckle escaped his lips. "Where do I begin? There's so much I should have told you, so much I should have . . ."

His throat closed abruptly and his words drifted into the deep silence of the cavern.

"And now, it's too late, and I will never stop grieving that. But I'm on the path, Asajj. You bought my chance with blood, and I won't waste it, I swear I won't. Every day, every minute of my life, I'll live it. For me, *and* for you. I'll fight, because you can't, and I'll laugh, and I'll do everything I possibly can with everything I have in me to make things better, because this galaxy has seen too much of darkness."

Vos gently stroked her cheek. "Rest, now, my love. I brought you to Dathomir. Your sisters don't have to wait any longer. You told me you were reborn, here, in this pool. I hope it's all right for me to return you to its waters."

He took a shaky breath. He had thought he would dread this moment, but he was surprised to feel more a sense of quiet peace than pain. This was the right thing to do, and he knew it, bone-deep. Slowly, reverently, he lifted his arms as if he were holding Ventress in them. Her body rose into the air in response. Vos bore her in the Force to the still, dark pool and gently lowered her. Slowly, the black water closed over her, accepting her into its embrace. Her face was the last of her to disappear, pale and bearing an expression of serenity she had never known in life.

He blinked. Was the water . . . changing *color*?

Tendrils of mist began to rise, green and glowing. Green, like the Dathomiri magicks Ventress had spoken of; green, like the Water of Life. Vos caught his breath. Soft susurrations reached his ears, sounding almost like—

Kenobi was beside him immediately, his lightsaber unlit but in his hand. "Vos, what's happening?"

Slowly, incredulously, Vos understood. His heart ached with a bittersweet joy.

"Listen," was all he said.

Kenobi's eyes widened. He heard it too, now, the whispers of women's voices. The Force had reclaimed Dathomir's wayward child, and as Vos reached out in it to send the woman he loved a final farewell, he thought he could make out a single word: *sister.*

Asajj Ventress, at last, had come home.

Read on for the short story

Kindred Spirits

by Christie Golden

This story was originally published
in *Star Wars Insider Magazine* #159.

"This enterprise is doomed to failure," Asajj Ventress muttered. Her hands were securely bound behind her, and she was sweltering beneath the blazing Florrum sun in a long dark robe and heavy cloak.

"Only if you blow it," Lassa Rhayme whispered back. The blue-skinned Pantoran wore Ventress's clothes: black boots with blue protective shin plating, leggings, and a black, high-collared shirt beneath a tunic. There was more plating on the left shoulder and across the hips, and plenty of places to fasten a variety of gear. The pirate captain looked born to it.

Ventress had no intention of "blowing it," but she was definitely having second thoughts about this scheme.

Taking the bounty had seemed like a good idea at the time. The job had appeared on the roster with an impressive number of credits attached to it, and Ventress had recently laid out a sizable amount for repairs to the *Banshee*.

Seeking half-dozen skilled fighter pilots to serve as escort for the cargo ship Steady On. *No questions asked. Half payment upon agreement, half upon safe delivery of* Steady On's *cargo.*

"Smugglers plus cargo equals pirates" was an equation Ventress had learned long ago, so the attack on the *Steady On* was not unexpected. What *was* unexpected was getting rescued by a *second* group of pirates, the Blood Bone Order, who had also intended to plunder the freighter.

"We've been planning this for weeks," Lassa Rhayme had told her. "You can imagine my surprise when, upon the *Opportunity*'s arrival at the proper coordinates, the only ships we saw were fighters floating dead in space."

Ventress had been the only survivor. Rhayme had brought the wounded woman to the ship's medbay and healed her injuries. She had also towed the *Banshee* in for repairs.

"Why?" Ventress had asked, curious.

"When your ship was in such bad shape and you were still alive, I had a hunch. It paid off. We found this." Rhayme had reached behind her back, withdrew Ventress's lightsaber, and tossed it to her. "I can use your help recovering the *Steady On*."

Ventress welcomed the familiar weight of the weapon in her hand. She had expected to miss her twin red lightsabers, but was glad now that they had been stolen. The old ones reminded her too much of Dooku, and she found she preferred the yellow light of this one. "I might be willing to help you—provided I get to keep a certain piece of cargo."

"What might that be?"

"That might be my business," Ventress had replied.

Rhayme's golden eyes had narrowed as she speculatively regarded the woman she'd rescued. "One item?"

"One item."

She nodded. "Help me get the freighter back, and whatever it is, it's yours."

Rhayme had sent a crew member to go undercover

on the *Steady On*. He had reported back that Hondo Ohnaka, the pirate responsible for the theft, was currently not on the Florrum base; only a skeleton crew led by an underling was unloading the *Steady On*. "It's a break for us—Hondo's sharp, and a nasty piece of work, even for a Weequay."

Weequay.

"Now you have my attention," Ventress said. "I am . . . not fond of Weequays."

It was an understatement. Ventress despised the species, with their leathery, wrinkled skin and sour dispositions. Weequay raiders had murdered both her slave master and, later, Ky Narec, the Jedi who had taken her on as his Padawan. Her hand had tightened on her lightsaber in anticipation.

"Don't get too free with that," Rhayme warned, nodding at the weapon. "*I'm* not fond of high body counts. We kill when needed, not for sport."

"You sound like a Jedi," Ventress had said scornfully.

"Don't insult me."

Jiro, the pirate put in charge in Hondo's absence, had been intrigued by Lassa's proposition when contacted via hologram, and permitted them to land in the flat, rocky depression in front of Hondo's complex. The area was cluttered with debris. Somebody had sniffed out this hideaway not too long ago, and it was definitely the worse for wear. Ventress had spotted the *Steady On*—noteworthy for being completely intact amid the rubble—being unloaded as they were "escorted" inside what remained of a large, multilevel complex at blasterpoint.

"I'm beginning to think this wasn't such a good idea," Ventress continued as they walked through a triangular door and passed from sunlight into gloom.

"Hey there, no talking!" One of the pirates shoved

a blaster into Ventress's midsection. She gritted her teeth to keep from Force-hurling the disgusting creature the length of the enormous and poorly named "grand hall."

A few of the pirates were engaged in activities such as drinking, flirting with the female members of the crew, fighting about flirting, betting on fighting, and the fine art of sliding off a chair completely smashed. But there were others, their cold gazes crawling over the newcomers, who speared food with knives as if they were simply practicing carving up flesh. Jiro awaited Ventress and Rhayme at the far end. Seated at a long table on a raised dais, he sprawled comfortably in an ornate chair that commanded the best view.

He was one of the ugliest Weequays that Ventress had ever seen, with a row of single locks of hair standing up in spikes on his overlarge head and two longer braids trailing down his back. The pirate who had brought in the two women handed him Ventress's lightsaber. Jiro looked at it carefully, then at Ventress, and finally at Rhayme.

"You must be someone special, to catch a Jedi. How'd you manage it?"

"The magnificent Captain Rhayme"—Lassa spat on the ground—"sends her crew off to scout for news of ships to plunder. That's how I came across her." She gave Ventress a scornful look. "I found her pretty badly injured, from what or whom I don't know, but still alive. I took her back to my ship, healed her up— enough to walk, at least—and contacted you."

Ventress gave Lassa a look that she hoped was both defiant and exhausted. Jiro leaned back in his chair, plunking filthy boots on the table. At the next table over, someone belched.

"I've heard of Lassa Rhayme. Sounds like she's not your best pal."

"Hardly," Rhayme said, with just the proper amount of loathing, her lip curling slightly. *She's good,* Ventress thought. "That witch is brutal. We boarded a Separatist ship once, and she stole its torture droid. Rhayme'd always been harsh to her crew, but now . . ." The "bounty hunter" shook her lavender head. "I'd do anything to get out from under her thumb."

"Like deserting your captain to join Hondo's Gang, eh? How could we trust a turncoat?"

Rhayme smiled sweetly. "Hondo gave *you* a second chance when you turned on him, didn't he?" Ventress stifled a smile as Jiro's face darkened at the reminder. She and Lassa had done their homework. Rhayme folded her arms.

"Look—I've got everything to lose and nothing to gain by lying. I'm giving you a *Jedi.* The ransom the Order will pay for her safe return will be staggering. Plus . . ." She placed her hands on the table and brought her face close to his. "I'll tell you everything you need to know about Lassa Rhayme's plans. Hondo will come back to find that in his absence, *you* have defeated a dangerous pirate captain, captured her ship, and gained a loyal new crewmember, with a Jedi prisoner in the bargain. He just might make you second in command."

Jiro considered this, removing his boots from the table and leaning forward. "Still, why not keep the Jedi yourself and collect the bounty?"

Ventress's patience had worn out. The more the Weequay grilled them, the more likely he was to simply order both her and Rhayme shot and claim all the glory himself. *Time to shake things up a bit.*

The lightsaber sailed from Jiro's hands into Ventress's just as she spun around to catch it. She could not use it to cut her bonds with her hands bound behind her, but she could fight. With a yell, she sprang over Rhayme, turning in midair and angling the lightsaber so precisely it singed Rhayme's lavender braid.

"What—" cried Jiro, then dived for cover under the table.

Rhayme gasped and stared at Ventress. Her brilliant gold eyes narrowed and she lunged for the nearest blaster, which happened to belong to the pirate who had brought them in. Ventress was therefore not displeased when Lassa used him as a shield while firing at the "Jedi."

The shots barely missed Ventress. Rhayme looked furious. Her color was up and her white teeth were bared in a grimace of pure hatred.

Oh, no. She thinks I've turned on her.

It was a perfectly reasonable assumption. There had been a time, not long ago, when it would have been the correct one. But not today. Ventress would have to hope that Lassa Rhayme would understand what she was doing—and that Jiro wouldn't.

With her back to Rhayme, Ventress used the Force to sense the bolts coming and bat them away. She heard a yelp behind her, but it was decidedly not feminine. Good. She jumped onto the table, whirling in a circle down its length and catching any stray arms or torsos unfortunate enough to be in her lightsaber's blazing yellow path.

"Stand down, Jedi!" came Lassa's clear, strong voice.

Has she caught on yet? One way or another, either to continue the plan or to end it, Rhayme would have to stop Ventress. Two Weequays charged the table, raising their blasters. Ventress leapt to meet them, kicking out with both feet. The toe of each boot caught a startled pirate under the chin. Their heads snapped back and they crumpled, either unconscious or dead.

As she landed, a powerful kick in the small of her back sent her sprawling. Her lightsaber was snatched from her hands, and a second later, pain blossomed in her wrists. Lassa Rhayme, pirate captain, planted a boot on her back. Ventress shifted her head to one side and looked up, still uncertain as to whether Rhayme was friend or foe. Rhayme brought the humming tip of the lightsaber so close to Ventress's face that she was forced to squint against its brightness.

She struggled for breath, and finally gasped, "I . . . yield."

"I didn't believe you were really able to capture her," Jiro said, somewhat grudgingly, as the "defeated Jedi" was led away. "I am . . . impressed."

Rhayme's shoulder ached, and she would have several bruises shortly, but she'd had worse. "No question, Jedi are tough to defeat. I'm lucky she's not at her best."

She casually fastened the lightsaber to her belt, as if there was no question that it belonged to her. Jiro noticed the gesture, but let it go, doubtless reasoning that the credits the gang would receive from the Jedi Council would more than compensate him for a lost lightsaber.

"So I take it we're agreed?" Rhayme continued. "You get the bounty on the Jedi and accept me as a crewmember, and I tell you where to find Lassa Rhayme's fleet."

"Well," Jiro hedged, "it's Hondo who has to make the final decision."

She took a seat without being invited, and again Jiro did not object. "I'm not surprised. It's his gang, after all. I'll wait. When is he expected back?"

That threw Jiro. "He didn't say. But I could put in a few good words for you if you were to tell *me* where to find this fleet. So I could, ah, prep the ships and get them all ready-like."

So you could send off your men now and take all the credit-like, Rhayme thought, amused. *And likely try to kill me in the bargain.* Rhayme pretended not to have come to this obvious conclusion.

"That's a great idea!" she said. Jiro visibly relaxed. "Now . . . let me start by telling you how many ships Rhayme commands, what kind, and their names." She smiled. "I think a drink might loosen my tongue . . . if you'll join me."

Jiro gave her a lascivious look, reached for a no-doubt filthy mug, and sloshed a bright green liquid into it.

The lightsaber burns on Ventress's wrists were exquisitely painful, but she didn't care. In taking Ventress down, Lassa had sufficiently damaged the stun cuffs so Ventress could break free—and that meant Lassa believed her. She could take a little pain.

Once the doors to the grand hall closed behind her and her escorts, Ventress wasted no time. She used the Force to shatter the remains of the binders and extended her hands, palms up, to each side. Two of the pirates slammed hard into the walls. She whirled on the third, who came at her with a fist raised and rotting teeth bared, and punched him in the throat. The fourth grabbed her arm. She twisted, using her momentum and the Force to hurl him over her head, landing a blow to his jaw on his descent.

They all looked to be alive, but out cold. Better safe than sorry, though. Ventress relieved the guards of their blasters, then paused. Rhayme had asked her to kill only when needed. Sighing, she set one blaster to stun, and gave the pirates a second shot of dreamland.

Now to take over the *Steady On*—and make sure the item she'd been hired to safeguard was still on board.

Once Lassa told Jiro where Captain Rhayme's fleet was supposedly based, he of course decided immediately to take the initiative and send what ships were on Florrum to attack. Lassa encouraged him to send all his men, but he stubbornly shook his head.

"Hondo said he wanted the cargo unloaded," he insisted.

That was really too bad, but Lassa took comfort in knowing that she'd just sent all the intact ships on Florrum and every pirate but Jiro, those sprawled snoring on the ground, and the few unloading the *Steady On* off on a wild caranak chase. With gusto, Lassa spun outrageous tales of the terrors the "evil Captain Rhayme" perpetrated upon her hardworking crew, buying time for Ventress. Jiro swallowed it all, apparently having decided that since she had defeated a Jedi, Lassa was entirely trustworthy.

A movement caught Rhayme's eye. Ventress's slender, robed figure blended so well with the shadows that she was easy to miss. *She's very good*, Rhayme thought.

"So tell me more about this ale that your Captain Rhayme hoards all to herself," Jiro prodded, plunking down his empty cup and reaching for a refill.

"Ale? Oh no, it's Tevraki whiskey," Rhayme said,

watching Ventress out of the corner of her eye while smiling at Jiro. "And a finer thing has never touched your lips."

Jiro leered hopefully at the implied invitation. Ventress made her way to the door and slipped outside. Lassa waited, continuing to exchange suggestive remarks with Jiro. She gave it a few minutes more, then unobtrusively placed both hands below the table, pressed a button on her bracer, and gave Jiro a bright smile.

"Well, I can't say this hasn't been fun, but I must be going." She indicated the cup of green liquid. "Thanks for the, ah . . . whatever that was."

Jiro's green eyes narrowed. "What're you talking about?"

"My ride should be here right about . . ." She cocked her head, and was rewarded by the unmistakable sound of a ship landing in the outside arena. "Now."

Faster than she would have given him credit for, considering the amount of alcohol he had imbibed, Jiro leapt over the table with a roar. Rhayme darted away, pressing the switch on the lightsaber. It activated with a *snap-hiss,* almost startling her with its speed. A sword was a sword, however, and Lassa Rhayme knew how to use one. Jiro grabbed for a blaster someone had left on the table, but Rhayme slammed the lightsaber down, slicing through both blaster and table with as little effort as if she were cutting through butter. Jiro growled and threw a stool at her. Again Rhayme waved the yellow, humming blade and cut the piece of furniture in half.

She laughed with sheer delight. What a glorious weapon! She swung it simply to hear the sound it made.

"Which of you is the Jedi?" blurted Jiro.

"Jedi?" came a smooth voice trembling with indignation. "In *my hall*? *Again*?"

Jiro and Rhayme whirled simultaneously to see Hondo Ohnaka silhouetted in the triangular doorway. Carrying an electrostaff that sparked magenta at both sharp ends, he stood like an aristocrat, head high, one hand on his hip, his duster billowing about him. The effect was spoiled by the Kowakian monkeylizard perched on his shoulder. Hondo strode forward, fairly vibrating with offense.

"Jiro! You *imbecile*! What have you done? Where is my crew?" He completely ignored the woman holding the active lightsaber. Rhayme stared from one to the other, unsure whether to attack or to burst out laughing.

"Oh, hello, boss," Jiro said miserably. "This lady here came saying she wanted to defect from the Blood Bone Order and join us instead."

"Of course she does. Everyone knows Lassa Rhayme is a tyrant. Am I not correct? Hmm?" He peered alertly at Rhayme, expecting confirmation. She nodded wordlessly.

"And—she brought us—I mean you, boss—a Jedi she'd captured. Said we could hold her for ransom and—"

"Da-da-da-da!" Hondo cut him off with an imperious, irritated gesture. "I leave you alone for half a day—half a day!—and look what you have done. No more ransoming Jedi! That never ends well. Bad for business."

"But . . . it was like this beautiful fruit just fell, right into my lap!" Jiro pleaded.

Hondo sighed and placed two fingers to his temple under his helmet as if in pain. "How many times must I tell you, Jiro. You cannot trust such unexpected gifts. Fruit never falls into your lap *unless you shake the tree first*!" He looked at Rhayme, spreading his arms in a helpless manner. "You see what I have to deal with."

"I certainly do," Rhayme said, not without sympathy.

"Now, then"—he turned to her—"what do you *really* want?"

Rhayme sobered and drew herself up, meeting his eyes evenly. "To take back what's mine." She pointed the lightsaber at him. "You stole my haul, Hondo Ohnaka. You see . . ." She smiled fiercely. "*I'm* Lassa Rhayme."

"You? The terrifying captain of the *Opportunity*?" He eyed her up and down. "Not what I expected. Not at all." He clucked his tongue and shook his head sadly. "Little girl," he said, "did you think I had come alone?"

And the hitherto empty chamber echoed with the sound of weapons being drawn.

Lassa smiled. "Did you think *I* did?"

Sudden perplexed cries of pain and anger came from the entrance area of the grand hall, followed by blasterfire. Hondo turned to look, and in that moment Lassa sprang.

She brought the lightsaber arcing down, but Hondo recovered in time to block it with his electrostaff. His eyes narrowed behind his goggles. "This is a fight you cannot win, my dear. You may have the laser sword, but you don't have the Force."

"Don't need it."

He swung the staff low, but she leapt up and it sliced only air. A second jump brought her onto the table, and she swung with the lightsaber. This time, he struck it hard and the impact jarred her injured shoulder. Gritting her teeth, Lassa kicked out and up, and the electrostaff flew from Hondo's hands.

"Not bad," Hondo admitted. He recovered the weapon and vaulted up to join her, shoving one of the sparking ends of the staff like a spear. She parried, but let him drive her down the table, pretending to be unsure of her footing. A smile curved his thin mouth, and he feinted, dodging her blow and bringing the staff down.

At the last second, Rhayme swerved and dived for a blaster someone had left behind. In one graceful movement she grabbed it, fired at Hondo, and flung the lightsaber toward the doorway.

Ventress —don't fail me . . .

Ventress had been using a combination of the Force and the pirates' own blasters to methodically mow them down. It was almost too easy. She'd already incapacitated the half dozen who had been unloading the cargo ship, and Hondo had brought only another ten back with him. There was an ample supply of things to hurl at them—pitchers, a crate and the sharp-edged tools it was filled with, mugs, stools; even the pirates themselves could be used to knock their fellows down. It was good exercise, and Ventress welcomed the chance to work up a sweat while fighting hated Weequays. Respectful of Rhayme's wishes, she didn't shoot to kill, but several of them were on the ground writhing in pain from blaster shots to their arms or legs.

Suddenly Ventress felt a quick, bright urgency in the Force. She whirled, looking toward the far end of the hall, and saw her lightsaber hurtling upward.

It turned end over end, still lit. Some of Hondo's pirates tried to grab it in midair, and paid with their fingers. Others, more wisely, dived out of the way. Ventress shot out her hand and the hilt smacked into her palm. She grinned as she sensed the tension in the remaining four pirates skyrocket. At that moment she heard the sound of another ship landing outside, and felt the presence of two dozen life-forms racing across the landing field.

She grinned, and set to.

"Not so fast!" Hondo warned as Lassa turned to fire on him. He struck her full in the chest with the end of the electrostaff and Lassa gasped, flailing helplessly as the jolts surged through her. She crumpled, gasping, and tumbled limply off the table, spasming on the ground.

He leapt lightly down and gazed at her. "A good effort, my dear. I'm impressed. You almost lived up to your—"

Rhayme lifted the blaster and aimed it directly at his chest.

"—reputation," Hondo finished.

"It's set to kill," she warned him. "Throw away the staff."

"Surely we can work this out like two civilized pirates," he protested, but he did as she ordered.

Lassa got to her feet, still feeling the effects of the staff but forcing herself not to show them. "On your knees, hands behind your head."

Again, Hondo obeyed. "Come now, Captain Rhayme, let us not be hasty."

She stepped forward, placing the tip of the blaster between his eyes. "You mocked me earlier. I think you've changed your tune."

"Most certainly," he said. To his credit, his voice was completely calm.

"I'm taking what's mine."

She fired.

* * *

"Hondo was rather charming, actually," Lassa said, finishing her account as she and Ventress sat in her cabin aboard the *Opportunity*. On the table beside the bounty hunter sat a nondescript metal box about a third of a meter high. "Of course I wasn't about to kill him, but he didn't know that. It'll be fun to hear what sort of rumors he'll spread."

"Well done," Ventress said as Rhayme uncorked a bottle of aged Tevraki whiskey. "So . . . I've been wondering something."

"Fire away."

"You don't have any tattoos." She'd noticed it immediately upon meeting Rhayme. All the Pantorans whom Ventress had encountered adorned their faces with bright-yellow tattoos. She wasn't sure what they signified—family affiliation, social rank, personal achievements—but Pantorans all had them.

"That's because I have no loyalties other than to my crew," Lassa said. "*They* are my family. Otherwise— I belong only to myself. I am my own woman."

Ventress nodded. She liked that. She thought of her own tattoos, and how much they meant to her. Rhayme's unmarred face obviously conveyed the same pride.

Rhayme raised her glass. "To success—and, perhaps, new friends."

Asajj was surprised at her reaction. She didn't have "friends." But she'd grown to admire Lassa, and the other woman had kept to every part of their bargain. And . . . she was good company. Ventress said nothing, merely gave a fleeting smile as their glasses clinked. The whiskey was delicious—a warm, slow comfort slipping down her throat.

"Much better than what they serve in the bars on

Thirteen-Thirteen," Ventress said. "I could get used to drinking this."

"Why don't you?" Lassa said. "I can provide erratic but profitable income, bed and board, adventure, fair treatment, and the company of the woman who beat Hondo Ohnaka in single combat." She winked a golden eye.

It sounded good. Very good. And for a long moment, Asajj Ventress was tempted. But then she thought of all the company she would bring along with her: the shades of the dead, the remnants of dark memories, and a wariness that would likely never fade. Ventress would never trust anyone, not really, not even this remarkable woman with whom she had partnered for a brief time. She would always be alone, and she accepted that.

"While that's a fine offer," she said, "I must decline."

She sensed Rhayme's genuine disappointment, but the Pantoran recovered quickly. "If you ever change your mind, the offer stands."

"And if you ever need a bounty hunter, I'm not hard to find."

"Deal." They shook hands. "In the meantime," Rhayme said, "let's take a look at this item that's been so problematic."

Ventress glanced at the box beside her. "Part of the deal was that I don't look at it."

"You've worked pretty hard for your bounty this time, Asajj. Go on. You can always say you were making sure it wasn't damaged in the fighting."

Ventress considered that. "Sheb does strike me as a dealer who'd appreciate that concern."

The lock was easy to pick, and Ventress carefully lifted the lid. A small force field in the box itself prevented unauthorized handling. Ventress was seldom moved by beauty alone, but this time even her eyes widened as Rhayme gasped softly.

The object that had given her so much trouble was no gem, or weapon, but a simple statuette. A sea mammal with four flippers and an elongated muzzle was caught in a moment of joyous freedom, its small gem eyes sparkling, its sleek body curled beneath it so its tail merged with the wave that formed the base. The stone from which it was carved was a breathtaking shade of blue. The entire image—its sense of action, of grace and power and playfulness, its delight in movement, even its hue—seemed to Ventress to be a reflection of the Pantoran woman sitting before her.

A pirate's life—but not for me, she thought.

"A pity you can't keep it," Rhayme said.

Ventress merely nodded. With unwonted gentleness, she closed the lid and locked it.

"I do my job," she said, and slid her glass over for a refill.